DANCING IN THE FLORIDA SUN

A NOVEL

KIM GRIFFIN

To the one who feels hopeless, or like you don't measure up, there is One who offers hope, sees all of you, and loves you beyond measure. May this book point you to Him and His great love for you.

For God so loved the world, that he gave his only Son, that whoever believes in him should not perish but have eternal life.
John 3:16

May the God of hope fill you with all joy and peace in believing, so that by the power of the Holy Spirit you may abound in hope.
Romans 15:13

So now faith, hope, and love abide, these three;
but the greatest of these is love.

1 Corinthians 13:13

CHAPTER

ONE

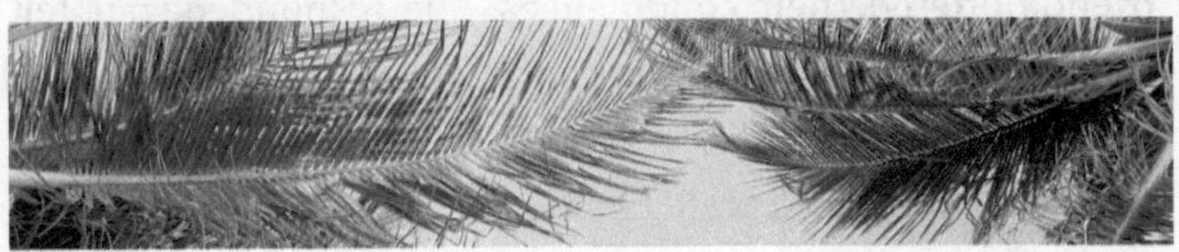

Achilly January wind whipped through the barren trees of the cemetery as Brooke stared, through tear-filled eyes, at her mother's casket. It seemed like a nightmare. Four days earlier she received a call, just after six in the morning, and found out her mom's car had slipped on the ice while she drove home after her twelve-hour nursing shift. Her mom fought for her life in the very same emergency room she had recently left. By the time Brooke arrived, it was too late.

Blinking back tears and trying to focus on the pastor's words, Brooke squeezed her sixteen-month-old son, Noah, tighter. She was a twenty-two-year-old single mom, and her lifeline had just died. She wanted to be strong for her son. He needed her. But this—surviving after her mother's death—seemed like an impossible task.

"Kendra Donahue Ferguson is not suffering, but is rejoicing before the Lord because of her decision to accept Him as her Lord and Savior," the pastor said.

Yeah, right. She knew her mom had turned away from God soon after she gave birth to her. She'd always taught Brooke not to be sucked in by those folktales. Where did that leave her now?

Her mom was a good woman. She'd supported Brooke every step of the way during her pregnancy, and after Noah's birth while Brooke finished college. Years earlier, Brooke was there for her mom when her dad admitted to having both an affair and a baby on the way before asking for a divorce.

Glancing around after the funeral, Brooke noticed a large crowd had moved from the indoor portion to the graveside service. Family and friends offered their condolences. She responded, but felt like she was in a dreamworld, waiting to wake up. Dizziness hit and she stepped back from the coffin to sit.

"Dear, you don't look well. Let me take Noah," Grams offered.

Brooke blinked and glanced down. Noah had squirmed out of her arms and into the seat next to her. "Oh!" Her eyes widened when she realized she hadn't noticed. "Thank you." She leaned down and pecked him on the forehead. "I'm so sorry, sweetie. I love you."

She hoped her mood and distraction didn't worry Noah. When he smiled and placed his chubby little hands on her cheeks, her worry eased.

"Momma," the toddler cooed.

"Come to Grams, Noah," Grams called to the brown-haired boy while holding out her hands. Once she had him in her arms, she looked back at Brooke. "We'll leave soon and get you home. The house will be filled with family for a few hours, but you and Noah can slip off and rest."

Brooke hoped she could hold herself together until then.

"I just laid Noah down for his nap," Grams said as she joined Brooke on the living room sofa at her mother's home after everyone left.

"Thanks." Brooke forced a smile.

Grams' forehead creased, and she placed a hand on her grand-daughter's knee. "Have you decided what you want to do?" When Brooke looked at her blankly, she continued. "Whether you want to stay here and live with your father and stepmom, or move to Florida with me?"

Brooke squeezed her eyes closed. She tensed when she opened them, fire filling her chest. "You know I'm not going to live with my dad and his new family. It's all his fault Mom's dead! If he had never cheated and left her, she wouldn't have gotten that stupid job. She wouldn't have gotten into that wreck!" Her body shook as she held back tears.

"I know this hurts, and what your father did was not right, but you can't blame him for your mom's death . . . and he does love you."

Grams pulled Brooke into a hug. When Brooke calmed, Grams leaned back and looked her in the eyes, speaking softly. "It's been over a week since Kendra died, and you've not gone to work. It's fine, but you are going to have to decide what you want, or your dad's office will have to look for a replacement."

Brooke clenched her fists until her knuckles were white, then let go and began weeping. "I can't do this without Mom." She sobbed as the dam finally broke. "I don't want to do this without her. How can I?"

Grams paused, then urged, "I think you should come with me to Florida. You can take as much time as you need off, and when you're ready, your dad can use his connections to help you find a job at a law firm in Orlando. Remember, he said one of his good friends from law school has a firm there." As she watched Brooke, she added, "In the meantime, we'll get passes to Disney, and we can introduce Noah to our favorite place. I think some Florida sun will be beneficial for both of you."

Brooke sniffed, wiped her tears, then glanced down and pulled at the hem of her shirt. She finally looked up, her eyes surveying the living room of the home she'd shared with her mom. She winced at the thought of leaving, but knew she needed a fresh start.

"Okay . . . I'll do it." Then, grabbing her grandmother's hand, she whispered, "I'm sorry for yelling at you. It's all so overwhelming. Thank you for being here. It means more than you know."

"I understand, dear. I'm hurting too and am no stranger to loss. We'll help each other get through this, then come out stronger in the end. You have such a great future ahead, and a precious son to share it with."

"I love you, Grams." Tears streaming down her cheeks, Brooke let go of her grandmother's hand and wrapped her arms around her.

"I love you too, precious one."

CHAPTER

TWO

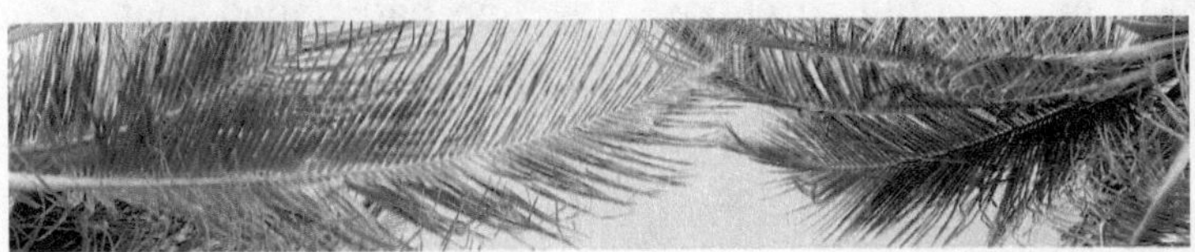

"I can't believe you would move with my kid to Florida!" Tyler shouted at Brooke. "I realize your mom's death is a loss. I'm trying to be sensitive here, but come on, you're going to have to suck it up and make Memphis work. That's too far!" He huffed, waving his hands in the air. "Good grief, your stepmom is a stay at home mom. Live with your dad and she can help with Noah. Just don't take him to Florida, I'll never see him. It's hard enough coming in from Nashville as it is. Med school is too demanding for me to give up any more time than I already do." Tyler's face was red with anger and frustration. "Won't you receive this house and whatever your mom had in savings? Surely you can stay here and afford childcare with that."

"You're making a huge assumption. My mom didn't have much in savings, and I think she still owes a lot on this house, so that's a moot point."

"Whatever." He shook his head. "And how can we consider marriage if you're living all the way down there?"

"Hmph," Brooke rolled her eyes while dropping to the sofa. While she was pregnant, he mentioned they would talk about marriage after he was born. Since that time, he periodically dangled it in front of her like a carrot, but never mentioned specifics or made it official.

She knew he would blow up about this, but she needed help with Noah and wasn't comfortable enough with her dad and stepmom to live with them. She certainly couldn't afford a place on her own. As she stared at the man she had loved for over three years, she realized he was never going to choose her. She had hoped that when he thought she might leave the state, he would step up and finally ask her to marry him—officially. It would be tough making ends meet while he was in medical school, but they would manage.

The problem was that his "plan" was ruined the instant she announced she was having his baby. He'd been wishy-washy about their relationship ever since.

"So you're asking me to marry you?" She challenged him. "If we get married soon, then obviously, I won't need to move."

Time stood still as she waited for his response. Before Noah, they had discussed a future together. Would he claim that future? Would he claim them? Sure, the plans would have to change a bit. They had a child, but he had once treated her like she was his world. Couldn't they get that back? She looked into his deep blue eyes—the ones that always melted her heart and pulled her under his spell.

Watching him rake his fingers through his dark brown hair, she felt as though she couldn't breathe. It shouldn't be this way. He should be sweeping her off her feet, begging her to marry him. Maybe, just maybe, this time he would want it too. She watched him hopefully.

"Well, no, not right now." Tyler shifted on his feet and looked at the floor. "I'm still not in a good place for marriage and a baby. You know that. I've got school loans for what my scholarships don't cover, and you certainly don't make enough to live on." Looking back up, his brows drew together in anger. "Why do I always have to rehash that with you?"

The spell was broken. "By the time you're in a good place financially, Noah's going to be in grade school. You've still got two and a half years of medical school, then a minimum of 5 years of residency for surgery, when you'll still make next to nothing.

"What am I supposed to do? Wait around forever while you decide if we're worth it? You've made it very clear that we are not! I realize that med school keeps you busy, but you rarely come here to see us. And when I offer to go there, you usually blow me off."

"Exactly! I'm always swamped with my studies! You can't hold that against me."

"I would expect nothing less than you pouring yourself into your studies, but you make no room for us at all. I've told you before we could stay for the weekend and be there to spend time together when you took breaks. Noah is a quiet little boy. You would hardly know he was there. For that matter, you never had to choose Vanderbilt in the first place! You were offered a full scholarship to UT here in Memphis, where we have our parents to help with childcare. But no, it wasn't prestigious enough."

It hurt to put her feelings constantly on the line, only to be rejected again. But for Noah's sake, she felt she had to try. She certainly wouldn't force it, though. She knew the outcome of that from her parents. Her mom always told her to make sure the man she married treasured her and was head over heels for her. She'd said to never marry for convenience or choose someone who didn't make her feel loved. Tyler no longer treated her that way, but it was hard to accept.

Tyler glared at her. "Whatever! It's too late to change now. Stop making this so difficult." He seemed to relax and reached out to touch her shoulder. He spoke more softly, "Just stay in Memphis . . . please."

Brooke's head dipped down. "It's too hard to stay. I need this. I need to get away." She looked up and saw his face tense again. "It doesn't have to be permanent. But it's what I need for now. It won't take much more time for you to get to us. Direct flights from Nashville are just under two hours, plus add the time at the airport and getting there, and you're about equal to the three and a half hours it takes to get here."

She knew time wasn't the real issue. If he wanted to see them, he would make time. That's part of why she wanted to get away. Being so close allowed her to get her hopes up that they would work out. After all this time, with so little effort on his part, she needed to move on.

Florida would give her a fresh start, a chance to move past all the pain—memories of her mom, seeing her dad and his happy new family, and the constant hope that maybe Tyler would put Noah and her first. The bright Florida sun always brought her happiness, and that's what she longed for.

She texted her grandmother, then looked up at Tyler. "Thanks for taking the time to come and talk. Grams is on her way back from the neighbor's with Noah, so you two can have some time." She paused and breathed deeply. "We will be going to Florida next week."

Tyler shook his head and huffed. "Whatever. I won't fight it. I'm sure you'll get your way. With your dad and his law firm behind you, there's no way I'd have a chance." His face reddened as he narrowed his eyes at her.

Brooke stood up and walked to the window, staring out at the gray skies. A tear slid down her cheek. There was no use in arguing. She knew it wouldn't matter whether they were in Kissimmee, Florida or Memphis, Tennessee. Either way, they would rarely see or hear from him.

THREE

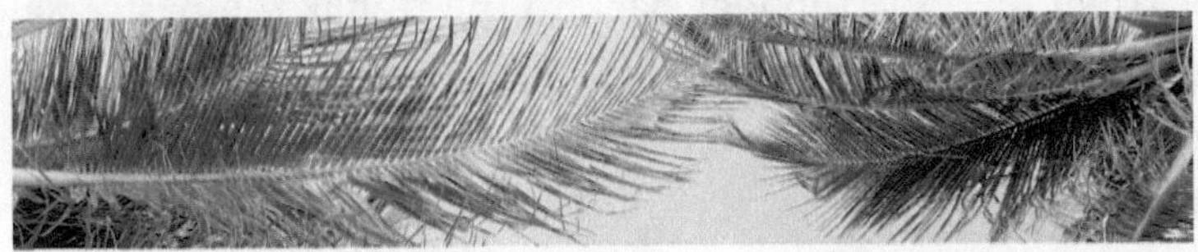

The scent of Tiffany perfume filled Brooke's nostrils, bombarding her with memories as she entered her mom's closet. She had not been in it since she picked out her mom's burial clothes. At that time, she'd been numb and going through the motions. Walking through the closet today, preparing to pack its contents up for donation, made it seem all too real. How could this be her life? Surely, any minute, her mom would come through the door and life would go back to the way it was.

Everything in the house held a memory, and it was more than she could bear. She had avoided going through things for the last two weeks, and with only two more days before leaving for Florida, time was running out. Thankfully, with the property needing to be furnished for staging to go on the market, she didn't have to get it all out. But this was the time to sort through each item that held sentimental or financial value. Grams helped, but was ultimately leaving the decisions up to Brooke about what to do with her mother's belongings.

Hours later, Brooke found herself growing angry. She still couldn't grasp how or why this happened. Her mom was a good person and a hard worker, yet had suffered through a marriage with a man who didn't love her the way he promised and cheated on her. To top it off, she died way too young. She still had so much life to live. She could have found love again, and watched her grandchild, and eventually maybe others, grow up. But no, now she would be nothing more than dust and bones. Why? What was the purpose of life? Just for people to go through it suffering and struggling, then die? She thought back to the things the pastor said at the funeral and scoffed. Some great God. He couldn't even give her mom what she deserved, and hadn't He done enough to torture Brooke?

She looked down and realized she'd thrown things into a box to dispose of without even paying attention to what they were.

"Ughh!" she screamed at no one, or maybe at God. She was glad Grams had taken Noah out for lunch. Tears erupted, and she covered her face. She needed this week to be over with. At least in Florida, she wouldn't see her mom at every turn.

Brooke rolled her window down for a minute to feel the fresh air as she squeezed the steering wheel, forcing herself to stay alert. The sky was brighter, and the air was warmer as they neared the Florida-Georgia border. It had been a long two days. Traveling with a toddler and a woman in her seventies meant frequent stops during an already lengthy trip. She was thankful they spent the night just south of Atlanta rather than trying to make the whole trip in one day. They had already traveled through four states and were almost to the fifth and final one. Every mile brought more release of the sadness and pain tearing through her mind and body.

The past two and a half weeks were a blur. They felt more like a lifetime. A lifetime since she had a "normal" day of getting up with Noah for her morning routine while preparing for work, then passing Noah off to her mom as she left. Dinner and playtime together in the evenings, and hanging out at the park on weekend afternoons with her mom and son. All gone, she thought longingly.

With her grandmother and son sleeping, it was quiet in the car and Brooke was left with her thoughts. Her mind kept rehashing the events of her mother's death, as if it was some puzzle she could solve, and it would end with a different result—her mom still living. What if she had checked the weather and warned her mom? What if her mom had driven an alternative route? What if her parents never divorced, and her mom had not had to work?

If there was a God who had all knowledge and power over all things, like her grandmother claimed, why would He have taken her mother, the woman that she and her son depended on? Why would a supposedly loving God allow that?

Brooke looked at the woman next to her, so strong and peaceful in the midst of this storm life had hit them with. She wondered how she held it together so well. Only four years earlier, her grandmother had lost her husband of almost fifty years. Grams missed him greatly, but handled it with her usual grace. Now here she was, dealing with the loss of her youngest child. A mother shouldn't have to bury a child. It should be the other way around. Yet she managed to not only handle her own life, but be the glue that held Brooke together.

"THE WHEELS on the bus go round and round, round and round, round and round..." Brooke, Noah, and her grandmother sang as they neared Kissimmee.

"Look, Noah, at the big Ferris wheel! That means we're almost there." Brooke called out as they barreled down I-4 through Orlando.

"Bye-bye?" Noah questioned.

"Yes, we went bye-bye, and now we're almost to our new home with Grams." Brooke tried to sound happy as she spoke to her son. He may not understand what she said, but he always picked up on her moods.

"Mams," Noah squealed and clapped, while kicking his feet against his car seat.

"Yes, precious, we'll all be together." Grams reached back and tickled his feet.

Brooke smiled and her hands relaxed on the wheel as she caught a glimpse of her son's joyful face in the rear-view mirror. The innocence of children. She would do everything in her power to keep him happy and save him from having to deal with all the sorrow and despair that filled her heart.

It was amazing how much happiness one little person could bring. Unfortunately, sadness over her mom and anger towards the men in her life still crept in. She usually pushed back unwelcome thoughts of her dad and Tyler, but the loss of her mom was a whole new beast to contend with. It left her spinning, unable to get a foothold on life.

She glanced over and saw Grams watching her. Grams placed a hand on Brooke's shoulder. "Everything is going to be fine, dear . . . more than fine. You have a wonderful life ahead of you. We'll cherish memories of your mom together, and you and Noah will live your best life because of all that she poured into you both. She has helped you lay a foundation, and now you'll build on it."

Tears began to trickle out, and Brooke smiled as she wiped her eyes with one hand and tried to focus on the road. "Thanks, Grams. I love you, and I'm so thankful we have you."

"I love you too, dear. I feel blessed you're both coming to live with me. I hope you realize that this is no burden for me, and I am truly looking forward to our time together."

FOUR

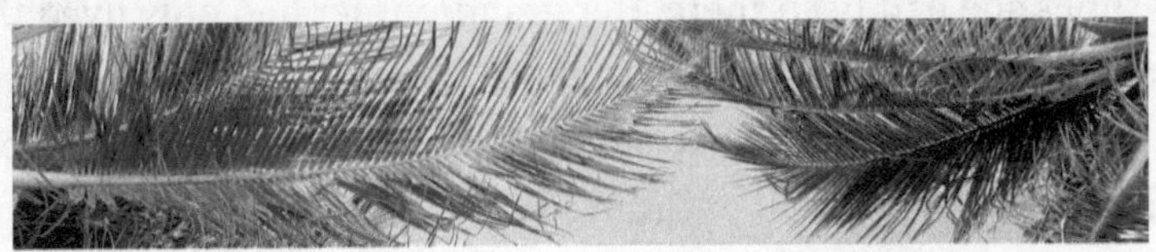

"Home sweet home!" Grams announced as they approached the gatehouse of her apartment complex.

Brooke checked in at the gatehouse. She would have to get a resident's sticker for the future. The property looked just the same as it had about two years earlier, when she came for spring break weeks after finding out she was pregnant.

The trip had been a last minute decision after Tyler flipped out about the pregnancy. They had planned to go to Panama City Beach with some other couples. She had felt off for weeks and thought it was from pushing herself too hard with school. But when she was sick to her stomach several days in a row, deep down, she knew she was pregnant. After a home test, a visit to the doctor confirmed she was nine weeks along. Brooke always had irregular periods, so had thought nothing of missing one. That positive pregnancy test turned her life upside down.

"Brooke? Brooke? Are you okay?" Grams looked at her granddaughter with a furrowed brow.

Brooke blinked back tears, then forced a smile and nodded as she parked the car beside her grandmother's building.

Grams looked doubtful and pulled her granddaughter into a hug. "We're going to make it, precious. The Florida sun is good for healing broken hearts."

~

STEPPING into the apartment brought back happy memories of the few times she had been there. Her grandmother had only lived there four years. Brooke looked around the place with new eyes as she analyzed everything to make sure it was toddler-proof. She noticed outlet covers and that all of Gram's breakables were moved to higher shelves.

"I was worried about Noah getting into things, but your home seems already childproofed." She looked at her grandmother with surprise.

Grams broke into a smile. "You remember my dear friend, Ann? The one that lives in the apartment diagonally across from mine?" Brooke nodded, then Grams continued, "She and her grandson came by and worked on things for me so it would be ready for our arrival. She even borrowed a portable crib for Noah to sleep in until the moving truck arrives tomorrow. It's in the bedroom that has the desk. We'll use that as Noah's room."

Brooke smiled, but envied her grandmother. "You're lucky to have such a true friend. I'd like to stop by and thank her after dinner."

She recalled how her own friends abandoned her after finding out she was pregnant and keeping the baby. A single pregnant mom didn't fit the image her sorority wanted.

Her last year at college, she buried herself in her studies, taking care of Noah and working part time at her father's law firm. Even at work, she felt ostracized as an unwed mom. For a fairly large city, Memphis sometimes felt like a small town. She hoped central Florida would offer her a new start where people didn't automatically judge her.

"That will have to wait, dear. Ann left yesterday to help her sister in Palm Beach. She took a fall and has a broken ankle, so Ann's staying there a few weeks, I think. We can certainly call her so you can thank her."

It took Brooke a minute to remember what they had been talking about, then she nodded before examining the photos on her grandmother's bookshelf. Pictures of her with her mom, and some of her grandparents before her Papa died. One that caught her eye pictured her when she was eleven, twirling around outside at her grandparents' home. The water glistened on the driveway from the rain that had just ended, and she danced with joy. Happy days.

It had been over an hour since Brooke texted Tyler to let him know they arrived safely. He had asked her to, yet he left her on read and didn't bother to respond. No surprise. She swallowed down the lump in her throat, wondering why she got her hopes up. Time and time again, he had let her down. He had told her he loved her and talked of a future with kids. She thought he was the one. But that was all B.N.—before Noah.

Her mind drifted to the last day they spent together before finding out about her pregnancy. They spent the afternoon downtown acting like Memphis tourists—biking around Mud Island, touring the museum there, going to the top of the iconic Bass Pro Pyramid, then making it back to the Peabody in time to see the ducks march out of the lobby fountain and up to their rooftop home. They planned to eat and go to Beale Street. When she started feeling nauseous and instead asked to go home, Tyler was attentive and worried.

Several days earlier, she had felt nauseous, but it had been in the morning and she thought she had low blood sugar from waiting too long to eat. The nausea went away after eating, just like when she'd had low blood sugar before. She told Tyler it was likely the same problem and suggested they grab a quick bite and spend the evening at home.

They went back to her apartment and snuggled on the sofa while eating Vietnamese food and watching Netflix. She remembered him waking her up, and when she discovered it was only 7:30 pm, she had a sinking feeling she was pregnant. Her mom had mentioned many times how tired she got during pregnancy, and that she fell asleep at odd times, whenever she sat still for very long.

Tyler had looked at her so fondly that night and kissed her like she was his world. But the next day, after taking the test and telling him, she saw only anger in those same eyes.

"Mama!" Noah patted her leg with a giant block, clearly wanting her to join him in his building project.

Brooke forced the sadness back down and smiled at her son. He was her happiness. She needed to be fully present for him. She picked up several blocks and added them to his creation, then watched him knock the tower down and giggle.

"Mo!" Noah brought his hands together, making the sign for "more."

"More? You want to do it again?"

Noah nodded and smiled. "Mo! Pease!" He circled his hand on his chest, signing "please," and then picked up two blocks and handed them to his mom.

"The sign language has been good for him as he transitions to speaking more, I see. I'm proud of you for working on that with him," Grams called out from the kitchen, peering over the counter top that separated the kitchen from the living room as she worked on dinner.

"It certainly kept him from screaming so much when he was younger and knew what he wanted, but couldn't quite get the words out. Mom was the best, though . . ." Her voice caught in her throat as she remembered their time together. "She really got into it once I decided to teach him. She taught us both so much."

～

WATCHING Grams pray with Noah made her nostalgic for the days when she was a little girl spending time with her grandparents and unaware of the issues her parents had. The bedtime prayers of Papa and Grams always left her feeling loved and secure. She longed to feel that again, but it would take a lot more than words to some far off deity to get her life back on track.

Twisting her hair while lost in thought, she watched her son. He was beautiful, with dark brown hair and green eyes. She was thankful they were green and not blue like Tyler's. It would be hard having his eyes stare back at her every day as a reminder of what she didn't have. Noah didn't get her strawberry blonde locks, but brown was fairly common and Noah had his own unique look.

An hour later, Brooke was lying in her room, exhausted from traveling for two days. The silence of her new reality engulfed her. In Memphis, she could look around her home and see her mom everywhere. Here, the loss was glaringly obvious. She didn't know which was worse. Her head told her being away would help her heal, but her heart grieved wherever she was. She longed for peace.

Her phone buzzed.

TYLER: I'm coming down in three weeks for my spring break.

WELL, that's interesting. Her heart raced. He was actually going to spend his break with them. Maybe leaving Tennessee would move their relationship forward, after all.

BROOKE: That will be nice. Just let me know your flight details and I'll pick you up from the airport.

. . .

SHE TRIED to play it cool and not sound too excited. Smiling, she drifted off to sweet dreams of a happy little family.

CHAPTER

FIVE

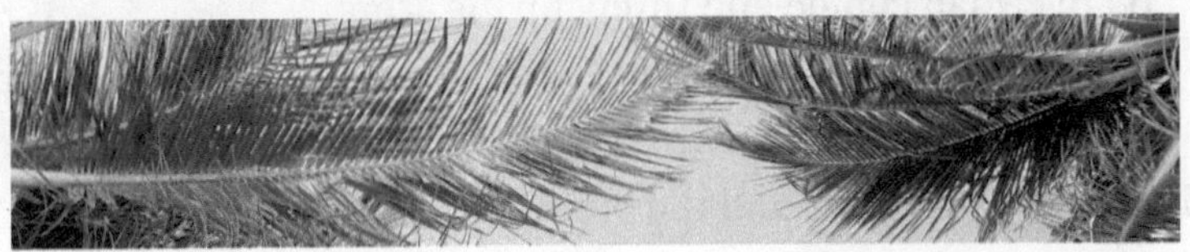

Sabrina, the wife of the pastor at Grams' church, sat across the living room on the sofa. She had kind eyes and a petite frame. Brooke scanned the room, trying to remember the names of the other visitors. Sabrina had brought her two daughters. Grace, the oldest, was babysitting age, and the younger one was . . . Faith—Brooke finally recalled. Sabrina's friend, Katlyn, sat next to her while her little boy, Benjamin, played on a mat with Noah and his blocks. The boys were close in age and getting along well. Grace and Faith fawned over them.

"Oh my gosh! Faith, look!" Grace called out to her sister as she pointed to her phone, then clapped her hand over her mouth as she looked at her mom. "I'm sorry. I didn't mean to interrupt."

"It's okay. What happened?"

"Leah just texted and said *Nine Days In* is playing in town next Saturday at House of Blues Orlando! It was a last-minute decision when they had a cancellation," Grace gushed with excitement.

"That sounds fun. I take it you're wanting to go?" Sabrina smiled knowingly at Grace.

"Mommm!" Both girls whined.

"Duh!" Faith rolled her eyes.

"Of course!" Grace spat out. "And Leah said her parents will go with us. She's planning to get a ticket for her sister, too. Can we go? We have to decide fast, because they'll sell out today, I'm sure!"

Sabrina looked at the calendar on her phone. "Sure. It looks like that will work." She winked at the girls.

"Yes!" Faith yelled and pumped her arms.

"Yeah!" Noah copied and threw up his arms.

Both girls laughed at him and squealed with excitement. Grace, glowing from the news, turned to Brooke. "Can Faith and I take Ben and Noah for a walk around the building? We'll stay close."

"Yeah, I think Noah would like that," Brooke answered.

"Sure," Katlyn agreed.

Once the girls left, Brooke couldn't hold back any longer. "Who or what is *Nine Days In*?"

"I won't tell the girls you asked that," Sabrina chuckled. "They are *the* most popular boy band right now. Even more than the Korean groups. Three of them actually play instruments, though, so they're a little different from most. Annnnd they just so happen to be from Orlando, so they play here pretty regularly. The young girls all go gaga over them. In fact, their group of friends inform each other if they see any of them around town, so they can 'just happen' to end up at the same place. They're sort of obsessed."

Brooke chuckled. "Okay, I've just learned something new. I guess I've been out of touch."

"That's understandable. They've only moved to international fame in the last couple of years, and it's mainly with middle and high schoolers. They're a bit after your time."

"I guess that makes me feel better," Brooke grinned.

"Their music is actually pretty good, and the media portrays them as overall good guys," Sabrina mentioned. "One of them even supposedly became a Christian a few months back. I haven't heard much about it since, but who knows? The girls, of course, remind me of that every time I give them a hard time about the group."

"It's all good fun, though. I remember being the same way when I was their age," Katlyn said before she took a sip of her water. "So, Brooke, I'm part of a group here in Kissimmee that takes our kids to different parks in town each Friday at 10 a.m. There are mostly moms with their kids, but some grandparents, nannies, and dads, too. It's a great way to get to know people. Plus, most of the kids are preschoolers, with a few homeschoolers that are a bit older in the mix, so it will be good for Noah to meet kids as well."

"That would be nice. Thanks for letting me know. I'm sure at some point we'll go, but it may be a few weeks before I'm emotionally ready to."

Katlyn's face fell, but she nodded in understanding. "This is my number, if you ever need anything." She handed Brooke a card.

Brooke tried to stifle a yawn. "I'm sorry. I've not had much energy lately."

"Emotional strain can be just as exhausting as physical exertion. We'll get going so you can rest. We'd love to see you at church when you're feeling up to it." Sabrina stood up and the others followed. She reached over to hug Brooke. "It has been great meeting you! Your grandmother always speaks so highly of you."

Katlyn hugged Brooke. "It was nice to meet you. I look forward to getting to know you and Noah better."

Brooke smiled at the two ladies. "Thank you both for coming, and for the food. The lasagna and pound cake look wonderful."

As they exited the apartment, they found the girls with Noah and said goodbye, leaving Noah with Brooke.

Though appreciative of their visit, her mind had wandered to the same dark place it had been going for the last couple of weeks. When that happened, she found it hard to put on a smile and make small talk, and needed to be alone. She was glad for Sabrina's awareness and couldn't wait to take a nap. Unfortunately, Noah's nap wasn't for another hour and a half.

"I can see you're exhausted. Let me take Noah to the park until his naptime." Grams offered.

"Honestly, that sounds amazing. That glider on the patio is calling my name."

"Consider it done." She held out a hand to Noah, and he wrapped his hand around her pointer finger. "Let's go get you ready for the park."

A few minutes later, Grams came out with Noah on her right hip and a backpack over her shoulder.

"Don't you worry about a thing. We'll be back in time for his nap."

"I won't argue." She turned to Noah and kissed him on the head. "Muah. Have fun with Grams at the park." Noah giggled and clapped his hands. "Love you both. Thanks, Grams."

"It's a privilege, dear. I love getting to show off my great-grandson." The older woman winked and grinned. "You can rest and have some time for yourself."

Brooke nodded, hugged her grandmother, and waved them off before heading in to put away the dishes from the dishwasher. Rest sounded wonderful as she eyed the glider out on the screened-in patio.

A CAR DOOR slamming startled Brooke awake. Lazily, she opened her eyes to see who had disturbed her long-sought sleep and was mesmerized by the most beautiful man she had ever seen. He stood on the sidewalk outside her grandmother's apartment building. Blinking once, then twice, to make sure she was awake, she realized this was not a dream.

The brown-haired man had just stepped out of a flashy, new red Porsche. In a black leather jacket, aviators, black jeans, and a grey T-shirt, he looked like a cross between a model and a James Dean bad boy wannabe.

He ran his fingers through his dark hair. Moments later, he was greeted by two teen boys with skateboards. She watched until he disappeared from view, pondering who he could be. *If someone could afford a Porsche, why would they live in an apartment and not own a house? Who wears leather jackets in central Florida? And why would someone who looked about her age be hanging out with kids so much younger?*

The rumble of her stomach pulled her from her thoughts and she went inside. After making a quick salad and grabbing a glass of water, curiosity got the best of her. She carried her food out to the patio in case the hot Porsche driver happened to walk back by.

After twenty minutes with no sign of him, Brooke scoffed at herself and mumbled under her breath, "What are you thinking? You're in no shape to meet someone."

Unsure of where things were going with Tyler, she needed her mind and heart to heal after all she had been through. He didn't even look like her type. She had only ever dated preppy, put-together guys. Yet somehow, she felt attracted to the stranger at first sight.

Gathering her bowl and glass, she stood up to go back in, when seemingly out of nowhere, Mr. Hot Guy appeared. This time with three teen girls and his sunglasses off. His eyes were dark and dreamy. Standing frozen, she watched as he waved goodbye to them and slid into his car.

As the engine roared to life, he turned his head and stared right at her, eyes lingering, before putting on his sunglasses and smiling with a cocky grin. Her eyes grew wide and her cheeks flushed as he drove off. Once she came to her senses, she retreated inside, feeling conflicted. Nope. She wouldn't get distracted by another man right now. Her priorities were being strong for Noah and herself, and figuring things out with Tyler. Anyway, the guy didn't look like the forever-after type—the only type she would consider.

SIX

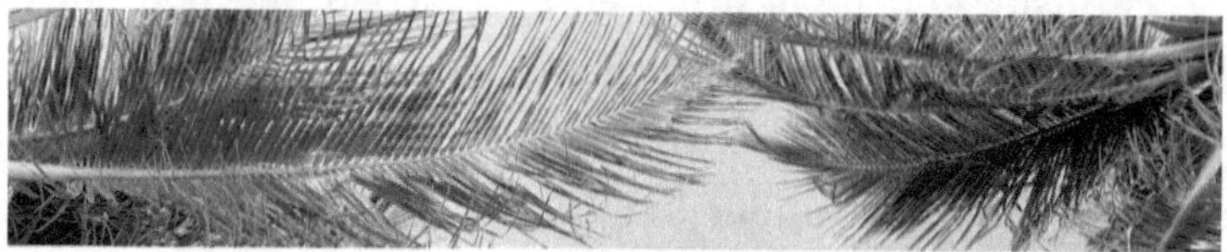

The days dragged on and Brooke struggled to have the energy to do much. She tried being cheery around Noah, but could only keep up the pretense for so long before needing time alone. Grams was understanding and always ready to jump in and entertain Noah. She seemed to thrive on taking care of both of them. Brooke was amazed at how much energy she had at her age.

They established a routine of Brooke hanging out around the apartment and the apartment grounds in the morning and spending time with Noah, then after lunch, they would nap. Once he was up from his nap, Grams usually took him out to give Brooke alone time. Brooke knew she was depressed, but didn't know how to get better.

Today she sat in her usual seat in the glider, watching the rain. It suited her mood. As she stared out at the parking lot, the Porsche guy came to mind, and she wondered who he was. The way he dressed, the fancy car, teens hanging around, it all pointed to the same thing —he must be a drug dealer. She couldn't get mixed up with a guy like him.

From her spot on the patio, she watched the mail lady fill up the mail compartments just as the sun peeked through the clouds and the rain stopped. Brooke wasn't expecting any mail, but headed out to keep her mind off other, more depressing things—like the fact that she had not heard from Tyler since his short text about his upcoming visit.

As she opened the box, the rain started again, and she hurried to relock it rather than get the mail wet. A shadow fell over her and she looked up to see Mr. Hot Drug Dealer holding his jacket over her head. She gasped and stared at him in confusion.

"You can get your mail," he leaned in and gestured with his head towards the box.

Panicking, she drew her eyes from his, pulled the mail out, then walked back to the cover of the building while he held the jacket over her. His masculine scent enveloped her, and her body tensed. What should she say?

Once they were out of the rain, she turned and looked at him with pursed lips, wanting to know more about this handsome, mysterious stranger, yet fearing what she would find. "Thanks," she blurted out.

Noticing his frown, she fled into the apartment. Her heart beat erratically as she leaned back against the door.

THE FOLLOWING DAY, Grams had a meeting during the time she normally took Noah out, so Brooke pulled herself together to take Noah out for ice cream. As she bent over to clip him in his car seat, she heard the rumble of a car pull up. She lifted her head and saw a shiny, new, royal blue, four-door convertible Mercedes park two spaces down from her. Mr. Hot Drug Dealer stepped out and grinned.

"It's a lot nicer outside than it was when I saw you yesterday." He chuckled.

Brooke's mouth fell open. That's two brand-new, expensive cars she'd seen him drive in the past few days. This guy had to be a drug dealer. Without answering, she hurried to the other side of her car and took off, barely glancing at the good-looking man staring back. Her heart pounded, and those beautiful brown eyes immediately appeared in her mind. It scared her. He scared her.

"Let's go get ice cream!" Brooke called out to Noah, hoping to calm herself by acting like everything was normal.

SUNDAY MORNING, while relaxing on the patio, Brooke scanned the parking lot. No sign of Mr. Hot Drug Dealer. She hadn't seen him since Thursday, when she took Noah out for ice cream. Thoughts of him made her anxious . . . *only because he might cause trouble in their apartment complex.*

Grams had taken Noah to church, but Brooke claimed she wasn't ready to be around people yet. Although true, she also had no interest in sitting around and listening to people talk about their "good God." She had seen the kind of things their good God had done in her life, and she didn't enjoy His kind of good.

The sound of a car revving drew her eyes to the parking lot. An older model Camaro pulled around the corner. It was black, with two bold white stripes down the top. She watched closely as it parked. Her heart raced as the door opened, but the moment a blond teenager emerged, her pulse slowed. She shouldn't have felt so disappointed. What was wrong with her?

MONDAY AFTERNOON, Brooke rocked on the patio glider, falling into her habit of bemoaning her sad and sorry life. With no hope in sight, she wondered how she could be there for Noah when she had no interest in even taking care of herself. Her appetite was practically nonexistent. Every morning, she dragged herself out of bed after tossing and turning at night.

When the hum of a car reached her ears, she didn't bother looking up. But once the car door slammed, curiosity overcame her. It was him. Mr. Hot Drug Dealer was back. She relaxed into the cushion.

This time, he wasn't mobbed by anyone as he climbed out of the Porsche holding a brown paper bag. Her eyebrows shot up. *Drugs?* Within seconds, he disappeared, and from the patio, it wasn't clear where he had gone. She stood up and moved back into the apartment, berating herself for being so hopeful about seeing someone who would likely complicate her already complicated life.

Her depression had taken hold of every facet of her being and was causing her to make poor decisions. The loss of her mom still tormented her. Maybe it *was* time to consider therapy, like her grandmother had been urging. If not for her own sake, she needed to get better for Noah.

Brooke held Noah's tiny hand as they strolled down the sidewalk of the apartment complex. He stopped now and then to pick up a leaf, a rock, or some other item he found nearby. They walked to the pond and Noah squeezed her hand in excitement when he saw the ducks.

"Next time, we'll bring food for the ducks to eat."

Noah clapped. "Duck eat!"

After Noah had his fill of excitement with the ducks, they headed back to the sidewalk leading to the apartment. Noah still held a rock and a leaf he had found along the way, but the rock slipped from his fingers. When it rolled into the street, he released Brooke's hand and toddled after it. Brooke rushed to him and panicked as he fell towards the road. In the nick of time, a masculine figure snatched him up.

"Hey, little guy. I don't think you should be in the road. You gave your mom quite a scare." He held Noah in his arms and looked at a worried Brooke.

She reached out for Noah. Mr. Hot Drug Guy's brown eyes searched her green ones.

"Th-thank you so much," Brooke shakily said as she gathered Noah into her arms.

She was hit with the same scent as the time he had covered her with his jacket in the rain. Her pulse quickened, and she had to admit she was attracted to the beautiful man before her.

She hurried past him and deposited Noah in the apartment. Once inside, she clenched her hands and groaned. She shouldn't feel anything towards him. She didn't even know him, but she had seen enough to realize he was trouble.

LATER THAT NIGHT, after putting Noah to bed, Brooke approached her grandmother. "I think you're right." Her grandmother raised an eyebrow. "I need to go to a therapist." It was difficult to admit. She had always been levelheaded and handled anything that came her way. But that was before she lost her mom—her anchor.

"I know the thought of opening up to a stranger with all of your feelings is hard, but you'll be amazed at how much it will help." Grams placed her hand on Brooke's. "I've got some names of a few therapists who I have heard good things about. I'll send their contact information to you, and you can look them up and decide." Brooke smiled hesitantly and nodded. "By the way, I spoke with Ann earlier, and she's coming home Friday."

"How did she work that out? I thought her sister needed help for a longer time."

"Her sister's insurance finally kicked in and will pay for her to have live-in assistance. So even though Ann offered to stay the whole time, her sister refused and insists Ann has already done so much and needs to come home."

"I look forward to knowing Ann better. She's always seemed like such a nice lady. The more you tell me about her, the more wonderful she sounds."

"I agree, and you can start getting to know her Friday, because I've invited Ann and her grandson, Jacob, over for dinner to thank them for checking on things and getting the place ready for us while I was gone."

"Good, I really am appreciative. It was nice not having to check everything over for safety. And having the portable bed took a huge burden off of me when I first got here."

"You can help me plan out the menu tomorrow, then I'll get the ingredients." Grams wrapped an arm over Brooke's shoulder. "I love you, dear, and I am so thankful for you."

BROOKE RELAXED into the sofa of the therapist's office. Her first session was going better than she anticipated. Her therapist, Heather, was a friendly woman, close to her mom's age. In fact, Heather's whole approach to Brooke reminded her of her mom. Instead of making her emotional, it relaxed Brooke, and she felt comfortable enough to open up.

Heather asked about her mom's death and her relationship with her mom, as well as her relationships with her dad and Tyler. Brooke gave her a brief overview of her life. She mentioned the challenges she'd overcome through the years, and ended with the thing that finally broke her—her mom's death. As she worked through all the traumatic events out loud, she wanted to laugh at herself and the fact that one person's life had so much devastation. Her life sounded like a farce, like some cosmic force poured out all its wrath on her. She shook her head and laughed.

"What do you find so funny?" Heather asked.

"Just listening to myself list out all the horrible events in my life. It seems like a cruel joke that the universe, or God, is playing on me."

"Do you really think that?" Heather questioned, and Brooke nodded. "Don't you know that no one has a perfect life, and this world is broken? We are all dying and it's just a matter of when and how. So many people suffer throughout their existence without even the basics, like food, clean water, and shelter. Others endure horrendous diseases or abuse, and some are not able to get medical care.

"What if Noah had been born handicapped, and you were tasked with raising him as a single mom? What if you didn't have a father or grandmother helping you through this? What if you had to go to work immediately after your mom's death, just to put food on the table?"

Thinking through the questions Heather asked, it dawned on Brooke that things could be so much worse. "Yeah, you're right. Deep down I know it, but my heart aches so much and I can't stop the negative thoughts."

"Acknowledging your depression and coming to me is a huge step towards healing. A lot has happened to you, but you have a beautiful life ahead, and have been gifted an opportunity many don't have." Brooke raised an eyebrow at Heather's statement. "You are getting to spend time with your grandmother. Someone who has lived through almost three of your lifetimes. Based on what you've said, she has great wisdom and experience to offer you and Noah. And because of her long and happy marriage with your grandfather, she may have a great deal to share that will give you hope for a healthy long-term relationship some day.

"I think you've sold yourself short and are accepting less than you deserve from Tyler simply because he's the father of your child. You've seen in your own life that it is possible to get by with an absentee parent, though it's not ideal. If you stop worrying about having a romantic relationship with Tyler, maybe you'll have more emotional energy to discover what brings you joy and, ultimately, emotional healing."

Brooke furrowed her brow at the idea of giving up on their relationship.

"I'll be honest. Tyler sounds like a narcissist. I could be wrong. At the very least, he is something close to that. I'll let you look it up for yourself to understand what you're dealing with. But suffice it to say, a narcissist is very self-centered and good at convincing others that his way is the best and only way. They tend to manipulate the people in their lives, including those they claim to love, even if it causes the other person pain or problems.

"Now is the time for you to grow into a strong woman who makes her own decisions based on her needs and those of her son. It appears that your grandmother and father are both willing to help you on your journey. A strong woman knows when to seek help and is open to receiving support from others."

Brooke watched Heather, but was at a loss for words as she processed everything she just heard.

"I'm giving you an assignment for the next few days, then we will plan to meet twice next week." She grabbed a sheet of paper and started writing. "You're going to work on getting out of the apartment and engaging in activities that bring you joy, both with Noah and without."

"What about handling my relationship with Tyler?"

"Let's not worry about that for now, other than for you to research what a narcissist is. If you happen to talk to him before we meet next week . . . remember you control the narrative. Don't let him manipulate you into anything you're uncomfortable with. It seems like you've done well with that so far by coming to Florida in spite of his tantrum. I may be wrong about him, and time will tell, but it's important that you stay true to what you feel is right for you and Noah. And if you need to speak to me before our next appointment, you can send a text to the office mobile number with an explanation of the situation and how serious it is."

"Thank you." Brooke smiled. After only one session, her outlook improved. Hope bubbled up.

~

Just as Brooke settled in bed, her phone vibrated.

Tyler: I'm sorry for not being there for your mom's funeral, and for the way I reacted when you chose to move. It's been a hard semester for me and I felt I couldn't get away, then the news about the move hit me wrong. That's no excuse, but it's the truth. Like I said before, I'll be there for spring break. I want us to take Noah to Magic Kingdom, so please don't take him before. I want to be with him when he first sees it. I'll video chat with you and Noah Sunday afternoon.

Brooke stared at her phone in bewilderment. For months, Tyler barely paid attention to them, and now that she'd left Tennessee, he'd finally apologized–a first–and wanted to spend time with them.

She had two days to prepare for their conversation and planned to look up what a narcissist was first. He had a habit of tearing her down. After experiencing a glimmer of hope, she refused to let him take it away.

CHAPTER

SEVEN

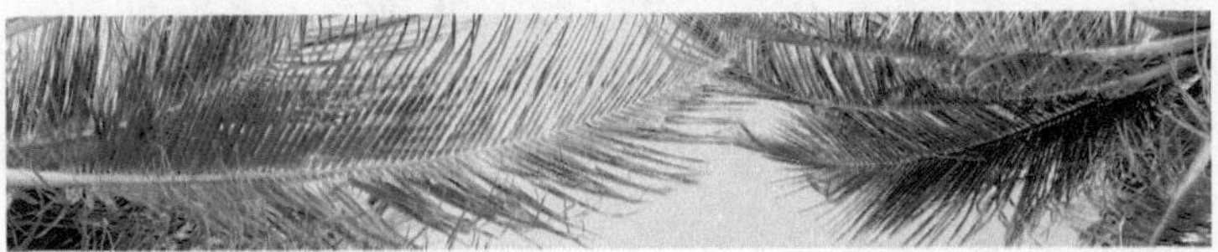

The doorbell rang and Brooke placed Noah in the playpen. She'd been looking forward to seeing Ann again and opened the door, ready to greet her. Instead, she found Mr. Hot Drug Dealer standing in all his glory on her doorstep, holding flowers.

Her brow furrowed and she swallowed hard. "Can I help you?"

"Brooke," he said with a crooked smile.

Her mouth dropped. "How—?

"Brooke! I see you've met my grandson," Ann said as she came around the corner. "Brooke, this is Jacob." Ann grinned and side hugged Brooke while balancing a cake with her other hand.

Still smiling, Jacob held out a hand towards Brooke. "Brooke." His husky voice shook her.

She stared at his hand for a few seconds before reaching out to shake it. When her eyes lifted to his, she couldn't read his expression. Realizing he still held her hand, she pulled it back.

Forcing a smile, Brooke reached out for the cake dish Ann carried, then stepped back into the apartment. She placed the dish on the counter and looked back at Jacob as he handed her grandmother the flowers.

Even as her grandmother greeted him, he watched Brooke's every move. Her mind was a jumbled mess as she tried to understand how the "perfect" grandson Ann had described when they spoke on the phone was the very same Mr. Hot Drug Dealer she had been running into. Had she misjudged him?

"Jacob . . . I'm glad to put a name to the face at last." She forced a smile and led him to the living room. "Come meet Noah." Once they were at the playpen, she whispered, "Why did you never tell me who you are?"

He frowned and ignored her question. "You don't like me, and I'm not sure why."

Brooke's face heated and her eyes darted down to Noah. She mumbled, "I thought youwereadrugdealer."

"What?" Jacob reached up and grabbed her shoulder, causing her to flinch.

"I thought you were a drug dealer," she said more clearly. When she saw his face had hardened, she asked, "You're not . . . are you?"

Jacob's hand fell from her shoulder and he laughed. "That explains all the dirty looks you gave me." He shook his head. "No, I'm not. I knew you were going through a hard time, so I had hoped that's all it was. I gave you your space because you always looked at me like . . . well, I guess like I was a criminal. Just . . . wow."

He frowned, stepped away from her, and reached down to pick Noah up. "Hey, Noah! Good to officially meet you." He tickled Noah under the chin and Noah giggled. Moving back toward Brooke, he leaned down to her ear and whispered, "Don't worry, I won't hold it against you."

A shiver raced down her spine, and when she looked at him, she noticed his grin was back.

Though Jacob said he wouldn't hold it against her, Brooke still felt embarrassed, resulting in a painfully awkward dinner. She had more questions for him, but not with their grandmothers present.

As the evening drew to a close, he pulled her aside and reached out to shake her hand. His hold on her lingered as he whispered, "Friends?"

"Friends," she agreed, but it felt like she was agreeing to more as she looked into his hypnotizing eyes. There was more to him than she imagined when she made her assumptions based on his appearance. She hoped he would allow her to get close enough to figure out all that lay beneath his bad boy exterior.

EIGHT

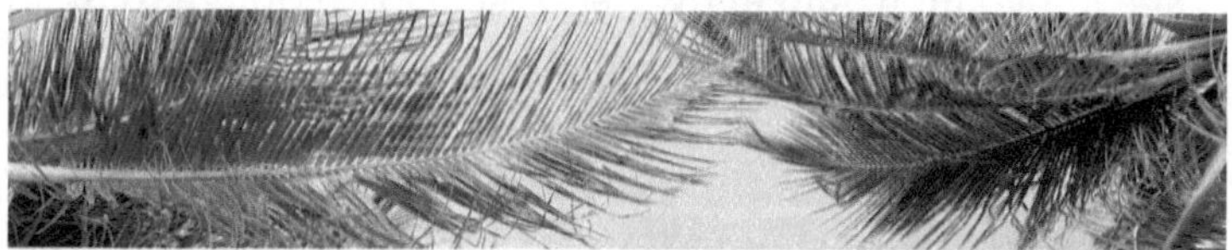

On Saturday morning, Grams left for Ann's to work on something for their church women's program. Brooke and Noah were on the patio. He was busy with his toy workbench while she scrolled through information on her phone about narcissists.

The more she read, the more she recognized Tyler. How had she missed it? How had he fooled her for so long? A knock on the door startled her. She picked up Noah before shuffling over and looking through the peephole. Jacob Reeves.

Brooke looked down at the old T-shirt she wore and frowned. She swiped at her makeup-free face to check for breakfast crumbs before shrugging and opening the door. Jacob held up a plate of cinnamon rolls.

"Um, hi." She looked down at the plate. "You made those?" Surely Mr. Hot Not a Drug Dealer didn't bake.

With a crooked grin, Jacob answered, "Nan did and sent me over with them. I have helped her make them in the past, though."

"I wouldn't have pegged you for a baker. Thanks," Brooke said flatly.

She reached out to take the plate, but Jacob pulled it back.

"Do you mind if I come in and chat with you guys?" He smiled at Noah and tickled his belly. Brooke frowned and didn't answer. Jacob sighed. "I thought we could get to know each other better. Last night, you seemed to hold back. I'm guessing it was because our grandmothers were there. It's obvious you still feel uncomfortable around me. If we're going to be together regularly, we should work through that, don't you think?" The side of his mouth quirked up.

Brooke's heart raced as she stepped back and let him in. She placed Noah on a floor mat and pulled over a basket of toys before sitting beside him. This man made her nervous. Jacob joined them, pulling out a fire truck and rolling it in front of Noah.

"Do you always judge people by the way they look?"

"Huh?" Brooke heard him, but wasn't sure how to answer.

"Do you always judge people by the way they look?" Jacob repeated. "I'm guessing something about the way I look made you think that about me."

Her eyes moved to his muscular arms, but she realized she was staring and looked down at Noah. "Of course not," Brooke quickly denied it, but the more she thought about it, maybe he was right.

"Well, I . . . it's possible that had something to do with it. I grew up going to a private school where everyone dressed—" she paused, searching for words. Basically, they all dressed like spoiled rich kids, including herself. "Um, different than you. I guess you could say preppy." She shifted on the floor, avoiding his eyes. "Then in college, in my sorority and with the fraternity I hung out with, it was more of the same. And before I moved here, I worked in a law office with a very strict dress code.

"So, yeah, the way you dress, combined with the different fancy cars, made my imagination run wild. I'm used to people with money dressing more preppy and tailored." She winced, knowing everything she said sounded awful.

Jacob frowned and stared at her as he shook his head.

Maybe she should tell him the rest. "Then when I saw you

hanging out with the teenagers, I worried you were selling drugs to them." He continued frowning, so she added, "Why else would a guy your age be spending so much time around teenagers?"

Pressing his lips together, Jacob looked away, then down at Noah, who was entertaining himself with toys. "It's true, I don't fit your mold, Brooke." He sighed.

The way he said her name this time made her flinch. Was he challenging her to take off her rose-colored glasses and see past the external?

"As a guy who grew up without a dad, and mostly, without a mom, I can't help but want to befriend and encourage the young people who are residents here. Every one of them I've met live in single-parent homes or with a grandparent. Most don't even have men in their lives."

For the second time in a month, it occurred to Brooke that she wasn't the only one who had a difficult life. Her therapist had pointed it out, but without faces and real stories, it was easy to ignore. Learning that this handsome man in front of her grew up without his parents, and the teens he hung out with were from broken homes, affected her deeply. All this time, she'd focused on her own hardships without seeing past the surface of the people surrounding her. Jacob was the opposite of what she had thought and much more compassionate than she was.

Her face heated. It occurred to her that the way she'd made assumptions and treated him based on outward things was similar to what she experienced from her supposed friends back home when word got out she was pregnant. "I'm so sorry. I had you all wrong, and I've been judgmental."

Jacob watched her, and seemed to be thinking. "I guess I'll have to show you what kind of person I am." He frowned and looked down. "I won't lie, there was a period in high school when I experimented with drugs. My mom died from a drug overdose when I was fifteen, and I got worse before realizing I was headed down the same path. I still had some big vices in my life for a long time after." His eyes found hers. "But last summer I became a Christian and started making changes in my life."

Her eyebrows shot up. That wasn't what she expected. "You too? If you're thinking of preaching to me right now, forget it. I've got a bone to pick with God, and refuse to listen to you extol His goodness to me."

A smile broke out on Jacob's face and he chuckled. "Don't worry. I won't say anything . . . today." He winked.

His smile disarmed her, and she no longer cared if he had a hidden agenda. She wanted to learn more about him. "So what do you do that allows you to drive all those fancy cars and have such an odd schedule? Do you work for a car dealership?"

Another chuckle erupted and he shook his head. "I work in the music industry. I write songs, so my schedule varies and sometimes requires extensive travel."

She side-eyed him. She'd heard it was challenging to earn substantial money in that industry.

"If you have the right connections, there's money to be made," he answered like he'd read her mind.

"Well, you're one of the lucky ones. I've met some people who tried it in Nashville, and didn't get that far."

He didn't reply, just grinned.

As she stared at him, she noticed he was dressed differently than usual. "I've not seen you wear shorts before."

He wore grey athletic shorts and a black compression shirt that showed off his toned upper body. Now she realized why it had been hard to keep her eyes off him all morning.

"Yeah?" He looked down at his shorts. "I'm going to meet my roommates to work out."

"Roommates? You don't live here with your grandmother?" He shook his head at her question. "But you were here when she was gone."

"I just get her mail, water plants, and check in with the neighborhood teens." He winked. "I do stay with her sometimes, though.

She's more like a mom to me than my mom ever was. Wherever she is, it feels like home."

He pulled a book out of Noah's basket and held it out to him. "Do you want to read a book?"

Noah's eyes lit up in delight. He crawled to Jacob and began climbing onto his leg. "Buh."

Jacob nodded and crossed his legs so he could pull Noah into his lap. Jacob's voice imitations amused Noah as he giggled and leaned back into Jacob's chest. Brooke was overwhelmed with emotion as she watched the scene. She longed for Noah to have that with his dad. Sadness and anger toward Tyler rose at the same time that amazement and thankfulness for Jacob grew. Jacob was quite different from her expectations. It scared her.

"Noah, say 'hi' to Daddy." Brooke waved her hand at the screen. Noah looked at her and copied.

"Da." Noah squeezed his hand closed, then opened it before touching the screen.

After her therapist visit, she analyzed everything Tyler said and did, wondering if he was truly a narcissist. Her hope for them to reconcile and be a family seemed like an impossible dream, since he had been so hot and cold with her.

Regardless of how things turned out for the two of them, she'd encourage Noah's relationship with his father, hoping it would thrive. She knew how rejection by your dad felt. The sound of her name drew her back to the screen.

"Brooke? Are you paying attention?" She nodded at Tyler. "We're going to have a great time at Magic Kingdom and see Mickey, aren't we, Mommy?"

Brooke bit her tongue to keep from saying what she wanted, then pasted on a smile and leaned into Noah. "Yay! Mickey Mouse!"

"Mimi!" Noah clapped.

Taking a deep breath, Brooke forced herself to continue. "Yes, and we'll ride the train, and the carousel, and see Buzz Lightyear . . ." Noah giggled at that. Tyler's parents had given him a talking Buzz. "And do all sorts of fun things!"

"It sounds like you're getting excited, too." Tyler smiled at Brooke, and for the first time in ages, she thought she recognized the smile he used to give her before Noah—like she was his whole world. It made her nervous, but raised her hopes again.

"Yeah, I really am. It's been a while since I've been, and I'm looking forward to sharing it with Noah. Maybe I'll take him to Disney Springs this week and get him some stuffed characters so he can recognize them at the park."

"Good idea." Tyler went on to tell her the specifics of his arrival on Saturday.

By the end of the conversation, Brooke felt better about the visit. He showed more interest in the two of them than he ever had.

She was most worried about the sleeping arrangements. Her grandmother would not let them sleep in the same room, so he would be in the bed in Noah's room. She knew he wouldn't be happy about that. In the past, it would have bothered her. But she needed to protect her heart and make sure he was committed to them if she was going to continue to give herself to him that way.

BROOKE LOOKED up from her laptop when she heard a knock at the door. Looking through the peephole, she was surprised to see Jacob.

"Hey." Brooke felt her face flush as she took him in. He was wearing shorts again, but this time they were khakis, paired with a fitted navy blue crewneck T-shirt. Was he trying to look more preppy for her?

Grinning, Jacob spoke up. "I was visiting Nan, and thought I'd swing by and see if I could take Noah to a park or something. You're welcome to come too, since you may not feel comfortable leaving him with me. Or I can take him to give you a break."

"Oh, um . . ." Brooke looked at him, wide-eyed.

"I'm sorry. You don't know me well enough yet. I just thought . . ."

"No, no. It's not that. I mean, I don't know you well, but he's not here." Jacob seemed to relax when she explained. She felt compelled to tell him why. "I've had a hard time with my mom's death, and Grams usually takes him out between lunch and his nap to give me a break."

"You're depressed." He stated. "It makes you sleepy." She looked at him with curiosity. "I went through that after my mom's death, too. Kind of surprising, since when she was alive, I sometimes wished she wasn't." He ran his hand through his hair. "It sounds awful. I was a kid and only thought about how things affected me."

He shook his head. "How about I take you out for ice cream, and we can go to a park, walk around, and get to know each other better?"

The request caught Brooke off guard, but flattered her. He was a good-looking guy, and she didn't mind spending time with him, though something inside urged her not to get involved. "I . . . uh, okay." She shrugged.

"Not as a date or anything, of course." He looked down at his feet and seemed nervous. "I figure since our grandmothers are so close, we should get acquainted."

She pushed aside her doubts. "You're right, we should." She nodded. "I need to shut down my computer first." At least she was dressed from taking Noah on a walk earlier. Sometimes she stayed in her pajamas all day. Maybe that needed to change.

He followed her in as she turned off her computer, slipped on a pair of shoes, and grabbed her purse and sunglasses. "It feels strange to me when I don't have to grab a diaper bag," she commented.

"It's good for you to have some time without Noah. You're a mom, but you're also a woman." She gave him a funny look. "Maybe that didn't sound right. You have needs and interests outside of Noah."

Brooke still wasn't sure how to take that. "I'm going to a therapist now, and one of my assignments for the week was to do things with and without Noah that bring me joy."

Jacob grinned as he held open the door of his Porsche for her. "That's what I'm talking about."

"So what's with having two, brand new, expensive cars?" Brooke had grown up with nice things, even after the divorce, thanks to her father's gifts and his help in supplementing her mom's income, even if it was out of guilt. But as a single mom working toward being on her own, she had gone through a huge learning curve about the cost of living. Now items that had once been necessary seemed extravagant.

Jacob glanced at Brooke before slipping on his sunglasses and backing up. He shrugged. "I deal with a lot of famous and wealthy people in my industry. When I drive them around, they expect a certain type of treatment."

Brooke watched his movements out of the corner of her eye, not wanting to openly stare. "I'm sorry. I shouldn't have asked that. There I go again, being judgy."

"It's fine. I'm sure it seems odd for someone as young as me."

"I'll get past it. Where are we going?" She noticed they passed the nearest park.

"There's a park further out. It's more of a local place, so it's not overrun with tourists. But first, I'm going to take you for some Puerto Rican ice cream."

"I'm up for that." She looked over at him, comparing his darker bronze skin to her pale skin. "Are you part Puerto Rican?" She knew his grandmother didn't look like it, and he didn't have an accent.

He chuckled. "Who knows, but it's good ice cream. My mom slept around a lot when she got pregnant with me. Lots of one-night stands, so she had no idea who my dad was."

"Oh." Brooke turned her face back to the road. "Did your mom ever marry?"

"Actually, she did, but it only lasted a couple years. When I was seven, she met this really great guy. She sobered up for him and got married. The times I visited, it was like the happy family I'd always wanted, so I went to live with them. It was the only time I ever lived without my Nan. Anyway, by the time I was nine, she started sneaking around and doing drugs again. Her husband tried to help her, but when he found her in their bed with her drug dealer, he filed for divorce and I went back to live with Nan. My mom couldn't keep it together."

"Wow. And I thought I had it bad growing up with married parents who hated each other. They finally got divorced after my dad cheated on my mom and got his mistress pregnant."

Jacob glanced at Brooke. "The hard stuff made us who we are today. We both turned out okay. I made it through. You will too."

Moisture filled Brookes eyes. When they parked outside of Coquitos Ice Cream, she noticed they were in downtown Kissimmee. "This is close to Grams' old house! The one she lived in before my Papa died." The memory brought a rush of emotions.

He scanned her face. "You have a beautiful smile."

She placed her hand over her mouth, but he reached to uncover it. Tingles shot through her fingers.

"Don't. It's the first time I've seen you smile," Jacob said.

She furrowed her brow. Surely not.

"You've pasted on a few fake ones, but that was the first genuine smile I've seen. If you want, we can drive by her old house after the park."

"I would love that." Brooke couldn't keep the grin off her face. "Are we going to the Lakefront Park on Lake Toho?"

"That's the one." Jacob chuckled at her newfound enthusiasm. He grabbed a ball cap and opened his door. Just as Brooke reached for the handle, he touched her shoulder. "Stay put. I've got it."

"You said this wasn't a date."

"It's not, but you deserve to be treated like a lady."

THE BRIGHT AFTERNOON sun shined directly on them as they strolled through the park. She was thankful when they found a shady oak, its branches hanging over a bench facing the lake. Even with sunscreen, she had to be careful with her pale skin. After winter in Memphis, she needed gradual sun exposure to avoid a bad burn. Not an easy task in the intense Florida sun.

The refreshing breeze from the lake and the Spanish moss hanging and swaying from the tree brought a familiar sense of happiness. The sound of a sandhill crane drew her eyes to the side. She smiled as it gracefully walked and pecked around for food.

"What's keeping you so quiet and thoughtful?"

Brooke had smiled nonstop since they arrived in this part of town. She played with the ice cream bowl in her hand and tilted her head as she tried to wrap her mind around her thoughts.

"This place." She waved a hand around at the park and lake. "I have so many happy memories here. Not just at this park, but this whole area of town around Grams' old house." Her mind drifted back to her first summer in Kissimmee with her grandparents, almost twelve years earlier. "Papa and Grams moved down here just before I turned eleven, and that summer I spent two months with them. My mom came down with me for the first two weeks, but it was just me, Papa, and Grams for most of the summer. It was the best summer I ever had. Lots of time spent at this park, the Denn John pool, and Disney with my season pass. I knew the Disney parks like the back of my hand, and most of the cast members recognized me."

"Sounds like a special time." He continued watching her.

Brooke nodded, took a bite of ice cream, then frowned. "Once I went home, everything started going downhill between my parents —or so I thought. I had no idea they had just been putting up with each other for years. Most summers after that, I came back down to get away from the tension. Kissimmee became my place of refuge. Every time I arrived and stepped into the Florida sun, it was like the pressures of home melted away."

The dam broke, and tears streamed down her face. Jacob placed an arm around her shoulder, and she began again shakily, "That's what I hoped would happen this time when I moved down here. It's just not working out that way." Sniffling, she attempted to regain control. She was a mom. She had responsibilities, and she hated feeling like a burden to others.

"I think you're going to be okay. Part of healing is accepting your feelings, so you can work through them and learn to live with them."

Brooke's mouth lifted into a small smile. "Are you sure you're not an old man in a young guy's body?"

He chuckled. "Well, according to my driver's license, I'm twenty-five."

Rain suddenly pounded down on them, and Jacob grabbed her hand as they darted towards the car. By the time they reached the car and climbed in, it had stopped.

"Look, a rainbow!" Brooke touched Jacob's shoulder and pointed. Her hand still felt tingly from where he had held it.

"Take a picture. I think God is giving you a sign of hope for your future."

At his words, Brooke felt a strange emotion. She was mad at God. Why would He give her a sign of hope? She pushed the thought down as she brought the camera into focus.

"Oh, good. It looks like no one's home, so they won't think we're creepers. Will you park? I want to take a picture."

Jacob pulled in front of Brooke's grandmother's old mid-century one-story ranch home. "They still have the orange tree in the front yard." She pointed to a mid-sized orange tree. "I wonder if the lime and clementine trees are still in the back, too. See the oak tree peeking above the house in the back? There was a tire swing on it that my cousins and I used." Brooke rolled down the window and snapped a photo.

She turned back to Jacob. "I guess we should go on, before the neighbors call the police."

He nodded, and his brow furrowed. "You're all wet and cold. I think I've got some things in my trunk." He hopped out and popped the trunk before returning with a beach towel and sweatshirt. "These should help."

Brooke chuckled. "Do you always drive around with a beach towel?"

"Pretty much." He grinned. "It's Florida and there's water everywhere, not to mention sudden showers like today's happen almost every afternoon. You never know." He shrugged.

During the drive back, a feeling of comfort settled on her. Thoughts of summers past, the day at the park, and the warmth of the sweatshirt combined with Jacob's scent was a heady combination. She sighed contentedly as she listened to Jacob point out places they passed.

"So, did today give you a little joy?"

"Hm?" Brooke glanced at him in confusion.

"Your therapist's assignment."

Brooke smiled. "More than a little. Thank you." She turned to the window, attempting to control her emotions, then looked back at him. "Seriously. You have no idea what today did for me."

"We should keep it up then. How about tomorrow we take Noah to the same park, so he can experience a place that holds so many of your happy memories?"

"I think he'd like that." Brooke took a deep breath before adding, "I would too."

CHAPTER
NINE

"You seem happy," Grams said when Brooke stepped into her room to let her know she was home. "You were smiling and humming."

Brooke tried to hide her smile, but it broke out again. "I had a nice time with Jacob." Her grandmother raised an eyebrow and smiled, but Brooke didn't want her to get the wrong idea. They were just friends. "It's just . . . he took me to Lakefront Park, and we drove past your old house off of Neptune Road. It brought back so many good memories."

Her grandmother patted the spot beside her on the bed and laid the book she'd been reading on the nightstand. Slipping off her shoes, Brooke climbed into the bed, snuggled up beside Grams, and they reminisced about summers past.

"Noah! Look at the dragon!"

"Da?" He questioned and pointed to the dragon in the water at Disney Springs.

"There's World of Disney," Jacob called. "We can go there first and then take Noah to the carousel and train before lunch."

"Are you sure you have time for all that? This is the third day in a row you've given up for me. I feel like I'm monopolizing your time."

He looked at her seriously. "I'm not a person who has trouble saying how I feel about things. If it's too much, I'll let you know. Besides, I leave town Friday and won't be back until the following Thursday, so I want to do something non-work related now."

"Okay, then." Brooke followed Jacob as he pushed Noah's stroller into the store. "I'm thinking some plush characters would help him become familiar before we go to Magic Kingdom." She pointed to a section near the entrance that had mini beanbag versions on sale. "Those look like a good size. They won't take up too much room in his toy box."

After sorting through them, they had a basket filled with Mickey, Minnie, Donald, Goofy, Pluto, Woody, Winnie the Pooh, Tigger, Eeyore, Rabbit, and Piglet. Jacob pulled Noah out of the stroller and held him up so he could see them. Noah squealed in excitement, then turned to Jacob and patted his face. He reached up and pulled at his cap, almost getting it off. Jacob's hand flew up to stop him. "Nobody wants to see my hat hair, Noah." Jacob made a sad face, and Noah giggled.

As they went to check out, Jacob stopped and picked up a couple of Winnie the Pooh books. "I want to introduce him to the fun of Winnie the Pooh. For the brief time my mom was married, my stepdad read the stories to me, with voices for all the characters. Those were some of my favorite childhood memories, and I want to do that for Noah."

"Th-thank you," Brooke whispered, barely able to get the words out.

This man, who had only known them a few days, was willing to invest time in her son's life, yet after nearly a year and a half, his own father was just now taking an interest in him. Her mind drifted to Tyler, and she wondered how the coming week would go. He was due in on Saturday, and deep down, she dreaded it. She'd had so many disappointments from him since her pregnancy and didn't want to get her hopes up only to have them dashed again.

Thoughts of Tyler quickly checked her emotions, and she tried making a joke. "So the bad boy has a soft side?" He kept surprising her.

At the front of the line, Jacob placed the basket by the register, and Brooke reached to pull out her credit card.

"Nope," Jacob placed a hand on hers. "Today is all on me."

"No, Jacob. That's too much."

He shook his head, "Please let me do this. I want them to be gifts from me. It's not like I can't afford them." Brooke frowned, but he slipped out his wallet and scanned his card.

"I THINK the train was his favorite," Jacob commented and Brooke nodded. "The look on his face was priceless." He pulled out his phone and showed her the pictures he took. "I'll send them to you."

Brooke lifted a spoon with ice cream to Noah's mouth, but he moved at the last second, leaving ice cream on his cheek. He smeared it around with his hand and offered it to Jacob, who pretended to eat it off his hand before grabbing a napkin and wiping him down.

Who is this man? Brooke wondered as she watched their interaction.

"I'd like to cook dinner for you guys tomorrow night, since I'll be leaving for a week. Your Grams is invited too, of course."

"Um . . . okay." She tried to smile, but the thought of him wanting to spend his last night home with them scared her. Not that she didn't like the idea. She liked it too much.

"My Nan said we can have the meal at her apartment. That way, when this little guy gets sleepy, we'll be close to your place. And before you get too excited, my cooking skills are fairly basic, so don't expect anything fancy."

A real smile broke through. "I think I can handle that."

"CAN YOU SPARE SOME HONEY?" Jacob waved Winnie the Pooh around in front of Noah, who grabbed it with excitement. While Noah held Pooh, Jacob opened one of the Pooh books he'd bought and began reading.

Brooke leaned against the doorframe and watched them, curled up together in the spare bed in Noah's room. Jacob patted the bed for her to join, but she shook her head and slipped out as moisture filled her eyes. She stood in the hall, listening and letting her tears flow freely. After cooking them dinner, he offered—no, begged, to help with their bedtime routine.

Fear gripped her. She felt drawn to Jacob—she had since the moment she first saw him, but it was too soon. And with Tyler flying down, she couldn't dismiss the possibility of reconciling with him—even if he was a narcissist. It was worth it, if it would be good for Noah. Rushing into the hall bathroom, she rinsed her face and patted her eyes. As she walked out, she heard Jacob call her.

"Mommy, come back and give Noah goodnight kisses. Right, Noah?" She heard Noah's soft giggles. "You need goodnight kisses." When she walked in, he added, "And tell her you've got a clean diaper, too."

After he passed Noah to her, he rolled up the dirty diaper and disposed of it, before washing his hands in the bathroom. He returned to the doorway, watching her put Noah down.

He waved. "Night night, Noah."

Her heart melted.

She softly sang *You Are My Sunshine*, kissed her son one last time, then laid him down and said her final good night.

When she entered the living room, she found Jacob sitting on the sofa and joined him.

"He went down easily."

"He's on a good schedule, thanks to Grams."

"It's not all Grams. You're doing an amazing job." He rubbed his hands on his pants. "So ... I hope you have a great week and figure out things with your ex."

The comment surprised her, and she watched his face for signs of what he meant. Did he want her to work things out because he cared about her as a friend? Had she been reading too much into things, thinking he felt the same attraction she did?

She gave a half-hearted smile. "I'm trying not to get my hopes up. My therapist thinks he's a narcissist. Like, not in the light-hearted, 'he's conceited' way, but in the manipulative, controlling, emotionally abusive, ruin-your-life sort of way." Jacob's brow furrowed as she described Tyler. "The first year and a half Tyler and I dated were wonderful. He treated me well, and we talked about our future. He wanted to be a renowned surgeon, and I was going to put criminals away as a lawyer. Our lives seemed to fit perfectly. When I told him I was pregnant, and was keeping it, everything changed. I saw a side of him I never knew.

"He was furious and no longer sure about us as a couple. He said I ruined everything, because a baby would just get in the way of our aspirations." Brooke's body tensed, remembering how he treated her. "The funny thing is, my dreams changed. Sure, I was sad at first —to give up law school and *settle* for an undergrad degree and being a paralegal, but providing for and having time with Noah became my priority." Tears flowed again and she rolled her eyes. "I can't seem to stop the waterworks."

Jacob slid closer and wrapped an arm around her, rubbing her shoulder. "It's okay, there's nothing wrong with crying. You've gone through so much. I don't know what will happen with Tyler, but God will be with you every step of the way. You can pray for wisdom, direction, and courage to follow through with what you need to do regarding him."

At the mention of God, Brooke tensed and wanted to scoff, but held her breath. This man had been a good friend to her, and she didn't want to insult him.

At her hesitance, he spoke again, "Why don't I pray for you right now?"

Brooke was surprised, but nodded.

He squeezed her shoulder. "Father God, I lift up Brooke to you. You know all she has been through better than me. Strengthen her for the journey ahead, draw her to Yourself and help her understand the love You have for her that surpasses all the brokenness in her life. Give her wisdom and clarity about the future of her relationship with Tyler, protect her heart from more pain, and help her trust You to provide love for her in the future if he isn't the one. And I pray for Noah, that regardless of how things work out with Tyler, he would never miss out on a father figure in his life. I pray that his childhood will be filled with joy. And I also pray for Brooke to have healing as she deals with her mom's death and other hurts from her past. Give her peace, God. In Jesus' name. Amen."

A warm feeling filled her body. All the cynicism left her. She may not believe in his God, but the prayer touched her heart, and she actually felt comforted by it. She opened her eyes and looked at him. "Thank you. I'm not a Christian, but I feel strangely better."

"I'm glad. I should get going. I've got to get home and get up early for my flight."

Brooke walked him to the door, feeling sad about not seeing him for a week. "I hope your out-of-town work goes well. Where are you headed?"

"A few different places in the Midwest."

"Hmm. Oh, I almost forgot! Tomorrow, I'm going to meet up at Denn John Park with a play day group that takes their kids every Friday. I found out about it from Katlyn, a lady who goes to Grams' and your Nan's church. She and the pastor's wife visited me when I first got here. Anyway, hanging out with you all week cheered me up enough that I think I'll be okay in a crowd of new people." Jacob looked at her with concern.

"I've never had a problem with crowds or new people before. It started at Mom's funeral. All these people wanted me to talk about my feelings, and I wasn't ready. And when I first got here, I was terrified of meeting new people and constantly rehashing everything that was tearing me up inside. Thanks to therapy and you, I think I'm ready."

Jacob smiled. "That's awesome!" He high-fived her. "I'm no therapist, but I'm glad I helped. It's been good to see you feeling better . . . happier. You deserve it, and it will be good for you and Noah to make some new friends." He leaned down and hugged her. "Goodnight, Brooke. Send me a picture from Magic Kingdom, maybe from the Pooh ride." He pulled back and grinned.

"I don't have your number."

"I guess you don't. We need to fix that. Hand me your phone." He dialed his number from hers. "It's fixed. I . . . " He ran a hand through his hair and met her eyes. "See ya." Shoving his hands into his pockets, he backed away while still watching her. "I'll send your Grams back home. Sometimes she and Nan get so caught up in their discussions, they don't realize what time it is."

"Safe travels!" She waved goodbye as he walked towards his grandmother's apartment.

Stepping inside, she wondered if he viewed her as a project, hoping she would get better so he could move on. Even though she had only known him a week, he'd filled an empty spot in her life. The thought of letting him go made her chest hurt. It couldn't be good to be so dependent on another person, but right now, she needed him.

THE SOUND of an incoming text drew Brooke's attention as she was dressing before getting Noah up for the morning. She glanced at it and saw an unknown number. From the screen, she could read some of the text.

· · ·

Unknown: At the airport and I had to get this—

Smiling, she realized it must be from Jacob. After saying good night to him, she had been distracted and forgotten to put his name in her phone with his number. Opening the message, she saw that he also included a picture.

Unknown: At the airport and I had to get this picture at The Magic of Disney store to send to Noah. Have fun at the park!

The picture was of him in front of a screen that showed the giant Woody in Toy Story Land at Hollywood Studios. Brooke chuckled— he was wearing his signature cap and sunglasses, even though he was inside. "Always trying to look cool," she said softly. It reminded her of the picture she took of him holding Noah in front of the Woody at the Disney Springs LEGO store. She hearted the picture before typing.

Brooke: Cute, or should I say cool, since that seems to be the look you're going for. Noah will love this. Maybe we can take him to Hollywood Studios so he can see it in real life. He would love all the bright colors and characters there. Safe flight!

As soon as she sent the text, she regretted it. It sounded like she asked him on a date. She rubbed her face.

While she prepared herself breakfast, her phone dinged.

. . .

Unknown: I would love to see his face when he goes to HS. I'll see if I can work it out.

I'll see if I can work it out. It felt like a rejection. She hadn't even mentioned a specific day or time. He had made time for her every day this past week, but now he was unsure. Evidently she *was* just a project for him.

She tapped her fingers on the counter while fighting back tears, but that only made her angry with herself. She had made progress this week and wanted to keep moving forward. She would be fine without him in the picture. It would force her to stand on her own two feet. *I can do this.*

She picked up her phone and tapped her mom's number. As it rang, she sucked in a breath. She couldn't have a conversation with her mom about Jacob, or about anything else. The reality stung.

Grams walked in as tears streamed down her face. "I just tried to call Mom on the phone. I miss her, Grams."

"I know, dear. Me too." The older woman sat down beside Brooke and pulled her close.

Noah fell asleep almost instantly after coming home from the park. Brooke silently closed his door, smiling. It had been a good day. She grabbed the baby monitor and sat down in the patio glider, thinking about the new friends she and Noah made. A woman her age named Andrea introduced herself, and their sons played well together. They planned to meet again the next day at a park closer to Brooke's apartment, since Tyler wouldn't be in until later in the day.

She opened her phone to look at the pictures she'd taken and saw some from the previous week with Jacob. Thoughts of her conversation with Andrea came to mind. When she had opened her phone to get Andrea's number, Andrea saw the airport picture of Jacob.

. . .

"Is that Noah's dad?"

"Huh? Oh, no. Just a friend."

Andrea giggled. "He's good-looking. Maybe he'd be a good fill-in."

"Noah's dad is actually coming to visit tomorrow. I don't even know where we stand. He's been stringing me along for a while. At this point, I'm starting to think I'm better off on my own."

"Don't sell yourself short. You can have love, and be a good mom."

"That's what people keep saying."

TEN

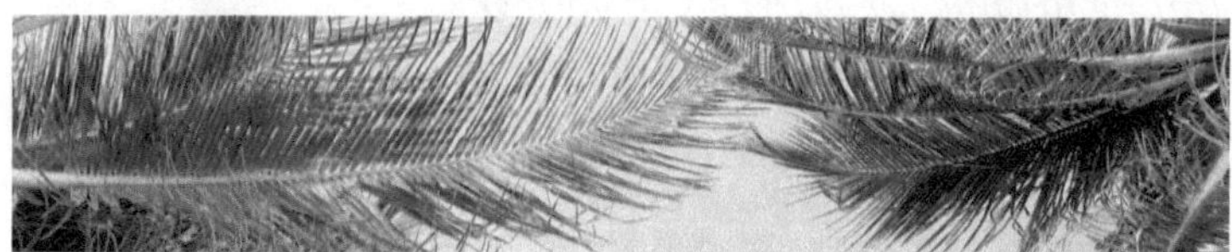

When Tyler arrived, he seemed happy to see Brooke and Noah, which surprised her. She wasn't sure what to make of his recent interest in their lives. Her therapist encouraged her to be careful and said if he truly wanted to fix things, she should let him prove it and pursue her. She was in agreement.

"Welcome, Tyler. How was your flight?" Grams had made it clear to Brooke that she was worried about the way Tyler had treated them in the past, but she promised to make him feel at ease. She was a southern lady after all, and skilled at laying on the charm.

"It was fine, Mrs. Donahue." Tyler knew how to turn on the charm himself.

"I have a chicken and pasta dish for you, if you're hungry, and also some pound cake. What would you like?"

"That's so kind of you. I've already eaten dinner, but I'd love some pound cake. Would it be possible for me to take a quick shower first, then eat?"

"Certainly, son."

"Oh, um, let me show you your room." Brooke forced a smile, and led him to Noah's room, where there was a guest bed.

"You sleep in here, with Noah?" Tyler furrowed his brow.

Brooke had been dreading this conversation. "No, I'm in the room we passed on the left."

Tyler's face tensed. "Is there a reason I'm not staying in your room?"

Stepping back from him, Brooke responded, "It's Grams' home, and she doesn't allow unmarried people to sleep together."

Tyler smirked and stepped closer. His eyes turned to Noah in her arms, and then back to her and he chuckled. "It should be obvious it's a little late for that." He tilted his body forward and whispered in her ear. "I'll be sure to come check on you after everyone's asleep, then." He leaned back and winked, before tossing his suitcase on the bed to gather things for the shower.

Brooke cleared her throat, "That's not a good idea, Tyler."

He walked back to her and ran a hand down her cheek, then lowered his voice. "Come on, baby, haven't you missed me?"

Had she? She recalled her past week with Jacob. The only times she'd thought of Tyler were when he had called or sent her information about the trip. If she was honest, she had not *missed* him at all. That was a first in the last two years. She felt proud of herself at the revelation. "I'm not going against my grandmother's wishes. If you aren't happy with the arrangements, you are welcome to stay in a hotel."

"Really? I come to spend time with you two, and you're going to kick me out?" Anger flared in his eyes.

"I'm not kicking you out. I'm happy for you to stay here . . . in this room . . . the entire night." She frowned, and her body tensed.

He gritted his teeth. "Fine, whatever. I don't want to start the trip with an argument." He went back to his suitcase.

～

SUNDAY WAS their first full day together, and Brooke planned for them to go resort hopping on the monorails and ride the boat on Disney's Bay Lake. She had booked lunch at Chef Mickey's in the Contemporary Resort.

In the morning, Tyler showed an improved demeanor. He acted as if nothing had happened the night before. Brooke was more than thankful to put it behind them.

On the drive to the Contemporary Resort, Noah seemed to sense the excitement and happily babbled along with the Disney songs on Brooke's playlist. She glanced over to find Tyler smiling and tapping his hand against the door to the beat. The happy domestic picture brought a smile to her face.

As they approached the Disney World entrance sign, Brooke felt her heart rate increase. Disney was another place with happy memories, and she was excited to share them with Noah. They planned to go to Magic Kingdom on Wednesday and she couldn't wait. "When was the last time you went to Magic Kingdom?" she asked. When Tyler didn't answer, she looked over at him. His eyes had narrowed, and he looked angry. "What's wrong?"

"I've told you before, we didn't have a lot of extra money for trips when I was a kid. I've never been. That's why it's such a big deal that I am the first in our family, not only to get a college degree, but to become a doctor. You wouldn't understand, growing up with your dad as one of Memphis's top lawyers. Everything came easy to you."

That conversation took a quick turn. What could she even say to that? She was unaware he'd never been, but she recalled his repeated claims of being the first in his family to graduate college. He'd told her never to mention it in front of others, as he didn't want to be embarrassed by his family's lack of social standing.

Thankfully, they were just approaching the parking attendant, and she avoided a full-blown argument. She provided the attendant with her reservation information, and he directed her to the Contemporary Resort parking lot. Within minutes, they arrived at the one-of-a-kind building with a monorail track running through it.

Tyler stared at it in amazement, causing Brooke to grin. He was in for a treat when he saw the inside of the Contemporary and the other resorts she planned to show him.

After loading up Noah's stroller, they headed off on their adventure. They briefly toured the Contemporary resort, before hopping on a boat to the Wilderness Lodge.

"You'll find it interesting that The Wilderness Lodge is designed with features similar to Old Faithful Inn in Yellowstone Park," Brooke explained as the boat approached the resort. "There's a geyser outside that spouts 120 feet into the air every hour." She looked at her watch. "It should go off a few minutes after we get there."

Tyler smiled. He looked happy and content—a dramatic change from when she'd seen him after her mom's funeral. She felt hopeful during moments like these, believing they could overcome the past two years of drama and reunite as a family. Even Noah seemed entranced in their little bubble as he happily turned his head into the breeze and imitated the sound of the blasting horn.

The towering evergreens shaded the path leading towards the geyser and the lodge loomed over them in the distance. It was easy to forget they were in Florida and not the wilderness of Wyoming. They made it to the geyser with time to spare, and within minutes, gazed into the air at the impressive blast of water.

Noah clapped his hands. "Yay!"

Tyler looked down at him proudly.

As they approached the main building, Brooke pulled up pictures of the lobby of Old Faithful Inn. "You need to see these before we go inside so you can compare."

"Wow, this is impressive," Tyler commented as they entered. "The similarities are astounding. Even the fireplace."

"Of course they've added the Disney touch to it, like hidden Mickeys in various places." Tyler looked at Brooke quizzically, so she explained. "Mickey head shapes that at first glance just blend in, but are strategically placed in things like a painting, picture frame, an imprint in a stone or framework, or even a post in the building."

"That's cool. Do you know where some are?"

"I remember a couple. They have a hidden Mickey scavenger hunt page at the front desk."

Tyler grinned. "I think it's time for a scavenger hunt."

～

"Mimi? Mimi!" Noah shouted when Chef Mickey walked up to the table next to theirs at the restaurant.

"We get to talk to him next, Noah." Brooke said as she wiped red sauce from his fingers and face with a wet wipe. "We don't want to get Mickey dirty, do we? Look! There's Pluto, Donald, and Goofy, too!" She pointed around the room, distracting him while they waited for Mickey.

"Mimi!" Noah squealed when Mickey Mouse arrived at their table. Mickey high-fived Noah, and he giggled in delight. He babbled to Mickey with what sounded like "Puhpuh, Duh, and Goo" and finished with smiles and hand gestures. The time with Mickey flew by and Noah happily waved goodbye after Brooke took dozens of photos.

"I'm stuffed," Tyler smirked as the last character left their table. "Hand me your phone, so I can send the pictures to mine." He reached for her phone. "This one's perfect." Holding out the phone, he pointed to one of the three of them where Noah was leaning over to give Mickey a kiss.

"I think that's my favorite, too." Brooke couldn't hold back her smile. "Next on the agenda is the monorail, with stops at the Polynesian Resort and the Grand Floridian."

Tyler grinned like a kid on a roller coaster as the monorail left the Contemporary Resort, passed the Ticket and Transportation Center, and stopped at the Polynesian Resort where they exited.

While wandering around the Resort, Tyler waved Brooke over to a hammock under the shade of a palm tree. He laid down with Noah in his arms and patted the spot beside him. Brooke froze. She no longer saw blue eyes staring back at her. Instead, she saw brown ones gleaming in amusement while reading "Winnie the Pooh" stories. She hesitated, disturbed by the image, before forcing herself to join Tyler and Noah.

~

"SINCE WE'RE NOT GOING to Magic Kingdom until Wednesday, I was thinking tomorrow we'd go to a park. There are loads of them around." Brooke tried focusing on the road home, but her mind wandered to park visits with Jacob. She wouldn't take Tyler to the Lakefront Park and her grandmother's old neighborhood. Those places were too special, and she wasn't sure Tyler deserved to be trusted with them.

"Sure, and while we're planning our days, Thursday I have an appointment with the Head of the Cardiothoracic Surgery fellowship at Orlando Regional. It's at ten in the morning. I'm interviewing for a clinical rotation next year."

He hadn't mentioned it before. It surprised Brooke that he was considering coming down for a rotation. She wanted to believe it was for them. "Oh, okay. We can hang out when you get back. How long do you think it will take?"

"I want to bring you guys with me to check it out. I'll have to step away for a few minutes for a one-on-one, I imagine, but I want you to come. They have a great program down here, and if all goes well, I'm hoping it might lead to doing my residency there. We could maybe make a go of it . . . as a family."

Her eyes went wide. Where was this coming from? The rest of the way home, Tyler continued showering Brooke with attention.

When they arrived at the apartment, they discovered Noah had fallen asleep and took him straight to bed.

"Today was perfect!" Tyler reached out to pull Brooke into a hug after they laid a sleeping Noah in his crib. He lifted her chin to him and before she could respond, he kissed her. "It's been too long," he said in between kisses. "I've missed kissing you . . . among other things."

Brooke was speechless. Did she miss it—this side of him? Not at all. The spark she used to feel was gone. When he released her, she stuttered something about needing to help Grams in the kitchen and he chuckled. Maybe it was more than a missing spark . . . his affection toward her seemed off.

~

BROOKE CONTINUED GRAPPLING with her mixed emotions throughout the day. Today Tyler was saying and doing nearly everything right, but she couldn't shake off the feeling that something was missing from his attention.

After dinner she pushed herself to focus on Noah and let her worries about Tyler subside. By the end of his visit she hoped to have more clarity on their relationship.

"It's time to go night night." Brooke nuzzled Noah's nose and he giggled.

"I'm going to take a quick shower while you change him and read to him. I'll tell him goodnight afterwards," Tyler said as he walked out of the room.

Nodding, Brooke turned away and frowned. As she settled on the bed, Noah grabbed Winnie the Pooh and said, "Pooh!"

"Sure. We can read *Pooh*." She smiled and pulled up the picture of Jacob in the bed reading to Noah.

"Da!" Noah pointed at Jacob, causing Brooke's face to heat.

"Jacob." She gestured to the picture.

"Da!" Noah repeated.

Brooke gave up, but scrolled to the picture of her holding Noah with Chef Mickey, then sent it to Jacob.

. . .

BROOKE: READING "POOH" to Noah for bed after he asked for Pooh when we got in. Had lunch at Chef Mickey's today and will have breakfast with Pooh and friends Wednesday at MK! Hope you're having a good week.

HER FINGER HOVERED over the keys to add "miss you," but she decided against it.

JACOB: ☺ Successful trip so far. Tell little guy I miss him and give him a hug from me. Expecting lots of MK pics! Especially from breakfast with Pooh!

JACOB SENT a picture of him in front of the St. Louis Arch, and she showed it to Noah before hearting it.

BROOKE: 👍 It's obvious he misses you, too! He clapped at your picture.

JACOB: 🤍 GTG

SHE COULDN'T BRING herself to mention that Noah kept calling him Da, or that she missed him, too. As she flipped the "Pooh" book open, she wondered what Jacob was doing.

"THANKS FOR WATCHING Noah while he naps, Grams." Brooke said with a smile before looking down and frowning as Tyler grabbed her hand

and pulled her out the door for a walk. She glanced back at her grandmother and forced another smile before shutting the door. Grams was obviously bothered by his show of affection. She had made it clear to Brooke multiple times that she didn't think Tyler was good enough for her, and she didn't see him as husband material.

"So, back to our discussion yesterday . . ." Brooke looked at Tyler as he spoke and a heaviness settled in her chest. "I know I initially said I needed to wait until after residency to think about marriage, but recently I realized that's not necessarily true. The program down here is one of the best in the nation, and from what I hear, they go out of their way to work with married residents."

Brooke stared at him. It certainly wasn't the declaration of love she had hoped for, to make up for all the heartache he had put her through. But maybe that would come.

He rubbed his neck, then put on his best diplomatic expression. "You know I've been buried with med school since before Noah was born, and you can hardly have expected more from me. But it's not that I don't care. You're a beautiful woman and an amazing mom. I always thought we would end up back together. It just wasn't viable before. You needed the support that your family could give you, and help while you worked. Don't look at me that way—you know it's true."

What could she say to that? He made it sound perfectly rational for him to leave her hanging these past two years. Was it rational? She hardly knew at the moment.

Tyler dragged her off of the sidewalk to the side of a building before pulling her into a hug. "Come on, baby. Don't be mad. You know I've always loved you. It was just a hard situation. We can make it work, just give us a chance." He leaned down, held her face in his hands, and kissed her forehead. He continued trailing kisses down her cheek before placing one on her lips. She pulled away, and Tyler blew out a breath. "For Noah's sake, we need to give us a shot."

"What do you think I wanted the last two years?" She narrowed her eyes. "I find it hard to trust you right now."

Nodding, Tyler ran a hand through her hair. "Fair enough, but I'm here now. Give me a chance."

"We'll see." Brooke took a deep breath. "We should head back."

THOUGH BROOKE HAD BEEN to Magic Kingdom many times through the years, it still felt new and exciting each time she walked down Main Street and saw Cinderella's Castle in the distance. She'd worked hard to get reservations at the Crystal Palace Restaurant before the park opened that day. It allowed them to get a few pictures around Main Street without hordes of park goers.

They'd barely sat down in the restaurant when music started up.

"Noah! Let's join the Pooh parade!" Brooke leaned over and unbuckled him from the high chair as the characters began marching to the music. She handed her phone to Tyler. "Will you—"

"I've got it." He grinned and waved her away.

They were able to get in right behind Pooh, which had Noah squealing in delight. Brooke looked over at Tyler and found him thoroughly engrossed in the parade. He winked at her and snapped some pictures. He seemed truly happy to be with them.

The next few hours were a blur as they bounced around the park between rides and shows, sticking with Brooke's carefully prescribed touring plan. She put in a lot of effort to ensure Tyler experienced all the best rides, reserving the ones Noah couldn't go on for his naptime.

"TRY THE GREY STUFF, it's delicious!" Brooke passed Tyler a "grey stuff" cupcake as they finished their lunch in the ballroom of the Be Our Guest restaurant.

His brow furrowed. "Grey stuff?"

"You've not seen *Beauty and the Beast,* I take it? We'll have to watch that before you leave. Basically, all the . . . hmm, I don't want to give away too much. The servants are singing and welcoming Belle to the castle, and that's part of the song. So they serve it here."

Tyler smirked. "Okay, then. Noah, what do you think? Should I try the grey stuff?" He pointed to the cupcake and Noah giggled and reached for it.

"That's Daddy's," Brooke chuckled and handed Noah his own.

"So, what's next on that list of yours?" Tyler asked in between bites of cupcake.

"The jungle ride, then I'm putting Noah down for a nap while you ride Tiana's Bayou Adventure—formerly Splash Mountain, Big Thunder Mountain, and Space Mountain."

"That's a lot of mountains!" Tyler wrapped his free arm around Brooke's shoulder and pulled her closer as he nuzzled his face in her hair. "Where is Noah taking his nap?"

"In his stroller."

Tyler looked doubtful at Brooke's reply.

"He does well napping in it. I just recline him, pull out the canopy over the top, and lay a blanket over it so it hangs in front and blocks his vision. Something about his vision being blocked allows him to sleep, even when there's noise." She shrugged. "It works for him."

"Interesting. I'm curious to see that."

After sending Tyler off to begin his mountain trek, Brooke found a shady spot around the corner from Tiana's and set Noah up for his nap. "Love you, Noah. Night night." She leaned into his little cocoon, kissed his cheek, then pulled back and covered the stroller. She walked around for a few minutes before sitting on a bench and flipping through pictures on her phone. The pictures with Pooh and friends from breakfast made her think of Jacob and his request. She sent him at least twenty photos from their day.

· · ·

BROOKE: Hope that's not too much. There were just so many good ones!

JACOB: Adorable! Keep them coming. Don't forget the selfies! Photogs need to be in pictures, too!

BROOKE'S HEART FLUTTERED, and she didn't know how to reply. She looked at her phone and saw he sent a picture of his hand across an acoustic guitar, mid-strum.

JACOB: Working on a new song right now. Be back tomorrow. Looking forward to seeing little guy.

BROOKE REPLIED and realized she was grinning.

BROOKE: You'll have to play it for us. 😊👍✈️

THE SOUNDS of people screaming as they descended Tiana's Bayou Adventure brought her back to the present, and she looked up just in time to see Tyler's log shooting down into the water. Quickly, Brooke raised her phone and caught it on video, along with a couple of photos. As she was looking at the video, a text came in.

JACOB: ✈️😊 See ya real soon! 😊

BROOKE: Okay, Mickey. 😊

. . .

BROOKE HEARD the Mickey Mouse voice in her head and laughed, but quickly stopped herself. She needed to stay focused and figure out what was going on with Tyler, not let her mind wander to Jacob.

Almost an hour and a half later, Noah called out from under the blanket. Brooke peeked in to see a grinning, stretching Noah reaching up to her. She pulled him out and snuggled close before she kissed him and passed him to Tyler, who'd just returned. She set his stroller upright and put the blanket away.

"I can't believe he slept through all that. You're like the baby whisperer or something." Tyler wrapped his arm around Brooke as Noah reached for her again, and kissed her on the nose. "I'm starting to think I was crazy for wanting to wait so long. Maybe we should make some more little ones."

Brooke looked up at him and felt her face flush. Months ago, she would have been overjoyed to hear him say that. But now, it left her uneasy. Should she shake it off and let him back into her life?

Tyler kept his arm protectively around Brooke as they waited in the Tomorrowland Transit line. Brooke shifted Noah to her other arm and Tyler reached for him.

"I'll hold him." He looked down at Noah and kissed him on the forehead. "You're getting too big for Mommy to hold so long."

Brooke smiled over at them. "He has grown a lot recently. Haven't you?" She tickled Noah's belly and noticed an older lady behind them smiling.

"You make a beautiful family. Enjoy them while they're young. It goes by too fast. Doesn't it, Ed?" The woman wrapped her arm around the white-haired man to her right.

"Indeed it does, dear." Ed smiled, somewhat sadly, down at his wife. "Our two are grown, and one is married. We're hoping for some grandkids. We'd have them here as often as they would let us."

"How long have you two been married?" the woman asked.

Tyler proudly grinned. "We've been together for over three years.

It's not official yet, but hopefully soon she'll make an honest man out of me." He turned to Brooke and winked.

Brooke was shocked by his response. He spoke as if they had never separated, even though he had left her in a holding pattern for the past two years.

"Oh. Well, best wishes to you both. It's certainly worth the leap. Ed and I have been married just over thirty-five years."

"Wow! That's wonderful, and so rare nowadays." Brooke couldn't help but think of her own parents' failed marriage. She wanted what this couple had, but it seemed unattainable, even with Tyler standing there looking at her like he was. She had a lot to discuss with her therapist after Tyler left.

TYLER STOPPED at the door to the apartment, a sleeping Noah in his arm, and drew Brooke close with his other arm. He leaned down and placed a tender kiss on her lips, then pulled back and stared into her eyes. "I'm coming into your room tonight after your grandmother's asleep," he whispered.

Brooke tensed. "We've already talked about this. I'm not doing that to her."

The arm around Brooke tightened and Tyler growled, his eyes narrowed. Brooke became nervous, but he finally released her, jerking the key out of her hand and practically throwing the door open, before handing Noah to her and trudging off.

CHAPTER

ELEVEN

Brooke looked up from her omelet as Tyler exited the bathroom dressed in khakis, a white Oxford, and a navy striped tie. She had always been weak for him when he dressed up, and today was no different. Though after last night, she wasn't sure what she should feel anymore.

"Good morning." Tyler grinned and pulled Brooke into a hug, as if the conversation the night before had never happened. She nervously smiled up at him, and he leaned down and kissed her on the lips.

Well, okay then. Maybe this was progress. "Are you nervous about the meeting at the hospital this morning?"

"Not really. I've got my good luck charm." He squeezed her waist.

NOAH LAUGHED as a breeze whipped through his hair and they bounced over a speed bump in a hospital golf cart, while Laura, the Assistant to the Head of Cardiothoracic Surgery, led them around the Orlando Regional Medical Center campus on a tour.

"Noah's going to love the inside of Arnold Palmer's atrium. It's the children's hospital and the atrium is sponsored by Disney. It's like stepping into a land of children's books." She pulled into a spot right next to the building and led them in.

They entered and stared in awe. Noah wiggled to get out of Brooke's arms. He ran right up to the three little pigs towering above him, and Brooke smiled as she joined him. Her gaze was drawn to the giant beanstalk climbing up the wall and ending almost at the ceiling, several stories high. There was Dumbo, and even a castle at the far end. It did feel like she'd stepped into a storybook.

Laura led them outside through another door and waved her hands around. "The pirate ship is a playground. There's also a meditation garden to the side over here," she said, pointing to her left.

Noah pulled Brooke toward the giant pirate ship. She looked at Laura and gestured to the ship. "Can we?"

"Sure. We can spare a few minutes for him to look around."

"Here, buddy." Tyler grinned and grabbed Noah's other hand to join them as they explored.

"So, Brooke—any questions?" Laura asked as they sat down with ice cream in the break room of the Health Heart Institute while waiting for Tyler and Dr. Gupta.

"How likely is it for Tyler to get the surgery residency if he does his rotation here? I guess I'm wondering if it will help."

"Well, I will tell you that we've looked at his transcripts and spoken with some of his professors. He gets excellent recommendations and has stellar grades. So unless he totally blows it with Dr. Gupta, or his academic performance drops off, it's highly likely.

"Also," her voice lowered, "as I mentioned to Tyler when I met him at the conference a few weeks ago, Dr. Gupta is a very family-oriented man, and the fact that you two are working toward marriage and have a little one already raises Tyler greatly in his esteem. Dr. Gupta feels that doctors with families of their own tend to have more empathy for patients—something most surgeons lack. So this cardiothoracic surgery rotation is already practically a done deal. Plus, he's brought in the head of the surgery residency to meet Tyler so they can discuss him doing a rotation with general surgery before the cardiothoracic one." Laura smiled. "That way, you would have more time together. Several months, in fact."

Brooke pasted on a smile as she processed Laura's words. Tyler knew Dr. Gupta would be swayed if he had a family—or in this case, appeared to have one. She wasn't sure how to respond and decided to keep her thoughts to herself . . . for now.

Once she got Tyler alone, she wouldn't hold back. The nerve he had to use them like that. It all made sense—his renewed pursuit after two years of barely acknowledging them. It hurt. She began second guessing every action since he'd arrived.

She wanted to call Jacob. He seemed to make everything better. She smiled, remembering he would be back in town that day.

"I see you're happy about that," Laura said as she watched Brooke.

Brooke's smile faltered, and she turned towards Noah to wipe his mouth and hide her frustration.

"Tyler! Noah and I aren't your Willy Wonka golden ticket! You're using us. Was any of this week real? I almost fell for it, thinking you had finally realized what you were . . . *are* missing out on." Brooke huffed and clenched her hands.

"Who knew the head of the cardiology department at the hospital with the best cardiovascular surgery department in Florida has a fondness for families and likes the idea of the surgery residents being married with children? And that top hospital just happens to be in Orlando. I met his assistant at a conference in Nashville, and she suggested I come down and meet him to discuss doing a rotation with him next year. If I get that, I'll be a shoe-in for their surgery residency, then the cardiothoracic fellowship." Tyler smiled at her and reached for her hands. "Don't be mad."

"But you did know. Laura said she told you when you met her."

He shrugged. "Yes, she did. But I've said all along I was considering marriage. I just didn't think it would be possible until I was further along in my training." He looked at her earnestly and gripped her hands tighter. "I've been torn at the thought of making you wait so long. It left me feeling helpless, and I didn't know what to do. But this . . . this changes everything. Don't you see? We won't have to wait. We can go ahead and plan for the future . . . for our marriage."

Brooke searched his eyes. Did he really mean it this time? Like nearly every other conversation they'd had since her pregnancy, she was left questioning herself.

"I DON'T LIKE the way that guy is looking at you." Tyler pulled Brooke in the opposite direction from where they were walking as they returned to the apartment.

She glanced up just in time to see Jacob, hands in his pockets, observing her with a grin that fell as Tyler pulled her away. "He's just a friend, Tyler. The grandson of Grams' good friend, Ann."

"He's not looking at you like a friend should."

Brooke rolled her eyes at Tyler's comment.

He squeezed her arm. "I'm serious, and he seems like a guy who's up to no good." Brooke laughed, and Tyler narrowed his eyes at her. "This is not funny!"

Trying to cover her mouth, Brooke shook her head. Finally getting herself under control, she spoke. "It's just that before I knew who he was, I thought he was a drug dealer." She chuckled again.

"See, I'm not crazy! And he probably is, so you and my son should not be associating with him."

"Our son. And no, we're not right about him. People are just different here. They aren't always so 'proper' in the way they dress and act. It's more laid-back. Besides, he writes music, and plays some himself, so he has a persona he wants to portray." Brooke shrugged.

Tyler's brows furrowed. "A musician? You definitely don't need to be hanging around him. Everyone knows that musicians are into drugs, drinking, and women. I don't want to hear about you spending time with him anymore."

Brooke stopped walking and put her hand on her hip. "That's not for you to decide. You should know me well enough not to believe I would expose our son to someone like that. I'm telling you, he's a good guy."

Frowning, Tyler sneered at her. "You like him, don't you? You're gone for three weeks, and you're already hooking up with someone! That's why you won't let me sleep with you this week." His face turned red, and he shook his head as he grabbed Brooke by the shoulders.

Eyes wide, she pulled back from his grip. "What is wrong with you! I am not that kind of person! It took me over a year before I slept with you, and I would talk to you if I was even going to consider a relationship with anyone else, because you asked me to give you time to figure things out. Can you say the same? Have you been abstinent since me?"

Tyler huffed, but didn't answer. Brooke folded her arms over her chest and looked away. Some of the neighbors walking on the side-walk were staring, and she realized their voices had grown increas-ingly loud.

"Let's go for a drive if we're going to continue this conversation," she said softly.

Tyler continued on loudly. "Nope, we're done here. You're not spending time with that . . . that drug dealer anymore, and that's final! Why don't you go back inside with your grandmother. I need time to cool down." He clearly didn't care if the whole apartment complex heard them.

"Enjoy your walk." Brooke angrily turned to leave, then stopped. "Oh, and I'm not going to stop hanging out with Jacob." She didn't wait for a response and hurried off.

She heard him curse and call out her name.

Nearing her apartment building, she clenched her fists and tried, yet again, to make sense of his hot and cold behavior.

The sound of Jacob's guitar filled the air as Brooke approached the apartment. It sounded like a ballad. He sang along softly, stopping and starting a few times. When he came into view, she noticed he was sitting on the same bench by the pond where she'd seen him on several other occasions. He appeared focused as he leaned over to write something down, so she looked on silently.

The music was soothing and lifted the pain that had settled in her heart. She closed her eyes and let it carry her away. Minutes later, she realized it had stopped. Brooke opened her eyes and found two brown ones gazing back at her.

"I'm sorry, I didn't mean to interrupt you. It was beautiful."

Jacob's mouth lifted into a lazy grin. "I don't mind. Come join me." He patted the bench.

Brooke walked closer, but froze and looked behind her, fearing Tyler might see. When she turned back to Jacob, he examined her with concerned eyes.

"Your boyfriend doesn't seem to like me. I'm sorry if I've caused any problems between you two."

"I don't even know if I would consider him my boyfriend at this point," Brooke commented sadly. Jacob's eyebrows lifted. "One minute he acts like he cares about Noah and me, and the next, he treats us like a burden." She explained what she had learned earlier from Laura about Dr. Gupta's preference for married residents, as well as Tyler's response, when she questioned him.

"That's not the way it should be, Brooke." Jacob shook his head. "I haven't known you long, but I can tell you are an amazing woman and mom. You should be treated like a treasure."

Brooke's face tightened as he spoke, and she tried to contain her emotions. The corner of her mouth lifted, and she murmured, "Tyler thought the same thing that I did about you when I first saw you."

Fighting back a smile, Jacob questioned her, "That I was a drug dealer?" Brooke nodded. "What is it with you Memphis people? You think everyone who dresses differently is into illegal things?" He chuckled.

Gazing at the ground, Brooke shook her head. "I'm not proud of it, and I'm trying to be less judgmental. But yeah, you don't exactly fit the mold of the crowd we ran with in school."

"Well, what do you think about me now?" Jacob smiled wryly, and his beautiful eyes bore into hers.

What did she think about him? There were things in her heart she was scared to admit. Her life was too messy. She raised an eyebrow and smiled. "That you're a drug dealer who writes songs, of course."

He laid his guitar down, reached out, and pulled her close, mussing her hair with his free hand. "You just wait, missy." He chuckled before smoothing her hair back down. His voice softened. "But seriously . . . " He pulled back and looked at her with a pained expression. "I'm here for you."

"Look, I don't know what to think," Tyler said as he folded his clothes into his suitcase. "I really want us to work, but it's hard when you won't stop doubting me and keeping me at a distance. Maybe time apart will do us both some good." He walked over and grabbed Noah from her arms. "Hey, buddy." He nuzzled his nose, then kissed his cheek. "I'm going to miss you. See if you can help your mom figure out what she wants. It would be great if we were able to be a happy family."

Brooke felt torn. He was right. She needed to decide what she wanted. She had never been so confused. All her life she had set goals, and the path to them was clear. Her current path was filled with mud, and at times, it seemed like quick sand.

TWELVE

"Tyler's gone?" Brooke nodded and let Jacob into the apartment, then watched as he joined Noah on his play mat. "I heard a suitcase rolling down the sidewalk earlier and figured it was him. I stayed at Nan's last night, thinking you might need someone to talk to after he left today." His eyes followed her as she sat down on the floor across from him. "How are you? How did you leave things?"

She shrugged and furrowed her brow. "He acts like it's up to me. Like I'm the one who has held us back. But up until now, I've been trying to get him to accept us and commit to us. To be honest, I'm confused." As she looked into Jacob's kind eyes, she felt safe exposing her pain. "I'm having trouble believing he's sincere after two years of him stalling our relationship. It seems like too much of a coincidence that after finding out Dr. Gupta's perspective, he suddenly wants us to be a family."

Jacob reached over and placed a hand on her shoulder. "I'm sorry you have to go through this."

As if Noah sensed his mom's need for compassion, he climbed into her lap, then grabbed Jacob's hand from her shoulder and placed it into his own lap. Noah patted it and looked at Jacob. "Da."

Brooke's eyes dropped to their clasped hands, and her heart raced. "I'm worried about letting someone in who will just let us down in the future."

Jacob tensed and shifted his gaze to Noah. "You deserve someone who will love you both and be there for you unconditionally . . . always."

Tears welled up in her eyes. "It's hard letting someone in, especially after all my mom went through with my dad. I waited a long time for what I thought was love. Now I'm confused and unsure."

"I get it. Watching my mom with so many guys left me cynical about love. I've never told a girl I love her. I've dated, but I put up walls. I've not let anyone past them." He picked at the carpet. "When's your next appointment with the therapist?"

"First thing Monday at eight. We'll see if I can get through the weekend without losing it." She frowned.

"You could try praying."

"To a God I don't believe in? You think He's like a genie and will grant my requests? 'Ask and you will receive' and all that? I know better. When I was a kid, I used to go to church with my grandmother. When I noticed the problems with my parents, I prayed for Him to fix it and nothing happened."

"You were praying for the wrong thing. You're right. He's not a genie. He doesn't work that way."

Brooke wanted to be angry with him. Why was he talking to her like this? "It's useless."

"Maybe you could start by praying for God to show Himself to you," Jacob suggested, and Brooke shook her head. "Do you remember when I stopped Noah from running into the parking lot? Before you knew me?"

She nodded at Jacob's question.

"Noah knew what he wanted, but you, as the parent, knew the potential danger that could result from him getting what he wanted.

It's like that with God. What we want or think we need isn't always best in the long run. Maybe the hard experiences we endure now prepare us for something in the future. Or maybe it lays the groundwork to help someone else. There are so many difficulties in so many people's lives, and God is working it all out. I've struggled with the same thing, and did some research on it."

"Research?"

He pulled out his phone and looked something up, then read, "Matthew 21:22. 'And whatever you ask in prayer, you will receive, if you have faith.'"

"John 16:23-24. 'In that day you will ask nothing of Me. Truly, truly, I say to you, whatever you ask of the Father in My name, He will give it to you. Until now you have asked nothing in My name. Ask, and you will receive, that your joy may be full.'"

Brooke looked at Jacob skeptically.

"Keep listening. James 4:2-3. 'You desire and do not have, so you murder. You covet and cannot obtain, so you fight and quarrel. You do not have, because you do not ask. You ask and do not receive, because you ask wrongly, to spend it on your passions.'"

"First John 3:21-23. 'Beloved, if our heart does not condemn us, we have confidence before God; and whatever we ask we receive from Him, because we keep His commandments and do what pleases Him. And this is His commandment, that we believe in the name of His Son Jesus Christ and love one another, just as He has commanded us.'"

A tear slid down her face, and she quickly reached up to wipe it. "I'm sorry. I don't know what's wrong with me." Embarrassed, she looked away from Jacob.

Noah pulled Jacob's hand and laid it on top of Brooke's, then patted them and giggled. Brooke gasped at the contact and looked up to see Jacob watching her with kind eyes. Was he looking into the depths of her heart? Did her expression reveal what she hid deep inside?

"—the beach?"

Brooke's eyebrows pulled together. He'd spoken while she was lost in thought. "What?"

"Have you ever taken Noah to the beach?"

She shook her head slowly. "No, I haven't. What does that have to do with praying?"

Jacob squeezed her hand and chuckled. "Nothing, but I figured you both might enjoy it. I'm working out-of-town tomorrow, and won't be back until Sunday. We could go after your therapy appointment Monday. Would you like that?"

Electricity shot up her hand and warmed her body. She wanted to say yes, but so much in her life was uncertain.

"Just as friends." Jacob smiled softly. "I know you're trying to figure things out with Noah's dad, and I won't get in the way of that." He pulled his hand away, then awkwardly added, "I'm not in a good place for a relationship, anyway."

How did he know that was one of her biggest concerns? And why did it make her sad that he wasn't interested in a relationship? She forced a smile. "You're right. The beach would be fun."

NOAH CLAPPED as the water rushed over his feet and back out to sea. He chased after it, with Jacob right on his heels to scoop him up before he got too deep. Jacob grabbed him and tickled him before setting him down next to Brooke.

"Here, you can put him in the pool float." She held out an inflatable ring designed for babies to sit in.

Once Noah was settled, they moved out to deeper water and bobbed with the waves.

"Did I tell you, I've got Noah signed up for swim lessons?"

"That's a great idea."

"With all this water everywhere, it seems necessary."

Jacob nodded. "What do you think, Noah? Do you like the ocean? Do you want to learn to swim?" Noah responded to Jacob's question by slapping the water and squealing.

As Brooke watched, she longed for more of what she felt today. Jacob easily anticipated Noah's needs, and hers, for that matter. He never made them feel like a burden. He seemed to enjoy spending time with them and making them happy . . . consistently. She didn't have to worry about a sudden angry outburst, or him turning on her because he didn't like what she said or did.

Did something specific about Jacob draw her to him, or was she drawn to him because he treated her the way she wished Tyler did? Brooke swallowed the lump in her throat and took deep breaths to keep her tears at bay, though a couple escaped. She hoped the water splashing on her face disguised them.

When Noah's fingers looked waterlogged, Jacob announced it was time to build a sandcastle. He had gifted Noah a complete set of pails, scoops, and castle molds. Noah enjoyed knocking down the castle more than building it, and Jacob patiently made tower after tower for him to destroy.

While Jacob kept Noah busy, Brooke worked on her own creation. She'd built three sides of the castle wall before the little destroyer discovered and besieged it. She grabbed her phone and videoed the fall of the castle. Jacob's eyes gleamed with mirth as he watched.

The beach that had been practically empty on their arrival was now filled with the chatter of people enjoying the perfect sunny Florida weather—most of them likely escaping the cold spring in other parts of the country. Brooke smiled at the thought of enjoying this year-round now.

When she looked back at the boys, she caught Jacob staring at her. He smiled as if he'd heard her thoughts. Their eyes locked until Noah dumped a bucketful of sand onto Jacob's lap. Jacob burst out laughing. Noah giggled and climbed into his sandy lap, clearly pleased with Jacob's reaction.

Brooke couldn't help but compare Jacob's response with what she imagined Tyler's would be. To say Tyler didn't like surprises was an understatement. Ironically, a surprise was the very thing Brooke had planned for him the next weekend. She wondered how he would take it.

Jacob adjusted his ball cap and pushed his hair back under it, looking around. "It's starting to get crowded here. Why don't I show you the jetty this beach is named after? If we're lucky, we'll see a manatee or even a tortoise. They like to swim around it." He stood up and wiped the sand off his shorts.

Brooke nodded and secured Noah with a safety harness. Jacob laughed at the contraption, but held onto it like a leash as they each grabbed one of his hands and headed toward the dock overlooking the jetty. When Noah squirmed incessantly to walk on his own, Jacob concluded it was ingenious.

A couple at the end of the dock excitedly pointed at the water. Jacob whisked Noah into his arms, and they hurried to see what it was. They were rewarded with the sight of not one, but two manatees, making their way between the pier and the rocky jetty. Jacob squatted down close to the water so Noah could get a better look, and the delight on Noah's face was evident. He pointed at the enormous animal and waved at it.

"Would you like us to take your picture?" the woman asked. "You make a beautiful family."

Before Brooke could correct her, Jacob handed the lady his phone. "That would be great. Thanks."

They smiled for several pictures. When Jacob held his phone up for Brooke to see, she silently agreed with the woman—they *did* look like a happy family. She felt guilty, knowing Tyler wanted them to patch things up and become that happy family.

As she watched Jacob with Noah, Brooke again compared Jacob and Tyler. Jacob was ruggedly good-looking, yet always appeared as if he hardly tried. He'd thrown on a fitted gray v-neck with his black board shorts. He had on one of his—apparently many—ball caps and sunglasses, which seemed to be his dress code for going out. It worked for him and his effortlessly cool vibe. No doubt about it, he was easily the most gorgeous guy she had ever seen. He had a messy past, but came out better because of it. The thought flitted through her mind that she hadn't seen him with a woman, or heard him mention a girlfriend. She shoved the little green monster down—she would finish things with Tyler before letting her thoughts drift to another man.

Tyler was Jacob's opposite. His style was professional and put together at all times. For a beach excursion, he would be dressed in the preppiest swim shorts available with an oxford shirt, and he despised ball caps. He was a nice looking, clean-cut guy who seemed to have it all together. That's what initially attracted her to him.

As she got to know Tyler, she learned he liked to have control and make everything in his life fit a certain mold. After her parent's divorce, she looked for certain qualities in a man. She'd appreciated the stability he offered. And because a broken family didn't fit the image of his ideal life, she believed he would always be loyal and steady.

Tyler's desire for control ended up being the very thing that made her pregnancy a problem. It didn't fit with his perfectly planned life. His recent change of heart, because of the potential residency, upset her all over again.

"Are you okay? You're scowling." Jacob squeezed her shoulder.

Brooke pasted on a smile. "I'll be fine. I just remembered something." Her conscience pricked—maybe honesty would be better. "I was just thinking about the situation with Tyler."

"Mm." Jacob frowned. "Do you want to talk about it?"

She reached out and rubbed Noah's hair as he snuggled deeper into Jacob's chest. The sight made her heart flutter. Closing her eyes, she thought about her therapy session and nodded. Jacob grabbed her free hand and led them to an empty spot on the beach where he spread out a towel for them to sit.

"So, what's going on?" He pried, while helping Noah make a mountain with the sand.

"I'm going to give Tyler one more chance," she blurted out, but as she said it, the words sounded absurd after all that had happened.

Jacob's brow furrowed. "Why? I thought . . ." His voice trailed off.

"Yeah, me too." She knew what he was thinking, because she had the same thoughts. "It's just . . . if I don't give it one last try, I'll always blame myself." She frowned and shrugged. "If my plan doesn't work, I'm done." He raised a brow. "Seriously. I've been 'that girl' holding on for two years, and I refuse to be her anymore. I'm taking Noah and surprising him in Nashville Friday night. I'll stay until Sunday." Jacob's eyes went wide. "My therapist says, if I insist on giving him one more chance, this is the best way. My dilemma is, does he really want to be with us, or is he just viewing us as a ticket into the residency program? He likes to have control over—well, everything, and his response to our arrival will give me an idea of his true feelings for us. I know it sounds crazy, but I'm giving it one last shot."

"Oh." Jacob looked at her, then turned back to Noah. "If that's what you want. As a friend, I'll be rooting for you . . . and praying, too, of course." He turned back to Brooke and smiled. "You both deserve good things."

The ride home was quiet, with Noah napping in the back and Jacob looking thoughtful. Several times, Brooke tried to make small talk, but unlike their usual easy banter, it fell flat. Brooke thought about their day at the beach and seeing the manatees at the jetty. She'd enjoyed those things, but it was the company that made it an amazing day.

"Are you okay?" Brooke questioned.

"Yeah. Sorry. Just got some things on my mind."

"This is what I needed. It was a good distraction, and you've come to mean a lot to Noah. Thanks." When Brooke spoke, Jacob glanced over at her with an unreadable expression.

"You're welcome. He . . . he means a lot to me, too."

Once they arrived at the apartment, Jacob helped take Noah's things in. After setting down the car seat, he quickly said his good-byes, hugged Noah, and left. Brooke wondered at his haste but knew she shouldn't dwell on it. He had made it clear he was just a friend.

As the week dragged on, Brooke was disappointed that she had not seen or heard from Jacob since Monday. On Thursday, during Noah's nap, she was reading on the patio when she heard the familiar rumble of his Porsche. He stepped out with a brown bag, and a couple of teen boys greeted him. He stopped and spoke to them before walking towards his grandmother's apartment. Brooke watched, hoping he would look up and speak to her—maybe even stop by. Instead, he kept his eyes down as he passed. When she heard no knock, her heart sank.

She'd missed their talks and spending time with him. She missed watching the way he interacted with Noah. Brooke rubbed her hands over her face and tried to remind herself to stay focused. She shouldn't have these thoughts. Tomorrow, she was flying to Nash-ville to see Tyler.

Upon waking from his nap, Noah ran inside the apartment and wouldn't stay still. Brooke decided a walk around the apartment complex with his safety harness was the best way to burn off energy.

As they approached the tennis and basketball courts, sounds of boys and a basketball echoed. Noah released Brooke's hand and charged ahead, but she stopped him with the harness. Before turning the corner, a group of teenage girls came into view. They were watching the game and cheering the players on. Brooke chuckled to herself, remembering what she was like at that age.

When they drew near, some of the girls noticed Noah, and turned to him to "ooh" and "aah." But the majority of the girls kept intently watching the game and flirting with the players. They appeared most excited about one specific player. When Brooke turned to see the object of their affection, she blushed. There Jacob stood, shirt off, tossing around the ball with a group of teen boys. She attempted to keep her eyes on his face, and not his muscular pecs and defined abs.

She had seen him shirtless at the beach, but keeping Noah safe distracted her, and she didn't want to be caught staring. She'd managed the whole day without more than a glance. With his focus completely on his game, she could now openly admire him. Several minutes later, he looked her way and their eyes locked. Before she could wave, the ball hit him right in the chest. Some of the boys broke out in laughter, but the girls turned their attention to Brooke, jealousy in their eyes.

They hit her with a barrage of questions.

"Do you know him?"

"Are you his girlfriend?"

"Whose baby is this?"

She attempted to answer them all. "We're just friends. This is Noah. His dad lives in Tennessee."

The girls seemed satisfied with her answers and went back to what they were doing before—cooing at Noah and Jacob. Jacob glanced her way again with a look of relief. She found it strange that all these young girls spent their time following around a twenty-five-year-old man. Even if he was really good-looking and drove around in cool cars, it seemed a bit much. He's just Jacob. The friendly guy with a flexible job who hangs out with the neighborhood boys, encouraging them to make good life choices.

As Brooke prepared to leave, the game ended. After some high fives, Jacob walked towards Brooke with his shirt back on and sweat seeping through. The girls, even those who had been enamored with Noah, all turned their attention to Jacob. Some called his name, trying to get his attention. As they gathered around, he stopped and said a few words, then told them he would see them later.

"Hey," he said to Brooke.

"Hey." She bit back a smile.

Jacob squatted down in front of Noah, who charged at him, wrapped his arms around him, and squealed, "Da!"

Looking up at Brooke, Jacob apologized, "Sorry, I'm sweaty."

"Don't worry about it. He'll get his evening bath."

He nodded, then picked Noah up. "Hey, little guy. I've missed you."

Then Noah did the sweetest thing—he placed his hands on both sides of Jacob's face, leaned up, and kissed his cheek. When Noah pulled back, Brooke noticed he left a wet spot. She winced, but melted inside.

Jacob's eyes welled up, but he blinked and shrugged. "There's already so much sweat pouring down my face. What's a little spit? So, I, um, I got some things for Noah for the flight. I left them with my Nan to give you. I'll be leaving town in the morning for work."

"Oh. You don't have time to bring them by yourself?"

He nervously ran his hand through his hair. "It's some toys. It might be more fun if he sees them for the first time on the plane."

"You're probably right. That was thoughtful. Are you heading back? I'm sure Noah would like it if you walked with us." *I would like it if you walked with us.*

Jacob nodded and walked with them, stopping at their apartment to say goodbye. It felt like more than a 'have-a-good-trip' goodbye. The way he gave them one last lingering look, it felt like a final goodbye.

Brooke sat, scrolling on her Instagram thirty minutes later when someone knocked on the door. She gasped when she saw Jacob through the peephole and opened the door.

He looked down at his feet before looking up at her. "I didn't like the way we left things earlier. You seemed upset."

She stared at him, unable to explain the thoughts floating around her mind, and hopeful that his return meant he wasn't abandoning their friendship.

"Anyway, here's the gift for Noah." He peered past her, looking for signs of Noah as he handed her the package he'd brought. "I still think you should wait to give it to him on the plane. And don't give him more than one thing at a time. When he gets bored, you can give him the next." Brooke's mouth curled up in a smile and she looked at him quizzically. "At least, that's what I heard is best," he added. "A friend of mine from church has a boy about his age, and has flown with him before. She pointed me in the right direction for what to buy." He smiled, looking embarrassed. "Oh, and there are a couple of suckers in there. I'm not promoting sugar, but it's supposed to help when you take off, to keep his ears from popping."

Brooke looked at him, not believing he had gone to so much trouble. At the mention of the girl he went to church with, she felt a flash of jealousy, and tried tempering it with thoughts of Tyler. "Why don't you come in for a minute while I look through everything?" She saw his hesitation. "Grams is giving Noah a bath, since some sweaty person hugged and held him." When his brow pinched together, she playfully punched his shoulder and grinned. "I told you he was getting one anyway."

He pressed his lips together and followed her to the sofa, where she pulled everything out of the gift bag. Two suckers, two grain bars, a pack of gum . . .

"That's for you," he said when she pulled out the gum.

Brooke continued pulling items out. A Winnie the Pooh board book with liftable flaps, a wooden toy that looked like a block of cheese with a shoelace to weave through it, and a fabric Montessori busy board bag. She stopped and looked at the busy board. It had snaps, buttons, laces, and other things to keep little hands busy. Deeper in the bag, she also found a coloring pad with invisible ink markers that turned into colors on the special paper. "Wow! Thank you. You've put a lot of thought into this."

She leaned over to hug him. He stiffened for a moment before wrapping his arms around her and pulling her close.

Brooke inhaled his scent and worked to ignore the thoughts invading her mind. Neither of them let go until they heard Grams coming out of the bathroom with Noah. Brooke quickly shoved the gifts back into the bag, and Jacob jumped up from the sofa.

"Okay . . . well . . . have a good trip." His smile faltered, and he left the apartment before Grams and Noah saw him.

Sighing, Brooke went to her room to finish packing for the trip.

THIRTEEN

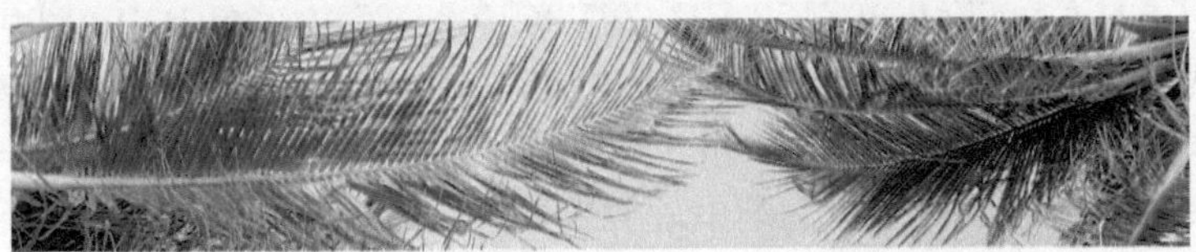

While riding up the elevator in Tyler's building, Brooke contemplated her plans for the evening. Tyler had a study group at his place until 9 p.m. They landed at 8:45 and with the time it took to make it from the airport to his building, they should have just left.

She thought back to their time together the week before. Much of it had been great, but their disagreements left her wondering if they could make it as a married couple. She didn't want to end up like her parents. She had been so determined not to repeat their mistakes, and yet, here she was. Tonight was a test. If he passed, she would give it a go.

Exiting the elevator, Brooke glanced down at Noah. He had been a trooper on the plane. The sucker Jacob gave him worked like a charm to keep him from crying at takeoff, and the gifts kept him entertained for the short flight to Nashville. Her mind wandered to Jacob, and she smiled. Shaking her head, she worked to focus on the task at hand.

She was nervous about surprising Tyler. Maybe everything would go off without a hitch. Her first challenge was remembering the door code to his apartment since she'd decided to sneak in. Hopefully he hadn't changed it since the one time he allowed them to visit. She pulled Noah out of his stroller, wheeled the suitcase up to the door, and punched in the code, relaxing when she saw the light flash green just before the lock clicked open. Once inside, she heard the television, and left the suitcase in the entrance to find Tyler.

As she peeked around the corner to assess the situation before announcing herself, she was the one surprised. There on the sofa lay Tyler and a brunette—kissing! Brooke gasped, but they didn't seem to notice until Noah called out, "Dada!"

Tyler jumped off the sofa, eyes wide with panic when he saw Brooke glaring back at him. "Brooke?"

The woman from the sofa stood up, confused, then with a sincere smile said to Tyler, "Why didn't you tell me Brooke was bringing Noah?" She crossed the room. "I'm Amber, it's so good to finally meet you and this little cutie." She reached out to squeeze Noah's hand.

Pulling Noah away from Amber, Brooke's angry gaze shifted to Tyler. "How could you? I can't believe I fell for it. You're such a liar."

"Wait a minute," Amber said with a hand on her hip as she turned towards Tyler and assessed the situation. "You said you broke up with Brooke last spring. So all these months we've been together, you've been two-timing me?"

Raising both hands in the air, Tyler backed up. "Brooke and I haven't been together—not really."

"Maybe not officially, but last week when you were down for spring break, you *again* confirmed you planned on marrying me. You said until this Florida residency came up, the only thing holding you back was the logistics." Brooke fumed, her hands shaking beneath Noah's weight.

"Wait! You were in Florida for spring break? You told me you had to spend time with your parents and that's why you couldn't go to the beach with me." Amber's face turned red.

"I said I had to spend time with family. Noah is family." Tyler frowned.

Amber clenched her fists. "What a liar! I can't believe you're acting like what you did wasn't intentionally deceitful." Anger showed in her eyes and furrowed brow, while moisture filled her eyes. Reaching up to her neck, she unclasped a necklace with a heart pendant and threw it at him. "We're over. Don't call. Unfortunately, I still have to see you at labs and classes, but you better stay out of my way." She stomped toward the door and stopped in front of Brooke. "I am so sorry. I honestly had no idea. I wish the best for you and Noah." She leaned in and whispered, "For both of your sakes, I hope you stay away from this jerk. He doesn't deserve a second chance."

Brooke shakily replied, "You and I are in agreement on that." As Brooke watched Amber leave, she assessed her options. Her first instinct was to leave and never come back, but with him being Noah's father, she knew it wouldn't be that simple, nor would it be fair to Noah.

If she stayed and tried to discuss things right now, she would say things she regretted and make poor decisions. "Tyler, we need to talk, but I can't even think straight at the moment. I'm going to a hotel and I'll contact you later to set up a time tomorrow to meet . . . probably in the morning, so don't make plans."

Tyler stared at her blankly before pointing at her, "You and I weren't official." His voice was harsh. Then, as if a switch flipped, he softened. Walking her to the door, he leaned over to hug Noah. "I guess I'll see you both tomorrow? Did you rent a car?"

"Uh, Uber," Brooke said, bewildered by his strange behavior. She couldn't get out of there fast enough. "Bye."

"Bye, Noah."

Noah tightened his grip on his mom, as if he sensed something was wrong. "Nie nie, Dada." Noah clenched and unclenched his hand like he always did when he waved goodbye.

Brooke didn't have the emotional energy to interact with anyone and was glad for an empty elevator ride down. She frantically searched her phone for a nearby hotel, then requested an Uber. Anger, hurt, and resentment battled with relief as tears threatened to fall. He'd strung her along for two years while cheating on her, and she'd blindly let him. All in the hopes that Noah would have a complete family. How did she not see what was going on? Something had felt off, but she'd been too busy with Noah and work. She assumed he was busy with school, so she'd never looked deeper into things. How could she have been so stupid?

Overwhelmed and tired, the suitcase, diaper bag, and convertible stroller-car seat she'd managed earlier suddenly seemed unwieldy. All she wanted to do was crash and take a hot shower.

At least the hotel was only a couple of blocks away. They were quickly able to get into a room and have it set up with a crib. Once Noah was asleep, only one thing came to mind. She had to talk with Jacob. He was so rational and understanding. He had a way of calming her and giving her hope. The call went to voicemail, so she texted and asked him to call her. She paced the room, looking at the time. It was 9:47 p.m. That was almost eleven in Central Florida time. Maybe he was in bed, though it seemed early for him.

After getting ready for bed, she sat down and leaned against the headboard, dreading texting Tyler. She finally grabbed her phone and sent a text, telling him to meet her at the hotel for breakfast at 9. He responded almost immediately, confirming that he would be there.

Brooke rubbed her face. What on earth was she going to say to him? The one thing she knew for sure, was that they were done romantically. There was no way she was giving him another chance. She closed her eyes and her ringing phone startled her. Jacob's name lit the screen.

Smiling, she softly answered, "Hey."

"Hey. Are you okay?" Jacob sounded out of breath and she heard a roar of background noise. "Just a minute. I can't hear you. Let me go somewhere quiet." The noises became muffled, followed by the sound of a door slamming, then silence. "That's better. What's going on? Are you with Tyler?"

"No. I'm sorry, is this a bad time for you? It sounds like you're out." She moved into the bathroom so she could talk louder without disturbing Noah.

"I am, but I can talk now. I was at a concert. It just ended."

"Oh. I didn't mean to interrupt your date. I'll let you get back to her." Brooke's stomach tightened. It felt worse than when she saw Tyler with Amber earlier.

"What? No. I'm here with my roommates. What's going on?"

She sighed in relief and explained the earlier events.

"Brooke, I'm so sorry. You shouldn't be alone. I can fly there right now. I'll tell the guys to go to the hotel without me."

"Hotel? Where are you?"

"Chicago. We're leaving for Milwaukee tomorrow, but if I meet back up with them there by two, it will be fine."

"Wow, you really do have a lot of travel with work. No, I can't ask you to do that."

"It's fine. I want to be there for you."

"No, seriously, I don't want you to come. It will make me feel guilty. I just need someone to talk to. The phone is fine."

"Okay. Only if you're sure. So are you going back home tomorrow? Surely you won't stay until Sunday now?"

"I hadn't thought that far ahead, but you're right. I'll change my return ticket for tomorrow."

"Good. That way you can be with Grams. Do you need help with expenses?"

"I'll be okay." Brooke wasn't about to take money from him. She had some savings, and money left over that her dad had given her for the move. The child support also helped, and Grams wouldn't let her pay for anything until she started working.

"Alright, but please let me know if that changes. I don't want you and Noah to struggle." She heard muffled noises in the background again, and then a door shutting. "Hey, I've got to go to the hotel with the guys. Will you be okay for a few minutes until I can call you back?"

"Yeah. If it looks like you can't, just text. I hate to take away from your time with friends."

"I'll call you. You're important to me. Talk to you in a few. Bye, Brooke."

Hanging up, she went back into the room and climbed onto the bed, already feeling better. A little over fifteen minutes later, Jacob texted.

JACOB: It's probably going to be about twenty more minutes. It took us a while to get to the car. I promise I'll call.

SHE SWITCHED her phone to vibrate and climbed under the covers, keeping her phone in her hand so she wouldn't miss his call.

BROOKE'S PHONE startled her awake, and it took her several seconds to realize where she was. "Jacob," she answered groggily.

"Hey, sorry it took me so long. Should I call you in the morning? It sounds like you fell asleep."

"No. It's fine, I want to talk to you. Can you hear me if I whisper? I don't want to wake Noah, and I don't feel like sitting in the bathroom."

"Yeah, I can hear you. Why don't we video chat? Then I can read your lips if I can't hear. Unless you're sitting in the dark."

"I'm not, but it's dim." She felt heat rise in her cheeks at the thought of seeing him. "I'll call you right back." She hung up and called him with the video app. At the sight of him, her stomach fluttered. "Is that better?"

"Much. Now I get to see you, so that's a bonus. Point the phone at

Noah. I want to see how he's doing." Brooke walked over to Noah's crib and aimed the phone at a sleeping Noah. She had to admit, she loved watching him sleep. Once she was back on the bed, Jacob spoke again. "Noah's adorable. Don't you want to just squeeze his little cheeks?" She quietly laughed and nodded. "So, how are you holding up?"

"Honestly, I'm doing pretty good." She tried stifling a yawn. "I think I'm more angry at finding him cheating, than I am hurt. After what he's put me through for the past two years, I guess I'm just over it. If that makes any sense?"

"Total sense. I didn't get a good feeling from him when he was down in Florida, and it wasn't just because he didn't like me. What you said about how he's been with you and what I saw were not encouraging. I've done some research on narcissists. It all lines up, and it's had me worried for you."

"Why didn't you say anything?"

He stared at her, seeming to struggle with what to say. "I barely saw the guy, and really only knew what you told me. How would it have sounded if I put him down, or warned you off him? And what if I was wrong, and he was meant to be your future? I didn't want to be responsible for keeping you from that. I'm sorry. You said that's what you wanted, and you're hard to say no to."

"Hard to say no to? I'll have to remember that. But it probably wouldn't have mattered. I'm not sure how I would have responded if you'd said something."

"So, you're meeting up with him tomorrow?"

"Yeah, for breakfast. Other than telling him there's zero chance of us ever getting back together, I'm not sure what I'll say."

"So you're really done with him?" Jacob questioned, and she nodded. "Good. He doesn't deserve you. You're a smart, thoughtful, sensitive, beautiful, and caring mom."

Beautiful. He thought she was beautiful.

Before Noah, she'd been confident in her looks—her strawberry blonde hair set off her green eyes—and she'd kept herself in good shape. Now it was harder to find time to work out, and she rarely felt pretty when she was constantly changing dirty diapers and had a toddler hanging on her. Tyler's treatment of her since she'd discovered her pregnancy fed into her poor self-esteem. Yet this man whose good looks put Tyler to shame, called her beautiful.

Without waiting for a response, he continued, "After you clarify the future, or lack thereof, regarding your relationship, you could tell him he needs to figure out how involved he wants to be in Noah's life, so you can know what to expect and work together to make that happen. Maybe tell him you'll get back with him in a week so he doesn't drag it out. Other than that, I don't think you have anything else to discuss. He'll have a chance to see Noah. That's it."

"You're right. There really is nothing else to be said right now. And it *would* help if he was more specific about how involved he wants to be in Noah's life." She became quiet. "I've also been thinking I'm ready to go back to work."

"Yeah?"

"Yeah. Mostly thanks to you, since you helped pull me out of my depression."

Jacob smiled. "I just wanted to be a friend, but I'm glad it helped you."

"So. What kinds of concerts do you and your roommates like to go to?"

"Um, we—"

"Jake, why are you in there? Come join us." A woman's sultry voice cooed in the background before the call was muted and the screen went black.

Moments later, Jacob was back on the screen, and she heard muffled music. "Hey. Sorry about that. I probably need to let you go so I can get my roommates to settle down. Are you okay for tomorrow with Tyler?"

"Sure. I, uh, I'll get through it. I was able to change my ticket to tomorrow, just after lunch. I'll talk to you later. Bye." She didn't wait to hear his response. Who was the woman, and what was going on at his hotel? She didn't know this side of him, and it made her uncomfortable.

~

BROOKE NERVOUSLY TAPPED her foot while watching the entrance to the
breakfast room at the hotel and keeping an eye on Noah, who was
happily eating beside her. She had quickly eaten her own food,
wanting to be done before Tyler arrived. His dark hair caught her
attention as he passed the outside windows. "I can do this," she
reminded herself.

Their conversation started with a discussion of everything but
the elephant in the room. She was determined to control the
dialogue and keep it focused on the important topics at hand. "Tyler,
just so you know, this conversation is being recorded." She pointed
to her phone, then added, "Do you understand, before we continue?"

"What? Of course, I'm not stupid! I was accepted to med school
at Vanderbilt, that should speak for itself," he said through clenched
teeth.

"Fine. I came to Nashville to see if there was a chance we could
work things out between us and get married in the near future." She
glanced around, glad for the crowd of people to keep Tyler's temper
in check. "Needless to say, I'm obviously not interested—"

"That's not fair. We weren't officially in a relationship, and you
caught me off guard. I—"

She held up a hand. "Enough, Tyler. There's no need to talk in
circles. We both know what you implied to me in Florida, and that
you've been alluding to getting married all along. It's fine . . . I'm fine.
You've done me a favor, actually. You're clearly not husband
material."

At the sight of his reddened face, she felt proud of herself for
being honest and making him squirm. "So, now that we've cleared
that up, how involved do you want to be in Noah's life?"

"I, you can't . . ." Tyler struggled to pull his thoughts together.

"It's okay. You don't have to decide today. I'll give you until next Saturday. That gives you a week. I'll talk with my lawyer and make sure we get everything in writing, so we're on the same page going forward. It will help to have a plan." The frown on his face showed he was not happy with the conversation, but she pressed on. "We can change the parameters whenever we want. But I don't want to set Noah's expectations too high, only to have him constantly disappointed. That's really all I have to say. You're welcome to hang out a bit to have some time with Noah before we leave."

Tyler furrowed his brow. "You came to see if we could work things out toward marriage?"

Raising her eyebrows, Brooke pressed her lips together and searched for the right words. "I hope that's not all you got from our conversation. Yes, I was going to give you a chance, and your response to our surprise visit was key to that chance. I got the message loud and clear. Now we're both free to move on. It's for the best, wouldn't you say?"

"Of course not, he's my son! And you . . . you're never going to find anyone as good as me." His face reddened and anger flashed in his eyes as he leaned in and lowered his voice. "You gave me your virginity. You're never going to be able to get me out of your mind. No one will ever feel as good as me or be able to take my place. You're mine."

Brooke shot up from her seat. "On that note, I think we're done here." She grabbed her phone and snapped Noah up from the high chair. "My lawyer will be in contact with you."

Once in the elevator, she lifted a shaky finger to choose her floor before finally letting out a breath. In the room, she sat down on the edge of the bed and squeezed Noah close. "It's all going to be fine. We're fine. We're better off without him." She rubbed his hair and rocked back and forth. "We're going to get through this, Noah. We've got each other. Mommy loves you so much."

FOURTEEN

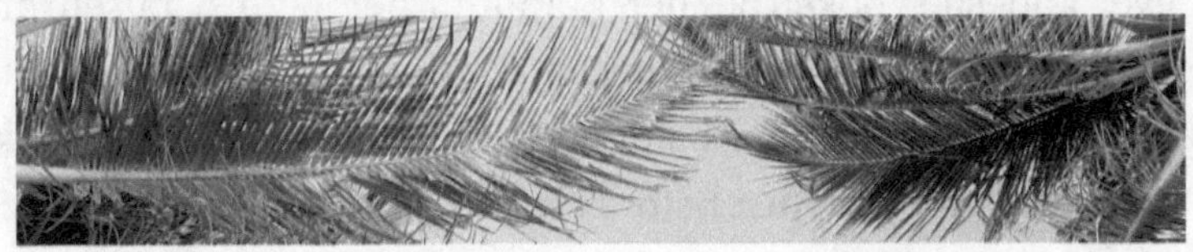

Brooke held it together up until she dragged her luggage into Grams' apartment, then she couldn't stop the tears and shaking. Grams set Noah on the play mat.

"I'm so sorry, dear." She enveloped Brooke in a tight hug. "I've always had concerns about Tyler. He's an awful man. I know it hurts now, but in the long run, you'll be glad you were spared from that relationship."

They walked to the sofa and Brooke pulled back. "The funny thing is, I'm not hurt because I lost him. I'm angry about the way he treated me, and embarrassed I let it go on so long. My mom raised me to recognize toxic relationships, but after getting pregnant with Noah, I so desperately wanted the perfect family I never had, so I overlooked his behavior. I was so stupid." She buried her head in her hands. "I guess I'm also disappointed, because I hoped that Noah would have a better home life than me, with two parents who love each other."

"Now, now, dear. If there's one thing I'm sure of, it's that you are not stupid. And he does have a good home life with someone who loves him. Don't forget that. The important thing is you didn't end up married to that jerk!"

"Grams?!" Brooke raised an eyebrow at the older woman. "I've never heard you say something so harsh about anyone."

"Well. Jerk isn't a bad word, and it's what he is. I couldn't hold back." Grams' voice was stern, but she looked a little embarrassed.

Relaxing into the sofa, a beautiful bouquet on the shelf caught her eye, and she looked at her grandmother with a raised brow. "Secret admirer?" She nodded toward the flowers.

"What? Oh, no," Grams said, noticing what Brooke was looking at. "They came for you. Just before I left to pick you up."

Brooke pursed her lips. "If Tyler thinks he can change my mind with flowers, he's got another thing coming." She walked over and ripped open the attached card. Her jaw dropped, and she blushed as she looked up at her grandmother. "They're from Jacob." She held back a smile as she read the message. She had avoided texting him all day after hearing a woman in his room the night before.

BROOKE,

Sorry about the way the call ended last night, but if I'd kept talking, the guys wouldn't have let us have any privacy. Just know I was praying for you this morning as you met with Tyler. Please call me and let me know how it went.

Also, I hope you're free on Tuesday. I want to take you and Noah to our park and have lunch. I'll be back Monday night.

As for the flowers and greenery, they all have meaning: yellow tulips—sunshine in your smile; white hyacinth—loveliness, prayers; ivy—friendship; marjoram—joy and happiness; daylily—mother; lilac—joy of youth; chamomile—patience in adversity.

Your friend always, Jacob

. . .

SHE SIGHED. It was a beautiful arrangement. Her hands traveled over the flowers as she contemplated what he'd written. There was that word again—friend. It bothered her more than it should when she'd just ended things with Tyler.

She texted Jacob and included a picture of the bouquet.

BROOKE: I'm home now. We're getting ready to eat dinner, but will be done in about 20. You can call anytime after. Thanks so much for the flowers! Lovely!

AFTER DINNER, she checked her phone. Nothing. Silently, she chastised herself for being impatient. He made it clear he wanted to talk, and he wasn't like Tyler. There was no cause for alarm.

Brooke curled up in bed and googled flowers and their symbolism. It was flattering that Jacob put so much thought into her bouquet. She found that some flowers had meanings you would guess, like the red rose meaning love or *I love you*. But some surprised her. True friendship was represented by oakleaf geranium, and sympathy by lemon balm. There were some peculiar ones like hostile thoughts or declaring war with tansy. Hydrangea signified frigidity and heartlessness, but also showed gratitude for being understood. She chuckled before her eyes fell on ivy. Not only did it mean friendship, like Jacob's card mentioned, but it also symbolized marriage and fidelity. Her stomach did that strange flipping thing, but she chastised herself. That's not why he put that in. He specifically did *not* mention those meanings.

Her phone rang, and the man himself was calling. "Hey," Brooke answered.

"Hey. Sorry about these late-night calls. That's just the way it works with my schedule. How did it go with Tyler?"

"Good. And thanks for the flowers. They're absolutely beautiful, and I love how you chose them based on their meanings. That's pretty cool."

"You're welcome. It's something I heard about a while back and have wanted to try. So . . . back to Tyler. What did you say, and how did he take it?"

She gave him the summary and Jacob said he was impressed by Brooke's handling of Tyler. He insisted she would come out of this stronger. "What I wouldn't give to have been a fly on the wall." He chuckled.

"Actually, I have the conversation recorded. Do you want to hear?"

"Absolutely!"

As the recording began, Brooke noticed her voice started out shaky and unsure, but within seconds, it was evident she had gained her confidence.

"Wow! You sound bad . . . as in someone to take seriously! I can't believe Tyler said those things to you. You don't deserve to be treated that way. I'm so sorry that was his response. But you did well standing your ground. You would make an amazing lawyer."

"That was actually my plan . . . or, was before I got pregnant."

"So why don't you go to law school now?"

"My priorities changed. I don't want to spend Noah's preschool years in school, always distracted with studies when I'm home. It's not worth it. Speaking of lawyers, I called my dad while I was waiting for my flight earlier, and told him I'm ready to go back to work."

Brooke became animated as she recalled the conversation. "He said he had already spoken with his friend, who is a partner in a huge law firm down here, and they have the perfect spot for me. One of the founding partners wants to go into semi-retirement, working only Monday through Wednesday. His current paralegal wants to retire completely. I'll go in on Monday for an interview as his paralegal, but they said after looking at my resume and contacting my references, they are confident I'm what they're looking for."

"That's awesome! Congratulations! I'm sure you'll be great. You are such a strong woman. I know you've gone through a lot of hard things, but you're pushing through. Noah is a lucky boy. So many people would let all of this swallow them up, but after taking your time to mourn, you're turning your life around. You should be proud. Can I pray for you?" She nodded at his question. His prayers had become a source of comfort.

Just after he ended the prayer, Brooke heard music in the background along with people laughing. "What's going on? Do you need to go?"

"No, it's fine. Just my roommates at it again."

She heard a door closing on Jacob's end of the line. "So. I don't completely understand. You're working, but your roommates are traveling with you?"

"Yeah. We work together. The problem is they're into the party scene, and I quit that a few months ago. I hang out with them some, unless it gets out of hand. I don't want to seem antisocial, and they've been my best friends for years. We've been through a lot together, so I love 'em anyway and manage to look past it."

"Do you tell them about Jesus?" Brooke thought out loud, knowing why Jacob had changed.

"Yeah, of course. God is the most important thing in my life now, and I want that for them, too. None of them are there yet, but I'll keep trying and I'm always praying for them."

"Oh. That makes sense." Truthfully, it hurt a little. If God was so important to him, why hadn't he shared Him with her? Maybe she didn't mean as much to him as she thought, or as she hoped.

"So how is little guy doing?"

The change of subject was probably good, since Brooke wasn't happy with where her mind was going. The day had held a roller coaster of emotions. She pulled her blanket up further and nestled into the pillow as they chatted until she couldn't keep her eyes open. Her last thoughts before drifting off were of Jacob and Noah playing at the park.

FIFTEEN

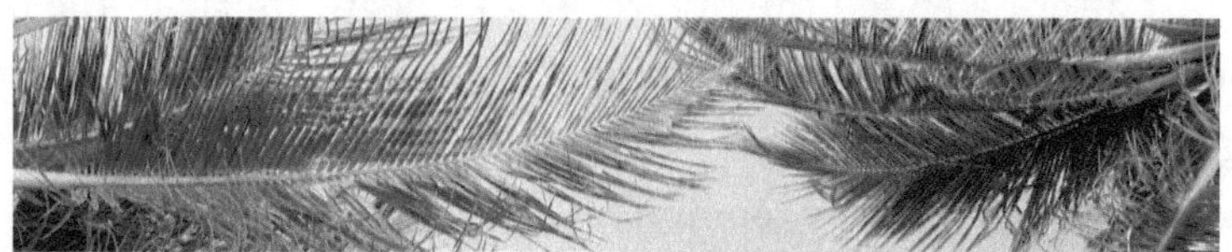

Brooke watched Jacob chase a giggling Noah across the playground.

"I'm going to get you! I'm almost there!" Jacob ran slowly so Noah could stay ahead, before suddenly darting forward, picking Noah up, and swinging him around. "I've got you! I've got you!"

Jacob brought him over to the blanket Brooke laid out for their picnic. Once placing him down, Jacob began tickling Noah, and the giggles turned to deep belly laughs. He leaned down and whispered something in Noah's ear, which was followed by even more laughter as the boy jumped into his mother's lap and tickled her.

How could Brooke contain such happiness? Only a couple of weeks earlier, she had felt utterly despondent. Her gaze shifted from the boy in her lap to Jacob. It was mostly thanks to him. This gorgeous man before her made them feel like they were the most important people in the world when he was with them. Could she dare to hope something more than friendship would develop between them—that maybe before, he was just holding back because of Tyler?

Jacob noticed her watching him and raised a brow. When Noah hopped off Brooke's lap and back into his, he looked between Noah and Brooke and smiled—the kind of smile that makes girls swoon.

"What?" Brooke asked.

"Noah's got your beautiful green eyes. They really stand out in the sunlight."

"Thanks." She felt her cheeks flush and moisture filled her eyes.

"Are you okay?"

She shrugged and blinked back the tears as Jacob scooted closer and placed his hand on hers. "I'm sorry. I'm such a mess. I have all this baggage, and you're always so kind to me and Noah." She wanted to say, "I don't know what I would do without you," but that might sound too clingy and drive him away.

"Lots of people have baggage, and most walk around hiding it. It's a result of living in a sinful, broken world. There's nothing wrong with you. You're handling it amazingly."

He rubbed his thumb over her palm and stared into her green eyes. A charge in the air between them sent sparks of life through her heart. Just as Jacob leaned toward her, Noah stood up from his lap, walked to his mom, and wrapped his arms around her.

"Mama!"

The moment passed.

"So . . . I'll be starting work next Monday." Brooke grinned as she stretched her legs out on the picnic blanket.

"Congratulations! I'm happy for you. From what you've said, you earned it by your own merit. Your dad just got you in the door."

"Yeah, they tried to make it clear that they wouldn't have hired me if I wasn't qualified. I appreciate that. I'll miss Noah during the day, but he'll have loads of fun with Grams. I am looking forward to something a little more challenging than changing diapers."

They laughed, which made Noah giggle and wave his cheese in the air.

"Tonight, I'm cooking you a celebratory dinner. I've already given your Grams and Nan a heads up. I figured you would get the job. We also need to make plans for another beach day tomorrow or Wednesday as your last hoorah before going back to work."

Brooke grinned and swallowed a bite of sandwich. Jacob's attention made her heart overflow. "All of that sounds perfect!"

Jacob cleaned up their picnic things while Brooke took Noah to the playground. He giggled as she gently pushed him in the baby swing, and the little girl in the swing next to him watched, mesmerized.

"My granddaughter can't keep her eyes off your son. He's going to be a heartbreaker when he's older," said the woman pushing the girl in the swing.

Brooke chuckled.

"He clearly takes after his dad." The woman gestured towards Jacob. "Such a handsome young man, obviously in love with both of you. He's a keeper."

Brooke blushed. "He's just a friend. My son's father is out of the picture." It felt strange to admit that about Tyler after trying to work things out for so long.

The older woman glanced back at Jacob and then turned to Brooke and smiled. "You shouldn't worry—I don't think he'll be *just a friend* for long."

Jacob walked up and tipped his cap to the woman, then looked back at Brooke. "Looks like you two made some friends."

"I was just saying her son is going to be a heartbreaker when he grows up. My granddaughter here is enchanted by him."

"He's a handsome young man. I'd say it's his beautiful green eyes that will have the girls doing a double take." Jacob snuck a side glance at Brooke and gave her a crooked grin.

Noah yawned, and his eyes drooped. Meanwhile, Brooke's heart fluttered. Did he say that because Noah had her eyes?

"How about we get him back home for his nap, then I can get things ready for our dinner tonight?" Jacob winked at Brooke.

She nodded and caught the knowing look of the woman at the next swing.

ALMOST AS SOON AS they hit the interstate after leaving the beach, Noah fell asleep. Brooke looked over at Jacob and sighed. It had been another perfect day. She was going to miss having so much time with Noah and Jacob once she started working.

"I see a lot of me in you," Jacob broke the silence.

Pulled from her thoughts, Brooke tried to process what he'd said. "What do you mean?"

"Anger at God because of all you've endured, and pushing Him away."

"But I don't believe in Him. How can I push Him away?"

He shrugged. "You told me you questioned how a good God could let these things happen. It sounds more like you're unsure, agnostic. Anyway, that's where I used to be. When my Nan became a Christian six years ago, after getting to know your grandmother, she started telling me things about God and pulling me into discussions about Him, but I had no interest. I had preconceived notions of who God is, and didn't want anything to do with Him. It was easier to pretend He didn't exist than to imagine He did and hated me. Most of my ideas were from things I had heard about Christians, or about God from non-Christians. I also saw hypocrisy in the lives of people who claimed to be Christians."

Brooke agreed. "Yeah, that sounds similar to what I've experienced. Where I was raised, a lot of people go to church and claim to be Christians, yet live horrible lives. There were tons of kids in my high school who would get drunk with me on Friday and Saturday nights, then wake up and go to church on Sunday morning. Or girls who went to church, but were quick to talk about people behind their backs and ostracize other girls because they didn't have money, or weren't pretty enough, or whatever they decided was worthy of gossip that day.

"It was the same in college. Some of the girls in my sorority who gave me the hardest time about getting pregnant out of wedlock and urged me to have an abortion were 'Christians.' They claimed I was an embarrassment to them and the sorority. Not that I was much better as far as being judgmental, as you learned firsthand, but at least I didn't claim to be something I wasn't."

Jacob turned and placed a hand over hers. "I'm sorry. That must have felt awful when you were already going through so much." Brooke nodded, unable to speak, and he turned back to the road. "The thing is . . . Christians are human and not God Himself. We make mistakes. Also, some people claim to be Christians because they think it gives them some kind of social standing, or maybe because at some point they were baptized, when, in fact, they never made a conscious decision to follow God, acknowledge their sin, and admit that Jesus is the only source of forgiveness for their sin. They never put Him first in their lives."

Shifting in her seat, Brooke's heart raced and moisture broke out on her forehead. Deep down, she wanted him to talk to her about God, because it meant he cared, but now that he'd started, she wasn't sure how she felt about it or how to respond.

Jacob continued, "The turning point for me began at a hotel. I woke up one morning, so sick and hungover from partying the night before with my roommates, and decided I was done with it. I was becoming my mom, and that shook me. That night, when the guys were at it again, I couldn't take it, and went back to my room.

"I couldn't sleep and found a Bible in the nightstand. I remembered my Nan urging me to read the book of John. By the time the sun was up, I'd read all the way through John. From that point on, I carried a Bible everywhere. It became my escape whenever my roommates were partying. In three months, I had read the whole thing.

"My roommates made fun of me and called me *the preacher*, but at that point I wasn't a Christian, and certainly wasn't preaching. I was soaking it all in and asking Nan and your grandmother loads of questions. After reading it all for myself, not just taking people's words about who God is, it started to make sense.

"One day, it hit me—this world is broken, and just because bad things happened to me, that doesn't mean God doesn't love me. It's the opposite. He made a huge sacrifice of His Son because He *does* love me. I also realized I didn't have to be perfect before He would accept me. It's impossible for me or anyone to be perfect. That's why Jesus had to die. The truth impacted me, and I haven't been the same since. I . . . I hope you'll give God a chance. It would mean a lot to me. But I don't want you to take my word for it, or anyone else's. You have to see it for yourself."

They were stopped at a streetlight, and Jacob watched her with those eyes that could sink a thousand ships. "You think I should read the Bible?"

"Yeah. Start with the book of John. We could talk about it as you go through it."

"Um." She wanted to say yes for his sake, but she feared what she would find. She turned and watched the passing trees.

"What do you have to lose?" Jacob reached for her hand and squeezed.

Her pulse quickened. If she said yes, she would follow through to the end. Her throat went dry. Why was this so hard? It's just a book. "Okay, yes, I'll do it," she finally said as she looked back at him.

He pulled her hand to his lips and kissed it. There wasn't enough air to catch her breath, and her hand heated where his lips had touched.

CHAPTER

SIXTEEN

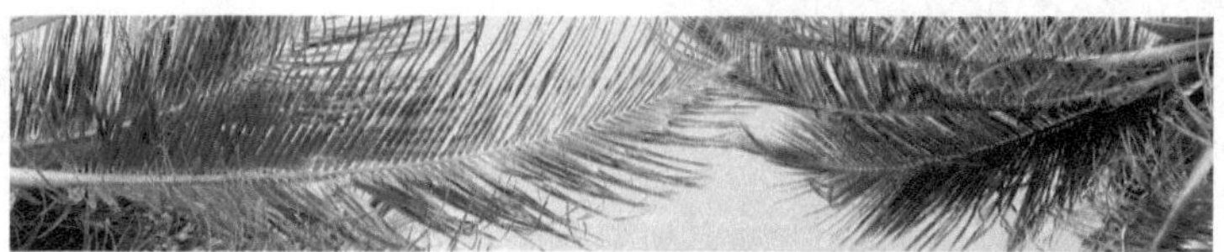

While towel-drying her hair, Brooke checked in on Noah in his crib. He was sound asleep. She was worn out too, after pushing his stroller all over Epcot for hours on end. It was worth it to see all the topiaries and try the different foods at the Flower and Garden Festival. She enjoyed *eating her way around the world* at Epcot and watching Noah's reactions to the characters, shows, and rides. He seemed particularly enthralled with the drummers at the Japanese pavilion as he banged the front of his stroller to the beat.

After saying goodnight to Grams, she climbed into bed to read some more of the book of John from the Bible Jacob gave her. *John* was a strange book that opened with a lot of figurative language. She was glad she had Jacob to discuss it with. John 1:1 said, "In the beginning was the Word, and the Word was with God, and the Word was God." It sounded so foreign. She'd heard people read and quote Scripture plenty of times. She was born and raised in the "Bible Belt" after all, but this was different. The first eighteen verses were written in a poetic style. As confusing as it was, she refused to be beaten by a book that had been around for thousands of years. She'd passed the

LSAT. Surely she could make sense of this. Opening her notes app, she put some things down to discuss when Jacob called later.

He'd left town for work again. He was enigmatic about what he did on these trips. He even mentioned an upcoming trip to Europe for a month. Why would a songwriter need to travel so much? Maybe he was a secret agent. She chuckled at the thought.

The vibration of her phone grabbed her attention, and Brooke realized she'd dozed off. "Hey. Jacob?" she groggily asked.

"Sorry, did I wake you? Should I let you go?" Jacob sounded energetic even though it was so late at night.

"No . . . no." Brooke sat up and wiped drool from the corner of her mouth. At least it wasn't a video call. "I just drifted off while reading *John.*"

"The Bible has got you that excited, huh?"

"We went to Epcot today, and it drained me." That part was true. She left out the part that the book of John had her confused, and she wasn't even halfway through the first chapter.

Brooke recounted her day before they tackled her Bible questions. "Okay, I get that it's referring to Jesus—He is God, and with God." And she was familiar with the concept of the Trinity, though it was as clear as mud. "But why? Why call Him *the Word*?"

"Good question," Jacob began. Was he placating her? "Do you have your Bible there?"

"Yes."

"Turn to Genesis one, verse one. It's the very first book."

She flipped to the front of her Bible. She did know that much. "Genesis one, verse one . . . 'In the beginning, God created the heavens and the earth.'"

"See how they both begin with the same phrase '*in the beginning*'? This first part of the chapter is pointing out that Jesus is one hundred percent God. It ties it all the way back to the beginning of all things. Once you get through this section, the rest of the book is a narrative about His life, which helps us understand that He is not only fully God but also fully man. As you read through the first chapter of Genesis, you read the expression '*and God said*' multiple times in conjunction with Him creating something new that never existed before. God's Word is so powerful, it creates, and in several of those verses it created life—plants, animals, man."

"That's an interesting perspective." She had never thought anything about God would be noteworthy, but it was, and not just because every word that came from Jacob's mouth made her want to swoon.

"Can you find Revelation? It's the last book."

After a minute, she found it. "Okay, got it."

"Turn to chapter nineteen and look at verse eleven." When she located it, he began to read, "Revelation 19:11-13. 'Then I saw heaven opened, and behold, a white horse! The one sitting on it is called Faithful and True, and in righteousness He judges and makes war. His eyes are like a flame of fire, and on His head are many diadems, and He has a name written that no one knows but Himself. He is clothed in a robe dipped in blood, and the name by which He is called is *The Word of God*.'

"The person on the horse is Jesus, which becomes apparent when you read the whole chapter. As an aside, the blood represents the blood from His death. His blood and death cover all of a Christian's sins when He stands before God to enter heaven. So here, at the end of the Bible, you see Jesus called the Word again.

"The Old Testament, all written before Jesus' life, ministry, and death on earth, was the Word of God, written to make people see mankind's sinfulness and need for a Savior. The New Testament is the Word of God lived out in the flesh through Jesus. It's the revelation of the long-awaited Savior that was previously only understood by the written word. There's a phrase someone told me, 'the Old Testament is the Word concealed, the New Testament is the Word revealed.'"

"That's deep."

"Are you making fun?"

"No, seriously, it is." Brooke chuckled. "I kind of get it, but I'll have to think about it some more. I never realized so much of the Bible tied together like that. I mean, the books were written by different people over thousands of years, right?"

"About fifteen hundred, so it is a long time. That's one thing that's so amazing about it. It all works together because of the third Person of the Trinity, the Holy Spirit. The Holy Spirit can actually be in many people and inspire them. In this case, He gave the writers the words. All Christians have the Holy Spirit in them."

"That sounds pretty crazy, you know."

"Yeah. Maybe that's enough for tonight. It sounds like you have a lot to process. So, are you going to the park for play day tomorrow?"

"I am. It's a good group, and they've made me feel so welcome. There are several other single moms, but even the married ones have been kind. It's nice to make some friends."

"You've come a long way these past few weeks. You've got a lot to be proud of."

"Thanks."

"How about tomorrow I call you just before Noah's nap?"

"Sure, I'll text you when we return from the park." Brooke grinned, thinking about what a good relationship Jacob already had with Noah. Monday couldn't come fast enough.

SEVENTEEN

"Good morning, Brooke. Excited for your first day?" Elise, the petite brunette receptionist sitting at the front desk of the law office, asked.

"I am. I'm eager to begin, though I'm a little apprehensive about a new environment and the challenges that come with that. Learning new faces and client names will keep me busy, I imagine."

"That's understandable, but I think you'll find Mr. Stearn easy to work for. The thought of going into partial retirement has mellowed him."

Brooke relaxed some at the idea as she glanced around the lobby, taking in the sleek, modern, yet inviting atmosphere, which was filled with cool grays, whites, and pops of blue. "Will you let Mr. Stearn know I'm here?"

"Actually, Susan Davis, his paralegal, called down to say that their morning meeting is running long, and they don't expect to be ready for you until about 9:30. She suggested you sit with me for a few minutes and learn the phone system." Elise noticed Brooke's raised eyebrows. "Not that you'll be doing what I do, but understanding the basics of the phones will be helpful. I'm sure she also didn't want you to feel abandoned." Elise pulled out the chair next to her.

"Thanks. How long have you been here, Elise?"

"Three years. After high school, I started out at community college for a year, but it wasn't really my thing, so I—" She stopped to press a button for the phone, and spoke into her Bluetooth, "Stearn, Hastings, and Associates, Attorneys at Law. This is Elise. How may I help you this morning? . . . Yes. Just one moment, please." She pressed some buttons before continuing, "Yes, you have a call from Mr. Bradford . . . Yes, sir, I'll put him through." After pressing even more buttons, she turned to Brooke. "So, where was I?"

"Community college wasn't really your thing."

"Oh, yes. I quit school and started as a receptionist at a pediatric dentist's office. I liked being a receptionist, but it was a small office and kind of boring. Except for the time this kid threw up in the waiting room and passed out, then the ambulance came. He ended up fine. Anyway, when I saw this job opening, I snagged it. It's been a perfect fit. I love it here." She answered the ringing phone. "Stearn, Hastings, and Associates, Attorneys at Law. This is Elise. How may I help you this morning?" After a pause, "Hello? Hello?" Another pause. "They hung up," she said, as she disconnected the call and shrugged.

Brooke watched the brunette as she pushed buttons effortlessly. She guessed Elise was close to her age. Her phone buzzed, and she looked down to see it was from Jacob. The gif he sent caused her to laugh out loud, and Elise turned back to her with a smirk.

"Someone just made your morning."

Brooke couldn't conceal her smile. "It's my friend, Jacob." Elise raised an eyebrow. "When we were eating dinner the other night, I mentioned my hours the first day were nine to five, and his grand-mother suggested we watch the movie *9 to 5* with Dolly Parton from 1980. We did, and it was hilarious. He just sent me a gif from the movie." Brooke held out her phone with the GIF of Dolly swinging a lasso.

Elise chuckled. "So, tell me about this guy! He must be more than a friend if you're hanging out with his grandmother, eating dinner, and watching movies." Brooke's grin grew wider. "Is he cute?"

"I just got out of a toxic relationship with my son's dad." Brooke frowned. "So I'm not in a hurry to start another one, but he might help me get over my ex faster." Brooke surprised herself with her admission. "And he's not cute." Elise raised one eyebrow. Brooke smiled slyly, and her heart fluttered as she pictured him. "He's absolutely gorgeous—the most beautiful man I've ever seen. He's got this rough around the edges, don't-give-a-care look." She sighed.

"Do you have any pictures of this Greek god?"

Brooke's face lit up. "Actually, I do." She pulled out her phone, but Elise held up a finger while she answered the office phone. Brooke continued searching for pictures with Jacob. "Here," she said, holding the phone out once Elise hung up.

"He looks hot! I need to see pictures where he's not wearing sunglasses and a hat so I can get the full effect."

"I'm sure I have some." Brooke scrolled through, but every one had a hat and sunglasses. She stopped and thought. She could have sworn they'd taken some. "They must be on his phone. I'll have to get him to send them to me."

"Well, at least tell me this—does he have dreamy eyes?"

Brooke batted her lashes and sighed dramatically.

"Okay, that look told me everything I need to know. And I'm totally jealous, by the way. Does he have a brother?"

Brooke shook her head and noticed a nice looking blond lawyer approach the desk. She recognized him from her first visit and racked her brain for his name, but came up short.

As he walked up, his blue eyes lit up, and he held Brooke's gaze. Heat filled her cheeks. He leaned his elbows on the counter and grinned. "Brooke, right? Good to have you working here."

Brooke nodded, and Elise cut in. "Hey Eric, how's your morning going?"

Not taking his eyes off of Brooke, he answered, "Great now.

Started off rocky, giving a client some bad news. Nice to see you again, Brooke. Let me know if I can help you with anything." He stepped back, gave a small wave, and headed towards the elevator.

Elise grabbed Brooke's arm. "Oh. My. Gosh. You've just broken his four years of showing no interest in relationships."

"What are you talking about?"

"He had a fiancé he was madly in love with, but she died four years ago. A couple of months before the wedding, her car was hit by a drunk driver. She died on the way to the hospital." She stopped to answer a call, then jumped right back in without missing a beat. "It was awful. They'd been sweethearts since undergrad. They were both in law school, and she died mere weeks away from graduation. I don't know how he finished after that trauma." Elise stopped for a breath.

"He's not noticed a woman or dated, not seriously at least, since then. I hear the few dates he has had were set up by friends. And I've seen him around some stunning models. Nothing. This is the first time I've seen him so much as turn his head towards a woman in my three years. He couldn't take his eyes off you. What are you going to do with two guys? Don't break Eric's heart. I would say give him to me, but if he hasn't looked my way in three years, I don't think it's going to happen.

"Oh, and did you know he's Mr. Stearn's son? From his second marriage, that's why he's so much younger than you would expect a seventy-year-old man's son to be."

Chuckling, Brooke laid a hand on Elise's shoulder. "That's a lot of information. I'll not be breaking anyone's heart. I need a break from relationships anyway, remember?"

Elise joined in the laughter. "Okay, yeah, I'll quit now. It's just, I've had a crush on that man since I started here, and he's not shown me any interest. I would say it hurts, but up until now he's not looked at anyone, so I never took it personally. Oh well. It was fun to see what he's like when he's interested. A girl can dream." Her eyes fluttered, and she fanned herself.

This girl was hilarious, and Brooke wanted to get to know her better. Elise made her feel at home, even though she thought the guy she had a crush on was flirting with her. Brooke couldn't imagine any of her old friends handling it that well.

She checked the time on her phone and realized she had never read or responded to the message Jacob sent.

Jacob: Hope your day is great and there are no "Mr. Harts" around. Praying for you.

Brooke chuckled and replied.

Brooke: Good so far. Haven't met any yet! Hanging with the receptionist while Mr. Stearn finishes a meeting. She's been great fun. Give you the deets tonight.

"Susan just called down for you," Elise spoke, drawing her out of her thoughts. "Do you remember how to get there?"

"I do." Brooke slid her chair out, then stopped and turned to Elise. "Thanks for making me feel welcome here."

Upon entering Susan's office, Brooke found an empty desk awaiting her.

"Sorry to keep you waiting." The older woman waved Brooke over to sit. "Mr. Stearn is finishing some paperwork, so we'll get started here. Susan showed her how their software worked and explained their basic procedures.

After Brooke felt confident learning her way around the

computer system, Mr. Stearn emerged from his office. "Miss Ferguson, I must say, I have heard great things from your previous office in Memphis, and I'm looking forward to working with you. How has your morning been so far?"

"It's gone smoothly and I've felt very welcome, thank you."

"Great. If you'll join me and Mrs. Davis in my office, we can discuss my current caseload." He held out his arm to usher Brooke and Susan in.

Just before Brooke walked through the door, Elise approached. "Sorry to bother you, but Brooke received some flowers." She held up a beautiful arrangement of purple hyacinth and pink tulips.

Brooke blushed at the thought of Jacob sending flowers for her first day and wondered about the meanings of each one. Elise gave her a knowing wink as she handed them to her and whispered, "I'm dying to meet this guy. He's clearly romantic."

Brooke laid them on her desk and walked away without opening the card.

"Go ahead, Miss Ferguson. You can look at the card. We'll wait in the office and give you some privacy. We've got time." Mr. Stearn smiled genuinely as he closed his office door.

Elise giggled and shot Brooke a questioning gaze. "I hope you don't mind if I don't give you privacy. I'm dying to know what the Greek god said."

"It's fine." Brooke already felt comfortable around Elise. She slipped out the card and frowned.

"What's wrong? Are you okay?"

"They're . . . um, they're not from Jacob. They're from my grandmother, wishing me a great first day. She forced a smile. They really are lovely." She meant it. The flowers *were* lovely, and she was touched by the gesture, even though she had hoped they were from Jacob.

Elise gave Brooke a side hug. "You obviously have a grandmother who loves you. Jacob can send flowers any time."

Brooke nodded and thought about the bouquet he sent when she returned from the breakup with Tyler. "He has sent me some before, when I broke up with my ex." Elise raised a brow. "He even chose them based on their meanings."

"I knew it! He is a romantic. Don't you worry. I'm sure there will be more to come from him."

WHEN IT WAS ALMOST time for lunch, Mr. Stern took Brooke to a small sitting area to meet some of the other staff.

"This is Dana Parker, Eric's paralegal. You will be working with her on the cases I share with him to assure that the larger corporate clients have access to a lawyer on the days you and I are off," Mr. Stern said.

Brooke shook hands with Dana and then was pointed towards another woman, who she recognized as Mr. Stern's assistant.

"And I believe you've met Gabriella Martinez. She's a shared administrative assistant for Eric and myself."

"Yes, I remember you from my interview." Brooke smiled and shook her hand.

"Great. Time for lunch." Mr. Stern clapped his hands. "Susan, and you"—he looked at Brooke—"will ride with me, and Dana and Gabriella will ride with Eric to our reservation."

Nodding, Brooke turned and bumped into Eric, who had just come around the corner. "I'm so sorry."

Eric's hands flew to her shoulders to stop her from falling, and he smiled warmly. "I don't mind at all."

Brooke stepped back, but his hold lingered. Maybe Elise was right. With her working on cases that Eric and his father shared, she'd have to be careful not to lead him on.

CHAPTER

EIGHTEEN

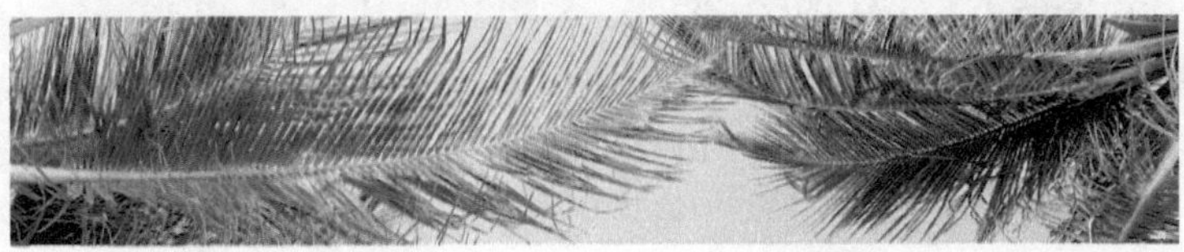

Tomorrow, Jacob was flying to Europe for a month. Wiping tears from her eyes to see the road, Brooke recalled their conversation from the night before.

"Brooke, I'm sorry for springing it on you like this. I mentioned the trip before, but failed to tell you when I was leaving. You've had so much going on that no time seemed good—your mom, all the stuff with Tyler, then your new job. I didn't want this to take away from your excitement about that."

He had pulled her into his arms and appeared just as upset about the situation as she was. Would he miss her as much as she would him? He had been a great friend, helping her through her hardest times. And she sensed a deeper bond growing between them—not to mention the obvious attraction. The looks he gave her, even when he didn't think she was paying attention, made her think he felt it, too. She wanted to take things slow . . . but a month was a long time.

. . .

A car behind her honked, bringing Brooke's attention back to the road as she exited I-4. She looked at the clock and was early to work as planned. Hopefully Elise was in. She needed a shoulder to lean on.

Elise was sorting through papers when Brooke arrived. She took one look at Brooke, waved her over, and pulled out a chair. "Hey. What's going on?"

Brooke's tears started again as she filled Elise in on the Jacob situation.

"How awful." Elise wrapped her arms around Brooke and gave her a motherly pat. "I have just the solution. My friends are in a band that's playing at a local bar on Friday night. You've got to go with me."

"I'm not looking to pick up a guy."

"I get it. I'm not trying to get you to replace Jacob, but I think you could use a fun distraction. How 'bout it?"

Brooke hesitated, weighing the pros and cons, but decided it was time she started living. "You're right." She finally smiled. "I'll go. Well . . . I have to make sure I have a sitter for the night. But I have several options. I'm sure I can make it work."

"Yay!" Elise clapped her hands. "You'll love it. The band is a lot of fun. We've all been friends since high school. Plus, it's at a local hangout and not packed with tourists."

Grabbing a tissue, Brooke dabbed her eyes and grinned. "Okay, it does sound fun. Send me all the details. I'll let you get to it, then." She waved and hopped on the elevator.

Exiting on her floor, Brooke caught sight of Eric. She smiled and turned away, but he called out, "Brooke, could you come to my office for a minute?"

She turned and followed. He offered her a chair and sat next to her with a look of concern.

"Are you okay?" He pointed to her face. "It looks like you've been crying."

Her eyes went wide. She didn't want a reputation for crying all the time. She'd hoped she was finally past that. "I'm sorry. I promise it won't affect my ability to work. I just-"

"That's not what I'm worried about. I'm worried about you. Something has upset you." He reached for her hand, but at the last minute patted her shoulder instead.

Brooke studied him and saw sincerity. "I've had a lot happen this past month. My mom died, which you know, but I also found my ex cheating on me just days after he told me he wanted to get married. Then, last night, I learned that the first friend I made here is leaving the country tomorrow . . . for a month."

He raised his brows. "Wow. Any one of those things would be difficult. Let me know if I can do anything for you. And if you need some time off, I'm sure my dad would be more than understanding, especially right now, while he still has Susan."

Brooke nodded, and his gaze lingered before he stood. "I should let you go. Like I said, if you need time off, don't hesitate to ask Dad. I hope your day gets better. The people who work here are friendly and often get together after hours. Maybe that would help you adjust. I could get something together for Friday or Saturday."

She recalled what Elise had said about his fiancé. He had his own share of difficult things, and yet he had compassion for her. It put things in perspective and tugged at her heartstrings. But she was determined not to lead him on. "Thanks. Elise invited me out Friday to see her friends' band play. I'd rather not be out two late nights in a row. My son will be up in the morning at the same time, whether I've had my beauty sleep or not."

"I understand. That's very responsible of you. You're a caring mom." He smiled and opened the door for her.

ENTERING HER APARTMENT, Brooke was anxious to give Noah a squeeze and love on him. She had grown accustomed to being with him nearly every moment he was awake. Instead, she was greeted by a table with flowers and two place settings, along with the smell of garlic and seafood. Nearing the kitchen, she found Jacob hovering over the stove.

He turned and grinned. "Scallops. Grams said you like them." Brooke nodded in shock. "I spent time with Noah earlier today and thought you and I should have some time, too." He turned off the stove. "I really am sorry for springing this on you." Stepping forward, he grabbed her hands. "We've become good friends . . ." He searched her eyes for confirmation. "This is my job, and I wish I could say it was the last big trip, or it's unusual, but it's not. We'll get through this . . . won't we?" His eyes searched hers.

"I don't understand why a songwriter travels so much," she admitted quietly.

"It's hard to explain." His brow furrowed before he turned and transferred the scallops to a platter. "Noah had a blast on the playground today. There was this little girl, and he was quite the charmer to her. That seems to be a pattern for him." Jacob grinned as he placed everything on the table.

They talked about Noah over their meal, but were relatively quiet as Brooke tried to process his upcoming trip. After dinner, Jacob led her to the sofa and pulled out his Bible. "Tell me what thoughts you've had as you read this week."

That was a loaded question. She'd had many thoughts and not all about the Bible. Pulling his Bible closer, she skimmed the passage she'd written about. "Ah, yes. John 1:14. It's saying that Jesus is full of grace and truth. What does that mean?"

Jacob opened up his notes app and shrugged. "I'm studying this again with you and trying to stay ahead so I can answer your questions. I'm still fairly new at this, but I've had some good mentors. Bear with me. There may be times I have to get back to you, but I think I've got this one. I need to pray first, though." He bowed his head and closed his eyes. "God, help me understand Brooke's questions and give me the words she needs to hear. In Jesus' name. Amen."

He looked up and leaned in closer. "First, let's talk about what grace means in the New Testament. In order to understand it, we need to know that all mankind, every single person, sins. None of us is perfect, or can ever be—not even Christians—until Jesus returns and all is made new." He paused, and although she was confused, she nodded.

He continued. "Because of that sin, we can never get to heaven on our own. Sin cannot be in God's presence. You're already familiar with the concept of Jesus dying on the cross to pay for our sins. That's possible only because He's sinless. And because of what He's done, we're able to go to heaven and have eternal life. Also, once a person becomes a Christian, she has the Holy Spirit living inside, which provides God's power to be better, and to follow His direction. Do we always utilize that power? No, because our sinful nature often holds us back from what the Spirit wants. So a Christian receives both the gift of the Holy Spirit and relationship with God for now and the gift of eternal life for the future, even though he or she has done nothing to earn them. That is grace. There is an acrostic, God's Riches At Christ's Expense, that helps me remember the meaning."

"Okay, wow, there really is a lot more to this Bible stuff than I ever dreamed."

"You're right, but don't let it overwhelm you. Can I talk about truth for a minute, and then we'll end? It's much simpler than grace." Brooke nodded for Jacob to go on. "You know what the meaning of truth is, so that's our starting point. The question, then, is why is Jesus truth? We're going to look at some other verses to understand it. That's always a good way to study the things of the Bible—let God's word explain other parts of His Word. Sometimes it's also helpful to go back to the language it was written in to better understand the original intent. I use the Blue Letter Bible app, because I sure don't know the Hebrew of the Old or the Greek of the New Testament.

"John 17:17 tells us 'God's Word is truth.' And as we've seen, Jesus is the Word. The verse reminds us that all Jesus said during His lifetime and the salvation He brings is true, even though most of the Jewish leaders of His day refused to believe and treated Him like a liar. Do you remember the verse from Revelation we looked at last time?" Brooke quickly flipped back to it. "Chapter nineteen verse eleven. Jesus is called faithful and true. Revelation was written by John also, so let me give you a verse by someone else before we quit. 2 Timothy 2:15 says, 'Do your best to present yourself to God as one approved, a worker who has no need to be ashamed, rightly handling the Word of truth.'"

Brooke smiled nervously. She enjoyed the challenge, and it made so much sense. But what she was learning both scared and intrigued her.

Changing the topic, she told him about Elise's invitation to go listen to the band. Part of her wanted to see Jacob's reaction. Would he show any jealousy that she might be out meeting guys? She also threw in Eric's offer to get a group together for her after work. Jacob shifted a bit in his seat, but she couldn't read his poker face. The sound of the door opening drew their attention, and Grams entered with a smiling Noah.

"This little guy is ready to see his momma and go to bed." Grams handed Noah to Brooke.

Jacob leaned in and ruffled Noah's hair. "Did you have fun with Grams?"

"Mams!" Noah squealed and reached for Jacob. "Da!"

Brooke felt a familiar warmth at his name for Jacob. She shrugged and passed Noah off.

"I've written a bedtime song for him." Jacob looked at Brooke with a raised brow. "Can I play it for him just before he lays down?"

Be still her heart. How could she say no to that? Brooke nodded, pulled Noah back on her lap, and choked back tears for what felt like the millionth time. Jacob started strumming his guitar and Brooke melted. The song was sweet and told of warm summer days, childhood play, a mother's love, and a loving father up above. It told of restful sleep and drinking deep of the water that quenches thirst for all eternity. It had an eerie, haunting quality that made her long for the happy days of her childhood, and simultaneously hope for an even happier future.

Her eyes dropped to Noah, who stared mesmerized by Jacob and his song. The tears slipped out. The thoughts of God, Jacob leaving, his song for Noah—it was almost too much.

CHAPTER

NINETEEN

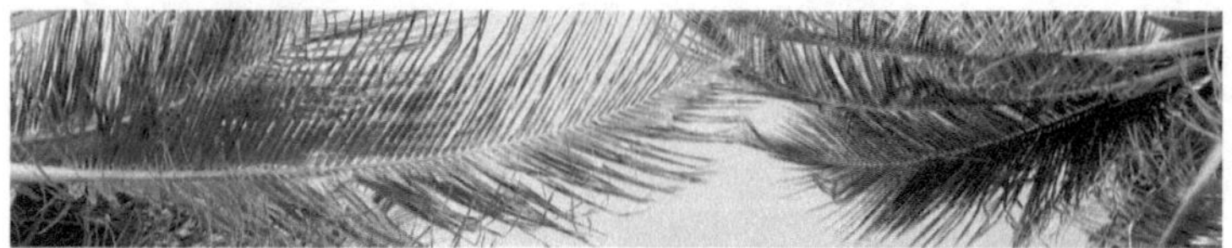

"**S**eriously, Brooke!" Elise said as she stepped back after applying winged eyeliner to Brooke's eyes while getting ready for their girls' night. "This Jacob guy sounds too good to be true. He wrote a song for your son? Surely that proves he's interested in you. He got up early to make your whole family omelets, then sent flowers to work the day he left!" She batted her eyelashes. "So dreamy! Who cares if he travels all the time? He more than makes up for it. I'll have to live vicariously through you."

Brooke rested a hand on her hip. "Now why would that be? My guess is you have plenty of guys after you."

"Maybe, but not the one I want."

Smiling at the discovery, Brooke prodded her friend. "And who might that be? Eric?"

Elise shook her head and pouted. "Brad Miller." She placed both hands on her hips. "Best friends since elementary school, and he has totally friend-zoned me. I don't know what to do to get out of that zone."

"I thought you had a crush on Eric."

"Oh, I do. He's dreamy, but it's just that, a dream. He's honestly not my type. I usually prefer a guy with a bit of a bad boy vibe, and maybe a couple of tats. Nothing too outlandish. Brad is perfect." Her eyes got a dazed look and she smiled.

Brooke chuckled. "The ironic thing is Eric *is* my type, but Jacob, the one with a little bad boy vibe, is not. Except he has no tats that I know of, unless they're hidden under his swimsuit." Brooke blushed when Elise wiggled her eyebrows.

"Here." Elise dragged Brooke to a full-length mirror. "What do you think?"

Brooke chuckled as she ran her hand down her smooth-as-glass strawberry blonde hair that Elise had straightened, and looked at herself in the rocker chick garb Elise convinced her to wear—a fitted black leather mini skirt, a gray T-shirt with the name of her friends' band, and a black leather jacket, complete with zippers and all. From the way Elise dressed at work, Brooke wouldn't have guessed she had a wardrobe like this. The jacket reminded her of the first time she saw Jacob, and she couldn't hold back a smile.

Brooke ran a finger over the word *Madness* on her shirt. It was the band's name. Elise said in high school, when the band first started practicing together, one of their moms said the whole idea was madness.

"Well?"

Brooke took in the whole outfit. "There's a first time for every-thing. What would my sorority sisters think now?" She chuckled. This might be a first, but Brooke would have fun with it. She doubted anyone at the bar would judge her based on the way she was dressed.

On the Uber ride there, Elise filled her in with details about the band. They had one female member, Maddie, who played keyboard, sang backup, and dated Rhys, the bass guitarist. They played a combination of their own music, current artists' songs, and they apparently had a thing for 80s music.

"What are your favorites?" Brooke asked.

"There's one Brad wrote, which is, of course, my favorite." Elise got that dreamy look again. "But they do a couple of *Nine Days In* songs I love. They sound almost exactly like them."

"I've heard of *Nine Days In*, but I've never listened to their music. I thought they were a boy band for younger girls? The girl who's babysitting Noah for a couple of hours tonight before Grams gets in is in love with them, and she's fourteen. Her sister feels the same way, and she's eleven."

"They started out as a boy band, but their most recent album and tour is geared toward a crowd our age—though I'm sure the young girls are still gaga over them. I have to admit, they are fun to watch. I've seen them live a couple of times. So good-looking—especially the lead singer. I might even give up on Brad, if *he* showed me some interest." Elise fanned her face.

"I've met them all." Her voice raised excitedly. "Our firm represents them, so they come into the office every now and then. I have all their autographs. Unfortunately, no sparks flew, and that wasn't the beginning of my beautiful rock star romance." She batted her eyes with a playful, forlorn look, then laughed.

"Seriously, though, my friends started their band a few years after *Nine Days In*, with a similar situation. They also met and put the band together in high school, here in Orlando. *Nine Days In* got lucky and was discovered playing the circuit of local bars and small venues, so that's what *Madness* is aiming for."

"How exciting. I hope your friends find a break like that. Next time *Nine Days In* comes to our office, I'll have to get their autographs for my sitter."

"That would earn you major brownie points! Gotta keep the babysitter happy." Elise grabbed Brooke's phone and stood back. "Need some pics of you to commemorate your first night on the town since Noah." Elise grinned as she snapped a few, moved in for a selfie of the two of them, then started typing.

"What are you doing?" Brooke questioned. Snatching her phone back, she noticed her message app was open and raised a brow.

Elise shrugged. "Have to make sure your man sees how hot you look and knows you can have fun without him." She winked, and Brooke narrowed her eyes. "Just wait and see."

Within seconds, Brooke's phone vibrated.

JACOB: 🔥 Seems I need to send someone to keep an eye on you for protection. Where are you going dressed like that? Didn't know you had that style of clothes. You've been holding out.

ELISE CHUCKLED. "TOLD YOU."

BROOKE: Elise is taking me to a bar to watch her friends' band, and these are her clothes.

JACOB: What's the name of the band?

BROOKE: Madness. It's local.

JACOB: I'll check them out. Stay safe. Stay together. Don't leave your drink unattended.

BROOKE: Yes, Mr. Bossy. 😉

~

THE BAR WASN'T FANCY—WORN booths and tables, exposed ceiling, and an unfinished concrete floor filled Brooke's vision. Elise led her to a table with four guys, close to the empty stage. In about fifteen minutes, her friends' band was scheduled to play.

"I'll introduce you to the band," Elise said when they stopped by the table.

"Elise!" cried a girl sitting in one of the guys' laps. Since she was the only girl at the table, Brooke guessed she was Maddie and sitting in Ryhs's lap. The girl turned to Brooke. "You must be Brooke. Elise has told me all about you. I'm Maddie. Glad you came out to hear us tonight!" Maddie had arresting blue eyes, short dark hair with red tips, and was dressed in all black. For someone who looked so intimidating, she seemed friendly.

The guys examined Brooke.

"Everyone, this is Brooke!" Elise announced to the table, then went around introducing the guys. On the left was Brad, an attractive guy with light brown hair, dark eyes, and several tattoos on his left arm. Brooke looked forward to getting to know him and helping Elise get out of the friendzone. Next to him sat Rhys, with Maddie in his lap. He had a dark brown faux hawk and tattoos peaking above his neckline. Then there was Liam, the guitarist, with blond hair shaved short on the sides, long up top, and a full beard. On her right sat Matt, the lead singer. He had short brown hair that was longer on top and swept over the side of his forehead. He wore a lopsided smile.

Matt's green eyes held Brooke's and he grinned. "Looks like all the seats are taken, so we'll have to get creative. I've got Brooke," he said, pulling her into his lap. "Brad, Elise is all yours."

Brad laughed and seconds later, Elise sat in his lap, looking content. Brooke watched Brad's expression, trying to determine his feelings, but it was hard to tell if he was just generally happy, or if there was something more hidden in his smile.

Meanwhile, Matt wrapped an arm around Brooke's waist and shifted her so he could see her face. "So tell us about yourself, Brooke. We only know you work with Elise and are beautiful." Brooke blushed and her eyes traced the tattoos on his arms. He was nice looking, and she was flattered by the interest, but her heart longed for a man on the other side of the Atlantic.

Elise pointed her finger at Matt. "Don't you get any ideas. She is not going home with you. She's my friend, not one of your groupies."

Matt chuckled. "Who said anything about just one night? I can do serious, too."

His hand moved up to her belly, where he rubbed her shirt. He looked up at her with what was clearly his signature smolder. Brooke felt the heat in her cheeks and hoped the band was ready to move to the stage.

As the thought entered her mind, Liam smacked the table. "We need to get up there, guys."

Matt groaned. "Sorry, babe." He tilted her chin toward him. "But I'll be singing every song for you." Then he lifted her and slid off the chair.

Elise rolled her eyes. "My apologies. I forgot to tell you that Matt acts like Casanova and is a total playboy."

"I heard that." Matt called out from a few feet away. "I'll have you know, I'd change for the right woman." He winked at Brooke, and she shook her head and laughed.

Scooting closer, Elise patted her on the shoulder. "Don't worry, he's really harmless. If you're not interested, he might still tease you, but he won't push it."

Madness's sound was impressive, and Brooke found herself up front, dancing with Elise and a group of girls who were going crazy for the guys—mostly Matt. True to his word, though working the whole crowd, he focused on Brooke. He even dedicated two songs to her—"Get to Know You" and "Mystery Girl." His groupies caught on to the direction of his attention and a few glared at her.

A melodic song came on that had Brooke entranced. It started soft and had an otherworldly quality, then towards the end, it picked up speed and intensity. The words had more depth than most of their other songs. It spoke of searching for answers, and during the more intense part, its message was about an approaching change.

When it ended, she felt sad, and turned, wide-eyed, to Elise. "That was amazing! Did they write that one?"

"Nope, it's by *Nine Days In*—off their new album." Elise grinned proudly and looked back at Brad, who gave her a wink. "Ah." She groaned and threw her hand over her heart. "That man! My heart can't take much more."

When the next song began, the crowd went wild and Brooke looked at Elise for answers.

"This is one of their own songs, from the early days. Everyone loves it."

It was upbeat, and she felt the energy in the room increase. Matt came to the edge of the stage and kneeled down, holding his guitar to the side and reaching out his other hand to the crowd. The girls went wild, grabbing it—and him. One even tried to pull him down to dance. "Sorry girls, all my dances are taken by the beautiful Brooke tonight." He pointed at Brooke and winked before standing up.

Brooke felt her face flush and rolled her eyes, but grinned.

When their break finally came, Matt made his way to Brooke as the filler music started. "I was serious about the dances." He grabbed her hand and led her back to their table, where he grabbed a drink the waitress had just dropped off, drank half, and pulled her to the dance floor.

"Wait!" Brooke urged, and he shot a questioning brow up. "If I'm going to dance with you, you need to get Brad to dance with Elise."

Matt gave her a grin and a knowing look as he tugged her back to the table and laid a firm hand on Brad's shoulder. "You need to go dance with Elise, so this beauty will dance with me."

"What?" Brad looked confused.

"You heard me! Go dance with your best friend." Matt nodded toward Elise, who was chatting with one of the bartenders.

Brad watched Elise for a minute, before nodding and walking over to her. Brooke saw Elise's eyes light up as she followed him to the dance floor.

"Happy?" Matt wrapped an arm around Brooke and guided her back to the dance floor.

TWENTY

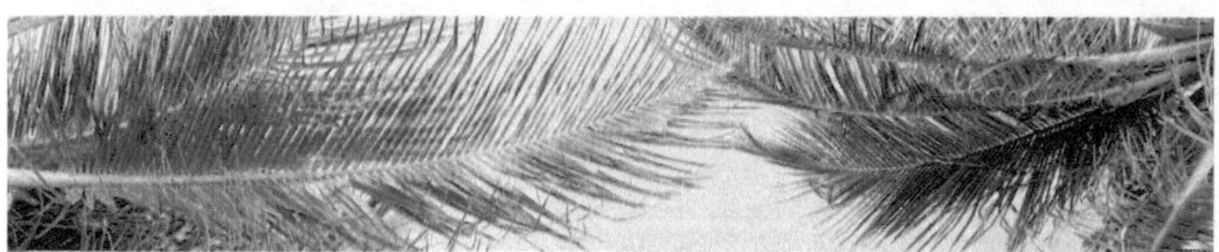

Yawning, Brooke stretched until her arm bumped into a warm body. Her eyes shot open, and she was momentarily confused until she remembered she stayed overnight with Elise. It had been two years since she had slept beside another person—Noah not included—and it was a strange feeling.

Rolling out of bed, she began quietly rummaging through her things, anxious to get home. This was her first overnight away from Noah and their longest time apart. She felt empty. Grabbing her phone, toothbrush, and facial products, she headed to the bathroom.

While brushing her teeth, she checked her messages and saw multiple ones from Jacob. Once finished in the bathroom, she slipped past a—still sleeping—Elise, and into the living room so she could sit down and see why Jacob was blowing up her phone. She was hit with a series of screenshots he'd taken from social media of her dancing with Matt, holding hands with Matt, and getting into an Uber with Matt. After each picture, he had included screenshots of some of the comments. "New girl thinks she can snag local heart-throb." "Mystery girl will learn Matt's all about the one-night stands." "Someone find this girl on insta so we can troll her."

"Matt's mine!" "New girl hogged Matt." "Learn to share like the rest of us!"

Brooke ran her hands over her face. This was crazy. She hadn't even looked at what Jacob said about it all. Checking the time, she calculated it was about four in the afternoon where he was. Just as she started dialing Jacob's number, she heard a key unlocking the door and jumped up, confused and looking for something to hit the intruder with. Grabbing a book from the table, she moved to a spot away from direct view of the door. As she began to swing at the invader, she realized it was Matt.

He grabbed the book. "Woah, there! I come in peace, and with donuts." He held up the box. "I texted Elise, but didn't get a response, so I planned to leave them on the counter. But this is even better." He grinned as he took her in and chuckled after seeing her feet.

Her brows furrowed. She followed his eyes and realized she was wearing her Minnie Mouse nightshirt and shorts with her fluffy Minnie slippers. With red cheeks, she stepped backwards. "I'm, um, I'm going to change, and then we need to talk!" she whisper-yelled and pointed at him. Brooke quickly turned and darted into the bedroom where she found Elise awake. "I was out there like this." Brooke gestured to her braless, super short shorts-wearing, fluffy-shoed self. "And in walks Matt, who apparently has his own key!"

Elise crinkled her nose. "Oops. Sorry. I forgot to tell you that since Brad and Matt live in the same building, we have each other's keys. You can never walk around indecent, because they're prone to pop in unannounced."

"Yeah? Well, moving on, there's also this." She tossed her phone on the bed for Elise to see what Jacob sent, then grabbed some clothes to change.

Elise's eyebrows shot up, and her hand went over her mouth as she scrolled through the images. After a few minutes, she spoke up. "At least he says he has someone who can get it all taken down for you."

"What?" Brooke plopped down beside her and looked at Jacob's message. "I was so distracted, I never got to his actual messages. There he goes, making me think he's some kind of secret agent again. Yesterday, he offered to send me protection for last night."

Elise's head tilted to the side and her brows pulled together. "That's weird."

"Tell me about it. I think I'll take him up on the offer for removing this from social media, though. Even though I closed all my social media accounts when I got pregnant, I don't like the thought that this stuff is out there."

"Good idea."

"I'm lonely eating donuts by myself out here!" Matt shouted from the living room.

"Will you go entertain him for a few while I get dressed?" Elise made prayer hands and Brooke rolled her eyes before chuckling and getting up.

"I'm just giving you a hard time. You were right, Matt really isn't that bad. Anyone who comes with donuts after I talked his ear off about missing Noah last night, is okay in my book." Brooke slipped on pants—and a bra—and left Elise to get ready while she joined Matt at the breakfast bar. He was drinking milk with a half eaten jelly donut sitting in front of him. "So, I have a friend that found all this on social media." She told him and handed him the phone.

Matt took it and burst out laughing. When Brooke glared at him, he threw her a sheepish look that turned into a lopsided grin. "Sorry, but some of these comments are hilarious." As she continued to glare, he covered his smile and made choking sounds as he tried to hold in his laughter. When she laughed out loud, he didn't hold back any longer.

"Thankfully, the friend who discovered it said he knows someone who can get it removed. I plan to take him up on the offer." She grabbed a donut and took a bite. "Yum."

"Who is this guy who takes so much interest in you?" he asked with raised brows.

After swallowing, she said, "A friend."

"Hmm. That's nice, I guess, to have someone who can do that for us." He looked hurt. "On another note," he said a few moments later and handed her back her phone. "I could tell you noticed the same thing I have—Elise and Brad are a perfect match." She nodded, and he leaned in and whispered conspiratorially, "Why don't we team up to help them get together?"

Brooke eyed him suspiciously. "And how do you suppose we do that?"

Matt grinned and tapped a finger on his chin. "We'll have to work the details out, but I've got some ideas." Brooke cocked an eyebrow. "We can start by having the four of us go out and conveniently leaving the two of them alone."

Placing a hand on her hip, Brooke narrowed her eyes. "Now don't you go getting any ideas about us." She waved a finger between them.

"Who, me?" Matt smirked. "But there is an *us*? Good." He reached forward to wipe some donut icing from the side of her lip.

"Matt!" She swatted at his wrist, and before she could think of a comeback, Elise walked in.

"We'll talk later," he whispered in her ear.

"I really need to get going, Elise." Brooke stood and hugged her friend. "Thanks for making my first night out since Noah, awesome." She opened the Uber app on her phone and saw that her driver was just around the corner.

"This won't be the last time. I'll make sure you don't forget you're a single woman and not just a mom." Elise winked.

"Here, here!" Matt held up his glass of milk.

Brooke turned to him and giggled. "And thank you, too, for making it fun. And for the donuts, but not for the pervy flirting."

"Aww, baby. You know you loved it!" He winked and chuckled.

Brooke rolled her eyes. "On that note, I really should leave. My car's here." She grabbed her bag and left with a wave.

It was now 4:37 p.m. Jacob's time. She dialed his number on the long distance app.

He answered almost immediately. "Brooke! I was beginning to worry. You didn't reply to any of my texts."

The texts . . . Brooke still hadn't looked at his messages. She switched him to speakerphone and began scrolling through. Apparently, he sent the first message while she was at the bar.

JACOB: I've checked out the band you mentioned. Beware of the lead singer, Matt. He lures women in for one-night stands. Doesn't do relationships. Have fun with Elise.

SHE SHOOK her head and pinched her nose.

"Did you . . . sleep with him?"

"What? Of course not!" She gasped, realizing the Uber driver heard that. As she continued scrolling, she saw that it was about four in the morning when he sent the screenshots from Instagram, followed by panicked messages.

JACOB: Are you okay? I'm worried.

JACOB: You didn't read your texts last night. I should have sent someone in person to give you this information. I've got someone who can take all this stuff down.

JACOB: You still haven't checked your messages. I'm trying not to call Nan or your Grams, but about ready to have someone find this Matt guy's place.

"BROOKE?"

"What?" She switched off the speakerphone.

"I was talking and you didn't respond. What's going on? Are you still at his place? Do I need to send someone to help you? If the answer is 'yes' to that last question, say 'Grams is taking Noah to Magic Kingdom today.'"

"What? Are you talking in code? I'm in an Uber on my way home. I didn't stay at his place. Why would you ask that?"

"But the picture—you were getting in a car with him."

"Elise, Brad the drummer, Matt, and I, were all in that same Uber because the guys live in the same apartment building. The picture cut out Elise and Brad."

"Oh. But you danced together and then it showed him holding your hand outside."

"I told him I would dance with him if he would help me get Elise and Brad to dance together. She's been in love with Brad forever. The holding-hands picture is him dragging me through his groupies to get to the Uber." A smile emerged as things clicked in her mind. "Are you jealous?"

"What? Of course not! Why would I be jealous of some guy who plays with girls' feelings? Anyway, if I didn't look like your type, he definitely doesn't with all those tats."

Brooke chuckled. "Mhmm. Not jealous."

"I'm not! So, what are you doing today?"

Brooke continued laughing at his change of subject. She stopped when she heard him groan in frustration. "I'm sorry. Nothing much, I'd say. Last night was long. We didn't get back to the apartment until after 1:30, and I haven't stayed up that late since Noah was born. I'll probably stay home and crash for a nap with Noah."

It was Jacob's turn to laugh. "That's a good idea."

"So can you stop worrying about me now?"

"Maybe." There was mirth in his voice. "Now that I know you're not mixed up with that Matt guy."

"He's really a nice guy once you get—"

"Brooke! You need to stay away from him."

"I have no interest in him that way, so his tactics are useless on me. But I'm sure I'll be hanging out with him more when I'm with Elise, since he's roommates with Brad."

"I don't like it."

"Don't pout. I'll be fine."

"How do you know I'm pouting? Maybe I should have a bodyguard follow you around."

"I'm seriously starting to think you are some kind of secret agent. All this talk about following people and having things scrubbed from social media—which, by the way, I *would* like those pictures removed. Also, you never tell me what you're doing on all these trips."

"I can't."

"Or you'll have to kill me?" she asked with a giggle.

"Something like that." He laughed dryly. "I'll tell you, eventually."

"I don't like being kept in the dark. But I won't force it out of you. I am serious about getting those pictures down from social media, though. This is exactly why I closed all my social media accounts. It was a nightmare with the Tyler scandal."

"Yeah, it's no problem. If there's anything else on the internet, we'll pull them, too."

"Thanks. We're about to turn into the apartments, so I should let you go. I . . . I'm sorry for causing you so much stress."

"I'm just glad you're safe. Talk to you later, Brooke."

She relaxed into the seat with a smile on her face.

TWENTY-ONE

While slipping a shirt over Noah's head to get him ready for church, Brooke's heart raced. Grams had repeatedly invited her to church, and she'd avoided it. But today she felt different and wondered if going would help make sense of her feelings.

Walking Noah into the living area, she saw Grams sitting outside on the patio glider with her morning coffee and an open Bible.

She took a deep breath before approaching her. "I'd like to go to your church today."

Grams' face lit up. "Wonderful! We have a great Sunday school for young singles if you'd care to try it."

Anxiety kicked in. "I'm thinking just the main service today. Maybe another time I'll check out that Sunday school." She shifted on her feet and hoped she hadn't hurt her grandmother's feelings. She just wanted to test the waters today.

Her grandmother hesitated, then smiled. "You know what, Noah and I will skip Sunday school today, so we can all go together." Brooke shook her head and opened her mouth to speak, but Grams held up her hand. "No, really. I understand, and I want you to feel comfortable."

~

BROOKE HELD Noah in one arm and clasped her Bible in the other as she approached the church building. Unlike the church Grams attended in Memphis, which was a huge brick building complete with white columns and a steeple, this one looked like a metal warehouse with a couple of exterior additions. Once inside, she was surprised by the contemporary decor. It wasn't what she expected.

Her eyes scanned the area and landed on a perfect little family. A young dad, holding the hand of a toddler with blonde hair and a pink dress, his other arm wrapped around his pregnant wife, who was absolutely glowing. Her heart clenched as she glanced down and saw they both wore wedding bands. Would she ever have that? As a teenager, she had promised herself she would be married before having a child, yet here she was. The woman looked up, caught her eye, and smiled.

She approached Brooke. "Hi! I'm Hannah. So nice to have you here."

Brooke smiled back. "Thanks, I'm Brooke, and this is Noah."

"Of course. I've met Noah with your grandmother." Hannah looked at Grams and grinned. "Clara is such a blessing to this congregation. We moved here a year ago. She's been like a second mother to me, and a grandmother to Charlotte." She pointed to her daughter. "This is my husband, Craig, by the way." Craig smiled and joined the ladies.

"Clara has told us some of what you've gone through." Hannah spoke softly while Craig and Grams chatted. "I've been praying for you." Noticing Brooke's surprise, she added, "Your grandmother leads a small prayer group with me and some other young married women. We share a lot of personal things. She's a great mentor. You're lucky to have her."

Tensing and holding Noah tighter, she waited for Hannah to give her the look that said, "I know you're a sinner, and you don't belong here," but it never came. Instead, she saw only sincerity and care in Hannah's eyes. She relaxed, and Hannah smoothed a loving hand over Noah's head.

"You're right. My grandmother is pretty special. I don't know how I would have gotten through the past month without her."

Taking her Bible and turning to Exodus twelve, Brooke listened intently as the pastor described the Israelite families preparing to leave from their slavery in Egypt once God enacted the final plague.

"They were to pick a lamb without blemish and paint its blood on the doorpost." Her stomach turned and her face contorted. "And roast the meat. They were to eat it and couldn't leave any for the next day, but were to be prepared to leave quickly. Even their bread was to be unleavened, because they would not have time to let it rise. God's final plague was to kill the firstborn of every family in Egypt, and the lambs' blood around the doors of the Israelites would be a sign for God to pass over the home without harming the first born."

The story was gruesome, and the pastor referred several times to the lamb's blood being a representation of the blood of Jesus. He pointed out that the Passover was to be celebrated yearly by the Israelites. Celebrated? Strange. She knew some Jewish families in Memphis who faithfully observed Passover, but had no idea that this was how it began. She also learned that Jesus was celebrating Passover with His disciples when He instituted communion.

After hearing the pastor talk about the lamb, Brooke's palms began sweating. She stared at the pastor. He was talking to her! She had been wondering why Jesus was called the lamb of God in John. This was weird. She looked around. Did everyone know he was talking to her? Thankfully, she'd brought the notebook she'd been using while studying John, so she scribbled down the things the pastor said and the questions she had.

She wrote down "Matthew 26" to look at later. It was the Lord's supper and said something about the wine representing Jesus' blood for their sins and the bread being His body. Glancing back at what she had written, she had a feeling there was so much more. It all went way beyond her knowledge gained from childhood visits to church with her grandmother. She had heard about Moses being saved from death by Pharaoh's daughter as an infant, and how Moses saved the Israelites from Egyptian slavery through God's plagues, but this . . . connection to Jesus, this was on a whole other level. This was deep stuff, and she wanted to understand it better. She was anxious to get back and video chat with Jacob to hear his thoughts on it all.

On the ride home, Brooke was silent, her mind full of everything she had just learned.

Grams looked at Brooke with concern. "Are you okay? You've not said a word since we got in the car. Was church uncomfortable for you?"

"No. It was great. It's just . . ." She searched for the right words. "It was weird. I felt like the message was just for me. I've been reading through the book of John and discussing it with Jacob. The next thing I was going to ask him about was why Jesus is called the lamb of God. Then your pastor starts reading from part of the Bible that happened hundreds of years before what I've been studying and says that they tie together. What's strange is I can actually understand some of what he's talking about, and I know there's more . . . a lot more, and I want to grasp it all. It's answering questions I never knew I had." Grams smiled in understanding and nodded. "As soon as we get home, I'm video chatting with Jacob. I've got to talk to him about it."

When they walked into the apartment, Grams offered to feed Noah. Brooke hugged them both and sprinted to her room. She spread out her Bible and notebook, then called Jacob with the video app. She couldn't wait to see his face when she told him what she learned, and . . . well, she just couldn't wait to see his face. Smiling, she watched her phone, but frowned when she saw him calling her without video instead of answering her call.

"Hey. Is this a bad time for you?" she questioned.

"No, it's just . . . not a good place for video. Sorry. So what's up?"

Brooke tried refocusing. This was too big to get off-track. "I went to church with Grams this morning!"

"That's awesome! You didn't even mention it yesterday."

"I know, right? When I was getting Noah ready for church, I felt this pull, like I needed to go."

"Really?" She could hear the grin in Jacob's voice and she tried imagining it on his face. "So, what did you think?"

"At first, I was worried people would look down on me for being an unwed mother and *defiling* their church. But everyone was so kind, and I knew quite a few ladies from the park playgroup."

"That's great!"

"Yeah, but the really amazing thing is what the preacher spoke about. He was going through Exodus, specifically chapter twelve. It's where God tells the people what to do for Passover, just before He sends the angel of death, or whatever it is, to kill everyone's first-born. I didn't think it was very interesting until he started talking about the lambs that were to be killed. Lambs without blemish. It's the same phrase I've heard about Jesus. When I was reading through John, I didn't understand why Jesus was called the *Lamb of God*. He also mentioned that the lamb was representative of Jesus, and he spoke about how the wine from communion represents His blood, and that Jesus was celebrating Passover with His disciples when He had the first communion and asked that they do it in remembrance of Him. It was like the whole message was for me! I know I'm missing something and there's more to it. But still, wow! I had no idea the Bible was so complex! I still have some questions. Do you have time to talk?"

"I have some time, but people keep coming in and out, so there's some background noise. Also, I'd like to put you on speakerphone so I can read my notes and use my Bible app. Would it be possible for you to call me before work tomorrow? You can message me your questions tonight, and I'll send you some verses I already had prepared about Jesus being the Lamb of God. What do you think?" Jacob paused when Brooke's phone vibrated. "Do you need to check that?"

"It's a text from . . . Matt?"

"Matt? As in the guy from the band? Why is he texting you?"

"I don't know. Let me check." Brooke put the phone on speaker and opened the text, wondering how his number got into her phone.

MATT 'THE ONE FOR YOU' Barrett: 😊 Hope you don't mind. I added my number when I was looking at those Instagram pictures so we can plan our date with Elise and Brad. 😉

"APPARENTLY, he put his number in my phone when he was looking at those Instagram photos yesterday. He wants to plan our get-together with Brad and Elise. Did I tell you about that? Elise has a crush on Brad, and we're scheming to get them together?"

"You mentioned trying to get them to dance Friday night, but not future plans. I don't like this. You know he's just looking for an excuse to go out with you?"

Brooke chuckled. "You're funny . . . and jealous. You saw the comments on insta. He's not looking for anything serious, just instant gratification. Once he realizes he won't get that from me, he'll move on." She heard Jacob sigh.

"I'm worried about you. I wish I were there. Please be careful."

"I will." She curled up on her bed and savored their conversation. One month couldn't pass fast enough.

TWENTY-TWO

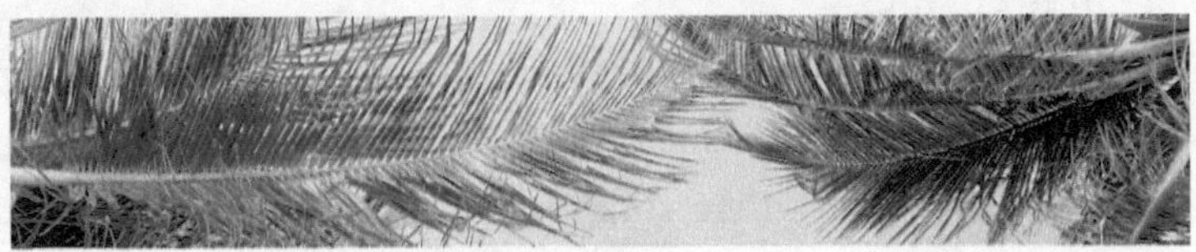

Isaiah 53:1-12. "Who has believed what He has heard from us? And to whom has the arm of the LORD been revealed? For He grew up before him like a young plant, and like a root out of dry ground; He had no form or majesty that we should look at Him, and no beauty that we should desire Him. He was despised and rejected by men; a man of sorrows, and acquainted with grief; and as One from whom men hide their faces He was despised, and we esteemed Him not. Surely He has borne our griefs and carried our sorrows; yet we esteemed Him stricken, smitten by God, and afflicted.

But He was pierced for our transgressions; He was crushed for our iniquities; upon Him was the chastisement that brought us peace, and with His wounds we are healed. All we like sheep have gone astray; we have turned—every one—to his own way; and the LORD has laid on Him the iniquity of us all. He was oppressed, and He was afflicted, yet He opened not His mouth; like a lamb that is led to the slaughter, and like a sheep that before its shearers is silent, so He opened not his mouth.

By oppression and judgment He was taken away; and as for His generation, who considered that He was cut off out of the land of the living, stricken for the transgression of my people? And they made His grave with the wicked and with a rich man in His death, although He had done no violence, and there was no deceit in His mouth. Yet it was the will of the LORD to crush Him; He has put Him to grief; when His soul makes an offering for guilt, He shall see His offspring; He shall prolong His days; the will of the LORD shall prosper in His hand.

Out of the anguish of His soul He shall see and be satisfied; by His knowledge shall the righteous One, My servant, make many to be accounted righteous, and He shall bear their iniquities. Therefore I will divide Him a portion with the many, and He shall divide the spoil with the strong, because He poured out His soul to death and was numbered with the transgressors; yet He bore the sin of many, and makes intercession for the transgressors."

JACOB'S TEXT said this was a prophecy about Jesus written about 700 years before His birth. She knew enough about Jesus to know He was rejected by the religious leaders of His people and tortured before being hung on the cross, and rather than defend Himself, He accepted all that they did. Just like a quiet lamb led to slaughter. "Upon Him was the chastisement that brought us peace, with His wounds we are healed." "Yet He bore the sin of many . . ." She flipped to her sermon notes and read Matthew 26:28. 'For this is My blood of the covenant, which is poured out for many for the forgiveness of sins."

She looked up Exodus 12 again. Exodus 12:13. "The blood shall be a sign for you, on the houses where you are. And when I see the blood, I will pass over you, and no plague will befall you to destroy you, when I strike the land of Egypt." The blood of the lamb . . . it was their protection from death.

The time on her phone said 6:00 a.m., so she picked it up to video call Jacob and walked out to the patio so she didn't wake Noah or Grams.

When he answered, she couldn't hold back. "The blood of the lamb in Exodus was their protection from death! Christians believe Jesus' blood, His death, gives them eternal life. That's it? Right?"

Jacob's face lit up at her excitement, and he chuckled. "Close. It's not just His death, but that He rose again—He came back to life. That's what makes His death so valuable. He rose again because He is God, so He is perfect. No one else's death could have the same value—worth the price of life for every person who has ever existed."

Brooke tapped her chin. "Hmm. Okay, I can see that. So what was the purpose in killing all of those lambs every year?"

"Actually, the Passover lambs were just a small number of the animals sacrificed by the people. There were other celebrations that required offerings and sacrifices—daily sacrifices—and they also had to offer animals regularly for sins. While traveling in the desert, God had them construct a tent called the tabernacle, and later build a permanent temple once they were settled in their land. The tabernacle was the place where all the animal sacrifices and offerings were done."

As Jacob spoke, Brooke's nose crinkled and she frowned. "That's disgusting, and it seems wasteful. Glad I already finished eating."

"Exactly! It was disgusting. But not exactly wasteful, because they ate most of the meat and burned the fat for incense with their worship. But yes, can you imagine the bloody, nasty, disgusting mess surrounding the tabernacle? And not only that, the priests had to do everything just right for it to be acceptable—ritual cleansing, special clothing, special equipment, and do it in the prescribed way. It would have been quite an ordeal."

His face got serious. "To God, our sin *is* a nasty, disgusting mess. Even worse, it is what keeps us separated from Him. Continually offering those sacrifices and facing all the ugliness involved with it was a visual reminder that our sin is awful, and won't go away, and nothing we try to do will ever make it go away. Enter Jesus—the once-for-all sacrifice. He Himself said, 'It is finished,' just before dying on the cross."

Sinking back in the glider, Brooke relaxed. "It brought peace," she said softly.

"It did. Can you imagine how the Jews who became Christians felt, knowing they no longer had to be fearful of sacrificing for every sin and doing them in the prescribed way? It was done for them. They were finished trying to atone for their own sins."

"That's beautiful." Brooke wanted to say more, but so many emotions bubbled to the surface, she wasn't sure where to begin. He nodded and silently watched her. Feeling self-conscious, she blushed. "So, I didn't even ask, where are you right now?"

"In my hotel room." Jacob turned the phone around so she could see the space.

"Nice, but I meant what city?" She took in the elegant, Danish modern look of the room.

"Stockholm, Sweden. Tomorrow the team leaves for Oslo, Norway."

"Doesn't that get old? Packing and unpacking."

"It does get tiresome. I'm working on making changes in my life, but I have some responsibilities to fulfill."

"I'm still trying to figure out what you do on these trips. Can't you give me a clue?" Brooke gave him her best sad look with a little pout.

With a chuckle, Jacob shook his head. "We'll talk about it when I get back. There are things I don't want you worrying about yet."

Brooke's eyebrows shot up. "Now, I *am* worried. My imagination tends to run wild."

Jacob's face lit up with a soft, pleased grin. "No need to worry. I don't anticipate any problems. Glad to know you care." His face turned serious. "Now, back to the Matt situation. Did you guys plan a time to get together with Brad and Elise?"

"Yeah, we're meeting for lunch today."

Jacob groaned. "I told you, he's using this as a way to hang out with you. I still don't like it."

"I'll make it clear I'm not interested in anything but friendship. I do appreciate the warnings, though, and I don't plan on doing anything alone with him." *Because I'm only interested in you*, she wanted to add. Jacob still hadn't made any declaration of his intentions with her. Though now wasn't a good time with him half a world away, she was determined to get the truth out of him when he got back.

"You're being so quiet. What's up?"

Brooke sipped her water and looked across the break room table at Elise. "Sorry. Lots on my mind."

Elise smirked. "Like the fact that Matt is a totally different person around you? Honestly, I've never seen him this way about someone. How he was acting around you at lunch, it's completely new for him. He's not usually interested in getting to know a girl—just looking for a fun time."

"I'm not thinking about him, but I agree. He has been nice to me. It's Jacob. I talked to him this morning." She shifted in her chair. "I keep pushing to find out what he does on these trips, and it's starting to worry me." Elise's brow furrowed. "He said he would 'talk to me about it' when he gets back. Hopefully that means he'll tell me. But he also said he's not told me yet, *so* I won't worry, and *that* makes me worry." Brooke shook her head as dangerous scenarios popped into her mind.

"Hey." Elise reached out to squeeze her arm. "That would be frustrating."

Brooke nodded. "The crazy thing is, I'm falling for him, but he's never asked me to be anything more than a friend. I feel like there's chemistry between us. But sometimes with the way he acts, I wonder if it's just me wishing it's there." She took a sip of water and gathered her thoughts. "I tried to tell myself it's too soon after Tyler, but I think I was falling even before things were over with Tyler.

"From the moment I first saw him, I've felt drawn to him. Part of why this is so crazy is at that time I thought he was up to no good, but I was still attracted to him. Who knows, maybe he *is* into something bad, and that's why he doesn't want to tell me. Maybe he doesn't work as a secret agent for the government, but he's working for some underground crime organization. Why else would he be traveling around the world so secretively?"

Elise threw her hand over her mouth before busting out laughing, and Brooke narrowed her eyes at her friend.

"I'm sorry," Elise said as she waved a hand in front of her face and tried to breathe. "But you come up with the funniest ideas. Why don't you just be a friend to him and get to know other things about him for now? Try not to think about what he does, and when he gets back, see what he has to say."

"I can try. It may be easier said than done. It's only been a week and a half since he left, and I'm already doubting everything with him."

Elise shrugged. "So, let's talk about Brad. What did you think after seeing us at lunch? Am I destined to be friend-zoned forever?"

Now it was Brooke's turn to laugh.

"What?"

"I'm picturing Brad and Matt when they came to pick us up at the office wearing button-down shirts and dress pants, trying to cover their tattoos and look professional."

Rolling her eyes and fighting back a grin, Elise placed a hand on her hip. "Brad looked hot and so did Matt. Brad, though . . ." She sighed and smiled dreamily. "But seriously, how did Brad seem around me?"

"To be honest, I haven't been around him enough yet to know what his normal interaction with girls is like. What's treating you as a good friend, and what's him flirting?"

Elise pressed her lips together firmly and furrowed her brow. "Cookie?" She held a baggy towards Brooke.

Brooke shook her head and munched the almonds she brought from home.

"Well, would you mind getting together some more with me and Brad and maybe Matt? I know you don't like Matt *that* way, but . . . would you? Is that asking too much?"

Brooke wondered if she should tell Elise what she and Matt were up to, but decided against it. "It's fine. Surely we can think of things that won't put us in an awkward position."

"Yeah?"

"Yeah." Brooke tried to hide her smile.

Elise leaned over and threw her arms around Brooke. "Thank you! Thank you! Thank you!"

TWENTY-THREE

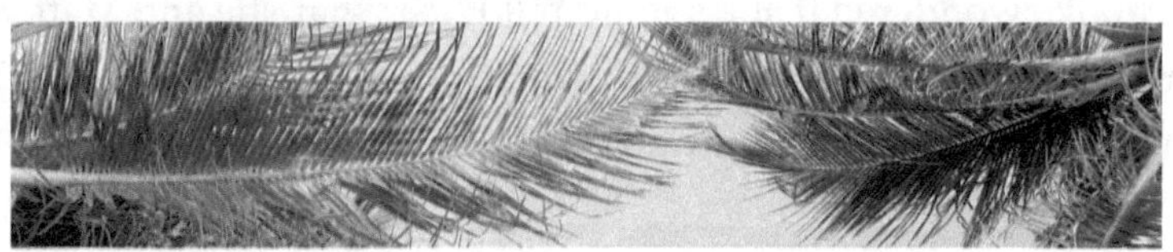

At work, Brooke and Eric sat side by side at the round table in the small conference room, going over his case.

"I overheard Tiffany," Eric said.

Brooke tilted her head as she tried to recall who he was talking about.

"She's an administrative assistant for three of our lawyers. Anyway, I heard her say you're dating that guy who's in a band. The guy I've seen here, who's been meeting you for lunch regularly."

Brooke rolled her eyes. One of the administrative assistants, apparently Tiffany, had been in the lobby when Matt and Brad came to pick the girls up for lunch, and of course, that was the time he chose to get touchy-feely and wrap an arm around her as if they were dating. Why was everyone so concerned about her dating Matt? Especially when she wasn't.

When she didn't respond, he continued. "To be honest, I'm worried about you. He doesn't look like your type. In the past, with Elise, I saw him in a short-sleeved shirt. Have you seen all those tattoos? I may have only known you a few weeks, but I can tell you're a classy woman. And I've heard your father talk about how you were raised. I think you should be careful. Elise is a great girl, but her band friends seem sketchy."

Brooke's mouth fell open in surprise and she furrowed her brow. Her eyes narrowed as she stared at him, wondering what to say, but not ready to give anything away. "Elise and I have been going to lunch with him and another band member. I don't think that's something for you to be worried about." She watched and waited to see how he would respond.

"I'm sorry." Eric frowned and held up a hand. "That was inappropriate, and I didn't mean to offend you. If he's who you want to date, it's your business."

"It's just . . . no, he doesn't look like my type, but I'm learning not to judge people by the way they appear on the outside." She gave him a pointed look. "I think I've done that for too long." Brooke shook her head. "And no, I'm not dating Matt or even interested in him, but he's Elise's friend and Brad's roommate, so we've been hanging out as a group." She didn't feel right sharing about Elise's crush on Brad, so she left it at that.

Eric bit his lip and nodded, but looked unconvinced. "Again, I'm sorry. I guess I felt responsible for you and your well-being, but that's not my job. It's hard for me not to worry about women I . . ." Eric shook his head and looked down at the papers in front of him.

"Women you *what*?"

"Nothing. We should get back to the case. I'm sure you have other things to do, and I shouldn't be meddling in your business." His cheeks were pink and he avoided her eyes.

Brooke sighed and touched his arm. "I'm not mad. Thanks for worrying about me. I have a tendency to doubt the intentions of guys after all I've been through."

Smiling softly, Eric placed his hand over hers. "It's good you're being careful. I really am sorry about what I said. You're right, I shouldn't judge a book by its cover. But if, I'm here. Will you forgive me for making assumptions?"

With a proud grin, Brooke nodded. "Sure, but as a lawyer, you should know better than to make assumptions without doing due diligence."

Eric winked. "Touché."

AFTER LEAVING THE CONFERENCE ROOM, Brooke's first thought was to call Jacob so they could laugh about him not being the only one who has been judged based on appearance. She also wanted to share her frustration with him about being the talk of the *Madness* groupies. But by the time she sat at her desk, she realized that would add fuel to the fire.

Jacob had requested she tell him every time she went to watch the band, or went out at night with Matt and had his coworker take down everything from the internet about her and Matt. So far, Jacob hadn't seemed too worried about the lunches she went to with Matt, Brad, and Elise. But that might change if things persisted with the groupies. And then what? Would he follow up on his threat to send a bodyguard to shadow her? She hoped he wasn't serious about that.

Looking down at the file before her, she tried to focus on researching corporate law for their client. Smiling, she decided to wait to talk to Jacob until their daily evening call—the one where they discussed the book of John before he would read Noah a bedtime story. Maybe she wouldn't bring up the subject of Matt at all.

BROOKE WAS CAPTIVATED by Jacob's dreamy, but tired eyes as she watched him on her tablet screen and held Noah in her arms while they snuggled together in the bed. Her eyes fell to his lips. What would it be like to kiss them?

"It's time to turn the page . . . Brooke? Brooke?" A pleased grin was plastered on Jacob's face. "Drawn in by my reading skills?"

Face red, Brooke quickly turned the page, thankful Jacob couldn't read her mind. Noah giggled and leaned back into his mom's arms. She found it unbelievable Jacob was willing—and even seemed to want—to do this every night, even though it meant he had to stay up until 2 a.m. his time. His selflessness added to the attraction she felt for him.

"ARE you sure there's not something going on with you and Matt?" Elise questioned after they returned from lunch with the guys the following day. "I've seen the looks you two give each other when you think I'm not watching. It seems like more than friendly gazes."

"I promise. Just friends. I'm still totally hung up on Jacob, so there's no room for anyone else in my thoughts but him. Not that I know if he reciprocates the feelings." Brooke leaned on the reception desk and avoided mentioning what the looks with Matt were really about.

"When does he get back?"

"Two weeks, I believe. He hasn't told me the exact day. I think it's still up in the air."

Elise winked. "Yeah, probably waiting to see what's next with his secret spy job. So . . . are you still talking to him every night?"

Lifting her head and nodding, Brooke thought about their calls and smiled. "Yep. And he reads from that children's book he sent to Noah. It's got a ton of stories, and Jacob's got the e-book version. You should see him. It's so adorable, the way he changes voices for the characters and stops to interact with Noah. He's beautiful . . ." Her voice drifted off. She longed to see him in person.

"Okay, okay. I get it, you're in luuuv with him. I see you with your dreamy eyes. I'll lay-off about Matt—for now. But if things don't work out when Jacob comes back, let me tell you, Matt is a changed man since he met you. Not a single one-night stand. You two would be cute together."

~

"I'M GOING to the bar to grab a drink. Need anything?" Brooke asked Elise as they danced to *Madness* on Friday night at their regular venue.

"Nope, I'm good."

Matt winked at Brooke and she grinned before turning toward the bar. She might not like him as more than a friend, but he was a nice guy, and she enjoyed his company. "Oof!" One of the groupies who had been dancing knocked her backward. She recognized the girl as the one who had given her a hard time the week before, claiming she was monopolizing Matt's attention.

"Oops." The girl smirked and shrugged.

As Brooke approached the bar, she saw a man out of the corner of her eye, watching her. Glancing his way, she realized she'd seen him earlier in the week when she walked to lunch with Matt, Elise, and Brad. Turning uncomfortably, she moved toward the end of the bar, away from him.

As she waited for her drink, a man strolled up next to her. Catching her eye, he smiled and held out his hand. "Logan. Nice to meet you."

Brooke eyed him warily. He looked friendly, but she was not one to give out her name to strangers. "Hi." Hesitantly, she shook his hand.

"I won't bite." He grinned and winked. "Unless you want me to." Brooke continued to silently evaluate him. "So, you like to be mysterious? Keep me guessing about who you are?"

When her drink was placed on the bar between them, she grabbed it and took a sip.

Logan set a hand on her shoulder and looked at her closely. "Let me guess. You don't regularly go bar hopping, but from the way you were watching the guys up there . . ." He pointed to the stage and pulled her away from the bar. "You know them, and that's why you're here."

She chuckled and nodded. "Okay, you've been paying attention. Yes, I know them."

Logan grinned. "How about a dance?" He motioned with his head toward the dance floor.

"I'm flattered, but, no, thanks."

"Has someone else claimed you, beautiful?" He looked around, as if checking to see if she had a date.

"I'm here with a friend, and she's waiting on me."

Shrugging, Logan smirked. "If you change your mind, let me know."

Brooke nodded and turned back to the bar to grab her drink, but it was gone. Placing her hands on her hips, she scanned the entirety of the bar and didn't see any lonely drinks. Funny how she was suddenly dying of thirst. What a weird night—as soon as the band was done with their set, she would have Matt wait with her for a ride. Her nerves were shot, and she was ready to go home.

"Do you get the Sunday paper?" were the first words out of Elise's mouth when Brooke video called her after seeing the text she'd sent while she was at church. It said, "Call me ASAP!"

"Um, I think so? What's going on?"

"Get it. There's something you've got to see!"

Once she had the paper opened to the page Elise told her, her mouth fell open and she felt sick. The article was titled, "Two Arrested For Possession of Drugs and Attempt to Drug Unaware Woman." It was the pictures that had her reeling. Mugshots of Logan and the girl who had bumped into her just before she met him at the bar.

"I . . . I know that guy in the mugshot. Logan. He was trying to get me to dance with him last night."

"Logan? It says here, his name is Jason."

"Really?" She looked at the caption. "He introduced himself as Logan."

"That's weird."

"Yep. That whole situation was weird. Just before I met him, that girl in the other mugshot bumped into me, and it didn't seem like an accident. She's the same girl who told me off for taking too much of Matt's attention last week. After I got around her, I went and ordered a drink and Logan—or Jason—appeared and started chatting me up. I took a sip of my drink as soon as it came, then Jason pulled me away and asked me to dance. I told him I'd rather not and turned back to get my drink, but it was gone."

Brooke swallowed the lump rising in her throat, realizing the implication of the situation. She saw her own fear reflected in Elise's eyes. "Do you think?" She shook her head, hardly believing it could be true. "What if they were putting something in my drink?" Her hand flew over her mouth.

Elise's eyes were like saucers. "Oh my gosh! I am so sorry! I feel responsible. I've been dragging you around with Matt and Brad, and some psycho chick has targeted you! I'm so, so sorry!" Elise began shaking.

"No, don't even think that. It was my choice to go, and it's not your fault that people are crazy." She attempted to calm both of them. Brooke had experienced the wrath of mean girls, but this was a whole other level. She looked back at the article, hoping to find something that might assure her she wasn't the target. No such luck. According to the article, the drink had been laced with gamma-hydroxybutyric acid, a drug commonly used for date-rape, and was discovered by an undercover agent before it could be ingested by the target.

"Did you read the article?" Brooke questioned.

"Yeah . . . Remember how Jacob told you he could have someone protect you? I think you should let him. He should know about this."

"Really? This seems so bizarre. I mean, Matt is just a local musician. I can't believe someone would go to such extremes over a crush on him."

"You're right, but if there's a chance Jacob can protect you, I'm guessing he would want to. Either way, you should let him know. I realize you aren't sure what he does, but from what you've told me, it sounds like he is in a position to help you."

Brooke nodded. "I guess you're right, but it's going to be humiliating to tell him. He tried to warn me off Matt. Not for this reason. He said it was because he learned Matt was a womanizer."

"Humiliating or not, it's got to be done. Yes? Nod your head."

With a half-smile, Brooke nodded, dreading the thought of that conversation.

THAT NIGHT, when Jacob called, he seemed off. Brooke decided not to let that sidetrack her and reluctantly went straight into the story of Friday night and the article in the paper.

"It was you," Jacob said softly.

"What?" The look on Jacob's face scared Brooke.

"You were the target."

"H-how do you know?"

"Look, just promise me you won't go watch the band, at least this week."

"Sure. I'm a little skittish about going right now. But seriously, how do you know I was the target?"

Jacob stared at her blankly, then rubbed a hand over his face. "The guy who has been taking down the pictures of you when you're out with Matt—last week, he found some comments that were . . . threatening."

"What? Why didn't you tell me?"

"I didn't want to scare you or have you think I was trying to keep you from having fun by asking you not to go anymore. Instead, I . . .

instead, I hired a bodyguard to follow you." He winced as her face fell.

"You hired a bodyguard and didn't tell me? Someone has been following me and I didn't know? Who does that?" Brooke dropped her tablet on the bed like it had leprosy, and got up to pace around her room. Rubbing her temples, she mumbled to herself, "What have I gotten myself into? I can't believe . . . what is wrong with people?"

"Brooke." Jacob tried to get her attention. "I just sent you a picture of Keith Woodhouse. He's your bodyguard."

Brooke angrily grabbed her phone and pulled up the picture. It was the guy she had seen when she was at lunch, and then again at the bar. Dropping back down on the bed, she grabbed the tablet. "I've noticed him a couple of times. He was at the bar Friday night. I can't believe you did that without even asking!"

"I'm sorry, I really am, but Keith is the one who saw what was going on. He's also the one that took your drink away to protect you. He tested it right there, and took samples, plus he's got video of them in action. The girl was the one who put the drug in, but he has video of them earlier that night and she was pointing you out. When they were arrested, the guy didn't take much convincing to tell the police everything. I don't think they intended to hurt you, but she wanted to scare you and 'send a message,' according to her accomplice."

Collapsing back onto the pillows, tears ran down Brooke's cheeks as the reality sunk in.

"I'm glad you're not harmed. I'd like to keep Keith on as your bodyguard for a while, if that's okay?"

Brooke blinked back tears. "I know you told me not to get involved with him, and I promise, we're just friends. I don't know why that girl got so bent out of shape that she would do something like that."

"So can Keith stay on as your bodyguard?"

Brooke furrowed her brows. "I'm still angry with the way you've handled this, but sure, it would help me feel safer."

Jacob let out a breath. "Alright, that's good. I'll give him your number, and he can come meet you today and discuss his plans with you."

Competing thoughts crowded Brooke's mind. She was targeted because of her relationship—that was only a friendship—with Matt. A bodyguard had been, and would continue, following her around. Jacob had hired said bodyguard without talking to her first. Could the bodyguard keep her safe? Noah! Would Noah become a target?

"Tell me what you're thinking, Brooke. I'll do whatever is necessary to make sure you're okay."

STILL SHAKING AND SOBBING, Brooke clung to her grandmother as she tried to take in the situation after hanging up with Jacob. The danger grew in her mind by the minute. Grams rubbed her back and spoke encouraging words.

When Brooke eventually calmed, she questioned, "Why don't you seem bothered by any of this? Bodyguards will be following me around. I'm some kind of target—you and Noah could be in danger, too."

"I was praying while I put Noah to bed and as you were explaining the situation, and God's given me a peace about it. It's going to be fine." She placed a hand over Brooke's. "Also, I trust Jacob has this under control."

Brooke looked closely at her grandmother. "You know what he does for a living, don't you? You know why he travels so much."

Grams nodded. "Yes, but that's his story to tell, and he has promised me he will as soon as he's home."

Past the lines of experience on Grams' face, Brooke saw peace and hope. The first would come to Brooke with age, but the last two seemed within her grasp. Remembering how her grandmother helped when she was younger, Brooke asked, "Grams, would you pray over me?"

"Nothing would please me more, dear." The older woman laid

her hand on Brooke's and prayed that she too would have peace in this situation and that she would know she can trust God. She asked for protection over all of them and that God would be glorified through this.

CHAPTER

TWENTY-FOUR

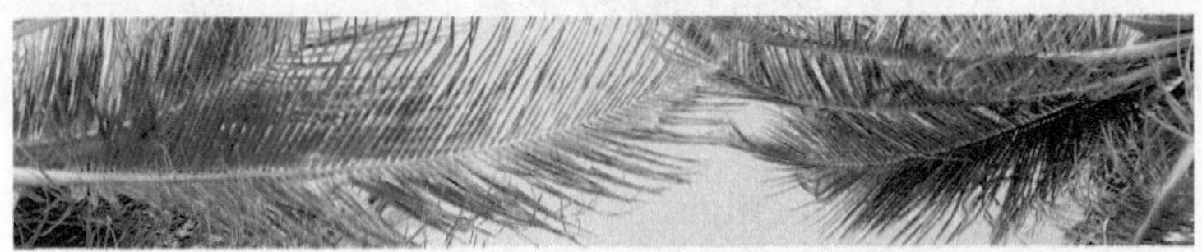

Walking into work while being followed by a bodyguard was a strange feeling. Brooke felt as if everyone she passed was watching her and thinking the same thing— *She shouldn't be involved with that Matt guy.* Thankfully, only her boss, Gabriella, Dana, and the other partners knew what he was really there for, and they had to sign a non-disclosure agreement.

Unfortunately for Dana, Keith was given a workstation in her space. Jacob had set everything up with Mr. Stearn the night before, and by the time they arrived in the morning, the desk was already set up. How Jacob managed to get so much accomplished from halfway around the world—in one night—she had no idea. Keith had a laptop with a direct interface to the security cameras and would monitor them throughout the day. He would also be informed about anyone coming up to Brooke's floor. As far as other employees were concerned, he was another assistant and sometimes helped with security. It sounded like a lame cover to Brooke, but what did she know about these things?

~

"Oh my gosh! What's going on? You said you had news," Elise commented as she walked into the break room for lunch.

Brooke waved her over and lowered her voice, even though no one else was with them. "It's about the people that were caught at the bar drugging drinks."

Elise's eyebrows shot up and she leaned in. "Yeah? What did you hear?"

"This is going to sound crazy, but stick with me. Apparently Jacob already had a bodyguard following me."

"No way!" Elise whisper-yelled and shook her head.

"It's true. In fact, that night at the bar I recognized him as a guy I had seen when we went to lunch, and I was so weirded out by it that I went to the opposite end of the bar to place my order. Anyway, the bodyguard saw that girl—I think the paper said her name was Kira—talking to Jason just before he spoke to me *and* after she bumped into me. She was pointing me out. Then when Jason pulled me away from the bar, my bodyguard saw Kira putting something in my drink. He took it and tested it right there, and they were apprehended as I was leaving the bar."

"That's crazy!"

"Keith, my bodyguard, said two undercover cops came in and coaxed them out the back, where they read them their rights and arrested them. Keith has them on video pointing me out and drugging my drink."

"I can't believe Jacob was having you followed and didn't tell you. Aren't you mad? I mean, yes, it protected you, but wow, that seems wrong."

"It bothers me, and I've gone through a spectrum of emotions about it. He said the chatter on social media was getting more aggressive toward me and it concerned him, but he didn't want me to panic. I'm not even sure how to deal with that. All I know is that right now, he's got me protected with Keith, and has a guy on call for Grams when she goes out, just in case there's any backlash on her."

Elise looked back toward the door. "Wow! Maybe he really is an undercover agent. So where is the bodyguard now?"

Brooke chuckled. "Funny story. He got in contact with Mr. Stearn yesterday and now has a permanent desk set up just outside my office in Dana's space."

"No way!"

Nodding, Brooke added, "Yep. All the partners know who he really is, as well as Dana and Gabriella—and you. But back to your question, he's at his desk. He has access to the office security cameras on his laptop, so he can see who is coming and going in the halls, and you or your fill-in during breaks has to let him know when someone is heading up to my floor. Also, the name of everyone who enters the building to come up to Stearn, Hastings, and Associates will be sent to him. He said I could come to the break room without him because there are no threats on the premises."

"Wow! Sounds like a lot of trouble, maybe even overkill. Hopefully it will keep you safe."

"I know, right? I hate the thought of . . ." Brooke's words trailed off when her phone rang and she saw Jacob's name. She showed it to Elise.

Elise waved her hand. "Go ahead and get it."

"Hey, what's going on?" Brooke's voice shook and she tensed.

"I was just checking on you to see how things are working out with Keith."

She placed a hand on her chest in relief. "Thank goodness that's all. I thought for sure you discovered something bad."

"No, and from now on, I have given Keith instructions to discuss any new information we receive with you immediately. That way if I'm held up and can't get to you, the two of you can determine a plan of action."

Brooke's heart raced, and she tapped her foot on the ground. Elise reached over and placed a hand on hers, then typed frantically on her phone.

"Jacob, I have to be honest, this is overwhelming and it's scaring me. I worry for Noah and Grams. My mind is filled with all the things that can go wrong."

"Please don't worry, it's under control. I deal with this sort of thing all the time, and the team I have working with me to investigate potential problems and protect you are the best. I have every confidence in them."

"I feel like I should be holed up in my apartment for a while."

"No. Nothing like that. It will be good if you stay close to home for a few days while we get to the bottom of this, but it's looking like Kira and Jason were the only ones involved. The police and my men are still investigating what they planned to do once you ingested the drug. Both of their apartments are being searched. I expect them to have answers within the next couple of days, and then you can return to your regular routine. With Keith, of course."

"Okay. Wow. How long do you think I'll need him?"

"We can talk about that when I get back home."

Home. Brooke liked the sound of that, even if she was still mad he didn't ask her about Keith first.

Her main goal needed to be keeping her son and grandmother safe, but she trusted Jacob. From the very beginning, even before she knew who he was, he had taken care of her . . . of them—toddler-proofing her grandmother's apartment, covering her in the rain, removing derogatory posts about her from Instagram, and now, the bodyguard.

She tapped her fingers on the desk. It was hard to accept his help. Over the past two years, she had become wary of the intentions of men in her life. Her troubles with Tyler now felt a world away. Unfortunately, her other troubles were just beginning. She didn't want to live like a hermit. She'd have to come to terms with the ups and downs of life, but her ups and downs seemed extreme.

"Matt Barrett is here to see you," Keith's voice said through Brooke's intercom, jarring her from her thoughts.

"Um, okay, send him in, please." Elise had told Brooke she was texting Matt while Brooke was talking to Jacob during their lunch break, but she never imagined he would come by.

"I am so sorry." Matt said as he burst through Brooke's door. "It's all my fault those crazies targeted you. Tell me what I can do to make it better?"

Seeing the bouquet of flowers he waved around struck a chord with Brooke, and in the midst of her fears and frustrations, she chuckled. "Well, that's a start! The flowers are lovely. Are they for me?"

"What?" Matt stopped moving his hands and eyed the bouquet. "Oh, yeah." He cocked a half-grin. "Sorry, I forgot those were in my hand. But seriously, I feel so bad."

"You're right, those two are crazy, but you're wrong about it being your fault. I'll get through it. I have a friend who is experienced with these types of things and is helping me."

"Yeah, I heard about the bodyguard." He pointed his thumb towards the door, "That's pretty wild. You would think that I was some sort of celebrity with all this commotion."

"Well, you are a celebrity in Central Florida."

Matt chuckled, but his face went serious. "Whatever. I feel bad, though. I want to help protect you, and I selfishly don't want to stop having you around, especially when the band plays."

Smiling, Brooke shook her head. "Give it a week, then I can probably go, just with a bodyguard for now."

TWENTY-FIVE

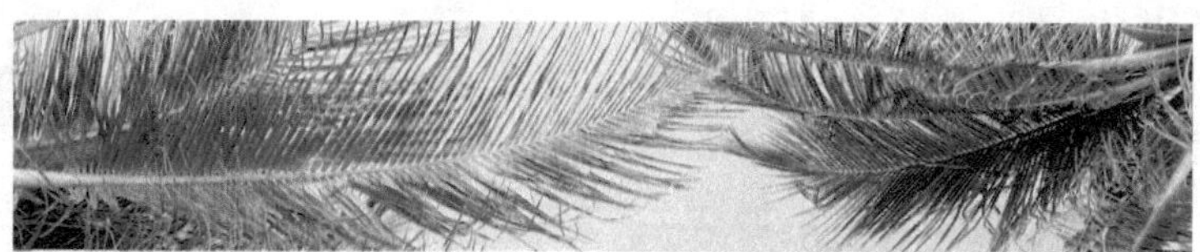

"Look at you grinning, Brooke. Somebody's happy. Must be because we're going out to watch the band tonight. Right, Keith?" asked Elise when Brooke exited the elevator from the parking garage with him.

"What? Yeah, we're going to the bar to watch the band tonight." Keith smirked as he turned to get coffee.

Brooke, still grinning to herself, looked up at Elise and shook her head, then walked up to the reception counter and leaned over on her elbows. "No. I'm happy because . . ." she glanced over her shoulder to see if Keith was paying attention. "In only three more days, Jacob will be back!" she whisper-yelled.

Elise grinned and whispered back. "Yeah, I see your dreamy face, I get it. I'm looking forward to meeting this guy who has you so smitten. He looks like he might be hot from the pictures, but it's hard to tell in the ones you've shown me. I'll have to judge in person."

Elise winked as Brooke chuckled and waved before turning to head up to her office, closely followed by Keith. She smiled as they silently rode up on the elevator with two others. Having Keith around was an adjustment at first, but now she hardly noticed, unless he was intentionally interacting with her. She appreciated that he was subtle about his real job. Being known as the new girl with a bodyguard was the last thing she wanted. She struggled enough trying to keep people from thinking she was snobby and pretentious in the past because of her school and who she hung out with—it was nice to get away from that stereotype.

~

"Hey, Keith." Brooke stopped at the entrance to her office. "Would you mind coming into my office for a minute?"

"What's up?" Keith gestured to the door, silently asking if she wanted it closed, and she nodded.

"Do you really think it's okay for me to go see the band tonight?"

"Sure. There is no current chatter, and the bar staff has instructions not to let Kira or Jason into the venue. Plus, those two are on bail while they're being investigated, so they'd be stupid to try anything. Also, we've talked about the drink thing, and between the two of us, someone's eyes will always be on your drinks. Don't worry, just enjoy yourself." Keith smiled, trying to ease her mind.

Brooke nodded. "Have you worked with Jacob long?"

"If you're attempting to find out what he does, my lips are sealed. He'll talk to you about that when he gets back." Keith smirked and shook his head.

Brooke pouted. "I guess I can wait, but honestly, I was just trying to get to know you better."

"Three years." Keith grinned.

"What?"

"I've worked for him for three years. Anything else you want to know?"

She tapped her chin. "Dating anyone?" One of the girls in accounting had asked about him.

Keith chuckled. "I think I have some work to do."

~

"Oh my gosh! Did you read the interoffice memo?" Elise rushed out, grinning from ear to ear as they ate in the break room.

Swallowing a mouthful of salad, Brooke shook her head. "No. What's got you so excited?"

"Only the hottest boy band in the world! Though, I do love my local *Madness* guys . . . especially one in particular." Elise's voice trailed off and she got a dreamy look that Brooke, herself, was very familiar with.

"Earth to Elise!"

"Huh? Oh, yeah! Anyway, they are famous, and they're so good-looking." She leaned in and whispered, "Especially the lead singer. Just don't tell Brad I said that."

"I'm still lost. What are you talking about?"

"Remember me saying our firm represents the band *Nine Days In?*"

Brooke looked at her blankly for a moment, and then it hit. "Oh, yeah, the group my babysitter is crazy over. What about them?"

"They'll be here Friday for a meeting! Didn't you say you wanted to get an autograph for your sitter?"

"I did. I won't be here Friday, though. Can I leave her name with you for an autograph?"

"What? You don't want to meet them? Maybe even get a picture with them? You could join me here for lunch at noon. They're supposed to be here at one."

"I don't really care about meeting a group of teen heartthrobs." Brooke shrugged.

"Oh, these guys aren't teenagers anymore. They're basically our age, and you wouldn't shrug them off if you saw them. Come on, surely you can get away long enough to come for lunch and meet them." She made puppy dog eyes at Brooke. "Please?"

Brooke held back a grin. "Okay, okay. If I take Noah home early from park day, I'll have time to get here. He should be worn out

Friday anyway, because we're going to Epcot for a few hours tomorrow with Grams."

Elise clapped her hands. "Awesome! It's a date. Make sure you're dressed nice, and not just in some 'park day mom clothes.'"

"What does that even mean?" Brooke chuckled. "I'm offended." She stood up. "On that note, I'm leaving." She moved toward the door.

"I didn't mean anything by it, I—" Elise stopped when Brooke looked back at her, clearly holding back a smile before she broke out in laughter.

LIGHTS STREAKED past as Keith drove Brooke and Elise to the bar where *Madness* was playing. To Brooke, it was all a blur. Her mind went to a dark place, imagining all the possibilities that could happen if someone else targeted her. Feeling pain, she looked down to see blood in her palm where she had squeezed her fist so tight, her fingernails broke the skin. She attempted breathing deeply, but her body tensed as the car approached the venue. Elise and Keith were talking, and she barely managed an "uh huh" and a "hmm" when it seemed appropriate.

Pray is the thought that crossed her mind. That's what Jacob and Grams would tell her to do. Silently, she tried it. *God, would You even listen to me? I hope so. Please help me overcome this fear. And please keep me safe. Noah needs me. Amen. In Jesus' name?* She had tacked on the "in Jesus' name" part, but wasn't sure if it was necessary. She'd have to ask Jacob why he said that. It felt strange conversing in her mind with Someone she couldn't see. Was it okay to pray while people were talking around her and with her eyes open? Swallowing, she glanced at Elise and Keith. Had they noticed she prayed? Would they think she was weird?

Elise turned to her and reached out to squeeze her hand. "Are you okay? You know Keith, the band, and I, all have your back."

A calm came over Brooke before she replied. Smiling genuinely, she answered, "I'm good, I really am." It was an unfamiliar feeling, and the most at ease she had felt since finding out about almost being drugged. Had God answered her prayer? And that quickly? Did He care about her that much? She hoped He did. That thought surprised her.

Rolling into her soft cushy bed after the long day, Brooke's mind wandered over the events of the evening. Everything had gone without a hitch. No one bullied her for being friends with Matt and having his attention. Keith said he didn't see any problems either, but the best part was being able to relax and have fun. She danced, sang to the music that she now had memorized, and enjoyed hanging out with her friends.

She was still overwhelmed by the instant answer to her prayer. Smiling, she found herself talking out loud. "God, are You really listening? To me? I'm extremely happy with my life here . . ." She thought about her time with Jacob and the way he fit into her life. And how glad she was for her friendships with the ladies at the park playgroup, and Elise, and the band guys. Noah seemed so resilient, and every day brought some new joy to his life.

She almost felt guilty. Guilty for being so happy with things, when she should be sad to have lost her mom so recently. Her breath caught and tears threatened to spill. "I still miss my mom."

TWENTY-SIX

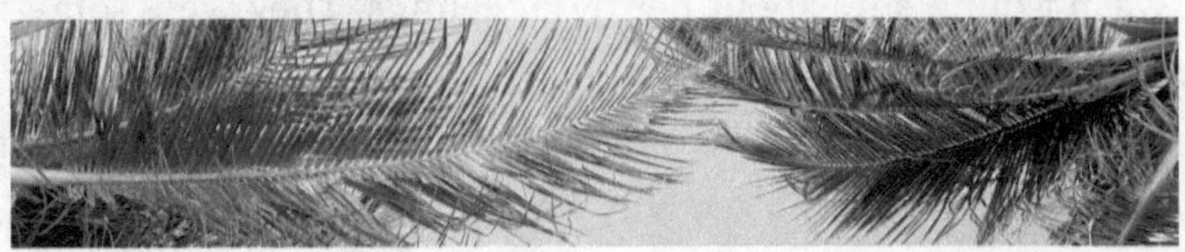

Keith looked at his watch, and Brooke spoke up, "I'm going to stay here a few minutes and talk with Elise, so you can relax for a bit if you want, since there's office security here close to the front desk."

"I'll just catch up on my emails." Keith nodded and walked over to one of the waiting room sofas.

Brooke turned to Elise and scrunched her nose. She didn't want to admit to Keith that she was hanging out to meet a boy band. She'd only told him she was meeting Elise for lunch on her day off. How immature would that sound, especially with all she was dealing with because of Matt. And she didn't want it getting back to Jacob that she was interested in other guys. Things might never progress between them if he thought that.

Luis, a top lawyer in the firm, stepped out of the in-office elevator looking intense and grave as he spoke with one of the office security guards before entering the elevator that led to the parking garage.

"He's the lawyer for *Nine Days In*," Elise whispered as soon as the elevator door closed. "He must be headed down to escort the band up." She grinned like a schoolgirl, then turned serious. "Remember, Luis's assistant has your request for autographs, so don't ask for one when you speak to them. They don't like to be bothered with that. When they get here, they have to sign in, so they'll come up to the desk. I'll let you hand them the tablet so you'll have a chance to meet them." She practically bounced in her seat.

Brooke chuckled, finding it amusing that Elise was so excited. She wasn't quite sure about her own feelings. They were something more along the lines of curiosity.

"Don't make fun, Brooke. I know you have Jacob, who is supposedly super hot, but you'll see why I'm fangirling soon enough." Elise shrugged and winked. "Who knows, you've got Jacob, and I might end up with a Jake."

"Maybe one day. You know as well as I do that I don't *have* Jacob. And who is Jake?"

"Only the hottest guy in *Nine Days In* and their lead singer. Get with it!" Elise smirked. "You really should—" The ding of the elevator drew their eyes up, and Elise squeezed Brooke's shoulder as her breath caught.

Brooke pasted on a smile. She'd seen how much of a headache fangirls were for her friends in *Madness*, and understood these guys didn't need another girl drooling over them. She tried to appear nonchalant while opening the check-in app. Standing up beside Elise, she grabbed the stylus and the tablet, then glanced up to see the group approaching. In the midst of them, she locked onto two brown eyes she knew well.

"Jacob!" she squealed, dropping the tablet back down, before running around to the other side of the reception desk with her arms thrown out for a hug.

"Brooke?" Jacob's eyes went wide and he frowned, then quickly recovered with a smile.

Brooke's own smile faltered and her heart sank. She heard Elise gasp, but it faded into the background as she zeroed in on Jacob.

Before she reached him, one of the men who entered with the

group held out his hand to block her from getting closer, but Jacob shoved the man's hand down and shook his head. "She's fine." He reached forward and pulled a stiff, confused Brooke into a hug.

Seconds later, Keith stood beside them. "Ryder, she's with me. This is Brooke."

Brooke finally reciprocated the hug, finding it difficult not to embrace the man she had missed for the past month. Yet the realization of what this meant began to sink in, causing her to tense.

"Dude! This is Brooke! I get why you've been hiding her. Afraid of a little competition?" a voice called out.

Peering over Jacob's shoulder, she saw a good-looking blond guy grinning at her as he spoke. When she pulled back to confront Jacob, his brow furrowed.

"Why?" Brooke mouthed at the same time Jacob spouted out, "I'm sorry."

Their eyes locked and he leaned closer, as if to kiss her. Her breath hitched, and she pushed against his chest, but he held her tighter, then looked back at the group watching them. "I'll meet you guys upstairs in a few minutes." A man in a suit nodded. Jacob grabbed Brooke's hand and dragged her to the corner of the reception room.

"Brooke, I was going to tell you everything tonight," Jacob urged, but she narrowed her eyes. "That's why Grams asked you to stay home tonight. I planned to surprise you and Noah by showing up early to explain things to you."

"What? Explain that you've been lying to me this whole time? That you're actually the lead singer of the 'hottest boy band in the world' according to Elise?" Brooke made finger quotes as she lashed out at Jacob.

Jacob clutched her shoulders. "And that's exactly what I hoped to avoid with you!" He whisper-yelled. "I didn't want you to think of me that way. From the first moment I saw you, I could tell you didn't recognize me, and I liked it. I wanted you to know the real me.

What's so wrong with that? As I'm sure you've figured out with your friend Matt, being idolized gets old."

Brooke's face softened. Maybe he was right, but she still felt wronged. She crossed her arms. "I don't know how I feel about this. But regardless, you've got a lot of explaining to do."

"I promise I will, but I really have to go to this meeting right now." Jacob shifted on his feet. "Do you . . . I hate to ask this, but can you wait about thirty to forty-five minutes for me? We've got to finalize some contracts and sign some papers." Brooke frowned. "Please? I don't want to wait until tonight to have time with you."

Sighing, Brooke looked down, knowing she couldn't think straight while staring into his eyes. But she didn't want to wait until dinner, either. She slowly nodded and lifted her head. "I'll stay."

A huge grin took over Jacob's face, and he pulled her into a quick hug. "Great! Perfect! Thanks for giving me a chance." He let go and stepped back, still watching her. "Okay, I'll be down as soon as I can. If you end up somewhere else in the building, let me know." Still grinning, he walked backwards towards the elevator, stopping to give Keith a pat on the shoulder.

Jacob had just stepped into the elevator when Brooke felt the dam break and rushed to the restroom. She barely registered Elise calling her name as she passed and glanced at her with glazed eyes. Bursting through the restroom door, the first tear fell, followed by a river. She dropped to the plush bench in the entrance and nearly doubled over. Anger. Hurt. Loss.

She finally let her guard down with a guy, and this was the result. Months of despair she thought she'd worked through rose back up with a vengeance until she raced to a toilet to vomit. Eventually, with nothing left but dry heaves, she dragged herself to a sink to sip water and splash her face before collapsing onto the bench and laying down.

Brooke felt her head lifted onto something soft and awakened to Elise's voice.

"Brooke, it's going to be okay." Elise stroked her hair.

Shaking her head, Brooke groaned.

"I know it seems bad, but give him a chance. He obviously cares about you."

When Brooke looked up, Elise frowned. "If Jake Reeves will be with you in a few minutes, we need to get you fixed up. Let's start with a swish of mouthwash and some gum." Elise stepped to the counter and dispensed some mouthwash into a tiny cup. After handing it to Brooke, she dug around in her purse to retrieve a piece of mint gum.

"Thanks," Brooke said after rinsing out her mouth. "A culmination of all that I've been through these last few months literally worked its way out."

"Understandable." Elise pulled a cosmetics pouch from her purse and emptied it. "Nothing a little makeup can't fix," she said while sizing up Brooke's face. "You know, when you gushed about how gorgeous your Jacob was, I thought you were exaggerating, but girl, you are the envy of almost every girl in the world!"

Brooke rolled her eyes and frowned. "I don't know what we are. He's never said, and now I'm honestly not sure if I can be with him. Maybe if it was just me, but I have a son. Is it fair to Noah to throw us both into the limelight like that? Is it safe for him? I've barely gotten past this garbage with Matt. And he's small-time compared to Jacob. Not to mention, I'm just friends with Matt and that happened. What would happen if things went further with Jacob? Who knows? If he just wants to be friends, it's a moot point ,anyway."

"It doesn't seem like nothing from what you've told me. It makes sense now, that all your pictures of him are with a hat and sunglasses."

"What do you mean?" Brooke thought about the pictures she had of him and recalled Elise mentioning that before.

"He wanted to prevent your friends, like me, from accidentally recognizing him and revealing who he is before he was ready."

Brooke frowned. "That, or he didn't want to be seen with me in public." She crossed her arms.

"Maybe for your own good. You need to let him explain."

"I guess. I just don't see any good coming from this. It scares me. I really do like him, but I don't want to be in the public eye. I also can't stand the thought of losing him." The tears began again and Elise wrapped her arms around Brooke.

"Good thing that mascara is waterproof." Elise squeezed Brooke harder. "No matter what happens, I'm here for you, and you've got lots of others who care for you, too."

Elise meant well, but giving up Jacob might throw her back into the dark place that held her before. He'd given her hope and brought her joy.

BROOKE STARED straight ahead at the road as Jacob drove her to his home in her car. At the stoplight, he looked at Brooke and begged her to talk to him. Expressionless, she faced him, and saw worry and anguish in his eyes.

"I don't understand. I thought you Christians weren't supposed to lie. It's one of the Ten Commandments."

Jacob's expression turned to shame. "It's true. But it's also true that no one is perfect. Becoming a Christian doesn't make you perfect. And it wasn't as if I never planned to tell you. I just needed you not to know for a while. I needed you to see *me*, not the rock star. I think that's different than lying to deceive."

"It still hurts and seems like you lied." She closed her eyes and tried to put her thoughts into words. "It feels like our whole relationship was a lie. It feels like you're just another guy I can't trust." She squeezed her eyes tight to hold back the tears. It had been the same with her dad and Tyler.

Jacob placed a hand on her arm. "You're mistaken. It was more real than nearly everything I've experienced since the band became famous." As he turned a corner, their eyes locked, and she saw sadness.

She pondered his words. They approached a gate, and he punched in a code and waved to the guard before entering the neighborhood. A few minutes later, they entered an estate at the end of a street and passed through another gate, leading to a long, landscaped driveway that ended in front of a Mediterranean-style, two-story mansion.

It was a nice distraction from their situation. "Beautiful. This is your home? I can't imagine ever wanting to leave. I'm surprised you stay at your Nan's as much as you do."

"Don't forget, I live here with four other guys and a couple of staff. It gets pretty crazy around here, and sometimes I need to get away for some quiet. I like to be there for the kids, too."

"Oh." His words stung. She recalled how familiar the kids in the apartment complex were with him. His time there wasn't just to be with her. Yet even though she was mad at him about hiding his identity and unsure if she was willing to be part of this life, she still hoped he wanted more with her.

"Come on." Brooke didn't realize they had stopped and Jacob stood at her door, beckoning her out. "It's time for you to officially meet my friends."

They entered through the front door, where a view through the gallery entrance and living room two-story windows revealed a huge pool and a lake beyond. It was a stunning tropical setting. Glancing around at the interior, she found a contrast of classical Mediterranean architecture with sleek contemporary furnishings in neutral colors.

"Hey, man! Welcome back to our home sweet home!" A guy with wavy sandy brown hair ran up to them, wearing only swim trunks. He turned to Brooke and reached a hand out. "Brooke, right?" She nodded and shook his hand. "Great to finally meet you. I'm Ethan." He looked between the two of them and grinned. "You guys gonna join us for a swim? The party's out back."

"Nah, but I'll introduce her to you guys before giving her the house tour. We're headed to Nan's after that."

Ethan frowned. "But it's our welcome back party. We're just pre-partying, but we've got more friends and girls coming soon." Ethan wiggled his eyebrows. "You guys should stay."

"Sorry, Nan's expecting us." Jacob shrugged and followed Ethan to the pool, with a hand on Brooke's back, guiding her. He seemed nervous. She definitely was.

"Now the party's finally starting! Hey, baby, jump in, the water's perfect! Ethan, turn on the music and bring me another drink!" Brooke recognized the blond guy floating on a water lounger as the one from the office who had commented on him hiding her.

Jacob's hand moved from her back to her shoulder as he walked her closer to the pool. Two guys tossed basketballs into a goal in the water and Ethan took a seat on the steps with a drink after turning on the speakers and tossing a can to the blond. "Guys, this is Brooke."

The blond opened his mouth, but Jacob held up his hand. "She's my guest and a good friend, so I'd appreciate it if you were all on your best behavior. *Ryan*." His eyes fixed on the blond.

"Hey, why you always picking on me?" He looked at Brooke and saluted. "Ryan, at your service. When you get tired of this nerd, you know where to find me." He grinned, and his blue eyes reflected the water.

The two playing basketball climbed out of the pool and walked over.

"I'm Anthony," said a dark-haired Latin American. He grabbed Brooke's hand and brought it to his lips, smiling as he kissed it. He lowered her hand, but didn't release it and held her gaze. "So glad to finally meet you. You'll have to come back again when you have more time. Maybe for dinner one day this weekend."

Brooke smiled, but stuttered over her words, "I . . . um . . ."

"That's enough, Romeo." Jacob pulled her hand from Anthony's.

The guy next to him rolled his eyes at Anthony and elbowed him.

"This," Jacob motioned toward the guy with green eyes and brown hair standing next to Anthony, "is Brandon."

Brandon shook her hand. "Saved the best for last." He smiled. "Anthony's right, though. You should come for dinner this weekend."

"Jake, is Mari back?" Ryan wiggled his eyebrows. "She's always a fun addition to our parties. You should invite her over. We'll keep her company even if you're a stick in the mud and don't stay."

Jacob shifted on his feet and moved away from Brooke. "She's not back." He sounded on edge.

"Hey, man! No hard feelings. I'm just picking on you."

He turned back to Brooke and pulled her away. "I'll show you the house."

Once inside, Brooke questioned him. "Who's Mari?"

Jacob pushed his fingers through his hair. "Just a friend I met through the band. She toured with us last summer." He pointed in front of them. "The kitchen's in here." He directed her to an enormous room with a sitting area by a fireplace, a large bay window looking out over the pool and yard, and a kitchen that looked like it was fitted out for professional chefs.

It was beautiful, but they needed to talk. "I told you I've been going to church lately with Grams. Maybe I can come visit yours sometime now that you're home."

"Um, yeah, I'll check."

What a strange thing to say. Brooke felt uneasy with the way he was acting. "What do you mean, check?"

"It's a small house church with mostly famous people who don't want to go to a regular church, to avoid the distractions that causes. They need a place to worship and learn without people begging for autographs and that sort of thing."

"Oh. Okay. Never mind, then. I wouldn't want to make anyone uncomfortable." She turned away from him and pretended to examine the stove. She wondered if this Mari person went to church with him, but stopped herself from asking. The jealousy rising inside of her wasn't a good feeling. Learning about Mari, whoever she was, added to the list of overwhelming news from the day.

"I don't mean to hurt your feelings. I know you're not that way, and I'm glad you're going to church now. But it's not my call to make."

Brooke nodded, her back still to him. "I get it. No worries." She forced a smile and turned around. "What's next on the tour?"

As she watched him lead the way, she realized there was a lot she didn't know about him, if she even knew him at all. Was it all a ruse? He had this whole other life she was just learning about. The thought of him being an undercover agent seemed laughable now, and almost tame compared to the truth.

The whole house was a gorgeous blend of architecture and furnishings befitting wealthy young bachelors who liked to party and entertain. Jacob said it had been meticulously planned and designed by an architect and an interior designer. Finally seeing where Jacob lived felt surreal now that she knew it wasn't just Jacob's home, but the home of a famous band. She didn't want to view him as *Jacob the rock star*, but seeing his home's practice room, sound booth, trophy room, and recording studio, made it hard to forget.

On the drive to the apartment complex, Jacob seemed anxious. He silently tapped the steering wheel and occasionally gave Brooke a sideways glance. When they parked, he turned to Brooke. "Are we going to be okay?"

Brooke stared at him, at a loss for words. She saw worry etched on his face and couldn't bear to disappoint him, nor could she imagine her life without him in some capacity, so she slowly nodded.

Dinner at Nan's was awkward. Tonight Brooke felt like an outsider to her own life, knowing everything was perfectly normal for the rest of them. Grams and Nan had kept Jacob's secret from her all this time. Both insisted it was not their story to tell. Even though they meant well, it still felt like deception.

Seeing Noah's excitement at Jacob's return eased some of her frustration with the man she thought she knew. In spite of the distance, the two had become closer through the nighttime story reading.

Before Jacob's jet lag kicked in, they did Noah's bedtime reading so Grams could take Noah home. Nan disappeared into her room, leaving Jacob and Brooke to talk in private.

Jacob's eyes drooped as he reached over to grab Brooke's hand. He rubbed circles on her palm. "I hope you can forgive me, Brooke. I didn't do it to hurt you. It was just such a nice change, having a friend who didn't make me wonder if they were my friend for other reasons." His voice grew softer. "I hope things will stay the same. I don't want . . ." He yawned and leaned his head on her shoulder. "Lose you . . . friend."

The movement of his thumb on Brooke's palm stopped. Looking down, she saw that his eyes were closed. She wondered if she should wake him so he could go to bed, or just stretch him out on the sofa and cover him up. Imagining how uncomfortable the plane must have been the night before, she lightly shook him. "Jacob," she whispered, then repeated a little louder, earning a grunt from him. He was out of it, but she finally got him to stand with her support. She led him to his room, eased him onto the bed, slipped off his shoes, and laid a blanket over him.

He was so beautiful, even in his sleep. She remembered being drawn to him the very first moment she saw him. Reaching up, she softly ran the back of her hand across his cheek and smiled, thinking about how she'd once believed he was a drug dealer. What must he have thought of her when he discovered that? Here he was, internationally famous, and she had been giving him dirty looks. His mouth drew up into a smile. She gasped and pulled her hand back, but her eyes locked onto his lips. Several times, she'd thought he would kiss her, but it was surely her imagination. He had his pick of women. He wouldn't be interested in her, a single mom, that way.

Her heart ached as she left Nan's apartment. It had been a painful and confusing day. What she wouldn't give to talk to her mom about it all.

TWENTY-SEVEN

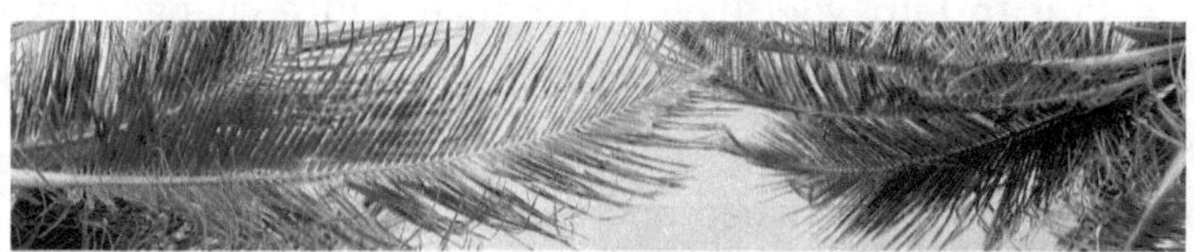

Elise: Call me when you're awake. I'm dying to hear how it went yesterday. Still can't believe your Jacob is Jake Reeves!!! 🔥😍

Your Jacob rattled around her mind, and Brooke sighed as she lay in her bed. She wanted him to be hers before discovering what he did for a living. Now it frightened her. It probably didn't matter how she felt. Yesterday, he made his feelings clear with his many references to her as a "friend."

Since Noah wasn't up yet, she stayed in bed and called Elise to give her a rundown of her time with Jacob, meeting the rest of the band, and seeing their house the day before.

"You are soooo lucky! This is just so amazing, don't you think?!"

"I guess," Brooke forced out.

"What do you mean, *you guess*?"

"It feels weird being with him now."

Elise scoffed. "He's still the same guy. You just know more about him. Isn't that what you wanted?"

"Yeah, but before, he was regular Jacob, and I felt like I was a big part of his life. Now I feel like I'm in competition with the whole world. He has a fast-paced life, and if I don't figure out what I want, I'll miss the opportunity. But I also wonder if everything I thought we had, I misinterpreted, and he was just being his normal, kind self. Maybe there's no *opportunity* to miss. It's possible Noah and I are like a charity case for him. I told you how he hangs out with the youth at the apartment building, didn't I?" Elise nodded and Brooke added, "He said it would have meant a lot to him to have a man in his life growing up. He probably thinks Noah needs a man in his life. I don't know . . . it's so confusing!"

"I seriously doubt you guys are a charity case to him. He seems too invested in your lives."

"Maybe. But what if he gets bored with us? He's got this glamorous life, jet-setting all over, but when he's with us, it's just parks and picnics. That's what he's doing with us today, by the way."

"Who suggested it?"

"He did."

"Enjoying a regular life with you might be something he likes about being with you guys—part of why he didn't tell you what he does. Maybe he wanted to do the regular *boring* stuff."

"That's essentially what he said. Time will tell, I guess. I don't think I can take getting hurt again, and it's hard not to let my heart get involved when I'm near him. I also worry Noah will get so used to having him around, and then when Jacob moves on, it will hurt him, too. That actually worries me more than my own emotional issues."

"I'm not sure what to say, other than give him a chance to show you what his intentions are."

"I can try. But I have a habit of putting my walls up when I have these kinds of fears."

"You really have a hard time letting people in, don't you?"

"I've lost too many important people. Some left on purpose, like my dad and Tyler, and some didn't intend to . . . like Mom. It makes me hesitant to let anyone get too close. Especially when they are people I depend on."

"I understand, but what if you miss out on the best part of your life because you're too scared?"

"What if . . ."

As they sat on the picnic blanket in the park, Brooke watched and pasted on a smile as Noah climbed on Jacob and giggled while Jacob tickled him.

Jacob's eyes found hers. "You're so quiet. What's on your mind?"

"Just a lot to take in."

Jacob nodded in understanding, and Brooke looked at his hat.

"Now it makes sense that you're always wearing a cap and sunglasses when we're in public." Brooke frowned.

"Actually, I did it more for you and this guy." Jacob gave Noah a squeeze. "I'm used to being ambushed and photographed, but you two deserve your privacy. And . . . I also didn't want you to find things out that way."

Brooke didn't respond.

"I'm still the same person. You can talk to me, just like you always have."

Chuckling nervously, Brooke looked up and noticed Keith sitting on a bench. "Was Keith nearby when we came here or went out in the past?" She was trying to wrap her mind around Jacob's celebrity life, and now she analyzed all of their previous interactions.

Jacob glanced at Keith. "Yeah, why?"

"It seems strange that I never noticed him until the week I had the incident at the bar."

"Part of his job is to blend in so he's not a distraction for me and whoever I'm with, but also so he doesn't draw attention to me when I'm not somewhere in an official capacity. I'm sure you've noticed his outfits correspond with wherever you'll be, so he looks like any other person. The only time he dresses like a bodyguard is when we're at an official function where everyone knows who I am, so his presence will be a deterrent for people."

"Hmm. Guess that makes sense." Her phone buzzed, and she looked down to see a text from Matt.

MATT: You should come to see our band tonight. Please, please, please :)

BROOKE CHUCKLED and shook her head before texting back.

BROOKE: Can't. I'm hanging out with a friend who just got back in town.

MATT: Bring her! I'm sure she'll love us!

BROOKE: Him, and not staying out late tonight. He has jet lag from Europe.

HE DIDN'T REPLY to her last text, and Brooke glanced back up at Jacob. "Sorry. Matt was bugging me to go to see his band tonight, but I know you'll be too tired for a late night."

Jacob's face became unreadable. "You should go. I'll be going to bed early, anyway. Don't let me hold you back from seeing him."

"No. It's fine. I really have no desire to stay up late tonight either."

"So, you're using me as an excuse?" Jacob smiled knowingly.

"Maybe," she chuckled. Her eyebrows flew up. "You know, his

band plays some of your band's songs. That's how I first heard your music. It's funny to think about now." Jacob gave her a questioning look. "I kept hearing your music and really enjoying it. *Madness*'s renditions of your songs impressed me so much that I started listening to your band, but I had no idea it was yours. You're really talented with words and musical compositions." Jacob grinned and she added, "It's strange to consider that the writer and composer was part of my life all this time."

"You like my music, huh?" Jacob's grin grew. "I knew you enjoyed the song I wrote for Noah, but it's good to hear you appreciate my other work."

"Don't go getting a big head." Brooke grinned back at him and playfully shoved his shoulder. "You know, your band should meet Matt and his band, *Madness*. They would be thrilled to talk to you guys. They really look up to you and are working to follow in your footsteps."

Jacob's smile faded. "Sure, that can be arranged. Or do you think they might like backstage passes to our next local concert?"

"I'm certain they would love that. But I'd be kind of jealous if you don't get them for me, too. I've not gotten to see any of your concerts."

A small smile appeared on Jacob's face. "Of course. I figured you and Elise would want to join them. I wouldn't let such a good *friend* get by without seeing my band in action."

He had emphasized the word friend, and Brooke flinched. It stung more than she cared to admit.

Running fingers through his hair, then pointing to the slide, Jacob asked, "Noah, do you want to ride on the slide?"

Noah's eyes followed where Jacob pointed and he squealed in delight, reaching for Jacob's hand. "Sli! Sli!"

Jacob placed some of their containers in the picnic basket. "Hang on, Noah. I'm helping your mom clean up."

"I've got it. You go on, I'll be there in a minute."

Nodding, Jacob swept Noah into his arms and hung him down to Brooke. "Give Mommy a kiss, and we'll go slide."

Noah giggled and leaned over to kiss Brooke's forehead.

"Love you, baby." Brooke blew one back to him with her hand.

"It always amazes me how Noah can fall asleep so easily in a public place with all the activity and noise around him." Jacob looked down at the stroller as he pushed it. "Seriously, how does he do it? And how does this blanket covering the stroller make that much of a difference?"

Brooke shrugged. "I don't know. My mom is the one who gave me the idea. She said she did that with me. It blocks his vision from what's happening around him, and it works. It probably wouldn't if it wasn't his normal naptime, but he's on a good schedule. He's always been an easy baby. If I ever have more, I hope they're like him, but I have a feeling I won't be so lucky."

Jacob smiled and raised an eyebrow. "You're a great mom. You should definitely have more."

She felt her face flush. "Thanks. Next time, if there is one, I'm making sure I'm married first."

He held her gaze and his look became serious.

"I learned my lesson with Tyler, and I'm not falling for that again," she said.

He nodded. "You deserve better."

His eyes didn't waver from hers, and her chest tightened. Did he know how much he affected her, and that she was imagining marrying him? She tripped over a rock on the sidewalk, and the moment was broken.

"So, the guys have invited you and Noah for lunch at the house tomorrow after church."

"The guys, huh?"

"Yep. They want to get to know you better. They would invite you for dinner tonight, but they're having another party today and it will go into the evening, I'm sure." He rolled his eyes.

"Sounds like they party a lot."

"They do. It's kind of crazy that just last year, I was right in the middle of it all with them. Usually, I was the one planning them." Jacob cringed as he spoke.

"I take it you changed when you became a Christian?"

Jacob nodded at Brooke's question.

"When I found out I was pregnant, I gave that lifestyle up. Now motherhood has changed my priorities permanently." Brooke wondered out loud, "With your roommates being so big in the party scene, do none of them have girlfriends?"

"Actually, Brandon's been dating his girlfriend for over two years. She parties with him when he's in town, but they're not quite as wild as the other three. Though, since I became a Christian and had a serious talk with all the guys about the drugs, they've kept it a lot cleaner. They were cool about it and don't have drugs at the parties anymore. We never did the hard stuff, and it's not like any of us were addicts, so they weren't devastated giving them up." Something flashed in his eyes.

"But back to your question, Ryan has never had a steady girl-friend. He's sworn he never wants to commit. Ethan has been in and out of relationships, but is currently single. Then there's Anthony. He's a romantic at heart, but he's never managed to get past about three months, because he always finds flaws with the girls."

He left out the one person she was most curious about. Brooke raised an eyebrow and wondered if it would be too weird if she asked about him. She decided to, anyway, before she lost the courage. "So, where on the spectrum do you fall?"

Jacob pulled a hand through his hair and winced. "Well, as you know, before I became a Christian, I was pretty messed up, and that goes for relationships, too. Or lack thereof, I guess. Growing up and seeing how my mom was with guys, and even Nan never being in a serious relationship because she used to be such a women's libber, I just considered girls as a form of pleasure. An actual relationship never crossed my mind. I was probably worse than Ryan. He at least cares about girls' feelings. I never thought about how my actions made them feel."

Brooke glanced at him and tried to imagine what he was like before. It bothered her to imagine him being with lots of girls, and it was hard to consider him that way now, when all she had seen was a guy who cared deeply about the feelings of others. "That's hard to picture." She looked at him skeptically. "You are probably the most thoughtful guy I've ever met. You do so much for me and Noah, and you spend so much time with kids in the apartment complex when you're in town. It seems like you devote more to others than yourself."

He blushed. It was the first time she had seen him blush, and it made him seem more attractive. How that was even possible, she didn't know.

"It's just hard for me to imagine you the way you described. I don't understand how a person could change so much."

Jacob smiled awkwardly. "I know it might sound cliché, but God really did make a difference. After reading the Bible all the way through and committing my life to Jesus, I knew I needed to represent Him better, or I had no business calling myself a Christian. I prayed about it a lot, and I started to think of people differently than I ever had. I actually considered their feelings, and I had a desire to show others that they were important. It was strange for me at first, but now I realize that's how God works. He changes us from the inside—changes our desires. I'm not living differently to try to earn salvation, or keep it, because I can't. That's all Jesus. I'm living differently because I understand He wants and knows what's best for me, and also because I want to please Him."

With wide eyes and an open heart, Brooke listened and felt moved by his words. She had been preached at plenty of times through the years. Living in the Bible Belt, it was hard to avoid. But when he spoke about God, it felt different. It drew her in and caused her to wonder if she'd been missing something all these years. It made her long for what he had—a sense of contentment and peace with his life that he didn't have before, even with the money, women, and fame she now knew he had. As she contemplated these things, it hit her that he hadn't mentioned a woman in his life currently, and she smiled.

"What are you smiling about? I just poured out my awful past, and you're smiling."

"Nothing. Just enjoying the day."

CHAPTER
TWENTY-EIGHT

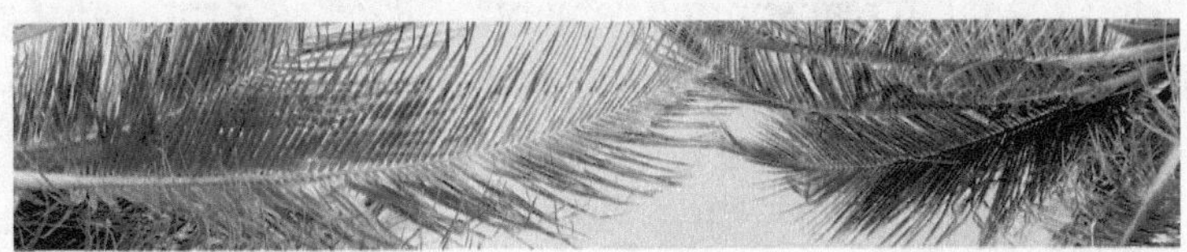

Brandon ran across the patio, holding Noah on his shoulders. Brooke wasn't sure who enjoyed it more.

"If he pukes up the lunch you guys just fed him, you're cleaning it up." Brooke chuckled. "Actually, it's almost his naptime, so he really does need to settle down."

"Party pooper!" Ryan bellowed.

Anthony threw a beach ball at Ryan. "Hey, she's being a good mom."

Rolling his eyes at the guys, Jacob turned to Brooke. "You relax, and I'll put Noah down for his nap in the portable playpen in the guest room."

He lifted a giggling Noah from Brandon's shoulders and left the lanai to take him inside.

Ryan chuckled. "That has got to be the funniest kid ever. I can see why Jacob likes having you guys around." He winked. "Who knows, after spending more time with Noah, I might even decide it's worth it to settle down at some point."

Slapping a hand down on the coffee table, Ethan broke out in laughter.

Ryan's chuckle became full-blown laughter as well. "Yeah, nah, I could never." He elbowed Ethan.

"One day, you two are going to meet the right woman, and your tune will change." Anthony shook his head.

"Where's your special woman, Mr. Know It All?" Ryan questioned.

"Still looking, but at least I'm realistic—and a romantic."

"Hey, man, I'm realistic and romantic," Ryan said through a grin. "There are just too many beautiful women to settle down with only one. I've got lots of love to share." He wiggled his eyebrows.

Thoughts of marriage and children swirled in Brooke's mind, but clicking heels drew her attention to the house.

"The party's here, you can turn on the music!" A woman's voice floated outside. Moments later, a dark-haired beauty with golden skin and curves in all the right places joined them on the lanai.

"About time! These guys are messed up! Let's have some fun!" Ryan shouted.

As the woman looked around, she noticed Brooke and her eyes lit up. "You must be Brooke!" Walking to the sofa, she held out a hand. "I'm Isabel, Brandon's girlfriend. You can call me Izzy, though." Izzy slid into a chair and joined them. "So, are these goofballs keeping you entertained?"

HALF AN HOUR LATER, the group was on their way to the practice room. Izzy offered to show Brooke how to use the equipment in the sound booth while the guys played for them. Jacob pulled Brooke aside and asked her which songs she knew. He promised to play them for her, along with a few she hadn't heard before. When they began playing "Searching," her heart raced. It was the first song of theirs she'd ever heard. *Madness* did a good job with it, but this was on a whole other level. The words and the rhythm always made her emotional, but today, tears welled in her eyes.

"Are you okay?" Izzy asked when she saw Brooke dabbing at her eyes.

Brooke nodded and smiled, knowing her watery eyes said otherwise. "For some reason, this song makes me want to cry." She fanned her face.

"It's okay, I get it. Jacob writes some pretty great stuff—not just fluff, like a lot of pop artists. I think that's what sets them apart."

"Give us a few minutes to work some things out on this new song," Jacob called from the music room, and the girls nodded.

"So, Jacob said you guys met through his Nan?"

"Yeah, she and my grandmother are close. Did he tell you about my confusion over who he was at first?"

Izzy nodded. "He told me you just found out Friday that he was part of the band."

Brooke laughed. "Actually, that was the second revelation. When I first moved down here, his Nan was out of town, and I kept seeing him at the apartment building, but I didn't know who he was. I made assumptions based on the fact that he was young, dressed hip, drove multiple expensive cars, and hung out with the teens in our apartments."

Izzy's eyebrows shot up. "Yeah? Why do I sense something crazy's about to come out of your mouth?" She raised a brow.

"Well . . . the truth is, I thought he was a drug dealer." Brooke made a face, waiting for Izzy's response.

Izzy looked serious and placed a hand over her mouth, but suddenly broke out in laughter. "I can see you felt bad, but that's actually pretty funny. Jake, every teen and adult woman's dream guy, a drug dealer. That's great. You don't mind if I tell Brandon, do you? That's too good to keep to myself."

"I don't know. I'm really embarrassed about it, but it will probably come out at some point." Heat washed over Brooke's face. "What about you and Brandon? How and when did you two meet?"

One side of Izzy's mouth quirked up. "I've known him since I was a little girl. His family moved next door when I was five. Brandon and

Martez, my brother, quickly became best friends. They're both two years older than me, so they were in classes together and completely inseparable. I was the irritating little sister who followed them around since there weren't any girls my age in the neighborhood."

Izzy explained that the summer after both boys graduated, the guys shared an apartment. Then she and her mom moved because of her parent's divorce, and with Brandon and Martez running in different circles, she didn't see Brandon for a couple of years, until just before *Nine Days In* became a big hit. "Forget the cliché about the guy being scared to date his best friend's sister." Izzy chuckled. "He came after me hard, and it was almost a year before I accepted a date with him."

"That's awesome. Make him work for it." Brooke was impressed with Izzy.

The music started up in the practice room and they both turned back to watch.

AN HOUR LATER, Jacob climbed out of the pool. "I'll help you get Noah up from his nap. I love seeing him when he first wakes up with those sleepy eyes."

A chorus of "aw's" filled the backyard. Izzy's was sincere, whereas Ryan's was laced with sarcasm.

"Giving up the man card, Jake?" Ryan chuckled.

Grinning, Jacob shook his head, then placed a hand on Brooke's back to guide her into the house. As they walked to the guest room, the sound of Noah's voice came through the monitor. Jacob stopped to turn off the monitor and held his finger to his lips as they drew near the door and leaned in. They couldn't make out what he was saying. It sounded like happy gibberish. Jacob had a gleam in his eye as he held Brooke's gaze and mouthed *"adorable."*

Quietly, they opened the door and approached the playpen. When Noah saw them, he turned his head and started giggling. "Da!

Da!" He stood up and reached for Jacob, who looked back for Brooke's approval before picking him up.

Brooke knew he had missed Jacob. It simultaneously warmed her heart and scared her.

~

IZZY FOLLOWED Brooke as she went to change Noah. "So, what do you think of living in Florida?"

"It's been great so far. I've had a rough year, and it's good to start fresh. So many people have made me feel welcome, and I have my grandmother and Jacob constantly supporting me. I'm glad I made the decision to move here." Brooke looked down at Noah and grinned. "It's been a good choice, hasn't it, baby?" She slid a romper over his head and snapped it at the bottom, before lifting him into her arms and turning back to Izzy.

A look of concern clouded Izzy's face, and she fiddled with her necklace. "I . . . uh . . . I'm a little worried about you."

"What do you mean?" Brooke's brow furrowed.

"You like him, don't you?"

"Jacob?"

Izzy nodded.

Tensing, Brooke shrugged and replied, "He's a good friend." She didn't feel comfortable baring her soul to someone she'd just met.

Watching her, Izzy hesitated before speaking. "No, you like him romantically. I see it in your eyes when he's around."

Brooke didn't respond and fiddled with Noah's outfit.

"Jacob's a great guy and all. He seems to have turned over a new leaf since he started with this "Christianity" thing. But I should warn you." Izzy looked away and took a breath before continuing. "He's past the one-nighters, but I'm just not sure he's ready to settle down with one woman yet."

The turn of the conversation caught Brooke off guard, and her face contorted. Did Izzy not think she was cool enough to hang with their crowd, and this was her attempt to get Brooke out of the picture?

"I realize I'm not the type of person you'd expect to hang out with an international pop star, especially toting a toddler around," she nodded toward Noah, "but like I said, we're just friends—"

"It's not that!" Izzy interrupted. "I don't think you're not good enough for him. In fact, it's quite the opposite. I just . . . don't want you to get hurt."

The blood rushed from Brooke's face, and she fought to maintain her composure as she gathered Noah's things without looking at Izzy. She knew if she did, the dam would break. "Thanks." She forced out. She needed to leave quickly. What was she to think from these cryptic comments?

Forcing a smile for the others, Brooke somehow said her good-byes, let a confused Jacob lead her to the car, and headed home.

In the car, tears began flowing, and she called Elise. "Hey. Jacob emergency. Can you come to my place?"

"I'm glad Grams isn't here, to be honest. I love her, but I don't want her to know how I feel about Jacob. She's been so close to him through his Nan, I'm not sure how she would respond, or if she would try to say something to him. I'm having enough trouble figuring out how I feel and what I want without outside pressure."

Elise lay back on Brooke's bed and pulled Noah on top of her. "Your Grams seems nice, but I get it."

"Yeah, she really is great, and she's got a lot of wisdom. I'm just not ready to tell her yet."

"So what's going on?" Elise asked after blowing raspberries onto Noah's belly and sending him into a giggle fit.

Brooke grinned and shook her head. "It's hard to be serious with you when you're making faces at my kid and blowing raspberries." Elise looked like she would explode as she tried to keep from laughing. Brooke rolled her eyes and handed Noah two little cars to distract him. "So, I met Brandon's girlfriend today, Isabel, and she seemed nice."

"Brandon, as in *Nine Days In* Brandon?" Brooke nodded at Elise's question and Elise said, "The face you're making tells me you're not so sure about her."

"That's the thing. Right before I left, she started questioning me about whether I liked Jacob as more than a friend and told me she was worried about me and needed to warn me. She told me she doesn't think Jacob is ready to settle down with one person." Brooke stopped and looked down at Noah, running her hand over his hair.

"She wouldn't say more, and insisted it wasn't because she thought I wasn't good enough for him." Rubbing a hand across her face, she continued, "I don't know what to make of it. Is he involved with other girls? Or maybe I've been reading way too much into our relationship and it's purely platonic for him. It could be he hangs with us for Noah's sake. I don't know." She threw up her hands. "I was just beginning to adjust to his international fame and feeling hopeful about things. I'm so confused!"

Noah stopped what he was doing and climbed onto Brooke's lap while patting her leg. "It's okay, baby. Mommy's okay. And to top it all off," she shifted her focus back to Elise, "I've got little guy here to worry about. Whatever decision I make affects him."

Elise frowned and leaned forward to wrap an arm around her friend. Pulling out her phone with her free hand, she began searching. "There's something I found that you need to see. I was waiting to show you in person." She opened a website and passed her phone to Brooke.

Glancing down, Brooke was stunned by a picture of Jacob with a familiar-looking, gorgeous woman hanging on his arm, quite cozily. Gasping, she checked the article date and noticed it was from ten days earlier. The headline read, "Mari Stephens spotted in Norway on the arm of Jake Reeves." Quickly scanning the article, Brooke saw that it referred to speculation about their relationship over the past year. "Mari?" Brooke asked.

"Are you familiar with her music?"

"No. What music?"

"She was with the girl band *Eternal*, but went solo. Apparently, she's with the same record label as *Nine Days In*, so they had her tour with them last summer to promote her new solo album. Then at the end of the summer, she was Jake's date to the MTV music awards. After that, they were frequently seen together. Talk was that they were dating. They also went to a couple of other award shows together, including the Grammys this past January. I hadn't heard anything about them in a while, but when I learned who your Jacob really was, I checked to see if she was still in his life." She placed a hand on Brooke's shoulder. "I will say, they have never confirmed an actual relationship, so who knows."

"Yesterday, Ryan asked Jacob if Mari was back, and at the time, I didn't think much of it. I wondered who she was, but it was said offhandedly, and Jacob changed the subject. Now I know why." Brooke sank into her pillow. "Here I was, worrying if I was willing to keep moving forward in our relationship with him being a celebrity, and he wasn't even viewing me as relationship material."

Placing a hand over her mouth, she started shaking her head, and her eyes glazed over just before the steady stream of tears began. "I had no idea." She continued to shake her head. "I mean, I know nothing was officially said, but he just . . . he seemed so committed to me . . . to us. I thought he was just taking it slow. I can't believe I've been so stupid."

Brooke's phone buzzed, and she looked down to see Jacob trying to video call. She stared at the phone like it was on fire.

"Do you want me to tell him you're unavailable? Or you can ignore it," Elise commented.

"I . . . he . . . he's calling to read a bedtime story to Noah. It's not fair to Noah." Brooke bit her lip.

"Okay, you run to the bathroom and freshen up your face. I'll answer and get them started. You can slip back in partway through and maybe get by without saying much."

Nodding, Brooke handed her phone to Elise and raced to the bathroom. After splashing water on her face, wiping her eyes, taking a few deep breaths, and saying a silent prayer, she walked back to her room. There in her bed, Noah smiled next to an awkward, flushed-looking Elise, who quickly switched places with Brooke. Brooke held her breath, hoping Jacob wouldn't ask to see her. She was relieved when he continued reading the story.

After the story was over, Jacob spoke to Brooke. "So, why'd you run off so fast from the house earlier?" Jacob questioned before she could hang up.

"I . . . uh . . . Elise needed to talk to me about some things."

"Oh." Jacob's mouth curled into a smile. "Girl stuff? Is she wondering what to do about Brad?"

Elise looked over at Brooke and her face turned red as she mouthed, "*You told him?*"

"Just girl stuff," Brooke repeated mysteriously, while ignoring Elise's comment.

"Okay, well, I guess I should let you go so you can get back to it." Just before Brooke ended the call, Jacob spoke again. "Wait. I almost forgot. On Thursday, me and the guys are going to Arnold Palmer Children's Hospital to chat with the kids and play a couple of songs. I want you and Noah to come. You mentioned you'd like to visit again."

Brooke had no words.

"We're supposed to be there at ten in the morning, so it should work with Noah's nap schedule. I'm guessing it will last about an hour and a half, then we can grab some lunch."

Furrowing her brow, she tried to decide what was best. Her mind pulled her one way, and her heart, the other. She glanced up at Elise, who furiously nodded her head. "Um . . . I guess we can go." As soon as the words came out, she second-guessed herself.

"Awesome! Okay, then I'll talk with you tomorrow. Enjoy your time with Elise. Goodnight, Noah." He waved at her son. "Goodnight, Elise!" he called out a little louder, before looking at Brooke with an expression she couldn't read. "Sweet dreams, Brooke." Then he was gone.

Brooke let out a sigh.

Elise looked flushed and fanned herself. "I can't believe I just got to watch and listen to Jake Reeves read a children's book." She grinned at Brooke, who rolled her eyes.

Brooke was thankful Noah went to bed easily, because it gave her more time to vent to Elise. She plopped down on her bed and threw up her hands. "See what I'm dealing with! I have no idea what is going on with us. Ugh. What should I do?"

"He's got to have *some* sort of feelings for you. I can't imagine him going to so much trouble if he didn't."

"Yeah. *Some* sort of feelings . . . like that of a friend."

"You know what I mean, and it's not as a friend. Maybe we just need to make you seem irresistible to him."

"What are you even talking about? I am not throwing myself at him like one of his desperate fans. Plus, if I learned anything from my parents and Tyler, it's that love is fragile enough, even when both parties start off caring. I want someone who can't do without me, not someone I have to coerce into being with me."

"Yeah, you're right. Not really sure why you're asking me for advice." Elise chuckled. "Here I am, scared to make my own moves on the drummer of a local band. I'm not exactly the poster child for pushing a relationship forward."

"Whatever, you goof!" Brooke tossed a stuffed animal at her. "It's sometimes easier to help others with their problems than it is your own." She folded her hands under her chin and batted her eyes. "Maybe we just need to make *you* irresistible," she said in a sultry voice, then broke out in laughter. "I've got to laugh, or I'll cry."

TWENTY-NINE

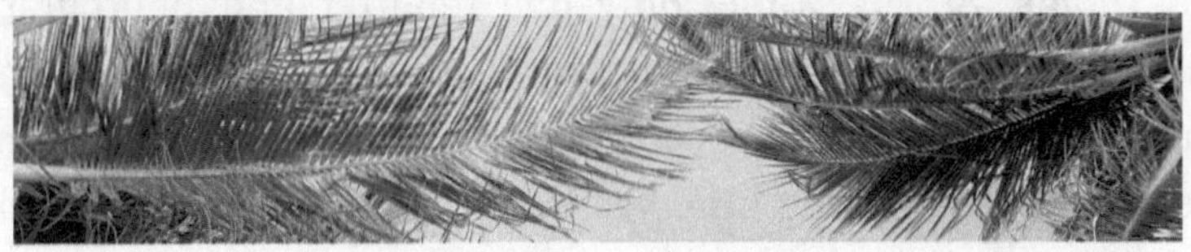

"I can do this . . . I can do this," Brooke whispered to herself as she drove to Arnold Palmer Children's Hospital.

She'd seen Jacob at Nan's on Tuesday, and they all ended up having dinner together. That had been rough. Throughout the night, he kept asking if she was okay. How could she answer that when he was the problem?

After dinner, she and Jacob washed the dishes together, and when she wouldn't talk, he grabbed her hand. The electricity she felt when he began caressing her palm as he stared into her eyes came rushing back. She'd tried hard to keep her walls up, but she nearly told him everything. It was obvious he cared, but the thought of being *just friends* made her feel sick. And the thought of not even being that would destroy her.

KEITH MET her in the parking lot and led her through the added security. When they entered the lobby, there was a crowd gathered around the band members. Jacob and his band were talking to some of the more mobile children and their parents, with the press standing further back, taking notes and pictures. Jacob's eyes soon found Brooke's and his face lit up. A couple of the reporters noticed and turned to see what he was looking at, causing Brooke to hide behind a mom and son.

Moments later, Keith appeared by her side to inform Brooke they would soon be going up and visiting individual patients in their rooms. At that time, only one reporter and photographer would be allowed to accompany each band member. Jacob requested that Brooke also accompany him and promised to make sure the press following him was informed not to include Noah or her in any pictures or written statements. He suggested that while they were in the lobby, she remain in the background for their privacy. It made sense, and Brooke sent word back to Jacob that she would follow his advice, yet she wondered if he worried people might think they were together. Her mind floated back to what Elise told her about Mari.

As Brooke scanned the room, she recognized Laura, Dr. Gupta's assistant, who had given her a tour of the hospital the last time she was there. "Laura!" She waved and made her way through the crowd. "Laura, nice to see you again."

"You're a fan of these guys, too?" Laura couldn't keep the grin off her face as she gestured to where the band was hanging out with children.

"I'm actually good friends with Jacob—Jake." She remembered that's what everyone else knew him as. "He recently introduced me to the rest of the band when they got back from Europe."

"That's so cool! I can't believe Tyler didn't say anything to me about it."

Brooke's eyebrows shot up. "What do you mean?"

"Last week, when we were going over the details for his rotation here, I remarked that *Nine Days In* was coming to the hospital this week and I couldn't wait. I would think he might have mentioned you being good friends with their lead singer."

"Oh. Tyler and I aren't talking. I haven't spoken to him since about a week after he was down for his visit here."

"What?" A look of confusion spread over Laura's face. "I've talked to him about you several times and he's acted like everything is fine. Just this last week, he even went on about ideas he had for proposing to you. I don't understand."

Brooke's face darkened, and she fought to maintain her composure. "We're not together anymore."

"He must still think he has a chance."

"Oh, no. I made it very clear that after what he did, we were done."

"What did he do?"

Brooke's hand flew to her mouth. "I'm sorry, I shouldn't have said anything. That's not really my place. Just because I'm mad at him doesn't mean he won't do a good job for you here." She refused to let her anger be the reason he didn't get into the clinical rotation or internship at the hospital.

Laura watched Brooke closely. "He cheated on you, didn't he? I can see it in your eyes."

Brooke stared back, unsure of how to respond. She didn't feel right about saying more, even though she wanted to.

"You don't have to say anything. Your silence says it all." Laura's mouth pursed and she laid a hand on Brooke's shoulder. "I'm so sorry. You deserve better than that. If it's any consolation, I can guarantee you he won't be coming now for a rotation. Dr. Gupta will be disappointed to know what he's done to you, but more than that, he absolutely will refuse to have someone who is lying to him. He won't want a person he can't trust."

"Thanks for the encouragement." Brooke gave a small smile. Wanting to change the subject, she offered, "So, ready to meet the band?"

Grinning, Laura glanced over. "Looks like your friend, Jake, has been watching us."

"He's pretty protective of me."

"Seems like a good guy. I'd say you're better off now." Laura wiggled her eyebrows at Brooke before pulling her closer to the guys.

"It's not like that," Brooke said softly as she felt her cheeks heat up.

"Uh-huh." Laura grinned. "Don't worry. I won't say anything."

"Okay, well, I would introduce you to the guys myself, but Jacob has suggested I lay low until we get upstairs and there aren't so many cameras focused on him. But when you go up, tell them you're a friend of mine, and I'm sure you'll get some special treatment." She caught Keith glancing their way and subtly motioned him over. "Jacob's bodyguard, Keith, can get you up to them. Here he comes now." She wasn't about to mention that Keith was currently *her* bodyguard.

"Thank you, and good luck!" Laura grinned just before walking off with Keith.

"Oh, and Laura—" Brooke stopped her and urged, "Please don't tell Tyler I told you we aren't together when you speak with him next. I wouldn't want him to blame me."

"Of course not." Laura's face held concern. "Did he . . . hurt you?"

Brooke looked at Laura, then at Keith, hesitant to expose her past. "Verbally . . . emotionally."

Laura nodded and hugged her. "I'll let you know when I call him."

Keith's brow furrowed as they walked off.

ONCE OFF THE ELEVATOR, Jacob excused himself to an empty room and had Keith bring Brooke and watch Noah for her. "You know her . . . Laura? What's going on? Keith said you were talking about Tyler with her and asked her not to tell Tyler something. I noticed you looked distressed." He wrapped an arm around Brooke and lifted her face to his.

"She . . . she was the woman who guided Tyler and I through the hospital when he was down for his visit. Apparently he's been acting like he and I are still together when talking to her about his rotation in the fall. He even went as far as telling her about his plans to propose to me."

"Do you think he would? Propose to you?" Jacob's brow furrowed.

"No. We haven't spoken since my Nashville visit. He's just trying to secure his spot and thinks that will help." Brooke shook her head and glanced away from Jacob's penetrating gaze. "But Laura said he will be declined for sure now, because the doctor in charge won't feel he's trustworthy."

"And you're worried there will be backlash from Tyler when he finds out?" Jacob's hand moved up to her cheek.

Brooke nodded, closing her eyes and trying to keep her emotions in check. "Yes. She said she won't mention us not being together, and she'll let me know when she contacts him."

"Promise me you'll let both me and Keith know when that happens." Jacob's face turned serious. "I know he's never physically harmed you, but I don't want to take any chances. Even if he doesn't realize you spoke with her, there's no telling what a desperate person will do. There's no reason not to take precautions." Brooke stared up at him blankly. "Please?"

"Okay . . . yes, I promise. It still feels so strange to me, having a bodyguard. Maybe he should go back to protecting you, now that things have calmed down with Matt."

"Nope. He stays with you. Please don't argue with me on this. I know he's good about being discreet."

"He is. I just don't think it's necessary anymore." When Jacob acted like this, it made Brooke feel like there was more between them, but she knew better than to get her hopes up. He was a gorgeous superstar. Why would he bother with her?

Shaking his head, Jacob reached for the doorknob. "Like I said, he stays with you. But right now, we need to go." He gave her a reassuring smile. "There are kids waiting."

CHAPTER

THIRTY

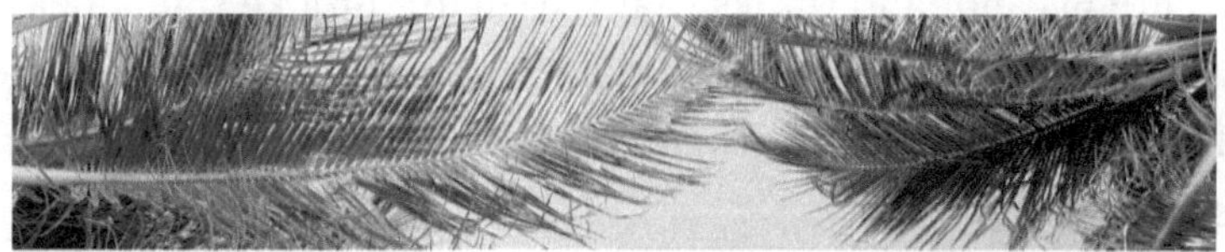

"Brooke?"

"Yeah? Why are you calling, Tyler?" She waited to hear his excuse.

"I wanted to catch up, and was hoping to talk with Noah, too."

"There's no need to confuse him."

"I won't, I promise. But I'd still like to be part of his life."

Brooke rolled her eyes. "Could have fooled me."

"Is that him chattering in the background? I hear him. Please let me speak to him. You can put me on speakerphone."

Brooke looked at the boy happily playing next to her. She hated the thought of Noah growing up with a father who wasn't consistently there—like she did. But she also knew it wasn't right to keep him completely distanced from Tyler.

Sighing, she pulled the phone back to her face. "Okay." Laying her phone down, she hit the speaker button. "Noah? Come talk on the phone."

Noah's eyes lit up. "Da? Da?" He scooted closer to the phone.

"Noah?" Tyler began chuckling. "He called me Dada. He called me Dada. Noah, it's Dada!"

Noah's eyebrows shot up and he looked at Brooke. "Da?" He crawled away from the phone and onto Brooke's lap. "Dada?" He looked about, as if searching—for Jacob.

All this time, he'd been calling Jacob "Da." She'd guessed it was because he couldn't make the 'j' sound.

"I think that was more of an accident, Tyler. You've not been around enough for him to call you that." She didn't want to tell him Noah thought it was Jacob on the phone and start an argument in front of Noah, so she bit her tongue.

"Well, we can change that. I'll make more of an effort to be around. In fact, why don't I come down this weekend?"

"N-no, I don't think that's a good idea, Tyler." He'd caught her off guard, and she wasn't prepared to see him again so soon.

"I think it's a great idea. You can't keep him from me. That's not your plan, is it? Just because—"

Tyler continued talking, but an incoming text from Laura distracted her.

LAURA: Just wanted to let you know that I spoke to Tyler a few minutes ago. He didn't take it well, and tried to convince me he could come down and work out whatever the issues were with us. He insisted he's a great fit for the program. I told him Dr. Gupta's decision is final, and he can expect a formal letter in a couple of days. Hope he doesn't give you a hard time. Nothing was said at all about you, Noah, or your relationship as the reason. Thanks again for the help with meeting *Nine Days In*! Jacob is so dreamy! Lucky girl. Keep in touch.

"UH, Tyler, I've got to go. Thanks for calling. Bye." Brooke hung up the phone.

She was shaking as she typed out a text to Laura. He had almost convinced her he was really calling to stay connected with his son.

. . .

BROOKE: Thanks for the heads up. You saved me. Tyler just called begging to speak to Noah, and I almost believed he was really interested in him until I saw your text. That was the first time he's tried to contact me since I saw him last and discovered him cheating on me a month and a half ago! I hung up quickly after your text.

LAURA: You're better than me. I would have said some choice words first! Sorry he's such a jerk, but glad you're away from him.

BROOKE: Absolutely! Thanks again.

~

"HI." Jacob grinned at Brooke and Noah at the door to Grams' apartment. He'd rushed over when she told him about the conversation with Tyler.

"Hi." Brooke blushed, wondering how she got so lucky to have this amazingly sweet and good-looking guy in her life. Though doubts still lingered and she worried he was too good to be true.

"Dada!" Noah reached for Jacob, almost falling out of her arms.

Jacob's brows shot up and he glanced at Brooke while he took Noah from her.

Her cheeks flamed. "Um, when Tyler called earlier, he, um— Tyler kept saying Dada. And you know how Noah always calls you Da." She shrugged. "I guess he decided he likes the sound of it."

Jacob's face gave nothing away as he looked from Brooke to Noah.

"I'm sorry. I'll tell him to stop." She felt so embarrassed.

Jacob tussled Noah's hair. "It's fine. He already called me Da, so it's not much different." He smiled sincerely. "Have you heard back from Tyler since you hung up on him?"

Brooke walked into the living room and checked her phone. "Nope."

"Okay. Please make sure you have Keith with you whenever you're out. I know Tyler's out of town, but I don't trust him."

"Sure, but I really can't imagine him doing anything to harm us physically."

"It's not worth taking chances, especially when Keith is at your disposal." His mouth pulled up into a lopsided grin. "Okay, enough about that—beach trip tomorrow? What do you say?"

"Beash!" Noah squealed.

"I'll get Noah changed while you pack his beach bag." Jacob lifted Noah high into the air while making airplane noises and sending Noah into one of his giggle fits.

Brooke watched Jacob walk off. Never in her wildest dreams did she imagine that this handsome man who had been changing her son's diapers and reading him bedtime stories every night was actually a superstar. She wondered if she'd ever get used to the idea. Just as he turned the corner, the doorbell rang.

"I've got it!" Brooke called. "It's probably Grams coming back to get something she forgot." Quickly opening the door, Brooke prepared to tease Grams. Instead, she was shocked to find Tyler.

"Hey, babe! I thought I'd surprise the two of you!"

Brooke's mouth hung open in shock, but she soon recovered. Anger boiled over, knowing Tyler was only there to try to win back his hospital rotation.

"Noah's ready! Aren't you, buddy? Did Grams find—" Jacob's voice stopped at the sight of Tyler in the doorway.

"What's he doing here?" Tyler angrily pointed and pushed past Brooke. "And with my kid! No way! You need to leave!"

"No, Tyler, you have no say about who is in my life. *You* need to leave. I don't even know how you got through the gate." Brooke firmly stated.

"The guard remembered me." Tyler smirked. "And I'm not leaving. I have a right to be here with my kid—who I send child support for."

"You can't just show up whenever you want, unannounced, and expect me to let you spend time with him. And you definitely can't push your way into my house." Brooke grabbed his arm and tried to pull him back out of the apartment. He shook her off and walked up to Jacob, who was placing his phone in his back pocket while holding Noah.

Seconds seemed like minutes as the two men stared one another down. Suddenly, Tyler made a move. Poking a finger at Jacob's chest, Tyler demanded Jacob give Noah to him.

"Hey, man. If Brooke says *no*, you need to accept it and leave. Why don't you go back to wherever you're staying and contact her from there. I don't see anything being accomplished right now."

Jacob calmly stepped away, trying to diffuse the situation, but Tyler kept moving forward, with his finger jabbing Jacob's chest. When Tyler reached for Noah, Jacob pushed him backward. "Back off! You're about to find yourself in trouble for assault."

"Right." Tyler smirked. "Just give me my son, wimp, and I'll leave you alone." He lurched forward and grabbed at Noah again, causing Noah to cry.

A tug of war ensued over Noah. Brooke fumbled with her phone for 911. "Get out, Tyler! Let go of Noah!" When Noah's crying increased, she dropped her phone and moved into the fray to help get Tyler's hands off of Noah.

"He's my son! I have the right to take him!" Tyler bellowed.

"Tyler Edmonds! Hands in the air!" a uniformed police officer called out as he entered the living room. "You have the right to remain silent. Anything you say can and will be used against you in a court of law."

Tyler raised his hands and slowly turned around. "I'm just trying to get my kid from this stranger who is accosting him!"

The police officer smirked and raised an eyebrow, then looked at Jacob. "Is this guy for real?" He shook his head. "Mr. Edmonds, this *stranger* is the one who reported you. And according to my source, he's the one who is supposed to be here. *You* are not."

The officer cuffed Tyler and moved him toward the door. "As soon as he's in the squad car with my partner, I'll be back for your statements."

Though Brooke was angry with Tyler, she didn't see the need to press charges. "Officer, I don't—"

Jacob grabbed her arm and shook his head. The officer turned and left the apartment.

"I don't think we should press charges. He didn't actually do anything," Brooke urged Jacob.

"That may be true, but this should be reported. He needs to understand the reality of what he did and have some fear put in him. If he's let off scot-free, he's likely to try something again. Maybe even worse. Let the officer do his job."

"Okay." She was surprised at how quickly the police arrived. "When did you call 911?"

"I didn't. I texted Keith saying Tyler broke in and was making threats. Keith was on his way over and he's trained to call 911 in a situation like this." Brooke tried to make sense of what he'd said. He explained further. "We have a number system for emergencies. It's faster than me texting specifics. I'll send you the number system. You should have it, too."

Brooke nodded and began shaking.

"Hey. It's going to be okay." He wrapped his free arm around Brooke and pulled her into a group hug with Noah while soothingly rubbing her back. "I've got you, and more importantly, God's got you. I was praying from the moment I saw him, and God protected us."

The officer came back in, Keith trailing behind. He explained he was taking Tyler in for trespassing, aggravated assault, and intent to kidnap. The officer said he'd heard and seen enough to file the report on his own. After being told Tyler would most likely serve very little time before receiving probation, Brooke was convinced to report him, too. Tyler's hold on her was difficult to break away from.

When Jacob made his statement, he showed the officer and Brooke his original text to Keith, and explained the emergency number system he had with his bodyguards. Brooke drew closer, intrigued. All the text said was '2/6 *Ty*.' Keith said he used that message and his tracker on Jacob's phone to know Tyler had forced his way into the apartment and was threatening them.

Thirty minutes later, the police car left, with Tyler in tow.

Brooke felt frazzled. "I guess it's too late for us to make it to the beach. We could just go to the park. I hate for Noah to miss out completely."

When Noah piped up with "beash!" Jacob's brow furrowed. "Do you have anything planned for tomorrow other than church?" Brooke shook her head. "Okay. Give me a few minutes to check on something." Jacob stepped into Noah's room and closed the door, and Brooke heard his muffled voice.

In a matter of minutes, Jacob came out and clapped his hands together. "We're going to the beach! I've got us a house."

"What?" Brooke questioned.

"Yep, on Anna Maria Island! You'll love the house. It has a pool and is right on the beach, with only the owner's house nearby. My travel agent will get them to sign a non-disclosure agreement and we'll have all the privacy we want. I've got it rented for two nights, so we can drive back early Monday to get you to work, or later tomorrow night, or . . . you can see about going to work a couple of hours late on Monday. Your choice."

Brooke's eyes went wide and she shook her head. "I can't! That's too much!"

Her emotions were wrecked after the events of the morning. A beach trip with Jacob for a whole weekend would test her already fragile heart. How could she think clearly about what she wanted or needed when faced with him in only swim trunks for multiple days? On the other hand, maybe it would force them to clarify what was going on between them.

"It's done and paid for. If you don't come with me, it will go to waste, because I'm not going if you don't." While Brooke paused, he glanced at Keith. "Come on, it will be fun, and you'll get some down time. If Keith comes and I get Ryder or Ben to meet us out there, we can even go out together when Noah's napping."

"I can do that." Keith spoke up and grinned. "A beach getaway sounds nice."

Jacob's questioning gaze moved to Brooke, and she smiled, but shook her head. "Looks like I'll be the bad guy if I say no." She laughed. "I guess I *could* use the time away after this morning."

"That's what I thought." Jacob grinned. "Alright! We need to pack more clothes, then. I'll pop over to Nan's and grab a few things. Keith, good thing you carry an overnight bag everywhere." He smacked Keith on the back.

"With your crazy schedule, I have to be prepared for all sorts of surprises."

CHAPTER
THIRTY-ONE

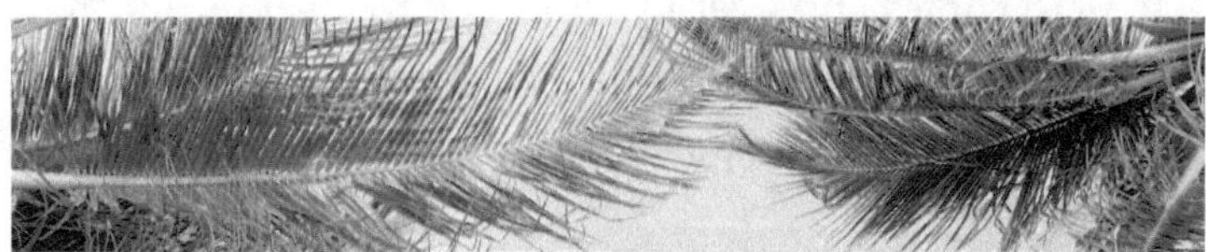

"This is your room." Jacob held out his arm for Brooke to enter, and her eyes were immediately drawn to the floor-to-ceiling windows framing the turquoise water beyond.

"You should have it. It's the largest room, and you paid for the place. Please take it."

"Nope. I insist. You deserve to be pampered for a couple of days. You're a working mom and rarely have time to travel. I do that for a living and constantly stay in enormous suites in the nicest hotels. It's your chance to live a little. Let me spoil you." Jacob laid her overnight bag at the foot of the bed and watched Brooke examine the room.

Brooke hesitated, then finally gave in. "Okay . . . thank you so much. I still can't believe you're doing all of this for me."

Jacob smiled softly and opened his mouth before closing it in frustration. He pointed to the bathroom. "You should check that out, too. It looked nice online."

Nodding, Brooke moved to see what he was talking about. She squealed in delight. "Jacob! This bathroom is to die for!"

He followed her in and grinned.

"Thank you! Thank you! Thank you!" She ran up and threw her

arms around him, then turned around to check out the freestanding tub in an alcove with windows overlooking the water. Peering into the tub, she said, "It's jetted. I'm definitely having a late-night soak in here. Just imagine the moonlight and stars reflecting on the water." She turned around to find him watching her with a half-grin. She suddenly felt nervous and softly repeated, "Thank you."

Noah's little arms stuck out from the child's seat on the back of Jacob's bike as he pointed to things they encountered on the road. Noah looked so proud.

Crickets chirping as the evening approached was music to Brooke's ears. They passed an older couple on the sidewalk, who smiled and waved. Noah cheerfully waved back. It was the perfect domestic bliss she'd always wanted. An aching twinge filled Brooke as she registered that this was only temporary. Yet the more she experienced with Jacob, the more she longed for it to be real.

Returning to the beach house in time to watch the sunset, they parked the bikes and strolled out to their beach chairs. Noah tugged Jacob's arm and pointed to the water, and Jacob followed him to the edge.

"Look! A crab!" Jacob gestured to a little white crab that nearly blended in with the soft white sand.

Noah squealed and chased it until it buried itself in the sand. Following them with her phone in hand, Brooke captured him on video, then switched to her camera app so she could get stills of the sunset in all its orange and pink glory as it sank closer to the water. Jacob swooped Noah into his arms and pulled Brooke close for a group selfie.

The whole day had been perfect. They'd spent hours on their quiet section of the beach, enjoyed a bike ride, and eaten so much seafood. But her favorite time was paddle boarding with Jacob after lunch while Noah was sleeping. Brooke couldn't imagine anything making it more wonderful . . . unless Jacob told her he wanted more than friendship.

~

"Come sit outside on the balcony with me," Jacob urged after they put Noah to bed.

The tub could wait. Brooke anxiously followed Jacob out and they settled in loungers with a view of the gulf that reflected the night sky. Leaning back, they stared at the stars and listened to the sound of the surf gently washing against the shore.

"Does it get old having to worry about being recognized every-where you go?"

Jacob turned and looked at Brooke. "At times. Often I forget about it, but when I want privacy, it becomes an issue. Like when I'm out with you and Noah. I don't want there to be speculation, so I feel like we have to be careful. But when it's just me and the guys or other people in the business, it doesn't seem like a problem, because I know they're used to it, and even if the media is involved, our people will work it out." He stopped and shook his head. "The crazy thing is, I used to love all the attention. The only concern I had then, was being caught doing something that would turn into a scandal. Since I've become a Christian, my priorities have gradually changed."

"I think I know what you mean. Now that I'm reading the Bible, I've started looking at things differently. I had already changed my lifestyle so much when I became a mom, but it was more for Noah's sake. Now I'm wondering if there are other reasons I should be making those choices."

"What kinds of things?"

"Getting drunk, sleeping with someone before marriage. Even little white lies feel wrong, and not just because I might get caught."

Jacob smiled softly. "God's working on your heart. Are you ready to trust Him as your Lord and Savior?"

Brooke froze. "I think I've still got some issues to work through before I get there . . . some things to fix inside myself." Though she was changing, she still didn't feel good enough for God.

Jacob looked at her. "That's where you're wrong. You can never fix yourself enough. You'll never be good enough."

Brooke's eyes opened wide. That was harsh. Did he really just say that?

"I know I've mentioned this before," Jacob said. "But it's an important truth. God doesn't expect you to be perfect when you come to Him. A Christian is never perfect until she's resurrected. To become a Christian, you repent of the sins you have already committed and believe He is who He says He is—the Creator and Lord of all, as well as mankind's Savior, offering the only hope for salvation by His life, death, and resurrection. Then, you confess Him as Lord of your life.

"He'll place His Spirit in you and begin helping you change. Unfortunately, and I say this from experience, we sometimes falter in our trust and try to keep parts of our life away from His influence. He doesn't abandon us, but often lets us suffer until we release it to Him." Jacob looked ashamed. "I'm still learning that, and I know I've got a lot more to learn."

As Brooke studied the handsome man before her, she only saw perfection. He was a man who could do and have whatever and whoever he wanted, yet he did things like take a single mom away for a weekend after being accosted by her ex. It was hard to imagine him being any better, and he'd only been a Christian for about a year. How could she compare to that? She still didn't feel like she qualified for what he was talking about. It didn't make sense that God would want her with all her baggage and imperfections.

"I . . . I'm just not ready," Brooke said softly. She hated to admit that to him, but it was true. Hopefully, it wouldn't lessen his regard for her.

～

THE SOUND of a guitar and Noah's little voice on the balcony woke Brooke the next morning. Climbing out of bed, she peeked out her window. She saw Noah clapping and standing next to Jacob on the sofa while he played his guitar and sang—it sent chills through her body. She could never get enough of watching Jacob with Noah. It had to be the sweetest thing she ever witnessed.

Quickly dressing and freshening up, Brooke joined the boys. "Hey, guys."

"Mommy!" Noah jumped up and down while Jacob wrapped an arm around his waist so he wouldn't fall.

"Good morning, baby." Brooke tousled Noah's hair and sat next to them.

"We're having a little Sunday morning worship. Want to join?" At Brooke's hesitation, he added, "I'll teach you the songs. Or just listen to Noah and me." His mouth pulled into a lazy grin.

"You guys sing it for me, then we'll see." Brooke had a decent voice, but didn't relish singing an unfamiliar song in front of a man who was internationally praised for his vocal abilities.

Jacob sang a song about mercy, boundless grace, and Jesus being a living hope. His voice was strong, and Noah repeated a few of the words while trying to imitate his inflections. It was precious. Clearly, they'd been working on it.

As she listened to the words, she was surprised to understand their meaning. They fit with what she had been reading in the Bible. She wanted what the song talked about—for God to call her His own —but something held her back. A fear that God would examine her and decide she was unworthy. Other men in her life had—even her own father.

When the song ended, Jacob reached down to the coffee table for his Bible. "I'm going to read from chapter one of Ephesians. It was written by Paul, who had been a persecutor of Christians until just after Jesus died and rose. Jesus came to him after His resurrection and called Paul to follow. From that time on, all of Paul's fire against Christians turned into zeal to spread Christianity. Anyway, I'll start at the beginning and read the first fourteen verses, then we can talk about them. They're packed full of insight into how God views us and what He has done for us."

Brooke watched his face as he read and saw the earnestness and excitement he had for God's Word. Words began to jump out at her. "He chose us before the foundation of the world, that we should be holy and blameless." That's what she was afraid of. "In Him we have redemption through His blood, the forgiveness of our trespasses. Riches of His grace . . ." How could that play out in her life? Did He really offer those things to her?

After voicing those thoughts to Jacob, he pointed out verses thirteen and fourteen. "First of all, do you see in verse thirteen where it says, 'In Him you also, when you heard the word of truth, the gospel of your salvation, and believed in Him, were sealed with the promised Holy Spirit'? It's really that simple to become a Christian."

He flipped some pages. "Here in Romans 10, verses nine and ten, it says, 'If you confess with your mouth that Jesus is Lord and believe in your heart that God raised Him from the dead, you will be saved. For with the heart one believes and is justified, and with the mouth one confesses and is saved.'

"Obviously, God knows if you really believe or are just saying it and going through the motions. But back to Ephesians. It says when you become a Christian, He gives you the Holy Spirit. The Holy Spirit is the part of God that stays with a Christian at all times and helps them understand God's will. It's mentioned in verse nine of Ephesians 1. The Spirit also pricks our conscience when we go against God's will. And more than that, He is the power of God in a Christian. He gives us power to overcome the sin that tempts us. For all of those reasons, it says He, the Holy Spirit, is the guarantee of our inheritance."

"What inheritance?"

"The guarantee of heaven—to be fully in God's presence forever, with a new body that is free of defects and sin, because Satan and all evil will be bound and thrown into the pit of hell. There will be a new heaven and new earth that also have been cleansed of sin with its ravages and imperfections."

"That's a lot to take in. It sounds so *out there*."

"Maybe, but the Holy Spirit, as the guarantor of these things, gives Christians a taste of the things to come. Before I became a Christian, those things sounded *out there* to me, too. I couldn't imagine them being anything more than someone's overactive imagination. But since becoming a Christian, and even a few times before when God tried to get my attention, I've started to understand it. I can tell there's more going on than just the physical things we see and feel. I've been praying God would give you glimpses of that."

A lump rose up in Brooke's throat and she stared at Jacob. She had started to have a sense of exactly what he spoke of, and it scared her.

Jacob grabbed her hand, and Noah settled onto his lap. "You can pray and ask God to show Himself to you. I have no doubt He will honor your prayer. Can I pray for you?"

Brooke tried to speak, but her throat constricted, so she nodded.

Bowing his head, Jacob prayed, "God, I thank You for placing Brooke and Noah in my life. You know how much I long for her to be my sister in Christ. Reveal Yourself to her in a way that is meaningful to her. Help her to see You and believe. And for Noah, I pray he would believe at a young age and become a man of God. In Jesus' name. Amen."

After dinner, Brooke sat on a balcony lounger watching the waves crash. With Noah in Jacob's lap next to her, she felt complete and at peace. Jacob had connected his phone to the speakers, and the music switched from slow to upbeat. Noah climbed down and started a crazy toddler dance. He had surprisingly good rhythm. Jacob joined him and Brooke broke out in laughter at the pair. Jacob had some amazing moves himself—as she expected from someone who regularly worked with a dance choreographer. Observing him dance with Noah had her heart overflowing. Noah waved his mom over, and she giggled when the boys pulled her into the dance party.

Noah's arms flew up toward Jacob in the universal toddler sign for 'pick me up.' His demands didn't end there, and soon he called out to Brooke, wanting them all to dance together with himself smashed in between. As they swayed to the music, with Jacob's arms wrapped around them both, Brooke's heart fluttered. Her eyes found Jacob's, and she thought she saw her feelings reflected—like he wanted this—them—in his future. If her worries were misguided and what they had *was* leading to something more than friendship, she should stop holding back her feelings and questioning his.

"THANKS, JACOB, FOR READING TO NOAH." Brooke reached to take him from Jacob's lap. "Okay, Noah. It's time for your nap."

"Dada!" He clung to Jacob's neck.

Jacob chuckled. "I've got you, little man." He stood up and looked back at Brooke. "I'll take him. We still on for paddle boarding while he's down?" His mouth pulled into a grin that had Brooke melting. She nodded, smiling to herself as he walked off.

Almost as soon as Jacob left the room, Brooke felt a vibration by her thigh and looked down to see Jacob's phone. She couldn't help but notice the text on the screen.

MARI: Just landed. Can't wait to see you!

BROOKE'S HEART SANK. She was just beginning to have more confidence that they had something more than friendship. But maybe he didn't return Mari's interest. Leaving his phone in its spot on the coffee table, she rushed to the kitchen, distracting herself by cleaning up from lunch. From where she was, she saw Jacob return, pick up his phone, and read the text.

"Give me a few minutes to make a call, then we'll head out." Jacob waved the phone in the air before walking outside to the balcony.

It was hard to keep from watching him as he paced around the balcony. She was curious about his interaction with Mari. His face lit up at first as he spoke, then became serious. When he turned and looked toward the kitchen, she glanced away and focused on wiping the counters. Moments later, she heard laughter, and her eyes were drawn back to the handsome man standing on the balcony. His easy-going demeanor with Mari made her doubt everything she'd thought about his affections for herself. He seemed to be just as happy speaking to Mari as he was when he spoke to Brooke. Maybe happier. She wasn't as special as she thought. Why did relationships have to be so complicated? She found herself whispering in desperation, "God, can't You just make it clear to me? And if he's not the one, help me to turn off these feelings."

A FAKE SMILE had been plastered to Brooke's face for the last hour as she paddle boarded alongside Jacob. Ever since his phone call, he had been in a good mood—a great mood, actually, and the longer his good mood persisted, the worse Brooke felt. It was increasingly hard to cover up. This was supposed to be a fun time for her to be alone with Jacob, but she felt the presence of Mari, who she had never even met.

She wished she could go back to the way she was before— enjoying his company, but not expecting or hoping for it to become more than friendship. At this point, she was too far gone.

Minutes later, Jacob suggested they head back in and get ready to take Noah out to build a sandcastle. Once the paddle boards were stowed, Brooke trudged up to the house.

"What's wrong?" Jacob questioned, pausing at the door.

Brooke stared at him. "Huh?"

"You look worried. You've got that furrow between your brows." He touched the spot he was referring to. "You get that expression when something bothers you. Are you thinking about Tyler?"

"Um . . . I . . . maybe." She didn't want to lie, but she couldn't admit the truth.

He pulled her into a hug before sliding open the door and guiding her through. "I'm sorry. I know there's so much going on with you. I hoped this weekend would take your mind off of things."

"No, no! This has been wonderful! It really has. Thank you. Are you sure you don't want to go back tonight?" She felt guilty. He had spent so much money and gone to so much trouble to ease her burden. But now that Mari was home, he might wish he hadn't given up the whole weekend. He had surpassed what she would expect from a friend, and she didn't want to take advantage of that. She smiled, truly meaning it this time.

Shaking his head, Jacob responded, "You and Noah are enjoying yourselves, your boss gave you permission to return to work a couple of hours late tomorrow, and both Ben and Keith seem to like the change of pace. It's all good. We're staying."

"Okay." She nodded up at him. He never actually answered the question by saying he didn't want to go back early, but she wouldn't argue. His compassion for others once again trumped his personal desires.

THIRTY-TWO

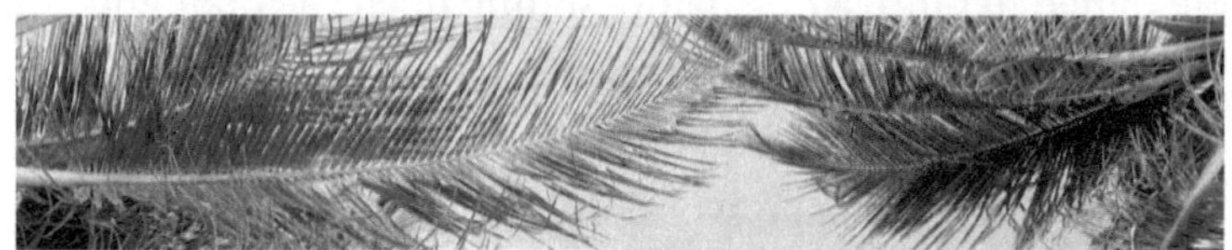

The ride away from the beach house on Monday morning was bittersweet. It had been a wonderful weekend in so many ways, but her brief hope that they could be more than friends was tempered with reality. Looking across the car at Jacob, she shoved down the feelings she'd let bubble to the surface.

"I think it turned out to be a great mini-break for all of us, wouldn't you say, Brooke?" Jacob asked.

Brooke nodded. "It really was a blessing. Thank you so much. And it was nice having the extra help with Noah, so I could have some free time." She smiled, thinking of her time in the soaking tub in her own private bathroom overlooking the ocean, and moments alone with Jacob. Things would probably change now with Mari back. She had seen his phone light up periodically with texts from her, and guessed that was who she saw him texting throughout the day.

When they parked in front of her office, she took a deep breath and turned to thank Jacob once more. Keith slipped out with a quick goodbye. Jacob nervously smiled at Brooke and leaned onto the center console. Brooke reached over and hugged him. He stiffened, then placed his arms around her, with one arm holding her head to his chest. It felt like time slowed, and she wished it would stop altogether on their moment.

"You're welcome. I hope you have a great day."

When his car finally pulled away, it took her heart with it.

"TELL ME EVERYTHING! How was the weekend? And by the way, I still can't believe what Tyler did," Elise said the minute Brooke walked into the office.

Brooke guided her friend to the bathroom, checked that the stalls were empty, and said, "I'll summarize. It was perfect, romantic, and relaxing. Then he got a text from Mari, called her, and it seemed like everything changed."

"What? I'll need more details than that! Don't leave me hanging."

"I need to get to work and so do you. I'll tell you more when I take a break. I already feel bad for starting two hours late, so I really should get upstairs."

"Okay, okay." Elise rolled her eyes. "I don't know which is worse —you saying nothing, or you teasing me with this."

Brooke forced a smile, but her heart wasn't in it.

"I WANT you and Noah to come over on Thursday afternoon to swim and have dinner. Everyone will be there," Jacob said softly as they walked away from Noah's room, once he was in bed later that evening.

"That sounds nice. Will Izzy be there?" She enjoyed Izzy's company, but remembering their last conversation also made her anxious.

Jacob nodded. "Yeah, and Mari will be there, too. I want you to meet her."

"Oh, okay." Brooke looked away and tried to steady herself. She'd been dreading hearing more about her from Izzy, but that would have been easy compared to seeing Mari with Jacob. Although, this would be her chance to see if there was really something between him and Mari, or if it was just her imagination running wild. A glimmer of hope remained that she had a chance with Jacob. Whatever Jacob said next got lost in the rush of thoughts working through her mind. Part of her wanted to avoid the dinner, but another part knew she should go.

WITH NOAH's nap and the Orlando traffic, they didn't get to Jacob's house until half past three on Thursday afternoon. Ethan answered the door and it sounded like the party was in full swing by the pool.

"Noah!" Ethan held up his hand for a high five, stepping back to let them in. "I got you," he said as he grabbed the diaper bag from Brooke's arm.

Keith spoke up defensively, "She wouldn't let me help her out with that."

"Well you're already carrying the travel playpen," Brooke explained.

Ethan smirked. "I think he could handle it, although I have to ask, what is in this thing? A block of lead?"

Chuckling, Brooke replied, "Don't you know? Every mom has to be like MacGyver and carry around a bunch of random stuff in case she needs to make a hot-air balloon or lie detector at a moment's notice!"

Ethan broke out into laughter. "What?"

"You know, that 80s show that was remade a few years ago, where MacGyver was a secret agent and whipped out random stuff like duct tape and gum to diffuse a bomb or build a hang glider?"

Ethan shook his head and peaked into the diaper bag. "That's awesome! You're too funny. I think I remember seeing it a couple of times." He waved his arm toward the backyard. "This way. Everyone's at the pool."

From where she stood, Brooke watched Jacob standing beside the pool, putting on a show. He was singing along with the music playing through the speakers and dancing as if onstage, performing for thousands. A beautiful woman with long, sleek, dark hair, who Brooke recognized as Mari, sat on the side of the pool, watching Jacob, before getting up to join him in a duet. Brandon and Izzy danced in the water, and Anthony, Ryan, and a guy she didn't recognize cheered them on.

Jacob's eyes found Brooke's and lit up. He continued singing while watching her. Mari turned toward Brooke with a look of surprise, her voice trailing off. Izzy jumped out of the water to greet them. By the time the song ended, all heads were turned in Brooke's direction. Noah had squirmed out of her arms and was running to Jacob, who had Mari by his side.

"Dada!"

Leaning down to grab Noah in a bear hug, Jacob grinned. "Hey, little man."

Mari's eyes went wide, in shock at Noah's name for Jacob.

Ryan piped up, "Looks like you've got more duties than we thought, *Daddy*." He broke out in laughter.

Brooke's face went red. This is what she was afraid of. "His real dad, who he rarely sees, tried to get Noah to call him that, but Noah had always called Jacob 'Da' since he couldn't make the 'j' sound. This week he suddenly took to calling Jacob 'Dada.'" She winced, wondering if it sounded as lame to the others as it did to her.

Grinning, Jacob squeezed Noah closer. "I don't mind."

"Maybe, but that's how rumors get started," Mari said coldly while narrowing her eyes at Brooke.

"It's fine," Jacob responded, then turned back to Brooke. "I'll put on his swimsuit. You go ahead and enjoy the pool."

"Uh-hm." Mari made a noise and wrapped an arm around Jacob's free one.

"Oh, sorry. This is Mari. I think I mentioned her to you." Jacob looked at Brooke.

Nodding, she held out her hand and forced a smile. "Nice to meet you, I'm Brooke."

"Yes, I've heard about you. The mother of the kid Jake goes on about." Mari tightly smiled back and shook Brooke's hand.

While the women assessed each other, Izzy came forward, tugging the arm of the man Brooke didn't recognize. "This is my brother, Martez."

Brooke appreciated Izzy's intervention that spared her from continuing the stare down with Mari. "Izzy mentioned you were a long-time friend of the guys. So glad to meet you." Martez grasped her hand firmly. He wasn't much taller than her, but looked like a professional bodybuilder.

"I'll be back in a minute," Jacob excused himself and pulled away from Mari.

"So what do you do, Martez?" Brooke asked as she sat on a lounger and slathered on sunscreen.

"I own a fitness center—Aptitude. You may have seen it at the intersection of Vineland and Conroy Road. It's just before you get to this neighborhood, next to the Screaming Peach Café."

Brooke thought for a moment about the buildings at that intersection. "Oh, yeah. It looks like a nice place. Huge, and it always seems packed." Brooke recalled passing the impressive building on her way to Jacob's home. Now she understood why he was so muscular. "You must be an amazing businessman to be so young and already have a successful business like that. Congratulations."

Martez grinned proudly. "It's been hard work, but I'm finally to the point where I've got reliable, well-trained staff and can get away some now. I started it five years ago. I got a lease on a run-down place where I had worked out since I was a teenager. The owner was ready to retire and hadn't put much effort into it in over a decade, so he sold me the equipment for next to nothing. With a small loan, I brought it into the twenty-first century, and it took off. I ended up leasing more space, then decided to build. Of course, it wouldn't be as big and nice as it is, if these guys—" He motioned to the band members. "Didn't help me out by investing in it. We've been in the new building for almost a year. You should check it out sometime. I'll give you a free day pass."

"Mommy! Ship! See?" Noah squealed in Jacob's arm. In Jacob's other arm, he held an inflatable circular child's float designed to look like a spaceship.

On closer examination, Brooke saw it had a water gun attached. "Nice! Did you thank Jacob?"

"Tank oo, Dada." Noah followed it with a kiss on Jacob's cheek and clapped his hands.

Jacob set him down, and Noah tugged at the spaceship to pull it towards the pool. "I think we're swimming now." Jacob grinned and followed Noah to the water's edge before jumping in.

"Me swim!" Noah stated as he jumped in and swam to Jacob, who was several feet from the edge.

"Good job, little man!" Jacob took him and placed him in the spaceship seat, and Noah was ecstatic.

"I can't believe he just did that!" Izzy exclaimed.

"He's been taking swimming lessons. With so much water everywhere here, I wanted him to know what to do if he fell in," Brooke replied.

"Definitely, keep it up," Anthony chimed in. "It's working."

For the next couple of hours, Noah became their entertainment, both in and out of the pool. Mari was a fixture beside Jacob. At first Brooke stayed close as well, since he usually had Noah, but after a while, it became too much. Brooke gravitated to Izzy, with Brandon usually nearby. Martez inserted himself into most of Brooke's conversations, and throughout the afternoon, he was attentive to Brooke. She couldn't decide if he was just trying to ease the ever-present tension with Mari, or if he was flirting with her.

Either way, Brooke's eyes continually drifted to Jacob. Letting go of her hope for a future with him hurt. But the more she saw of his familiarity with Mari, the more it seemed likely there *was* something between them. For Mari's part, there was no question. It was more difficult to tell how Jacob felt. He seemed happy, but that wasn't unusual when he played with Noah. A few times, Jacob looked in Brooke's direction with concern, but someone, usually Mari, always distracted him before anything was said or done.

For dinner, Martez and Izzy had prepared a number of Cuban dishes requiring some last minute preparation. Brooke offered to help with the food, hoping to pick up some new recipe ideas. Three crock pots kept the dishes warm throughout the afternoon. One had rice, another contained Cuban black beans, and the largest held the main dish of ropa vieja.

"Ropa vieja is a traditional Cuban dish that literally means 'old clothes.' It's shredded beef in a tomato-based sauce with bell peppers, onion, and garlic," Izzy said as she reached for the dish.

"Smells delicious," Brooke said after Izzy lifted the lid, allowing the aroma to fill the kitchen. Brooke was busy arranging pastelitos de carne—meat pies—on a baking pan.

Meanwhile, Martez connected his phone to the wireless speakers and played Cuban music in the background while he sautéed plantains on the stove and swayed to the music. As he finished, Izzy wrapped them in bacon and placed them on another baking sheet. Brandon and Ryan set the dining room table, and the others were in the sitting area adjacent to the kitchen, entertaining Noah.

Once everything was in the oven, Martez reached for Brooke's hand and pulled her into his arms to dance. "Do you know how to salsa?"

"I've seen it, but never tried." Brooke's face reddened.

"Follow me," Martez urged. He placed one of her hands on his shoulder and grasped her other before stepping backwards and pulling her with him.

Izzy dragged Brandon into the kitchen and they joined the fun.

Brooke found herself laughing at her lack of salsa abilities. She looked up at Martez and then over at Izzy. They were both naturals. "I can't even begin to make my hips do what yours are doing," she chuckled to Martez and tried her best. "Guys aren't supposed to be able to do that with their hips. I'm envious."

Martez grinned as he continued to pull her along with him. "We grew up dancing. My family will make just about anything into a reason to celebrate. More often than not, we found our home crowded with people, food, and dancing in the evenings growing up."

"Mommy dance!" Noah called from the sitting room, drawing Brooke's attention to his own dance moves.

"Good job, baby!" Brooke chuckled, but her laughter faded when she noticed Mari and Jacob dancing next to him. Turning back to Martez, she tried focusing on what he was teaching her, though her thoughts were distracted.

The oven timer beeped and Izzy pulled the Cuban delicacies out.

"Smells delicious!" Ryan called and went to reach for the food that was sitting out to cool. Izzy swatted his arm. "Hey, I just want to sample one of these meat pies and make sure they're done." He laughed and grabbed one before darting out of the way and blowing on it. "Mmm. 'It is very gooood. You vill like it.'"

"The guy with the mustache in Oslo!" Mari and Jacob shouted in unison, then broke out in laughter. They joined the group at the island and Jacob settled onto a stool with Noah. Mari leaned into him and placed an arm around his neck.

Everyone seemed to understand the joke, leaving Brooke feeling out of place. With Jacob holding Noah in his lap, Brooke wasn't sure where to look.

"There was a waiter in Oslo—" Jacob offered.

"And whenever we tried to ask what a dish was like, he always said, 'It is very gooood. You vill like it.'" Mari finished his sentence, grinning, with a hand massaging Jacob's shoulder.

Dinner was casual around their dining room table. Brooke sat on one side of Noah, with Jacob on the other and Mari on his left. Everyone made her feel welcome and Brooke felt comfortable with them all—except Mari.

Dessert of dulce de leche cheesecake and flan followed the delicious dinner, then the group moved to the sitting room. Brooke found herself next to Martez on a sofa. Jacob sat in a chair with Noah on his lap. Unfortunately, Mari made herself at home on the arm of his chair.

After they'd been sitting around chatting for nearly thirty minutes, Noah yawned. Brooke decided that was her out. She broke off the conversation she'd been having with Izzy. "We should probably head out. It's getting close to Noah's bedtime."

"I picked up a new book for him. Let me grab it, and I'll read him his bedtime story in the living room where it's quiet," Jacob offered. Brooke nodded, knowing Noah would protest if she didn't let him. "Noah, say goodnight to everybody."

Noah blew kisses to all of his new admirers. "Nigh nigh!"

"Come join us," Jacob held his hand out toward Brooke.

"Um—" Brooke looked around the room. "I'll just stay and chat with everyone. I'll meet you there in a few minutes to get him." Sitting with him while he read to Noah was too intimate, and she needed to pull away from him.

Jacob nodded. "I'll message Keith and have him load up the car so he'll be ready to drive you home."

"Keith? That's *your* bodyguard. Why would he drive them home?" Mari questioned Jacob.

Shrugging, Jacob replied, "There were some concerns, so I've had Keith with Brooke."

Mari made a face. "That's why you got the new guy, Ryder? Seems a bit extreme. Keith was used to your routine."

"Don't worry about it." For a moment, Jacob seemed bothered, but then smiled and left the room with Noah.

Brooke finished the conversation she'd been having with Izzy before saying her goodnights, ignoring Mari's glare. With each step toward the living room, she was more anxious to leave and more angry at Jacob, but the sight on the sofa stopped her in her tracks. Jacob was praying, and Noah sat beside him with his eyes closed and hands together, attempting to repeat the words each time Jacob paused. How could she be mad at Jacob? The fists at her side relaxed as the anger turned to sadness and tears threatened to spill.

After the "Amen," Jacob opened his eyes and noticed Brooke. Smiling, he patted the empty spot next to him. Part of her wanted nothing more than to join him—to sit close by and feel his warmth. But she had to start protecting her heart, so she shook her head.

"Noah, it's time to go home." Brooke dared not step too close with moisture still filling her eyes.

Noah looked at her and leaned further into Jacob, grabbing his neck. "Dada."

"Come on, baby, don't give Mommy a hard time." Brooke's voice wavered.

Keith entered the room. "Everything is loaded."

While Jacob was focused on Keith, Brooke dabbed the edge of her eyes.

"Thanks, man." Jacob nodded in his direction, then stood and turned to Brooke. "How about I buckle him in?" Brooke could only nod and give a small smile before turning to the door.

"Alright, little man. It's time to go home," he said as he opened the car door. "You know Mommy is right, and I'll see you later. Don't worry." He buckled Noah in. "Goodnight, Noah. Be good for Mommy."

Noah grabbed at Jacob's arm as he pulled away. "Wuv you, Dada."

"Love you, too, Noah." Jacob patted his head, then turned to Brooke as he shut the door. "I'll talk with you in the morning, unless you want to call me tonight?"

Brooke shook her head and hurried into the car, without much more than a glance at Jacob. Anything more would break the dam.

Her heart had nearly fractured when she heard Noah tell Jacob he loved him.

"Are you okay?" Jacob questioned with a hand on her door, stopping her from closing it.

"Fine," Brooke barely choked out, not looking up.

"I can see you're not, but we'll talk later." He leaned down and looked over at Keith. "Get them home safely, and text me once they're home." Jacob hesitated, then sighed before shutting the door.

Keeping her face turned toward the window as they pulled out, tears burst forth. Brooke was thankful Keith didn't ask, and instead, turned the radio on. The volume was down, but it was enough to cover her occasional sniffs. Her head fell to the glass. The thought of pulling away from Jacob tore at her heart, especially when she considered Noah.

Her mind drifted to her mom. What she would give to be able to fall into her mother's arms and let out all of her worries and pain.

THIRTY-THREE

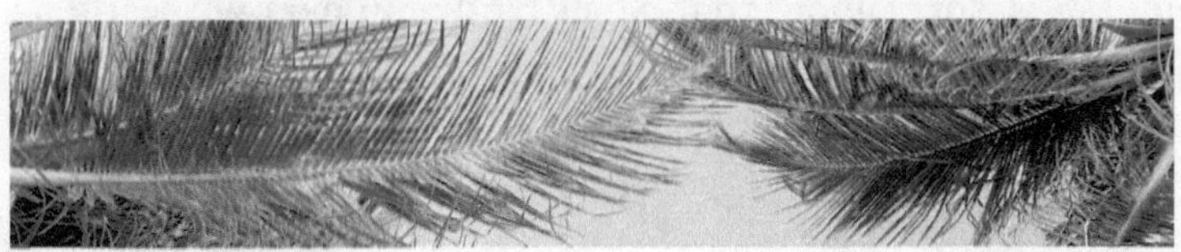

Brooke anxiously packed the diaper bag for their park play day. She was getting ready early, since she knew Jacob planned to call her before they went. Was she ready to talk to him? Thankfully, the night before, her grandmother had been there for her with open arms and no questions asked. How would she have put into words all she felt, knowing that Grams was best friends with Jacob's Nan? Talking to Elise later for nearly two hours helped, too. At least with Elise, she could openly talk about her issues with Jacob.

"I've got to run. Love you, dear. Hopefully this time out will cheer you up," Grams said with a hug to Brooke and Noah as she left to work at her church food pantry.

"Thanks. Love you, too." Brooke pasted on a smile. That smile disappeared almost immediately once the door was shut and her phone rang. Jacob's name filled the screen, and her stomach clenched.

Noah was pushing a toy around the family room, but stopped at the sound of her phone. "Dada?" He grinned when he recognized Jacob's ringtone.

His excitement and familiarity over Jacob felt like a punch to the gut. She knew what she had to do, but it would be like cutting off one of her own appendages. "You play, Noah." She swiped the screen. "Hey."

They went through the initial pleasantries before Jacob broached the subject of what had her upset the night before. "So what was going on last night?" He paused. "Was Mari making you feel unwelcome? I'm so sorry about that. She's kind of in her own world a lot of the time."

"It's . . ." *Yes, she totally was.* "That's not really the problem . . ." *But Mari's the root of it.* "It's just, I think maybe you don't need to spend so much time with Noah."

"What? Why would you say that? Have I done something wrong?"

"No." *That's part of the problem—you're actually too perfect, and it's breaking me.* "He's getting so used to having you around." This was the reason she and Elise decided would sound best. She could avoid touching on her own feelings for him and embarrassment over them, since he clearly didn't feel the same way.

"I mean, last night was a prime example. He didn't want to leave you, and it's only going to get worse. You're leaving again in a couple of weeks for your two-month tour. How's he going to handle that? I feel like I'm setting him up for disappointment, and it's not fair to him in the long run. It's bad enough that his own dad doesn't want to spend time with him unless it benefits him. He doesn't need another man who's unpredictable in his life." That part really was true and is what made this decision necessary.

"But I . . . Brooke, please, what are you saying? I promise I'll do everything in my power to be there for him. We made it work when I went overseas for a month. This time we'll mostly be in North America. I'll fly you guys out to me a few times, and fly back when I can. We can get through this."

There is no we, she wanted to say. If he hadn't made a commitment to her by now, he obviously only considered her as a friend. She shook her head, even though he couldn't see it, and held back tears. "I really think it would be better to reduce how often he interacts with you." She barely brought herself to say the words, but knew it was best.

"I . . . wow. Are you worried that my fame will affect his life negatively? Worried about him being seen with me, and you guys being hounded? Because we can be more careful."

Brooke held the phone away and tried to calm herself enough to speak. "No, that's not why. Look, I've got to finish getting ready for the park. Bye." She hung up before he could respond, and tears fell as she laid her phone down. "Oh, God! What have I done?" She softly cried, trying to keep from upsetting Noah.

Her phone rang with Jacob's ringtone and she sent it to voicemail. Minutes later she received a text, but didn't bother to look, and instead silenced her phone. She decided it was best to leave for the park, even though they would be there before the rest of the group. She needed a distraction. After messaging Keith, she gathered their things, and by the time she loaded Noah into the car, Keith was there. She would have to talk to Jacob about Keith. She didn't feel right about using his services anymore.

As expected, they were the first ones at the park, so she took Noah for a walk in his stroller. She stopped in view of a sandhill crane, knowing how excited he would get when he saw it. Her phone felt like an albatross in her pocket, and knowing she would check it eventually, now was as good a time as any.

There were five texts and a missed call from Jacob.

JACOB: Why won't you answer? Please don't shut me out.

JACOB: Can we just finish our conversation? You don't have to be at the play day for a while and even if you're late, it's not a big deal. Please stop avoiding me.

· · ·

JACOB: I thought this was for Noah's sake, but it's feeling like you have a problem with me. Please talk to me about it. We can work through it.

JACOB: Hello?

JACOB: Ok. Fine. Call me when you're ready to talk. I won't bother you anymore.

EACH TEXT WAS like a knife twisting in her chest, but the last one hurt the worst. She didn't dare listen to the message he'd left, for fear she would give in and call him. Wiping tears from her face, she pushed on. Surely, it would get easier.

~

BY LUNCH ON MONDAY, Brooke felt like an addict trying to quit cold turkey. She hadn't slept well in the four nights since the dinner at Jacob's house. Her boss even commented that she didn't look well.

"What's going on, girly?" Elise approached her with concern. "You don't look like yourself. Are you sure this no communication thing with Jacob is the best idea?"

Brooke's hand ran over her face. "I don't know why I let it get this far with Jacob. I miss him terribly, and so does Noah. And we have no right to. At least I understand my reasons for doing this, but Noah is hurt and doesn't. Friday and Saturday nights when it was time for his bedtime story, he asked for "Dada." It killed me, but we got through it. The worst, though, was last night . . . when I told him Jacob couldn't read to him, he started crying these sad, silent tears, and pushed the book away. He wouldn't let me read to him and went to sleep crying. It broke my heart. I don't know if I can keep this up, but I'm afraid if I give in, it will prolong the inevitable."

"I'm so sorry." Elise wrapped an arm around her shaking friend.

After talking with Elise all through lunch, Brooke still had no idea what to do next about Jacob. Walking back to her desk, she saw Keith and was reminded that she had to let Jacob know she didn't need him anymore. She smiled hesitantly at Keith, wondering if he knew what was going on with her and Jacob. The vibration from her phone pulled Brooke out of her thoughts, and when she noticed it was Jacob, her chest tightened.

JACOB: I've left your tickets and backstage passes for Friday with Grams. She was surprised I haven't been around. You didn't tell her what's going on? Anyway, guess I'll see you there.

BROOKE'S PALM went to her forehead. She'd completely forgotten about the live concert he had invited her and her friends to on Friday. Elise hadn't mentioned it, but surely she had been dying to ask if it was still happening. When Elise first found out, she'd been ecstatic. Thankfully, he followed through, even though Brooke had been ignoring him.

If she didn't text him before starting back to work, she would never be able to focus, but words eluded her.

BROOKE: Thanks so much.

SHE COULD SAY that at least. But she also wanted to say something about Keith.

. . .

Brooke: Thank you for your kind provision of Keith, but Mari was right. He is your bodyguard, and anyway, I really don't need his services anymore.

After hitting send, she second-guessed if she should have mentioned Mari. Did that sound catty? Too late now.

Jacob: Not happening. He stays with you.

"He's got to be kidding," she mumbled.

Brooke: Why?

No response. She shrugged. "I guess he can play the 'ignore texts' game, too." Only it didn't feel like a game.

THIRTY-FOUR

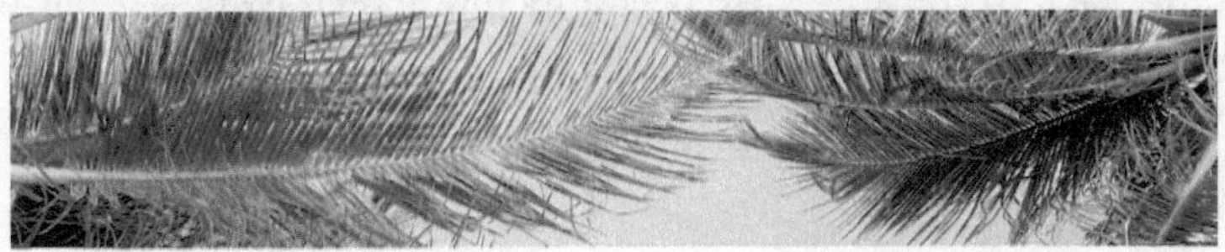

Eight days. One hundred and ninety-two hours. That's how long it had been since Brooke last saw Jacob. About twelve hours fewer since she heard his voice, the same voice now crooning out of the speakers at the concert venue. She swallowed, choking back sadness, pain, and emotions she couldn't name. It was the voice that filled her dreams. The lights were out for the first few words of the song, but from her front-row seat, she could make out his shadow—that shape she knew so well. The roars of the crowd faded as the pounding of her heart and the onslaught of her thoughts overpowered her senses, drowning out everything but him. The sensible side of her said she should never have come—this would set her back immeasurably. But her heart longed for one more night in his presence.

Bright lights flashed, leaving everyone momentarily blinded. Yet Jacob's eyes found hers and held them captive, as if he was communicating something, but she couldn't make it out. Sadness and disappointment swirled on his face. She hoped her eyes didn't reveal the longing she felt—exposing her soul, holding it out on a platter for him to consume. She was too transfixed to know.

Eventually, his gaze moved from hers and the spell was broken. The surrounding chaos resurfaced in her awareness. She looked behind her and saw screaming fans. Girls reaching out toward the band, and guys not quite as enthusiastic as their dates.

A hand touching her arm drew her attention from the stage. When she turned, Elise mouthed, *"You okay?"*

Was she? Brooke shrugged and pressed her lips together before turning back to the stage. He was only a few feet away, yet felt more distant than ever.

"How are you tonight, Orlando?" Jacob yelled after the first song ended.

The audience replied with a roar.

"It's good to be home. We missed you guys!" Ryan shouted into his microphone.

More screaming.

Jacob's dancing brought images of their time at the beach to the surface, and tears threatened to escape. Her heart rate sped up, and beads of moisture rose on her forehead.

Periodically during the concert, he looked at her. Several times, he came to the front of the stage and reached out to touch the hands of fangirls begging for attention. Brooke refused to go near.

When Jacob sang the song "Can't Explain," his eyes once again found Brooke's. It had a slower melody, reminding her of their song "Searching." As he pressed on with words detailing a love beyond explanation, Brooke tensed up. Was there still a chance he felt more than friendship for her? Was it her imagination that he spent most of the song gazing her way? Had she misjudged the situation with Mari?

"Oh my gosh!" a girl from behind squealed to her friend. "Jake keeps looking at you!"

"You've got to help me get closer when he leans down to shake hands!" the other girl responded.

Looking back, Brooke saw two girls who looked like high schoolers—one blonde, and the other brunette. She forced a smile, and the brunette spoke up, "Isn't she so lucky! Jake has been watching her all night!"

Brooke smiled again and turned around. Now she knew it wasn't her imagination that he kept looking in her direction. He certainly wasn't looking at the high schooler.

"We have a special surprise for you tonight! A guest singer is joining us for a couple of songs, and if you follow our music, you probably know who it is—" Screaming interrupted Jacob. "She toured with us last summer and joined us at two of our European stops last month. Welcome . . . Mari Stephens!"

Jacob held his arm out as Mari strutted onto the stage and gave him a hug. Arms still entangled, they turned to the crowd and belted out the first few notes of a duet. Sighs and screams ensued as they sang.

Brooke's heart sank and she moved toward her seat, but Elise wrapped an arm around her, holding her steady, and shook her head. Brooke was not prepared for this. She expected to see Mari at the after-party, but never dreamed she would have to watch her perform with Jacob. Mari danced around and interacted with all the band members, but most of her attention was on Jacob. When they began singing their next song, Brooke recognized it as "Love You Right Now" and cringed. Another stab to her heart.

As they continued performing together, Mari moved closer to Jacob and wrapped an arm around his shoulder, singing the final words of the song directly to him. After the harmony of their last note trailed off, she slammed her lips onto his.

Brooke froze and Elise grabbed her hand, squeezing tight. If it weren't for Matt and the rest of the *Madness* band, who were all anxious to meet *Nine Days In*, she would have left right then. She knew she should stay to make the introductions that they wouldn't have otherwise.

Their group hung back while the crowd exited, and Elise pulled Brooke aside. "Are you going to be okay? Would you rather me go home with you and leave the others?"

Without hesitation, Brooke shook her head. She had made up her mind. "No. I'm pushing through. I need to do this." She looked to the side and saw Matt watching.

He gave her a wink and walked over, placing his arm over her shoulder. "Thanks for sharing this with us."

ENTERING THE AFTER-PARTY, Brooke scanned the room. The vibe was relaxed and soft chatter filled the area. Brandon, Izzy, and Ethan were talking to two men, but she didn't see Mari, Jacob, or the rest of the band. A table with drinks and food sat off to the side.

Brooke ushered her friends over to begin introductions and Brandon looked up. "Hey! I'm glad you made it! When you weren't at the pre-concert meet-and-greet, I wondered if you were coming."

"I figured it would mostly be a bunch of fangirls fawning over you guys, with no real chance to talk, and decided to skip it," Brooke said and Brandon nodded in understanding. "I've brought some friends of mine I want to introduce you to. This is my good friend, Elise, from work, and my other friends who are all part of a local band called *Madness*. Matt's the lead singer, Ryan plays bass guitar, Maddie's on the keyboard and does backup, Liam does guitar and backup, and this is Brad, who plays drums." She pointed to each of them as she said their name.

Brandon and Ethan introduced the other two men as their manager and booking agent.

Ryan entered from a hallway and two women instantly flanked him. Moments later, Anthony and Mari walked in and joined the group. They were wrapped up in introductions when Brooke looked up and saw Jacob watching her. He was casually leaning against the wall at the entrance—one foot crossed over the other—with that tough, yet mysterious, James Dean look that had originally attracted her. His intense gaze unnerved her, and she wondered how long he'd been watching her. When he pulled away from the wall and walked in her direction, a million thoughts flitted through her mind.

Only a few feet away, Mari stopped him. "Jake, babe, we did it!" She threw her arms around his neck and placed a kiss on his cheek.

Trying to regulate her breathing, Brooke clenched her fists and looked away, only to catch Izzy giving her an apologetic look.

Matt walked over and wrapped an arm around Brooke's waist, then whispered in her ear, "She's got nothing on you. I've got your back. Play along."

When Brooke turned, she read sincerity in Matt's eyes and gave him a weak smile, knowing she was in for another long, heart-breaking night. All she had to do was paste on a smile and not ruin it for her friends.

"Jake Reeves." Jacob's voice broke through her thoughts as he held out his hand and introduced himself to Matt.

Matt kept his arm around Brooke as he replied.

Jacob's eyes bounced between them. "It's . . . good to see you, Brooke. How's Noah?"

"He's fine." Brooke wouldn't admit what a hard time Noah had been having.

Jacob glanced at Matt before running his fingers through his hair. "Brooke, can I speak with you alone for a minute?"

Her eyebrows rose. "I guess." She looked at Matt with worry, and he squeezed her shoulder. "Excuse me."

It felt strange to be near Jacob, yet feel so emotionally distanced from him. She watched him warily as he guided her to a corner. His touch on her back shot electricity through her body.

"Look, I don't understand what happened. You asked me to stop seeing Noah for a bit, and I've waited for you to tell me when I could see him, but you've not contacted me. I still want to be part of his life." His voice was shaky, and he rubbed the back of his neck. Pain flashed in his eyes. "I can make sure to avoid you, if that's what's bothering you. Please don't make him suffer, because you don't feel comfortable around me."

Brooke's breath caught in her chest. Was she that obvious? Maybe he was right. Noah really missed him. Her eyes drifted to Mari—who was watching them—and she knew she couldn't give in. She had to think long term. Right now, Jacob wanted to be there for Noah, but one day, maybe soon, he would have his own children and Noah would fall down in priority. By that time, Noah would be even more attached. No. She wouldn't let that happen.

"No," she said out loud. "That won't work. I—" She mistakenly looked at him and saw the pain in his eyes. Swallowing, she choked out her next words in a whisper. "I'm sorry." She turned and raced off to find a bathroom.

THIRTY-FIVE

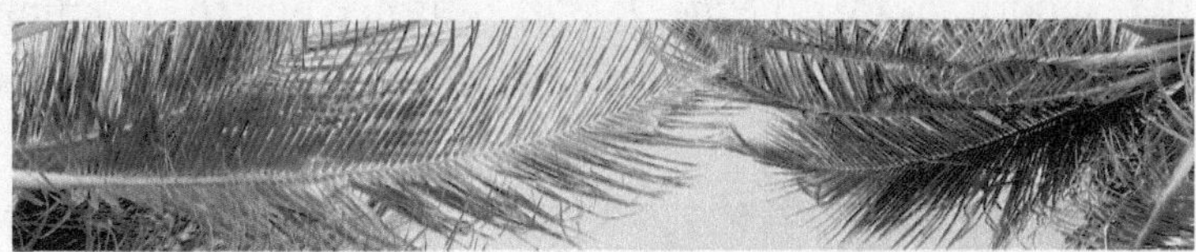

The slam of a door startled Brooke awake. "Where is she? She hasn't left yet, has she?" came Matt's voice from Elise's living room, followed by Elise's muffled response.

Curiosity pulled Brooke from bed and she noticed it was 11:15 a.m. At least after the restless night, she finally got some sleep. Searching for her bra, she slipped it on and shuffled out in her pj's. Eyeing Matt and Elise from the doorway, she grimaced.

"Are you okay?" questioned Matt.

Brooke nodded and pointed to her face. "Don't you see my smile?" She tried again.

Matt smirked. "Nope, that's not a smile. Looks more like you just ate something bad."

She shrugged. "It was supposed to be a smile. What's up?"

"So, I just got a call from *Nine Days In's* booking agent, Kurt. He listened to the music on our website and wants the band to audition for him later today. Thank you for giving me that chance last night to meet him! I know it wasn't easy for you, but I want you to know that even if nothing comes from this, your sacrifice did not go unnoticed." Matt swept Brooke into a hug and twirled her around.

When he released her, she giggled and covered her mouth. "Sorry, morning breath."

THE NEXT TWO weeks were a flurry of excitement. Not only did *Madness* impress the record producer, but they were asked to go on the two-month tour with *Nine Days In*. It turned out, the opening act had to be let go when their lead singer got arrested for drug possession. *Madness* was ecstatic.

Elise and Brooke both showed up to send their friends off on the tour. Things were awkward between Brooke and Jacob. They watched each other from a distance, but just before *Nine Days In* loaded their tour bus, Brooke walked over to say her final goodbyes, and Jacob reached out to shake her hand. He grasped it and held her captive with a piercing look, but she couldn't get out a word. When Brandon strolled up and cleared his throat, Jacob shook his head, released her hand, and headed to the tour bus.

Stunned and speechless, she felt an arm wrap around her waist. She turned to find Matt waiting with open arms. "I know he still wants me to let him talk with Noah," Brooke whispered. "But I just can't do it."

"It's okay. Noah's young and will snap back." Matt ran his fingers through her hair. "You're strong, and it might be hard, but standing firm and getting through this will make you stronger."

WITH JACOB OUT of the picture, Brooke began meeting with Sabrina, the pastor's wife, for Bible study and prayer. Sabrina encouraged her to view this as a time for growth, making her relationship with God her own, and leaning into Him for her fulfillment in life. She taught her that once we see God not just as a source for fulfilling our needs and desires, but as the treasure Himself, we find more satisfaction in the life we have. They continued through a study of Romans, since she had started that with Jacob and wanted to finish. She found that her relationships with other women at the church grew as well.

At home, she developed new routines. Ones that didn't include Jacob, and it was almost as if he had never been involved in their lives. Almost. Well . . . maybe only outwardly. Inside, it felt like she had part of her heart removed—not that there was much left after her mom's death. Occasionally, Noah came across a toy or book Jacob had given him, and he cried those sad, silent tears he'd cried in the beginning. Brooke tried hiding them all, but Jacob had been very generous and they turned up everywhere. It pained her to put them away, but she and Noah had to move past this. Then there was the ever-present Keith—a constant reminder of Jacob.

Yet, in spite of her tumultuous feelings, she found herself looking forward to her morning times with God in prayer and reading the Bible. She now had a real relationship with Him and wasn't going through the motions of religion like she had in the beginning. It no longer seemed she was on the outside looking in at what someone else had. She wanted, even needed, that time with God.

"I'M READY!" Brooke raced into the prayer room at church, where she met Sabrina for their time together.

"Ready for what?" Sabrina smiled a knowing smile.

"To become a Christian! What do I do?"

"You already know." Sabrina's reply was met with Brooke's confusion. "Remember the Scripture I had you memorize? Romans 10:9-10?" She smiled.

Brooke thought for a moment, then her eyes lit up. "If you confess with your mouth that Jesus is Lord and believe in your heart that God raised Him from the dead, you will be saved. For with the heart one believes and is justified, and with the mouth one confesses and is saved." She looked skeptically at Sabrina. "Really? It's that easy?"

Sabrina nodded. "It really is. Of course, that implies a real commitment to God in your heart. God knows the truth. But to be honest, as you mature in your faith, your understanding of what *Christ is Lord* means will grow. This is just the beginning. If you truly believe, it will change your whole life . . . how you view your circumstances, goals, and desires. You'll want to put Him before all other things or people, but you'll find your relationship with Him will give you more to pour into the lives of others. As a Christian, it's important to keep studying the Bible daily, and praying, just like you've been doing. You're also a missionary now."

Brooke looked at her with confusion again. "What?"

Sabrina explained, while flipping through her Bible, "Just before Jesus ascended to heaven for good, after rising from the dead, He made it clear to His disciples what He wanted them to do, and all Christians are His disciples. Look at this." She pointed to her Bible.

Brooke read, "Matthew 28:19-20. Go therefore and make disciples of all nations, baptizing them in the name of the Father and of the Son and of the Holy Spirit, teaching them to observe all that I have commanded you. And behold, I am with you always, to the end of the age."

"Good, now look at this." Sabrina flipped the pages again.

"Acts 1:8. But you will receive power when the Holy Spirit has come upon you, and you will be My witnesses in Jerusalem and in all Judea and Samaria, and to the end of the earth." Brooke's brow furrowed. "I need to go to these places? Jerusalem and the others?"

Chuckling, Sabrina shook her head. "They are representative. Jerusalem was the home of the people Jesus was speaking to, Judea was the region Jerusalem was in, Samaria was the region north of Judea, and then He basically says everywhere. Remember, too, that the church is referred to as a body, where each part has its own importance and job." Brooke nodded at Sabrina's words, remembering when she had first learned that. "It's not everyone's job to go to every place. You have to follow God's lead. He'll show you. Even the disciples who heard those words directly from Jesus did that. Some stayed, and some went."

"Okay. I'm ready to say 'the prayer.'"

"'The prayer' is not going to change you. God already has. Just be aware of that. We can and will pray, though, so you have a specific point in mind to mark when you became a Christian. Then, let's get you set up to be baptized this Sunday."

Brooke threw her arms around Sabrina. "Thank you so much for walking me through all of this. I love my Grams, and I know she could lead me with all this spiritual stuff, but the issue with Jacob would have come up, too. And I don't want to lay that burden on her with her being so close to his Nan."

"I understand. One day, maybe you'll be ready to share it with her."

LATER THAT NIGHT, after a long joyful conversation with Grams, Brooke settled into bed, feeling at peace for the first time in weeks. She knew what she had to do, and she grabbed her phone. Shaky fingers hovered over the keys.

BROOKE: I became a Christian today! Thank you for all you did to teach me and point me to God. I get it now! Jesus is my Lord and Savior. I hope things are going well for you on the tour.

THERE. She did it. She really did get it now. Jacob was trying to be a witness to her, just like Sabrina had explained. She had misconstrued his attempts at witnessing to her, combined with his striving to be a positive male figure for Noah, as romantic interest. It still hurt a little—actually, a lot, yet he was a good guy.

She felt stronger now, somehow. She knew God had a plan for her and she would take it one day at a time. Matt kept in touch with her and shared some about the tour, but he avoided the topic of Jacob. She also purposely kept from following the media, though she prayed for Jacob and the tour. She could finally think about him without feeling as heartbroken as she would have a few weeks earlier.

JACOB: I'm so happy for you! Praise God! I have been praying this for you constantly! Things are good here. Matt and his band are doing a great job and seem to be getting lots of media attention. Thanks for letting me know about your good news!

BROOKE STARED AT THE TEXT, deciding how to respond, when another text came through.

JACOB: I would encourage you to find a woman who has been a Christian for a while to mentor you in your faith.

BROOKE: I've been meeting with my pastor's wife. She's been a great encouragement and help.

SHE HADN'T WANTED to mention Sabrina before, so as not to lessen the part that he played in her becoming a Christian, but since he brought it up, it seemed appropriate. So much more came to mind that she could share, but she held back. It was enough that he'd responded. It was best to keep their communication brief. And spending more time with her Bible before bed would help, too.

THIRTY-SIX

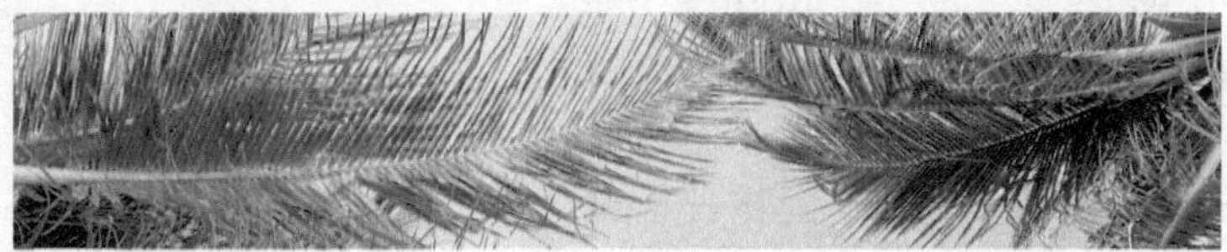

Walking through the grass on a warm June afternoon, Brooke smiled as she listened to Noah's giggles. He ran ahead with Chloe, the sixteen-year-old granddaughter of her grandmother's longtime friend, Mrs. Bronson. The two ladies were watching from the back porch while she and Chloe took Noah to feed the cows in the field just behind the enclosed yard.

She had been here numerous times when she was younger and recalled her amazement at this—and all the other cattle ranches—in Kissimmee. When she was younger, Mr. Bronson regaled her with many stories about his childhood days of driving the cows through open fields for miles—back before the Florida fencing law of 1949. Before then, the cattle roamed free. He even had stories of traffic halting because of cattle asleep on the roads. Of course, that was years before his dad sold land to Disney, resulting in the exponential increase to the central Florida population. Brooke shook her head, wondering what Mr. Bronson's father would have thought if he had realized the huge impact Disney would have on central Florida.

Mrs. Bronson called them back to the house for her homemade chocolate chip cookies and freshly squeezed lemonade, with lemons from their own tree. When Mr. Bronson walked out and kissed his wife on the cheek, Brooke's hand instinctively went to the new necklace Jacob sent to commemorate her becoming a Christian. There were other items in the package with it—a plaque with Scripture and a journal—but this was something she could take with her everywhere as a reminder of him, dangerous though it was. It had three silver rings, each with a word engraved—faith, hope, love. They were suspended from a black cord. He had written a note saying they represented 1 Corinthians 13:13. "So now faith, hope, and love abide, these three; but the greatest of these is love." The verse came at the end of a whole chapter on love. Her chest tightened at the thought.

How things had changed over the last month, and after a week and a half of being a Christian, she could truly say she was happier and more content. Yet something inside her would always long for what she briefly had . . . or believed she had with Jacob. Even though there were never romantic feelings on his part, it had felt real to her.

Hope bloomed in her heart as she pondered a possible hidden meaning behind Jacob's mention of the love verse. She recalled how, hours after receiving the package, she met with Sabrina.

Sabrina explained that love is paramount to God and cited Mark chapter twelve, where Jesus is answering one of the scribes' questions asking which commandment is most important. In verses 30-31, Jesus says, "'And you shall love the Lord your God with all your heart and with all your soul and with all your mind and with all your strength.' The second is this: 'You shall love your neighbor as yourself.' There is no other commandment greater than these."

Loving God is the most important thing. Jesus said it. Something in Brooke had still clung to the hope that he felt something more, but now she realized that love was just a common and significant theme throughout the Bible. That day, she'd prayed God would take the desire for Jacob from her. The desire wasn't gone yet, but she would keep praying.

"Okay, so what's it like there? Flip the screen and give us a tour!" Elise urged Matt. This was the fourth time they had video chatted with him, while he and the rest of *Madness* were backstage for one of their concerts. They had seen backstage in Jacksonville, Charleston, Atlanta, and now Charlotte. "I don't know. They're all starting to look the same. I think I prefer the outdoor video tours you give." She chuckled.

"How did your sound check go?" Brooke threw in.

"It was good! We're getting the hang of it. I'm looking forward—"

Brad grabbed the phone. "Elise! Brooke! I miss you guys!"

Elise was sure to monopolize the phone for a few minutes once Brad was on, but soon the other members of *Madness*, and even some of *Nine Days In*, were jumping in on the conversation. Matt quickly reminded them that this was his conversation with Brooke and they were horning in. About that time, Jacob strolled by, glanced at the phone, and walked on. It hurt Brooke more than she imagined it would.

Matt noticed Brooke's pained expression and commented, "Just so you know, Mari isn't touring with us. I think she's planning on joining for a couple of shows, but that's all."

"Thanks, but it doesn't matter." Brooke said the words, but didn't know if she believed them herself.

"Okay. Well, we still want you guys to come out to one of our concerts on the tour, and I'll make sure it's one she's not at."

Brooke nodded and gave a small smile. "You're a great friend, Matt. I don't deserve you."

"Friend. Ouch." He pounded his heart.

"Maaatt," Brooke drawled out, unsure of what to say. She truly did appreciate his friendship.

"What? A man can dream."

"You know, I think you're great and really attractive, but you're a good friend. Let's not ruin that."

"I know, I know. I'll just hold on to those first two thoughts." He winked at her, then his face changed. "Well, I wanted to talk to you before things got crazy around here. I love you." He winked again.

Brooke's mouth fell open, then she saw Jacob in the background and understood. She rolled her eyes. "Love you, too," then mouthed, *"friend."*

"I'll talk to you later. Bye." Matt grinned and blew her a kiss.

"Bye." Brooke shook her head. Matt was determined to make Jacob jealous. He really was a good friend. And even though he wanted to be more, he always prioritized her feelings before his own.

Brooke sighed and Elise raised an eyebrow. "Why can't I have feelings for Matt? Why do I choose the guy who sees me only as a friend? I can't seem to find the whole package at once."

"Just focus on Noah for now, and when and if romance comes later, it will be a pleasant surprise," Elise encouraged her.

"You're right. My mind knows that, now if I can only wrap my heart around it."

THIRTY-SEVEN

"I can't believe you finally agreed to go to one of their concerts on the tour!" Elise giggled and grabbed a bite of her Greek salad. "Mmandmweregoingfmmtonewyorkfmtoo!"

"Finish chewing. I didn't understand a word of what you said!" Brooke's stern face gave way as she chuckled.

Swallowing, she repeated her sentence, "And we're going to New York, too!" She clapped and a couple of guys sitting on the other side of the break room turned their heads to look. Brooke shrugged and smiled as her friend continued. "Thank you for agreeing. I honestly thought I'd have to go by myself, or get some rando to go. I'm not missing out on this opportunity."

Laughing again, Brooke looked over at Elise. "Well, thank goodness some rando is off the hook."

Elise pulled up the notes app on her phone. "Okay, so we fly up on Thursday and stay for . . ." She counted with her fingers. "One, two, *three* nights, and leave on Sunday. We need to find a hotel. Do we want to stay close to Madison Square Gardens, where the concert is, or closer to Times Square? Although they're not too far from each other. Or maybe we should stay closer to Central Park. We'll for sure want a cab to the concert, then. We should also figure out what plays we want to see. We have to see at least one play! Hopefully, two. Maybe we should stay in the theater district. So many decisions! What? Why are you looking at me like that?"

Brooke had another bout of laughter. Wiping a tear from her eye, she answered, "You've been talking a mile a minute. You need to breathe."

One of the guys on the other side of the room chuckled.

"I'll check out my trip app and see what kind of hotels with decent prices I can find for those days in the areas you mentioned. Maybe that will help make our decision. You find out what shows are running that you want to go to and think I'll enjoy too, then map out where those theaters are located. After work, let's book our flights. With only two weeks, the prices may already be outrageous." Brooke furrowed her brow.

"You think it's going to be too expensive? Maybe your Grams can loan you some money."

"No, it's not that." Brooke grimaced. "Do you realize this will be the longest I've been away from Noah? It makes me a little anxious, and sad."

"Wow, I didn't think about that. That's bound to be tough. I'm sorry, maybe I shouldn't have pushed you into this trip. You don't have to go. Seriously, I'll find someone else. It's no big deal. You'll already be stressed about Jacob, and with Noah, it might be too much."

"No, I need to do this. I'm going to do this. I have to face my fears and insecurities. I can't always be with Noah, and I have to push past the Jacob thing. He'll always be around to an extent, because of our grandmothers' relationship. It will require lots of extra prayer, that's for sure."

"How's that going, by the way?"

"What?" Brooke raised her eyebrows.

"The God thing. You becoming a Christian."

One side of Brooke's mouth raised up. "Really well, actually. You should come to church with me sometime."

Elise shook her head.

"Aren't you curious? Have you ever been to church?"

"My parents took me a few times on Christmas and Easter when I was younger. I don't think that's for me. All those rituals and religious mumbo jumbo. Nah, I'm good."

"I'm sure it seemed that way from a child's perspective. I was even put off by it as a teenager visiting a few times with friends. It felt like a waste, and I thought the people there were a bunch of hypocrites." Brooke shrugged. "Then when my mom died, it made me think. You know? Don't you ever wonder what happens when we die? What's the meaning of all this?" She waved her hand around. "It didn't start to make sense until I began reading what the Bible says about God for myself and stopped taking people's word for it. Of course, Jacob was an encouragement. He showed me how to study it and how different parts of Scripture help explain each other." She paused, feeling the clench of her heart as she remembered their times together.

Elise reached forward and squeezed her hand, giving her a small smile of understanding. "Hang in there. For now, let's just focus on this trip and the fun we'll have."

"You'll need to do a thorough study of all their employee manuals, to see if this corporate restructure will cause any legal ramifications with the things the employees had been promised at their time of hire," Mr. Stearn directed Brooke as she sat in his office, taking notes.

"Okay. Are all of their manuals available as PDFs or do—" A knock on the door interrupted Brooke.

"Come in," Mr. Stearn called out.

"I need to speak to Brooke, sir."

Brooke turned at the sound of Keith's voice. "What is it?" He rarely spoke to her during the day, other than to verify her schedule.

"It's urgent. May I talk with you privately?" He gestured for her to step out.

When Mr. Stearn saw her hesitation, he spoke up, "By all means, Brooke. Please do."

Brooke's chest tightened as she followed Keith out. "What's going on?"

"It's your grandmother. The ambulance has just taken her to the hospital, and they think she's had a heart attack. I'll take you to her."

Brooke's hand flew to her chest. "No, no, no. I can't lose her, too." She frantically turned to her desk and grabbed her things to leave. "Wait! She had Noah. Where is Noah?"

"Ben has him. He was at the park with them when your grandmother had chest pain and became dizzy. Noah was never in harm's way."

Tears threatened to burst forth. "Thank you, God," she said softly, before going back to let Mr. Stearn know what was happening. As much as she wanted Jacob to stop paying for bodyguards, today she was immensely thankful. Her prayer then turned to asking for healing for Grams and wisdom for the medical professionals working on her.

WARM HANDS SQUEEZED her shoulders and startled Brooke awake. A voice she only heard in her dreams whispered her name. Maybe she was still dreaming.

"Brooke. I spoke to the doctor, and he said Grams' angioplasty was a success. She should be able to go home in the morning."

She lifted her head from her grandmother's side and turned toward the voice. Her dream took form as she stared into Jacob's dark eyes and nodded, before jumping up and wrapping her arms around him, holding on for dear life. He set a huge bouquet of flowers down.

"You're supposed to be on tour. How? Why are you here?" She choked out in a whisper.

Jacob froze as she clutched him, but he soon relaxed and hugged her back. "I heard about Grams. Ben told me as soon as it happened."

Realizing she was wrapped tightly around him, she released him and stepped back. It didn't make sense that he would come. They hadn't spoken in weeks. "I don't understand. Matt said you were doing interviews all day."

Jacob winced and shifted on his feet, avoiding her eyes.

"What is it? What aren't you saying?" Brooke watched him carefully.

"Let's go sit over here, so we don't disturb Grams," he urged as he glanced at her sleeping body, then nodded to the sofa while tugging her arm.

"Tell me," she pleaded again, once they were settled.

His eyes flickered to hers, then to his hands as he clenched and unclenched them. "This probably isn't any of my business, but when I heard about Grams, I immediately told Matt about it."

Brooke furrowed her brows, wondering why he brought up Matt.

"I urged him to forgo the interviews and fly in to be with you. I explained that we could have him contact the interviewers separately by phone later and could send in pictures, or even take new ones for the media outlets." His hand went to the back of his neck, and he appeared pained. "He refused and said that if I was so concerned, I should go. He acted angry at me for asking." Brooke stared at him silently and he continued. "I tried, I really did. I offered to pay for his flight and everything, but I couldn't convince him. I'm so sorry."

Still confused, Brooke looked at him and shook her head. "It's fine, but I don't understand why you came. You could have told me that over the phone."

"I didn't want you to be alone."

"I'm not alone. I've got your Nan and some ladies from the church who offered to take turns with me here, and to help with Noah."

"But you should have had your boyfriend by your side."

Brooke's brows furrowed, then it hit her. It seemed that Matt had been more successful than she believed with his act. She shook her head again. "Boyfriend?" she questioned, in case she'd misunderstood.

Jacob looked as bewildered as she felt. "Matt." He made a face as if the word tasted bad.

Heat rose in her face as a mixture of emotions filled her. Once again, Jacob proved how thoughtful and caring he was. He skipped his own interviews to be with her when she was hurting, even though they hadn't spoken in weeks and he thought she'd had a boyfriend the whole time. Tears welled in her eyes. "I'm so sorry."

"Why are you sorry?" Concern etched his face, and he reached out, but pulled his hand back before touching her. "Matt's the one who should be sorry for leaving you to go through this alone. You don't deserve that, so I came. I hope you don't feel like I've intruded on your privacy."

Brooke shook her head as tears began to fall. "No, I could never think that. It's the opposite. I feel undeserving of your attention after I've ignored you for so long."

Again, Jacob reached for her and stopped himself. "I'm sorry. I have no right. I just . . . I still care so much about you. And maybe you don't want me as a friend anymore, but you are a sister in Christ now. So I at least have that claim on you. To be honest, though, Matt doesn't deserve you." He ran his fingers through his hair. "There, I said it."

"Um." The realization that she hadn't yet clarified about Matt hit Brooke. "No, you're wrong."

Jacob looked at her skeptically.

"Matt isn't my boyfriend. Never has been."

"What? I don't—I thought . . . but he—"

Brooke shook her head. "No. We've never even dated."

Jacob let out a breath. "So . . . are you hoping for something with him?"

Brooke held his gaze. "I don't have those kinds of feelings for him. He's asked for more, but I think he understands."

Jacob furrowed his brow and stared at her silently before speaking. "Can I pray for you and Grams?" She nodded, and he spoke words of hope, grace, and healing over Brooke and her grandmother. His voice faltered as he was seemingly overcome with emotion.

The prayer brought tears to Brooke's eyes. Thoughts of what they could have been, combined with thankfulness for his presence, however short it would be. After his prayer, they caught up on the last few weeks, before Jacob offered to get food from the cafeteria. He pulled his cap down lower to cover his face before stepping into the hallway.

Barely ten minutes later, Brooke turned to the sound of a knock and found Elise at the door. Elise pulled her friend into a hug. "I'm sorry. You've gone through so much!"

"It's going to be okay. It looks like they got her to the hospital before any permanent damage was done to her heart. She had an angioplasty, so they think after taking it easy for a couple of weeks, she should be fine. For once, I'm so thankful Jacob kept the bodyguards. It was Ben who called the ambulance and kept Noah until I got here." Elise looked taken aback at Brooke's words. "And get this, he called Jacob, and Jacob came immediately. He's here."

Elise pulled back and examined her friend. "How do you feel about that?"

"I don't really know. I feel like I'm on emotional overload. The other thing is, he was all torn up, because he thought Matt was my boyfriend and he refused to come see me when Jacob told him what was going on. Jacob's so thoughtful, and to be honest, I'm glad he came, but it scares me that it will be so much harder when he leaves again."

Elise's brows raised, then furrowed in worry and she stared

across the room at nothing in particular. Sighing, Elise turned back to her friend. "You're strong. It will be okay. Just enjoy him while he's here and be thankful for the relationship and the way it has grown you. I know it's been hard, but he helped get you through a difficult time when you first moved here. And because of him, you became a Christian. And even though I don't understand it myself, I can see it's made you into a more confident person and aided you in overcoming the worst of your emotional struggles. Wouldn't you agree?"

Brooke pressed her lips together and studied the tile floor before nodding. "You're right. Thanks for helping me realize that. I needed a reminder. It's just that every time I see him, I lose my footing."

Elise chuckled. "Who wouldn't? The man is a god who makes women weak just by being near him." Brooke blushed at the thought. "Oh, by the way. I'm sure Mr. Stearn will message you, but when he heard I was coming to visit, he wanted to let you know he's already contacted Susan. She said she can fill in for you, so you can take time off for your Grams. He didn't want you to worry you're letting him down."

"That's a relief. I hadn't even—" Brooke stopped at the sound of soft giggling. She turned and saw a nurse clinging to Jacob's side as they entered. He was writing on her clipboard.

The giggling stopped. "Oops, sorry. I'm here to check your grandmother's vitals." The young nurse wrote on a piece of paper and slipped it into Jacob's back pocket. He mumbled something to her, then stepped over to Brooke while the nurse checked Grams.

"Elise, good to see you," Jacob said.

He looked nervous, and Brooke wondered if he'd overheard some of their previous conversation. She tried to remember exactly what was said before the door opened.

Brooke had a hand on Elise's arm and squeezed tightly.

Elise's face tensed. "Um, yeah, you too." She reached up and tried to peel Brooke's hand off her arm.

"Jacob, do we need to worry about that nurse telling people you're here?" Brooke fought to hold in her jealousy at seeing the nurse act so familiar with him. It combined with thoughts that he would leave the hospital soon to see Mari. Closing her eyes, she waited for an answer, fearing that if she looked at him, he would know everything she felt.

"Ryder will take care of it. He's already contacted the hospital to make sure everyone working on this floor tonight and in the morning signs an NDA."

Before Brooke responded, Elise spoke up. "Well, I should get going. Just stopped by to bring those." She pointed to a balloon bouquet.

"Are you sure?" Jacob offered. "I have enough food to share if you're hungry and want to join us."

"Oh, no. I'm sure. It was great seeing you, Jacob." Elise smiled at him, then turned around to hug Brooke. "He's so hot," she whispered in Brooke's ear. "Just enjoy the eye candy."

Brooke chuckled as Elise left.

"What?" Jacob asked.

"Nothing. She's a mess."

"Well, I'm glad she's here for you. I know this has—"

"Brooke? Jacob?" Grams' voice called out weakly.

"Grams! We're right here." Brooke hurried across the room and offered her grandmother water. "How do you feel?"

"A little strange, but not in pain. Painkillers must be working." The older woman chuckled. "I thought I was dreaming when I heard your voice, Jacob. I should have known you wouldn't be far when Brooke had anything troubling her." She laid a hand on his.

He stood opposite Brooke, and their eyes caught. It embarrassed Brooke when her grandmother spoke like that, and she felt Jacob's eyes on her as she shifted her gaze to the suddenly interesting lint on the bedsheet. She'd had several conversations with Grams about Jacob ever since she had shut him out of her life. She tried to get her grandmother to understand that Jacob had other important things in his life and didn't need to worry about them. But her grandmother insisted he cared for her and that if she gave the relationship time, it would grow into more. It was apparent that both Grams and Nan had visions of the two of them together. Knowing it would never happen, she'd tried to steer them away from that idea.

"You're right, Grams, I couldn't leave her on her own for this, although I will have to go in the morning after we get you settled in at home."

Brooke's eyes flew up in question, and Jacob smiled.

"Are you staying the night?" Jacob questioned Brooke. "Or I can stay and you can go get some rest."

"Oh, no, I'll be fine here." Brooke couldn't imagine him willingly giving up his own bed after being away for weeks. "I'm sure you'll enjoy your own bed for a night."

"Actually, I'm planning to stay at Nan's." When he saw Brooke flinch, Jacob added, "Don't worry. I'll wait until Noah is in bed before I go by to see her, then I'll crash at her place and be back in the morning to help you with things here."

"You don't have to do that, but I appreciate the offer." Brooke felt guilty that even with him offering her all of this help, she still felt uncomfortable at the thought of Noah seeing him. And what's worse is Jacob knew it, but was still willing to help.

"I insist. Now, let's focus on you, Grams. We should probably have someone come check on you, now that you're awake."

AFTER PUTTING Noah down for a nap and checking on Grams, Brooke sat down on the sofa. Left with her thoughts for the first time in over twenty-four hours, shaky, unsettled tears made their way down her face. So much had happened. The fear of losing her grandmother, the relief that she would be okay—for now, Jacob's arrival to help, then his departure. Her mind tried wrapping itself around the competing thoughts. What if this was just the beginning of health problems for her grandmother? What if she couldn't shove her feelings for Jacob back down where they were safely hidden before this incident? "God,

I feel lost, weak, and helpless," she whispered, before opening her Bible and searching for wisdom.

In Isaiah chapter 40:28-31, she found words of hope and clung to them. "Have you not known? Have you not heard? The LORD is the everlasting God, the Creator of the ends of the earth. He does not faint or grow weary; His understanding is unsearchable. He gives power to the faint, and to him who has no might He increases strength. Even youths shall faint and be weary, and young men shall fall exhausted; but they who wait for the LORD shall renew their strength; they shall mount up with wings like eagles; they shall run and not be weary; they shall walk and not faint."

"Yes, Lord, I'll wait on You. Help me trust You in the wait."

THIRTY-EIGHT

Sipping ginger ale and leaning back into the leather seat on the plane, Brooke took a deep breath and closed her eyes. A week and a half ago, there was no way she would consider taking this trip, but with much convincing from her grandmother and Elise, she agreed. Jacob's Nan promised to sleep at their apartment so Grams always had someone if there was a problem. Sabrina's oldest daughter, Grace, would go by for several hours on Saturday and Sunday to give Nan a break. Sabrina even planned to send a meal for Saturday.

This morning, Brooke was a nervous wreck with the reality of leaving Noah and the thought of seeing Jacob again hitting full force. At least Matt had confirmed Mari wasn't scheduled to sing with *Nine Days In* at the New York concert. Part of her worried Mari would unexpectedly show up.

Once arriving at the airport, God reminded her He would get her through in a surprising way. While checking in, they were told someone had upgraded them to first class. Brooke and Elise guessed that everyone in *Madness* had splurged to make it happen. So there Brooke sat, relaxing on the plane as the other passengers boarded.

After sending up a prayer of thanks, Brooke pulled out a note from Sabrina and reread the verses she had been quoting all morning. "Proverbs 3:5-6. Trust in the LORD with all your heart, and do not lean on your own understanding. In all your ways acknowledge Him, and He will make straight your paths."

Brooke sighed and glanced out the window, watching the workers loading suitcases onto the plane. She was determined to enjoy this trip and concentrate on the positives. She was in first class with her best friend, about to have a blast in New York. *Yes, focus on that*, she thought as the flight attendant did the final checks and explained the emergency procedures.

"So, do you have your outfit planned for the concert tonight?" Elise asked, while thumbing through the SkyMall catalog.

"Sort of. I—"

"Oh my gosh! Are you guys going to the *Nine Days In* concert?" A girl across the aisle interrupted, and Elise slowly nodded. "Me too! And my friend here." She pointed beside her. "Our parents gave us this trip for graduation."

"From college?" Elise asked.

Nodding her head, the girl said, "Yep. We are super excited. They bought us backstage passes, too. We go to their concerts whenever they're in central Florida, and we've been to a few of their out-of-town ones. We finally get to meet them in person!" She happily sighed and fluttered her eyes. "They are all so hot, but I'm especially looking forward to meeting Jake. I don't care if he *is* dating Mari Stephens. It will be awesome talking to him. Who knows, maybe it will be love at first sight." She giggled and nudged her friend.

Elise opened her mouth to speak, but Keith sat in the row behind the girls and looked at her sternly, shaking his head. Brooke imagined she was ready to tell the girl all about how they were already friends. Elise seemed to rethink it and instead said, "That's great. Maybe we'll see you there."

"We'll be in the front row, near the center. If you're anywhere near there, be sure and give us a shout." She winked. "I'm Ally, by the way. And this is Laikyn."

"I'm Elise, and this is Brooke. I hope your trip turns out great." Elise smiled, then turned to Brooke and made a face before whispering, "Hopefully, she won't ask us anything else."

When collecting their luggage, they again ran into Ally and Laikyn, who informed them they were staying at the Renaissance Midtown Hotel two blocks from Madison Square Gardens..

Elise rolled her eyes as they walked away. "She's a talker! Thankfully, we'll be in Times Square at the Marriott Marquis. Now if we can just avoid seeing them at the meet-and-greet..."

They looked up and found their driver holding a sign with Brooke's last name, and minutes later, were in bumper-to-bumper traffic.

As their driver pulled to a stop in front of a hotel, Brooke examined the building in confusion. "Um . . . this isn't the Marriott Marquis."

"No, ma'am. I was instructed by the travel agent to bring you here. This is the Chatwal. It's where your friends are staying. Your reservation was moved here."

Brooke felt heat rise to her face and she looked at Elise, whose brow was furrowed. "Can you hold on just a minute before letting us out?" She was already dialing the travel agent as a man approached the car to help them out. "Pamela. What's going on? I appreciate the flight upgrade, but we had reservations right on Times Square. The Chatwal place is a block over."

When the valet opened the door, Brooke held up a finger.

Pamela said, "I promise you'll like this just as well. You've been upgraded to a junior suite with a terrace. Your friends wanted to have you nearby and have paid for your accommodations."

"Oh. Wow. That's really nice." She glanced back at Elise and shrugged. "I guess we're staying here. Thanks."

"Let me know if you need help setting anything up while you're there. I can get you tickets to plays and museums, or even meal reservations and tours," Pamela said.

"Will do. Thanks, again."

"So," Brooke said, glancing from Elise to the driver, "Our room is a suite here and has already been paid for by our friends, who want us close by, so I think we should stay. Are you okay with that, Elise?"

"Yes, ma'am! I won't say no to a free suite in New York!" She grabbed her purse and shoved Brooke out of the car giggling.

"Madness must get paid really well to afford all of this," Brooke said while touring the suite once the bellhop left.

Elise grinned and twirled around before falling on the bed. "This room is huge!"

"Check this out!" Brooke said as she peered out at the balcony. "We should eat breakfast out here each day!" She perused the garden-like terrace, complete with a table for four and an umbrella. "This has our basic room at the Marriott beat." She giggled and shut the door before stretching out on the sofa.

Elise nodded in agreement and rolled onto her belly, propping her head up. "I can see why the guys chose a place like this. It's just small enough and off the beaten path to keep them away from the chaos, but it's still close enough to walk most places."

"Agreed. Speaking of location, let's figure out what we want to do for the next three hours until we meet up with the guys."

"On it!" Elise grabbed her phone and clicked around, then joined Brooke on the sofa. "Look at this. I have a bunch of things in the area mapped out. We can go to Top of the Rock and then have dessert in this place." She clicked a heart on the screen and it brought up La Maison du Chocolat. "It's right there in Rockefeller Plaza. Then we can—"

"What's Top of the Rock?"

"It's the top of the Rockefeller Center. A viewing spot, like on top of the Empire State Building. Except the cool thing is, you can get a picture of the Empire State Building from it. Also, the lines are shorter. Let's book a time before we go to shorten the wait even more." Elise grinned. "Then, if we have time after all that, we can stop by Times Square for selfies."

"Thanks for planning things out." Brooke patted her friend on the shoulder. "It all sounds good to me. I'm especially interested in that chocolate place." She grabbed the phone. "Let me see that again," she said, wiggling her eyebrows.

As the girls approached Madison Square Gardens to meet up with the guys before the concert, Brooke stopped.

Elise kept walking, but a few steps later, looked back. "Brooke? What's wrong?" Her friend's face was contorted. "Seriously, Brooke. You don't look good."

"I . . ." Brooke shook her head. "I don't know if I can do this."

"What? See Jacob? You handled it great when he was at the hospital a week and a half ago." Elise wrapped an arm around Brooke.

"Yeah, but I was distracted with Grams and didn't have time to worry beforehand. He just showed up."

"Maybe, but you've got this. I know you can do it. You could, um, you know, pray. Maybe God will give you some superpower or something."

Brooke looked up at her friend and chuckled. "It doesn't work that way. He's not like a genie. I used to think that, too. But He does hear the prayers of His people and answer them in His will."

"In His will? What does that mean?"

Shrugging, Brooke replied with a sad smile, "I'm still trying to figure it out. But you're right, thanks for reminding me. God's got me and I don't need to worry. If you don't mind, I am going to pray."

"Whatever you want." Elise smiled awkwardly.

Brooke nodded and bowed her head. "God, I don't know what I need, but You do. Please get me through this. In Jesus' name, Amen." When Brooke looked up, Elise had a funny look on her face. "You can ask me questions about God, if you want. I'm still figuring things out, but I have a good mentor who can help me if I get stumped."

Elise smiled softly before grabbing her VIP ID badge and pulling Brooke to the door. She squeezed Brooke's hand. "You've got—Hey! Where'd you come from, Keith? You're like a ninja."

"Part of the job." He chuckled and led them to the room where *Nine Days In* was lounging.

"Look who the cat dragged in!" Ryan pulled Brooke into a hug. "Long time, no see. I thought you had forgotten about us. And you've brought your beautiful friend . . . I'm sorry, what's your name again?" He wiggled his eyebrows at Elise.

Blushing, Elise reached out to shake his hand and was pulled into a hug as well. "Ha-ha," she choked out, but Brooke saw the grin on her face.

When Brooke scanned the rest of the room, she noticed Jacob's eyes were locked on hers, then trailed down to her neck. Her heart raced and her face flushed as she remembered she wore the necklace he gave her. She reached up to touch it, and Jacob's mouth curved into a smile. The members of the band gathered around Brooke and Elise to greet them, but Jacob stood on the far side of the group. As she spoke with the others, her eyes continually sought Jacob's. More times than not, he was looking back at her, which left her feeling confused.

Anthony soon drew her into a debate with Brandon over which Broadway shows were worth attending. When she glanced back at Jacob, he'd vanished.

"How was your flight?" Jacob's familiar voice startled Brooke.

Turning to the handsome man, everything seemed to move in slow motion, including her brain. "Um . . ." She shook her head and blinked, trying to clear her thoughts. "It was really nice. We were upgraded to first class." She looked around. "Do you know where Matt and his band went? I think they paid for our upgrade. We got moved to their hotel, too. The Chatwal. Are you guys staying there?"

Jacob's brows raised. "Yeah, we are. Cool. I'm glad things are working out for you on this trip." The corner of his mouth went up. "And *Madness* is onstage right now, doing sound checks. They'll be back here any minute." His gaze traveled behind Brooke and she shifted her head to see what he was looking at.

"Matt!" Brooke called out.

When Elise realized *Madness* was entering, she raced over to Brad.

"Brooke!" Matt responded as he joined them, pulling her into a hug. He grinned and twirled her around, but stopped when Jacob cleared his throat.

"I'm gonna head over there with the band." Jacob pointed with one hand while rubbing his neck with the other. "We have some interviews before the meet-and-greet. There's food over there. You're welcome to it, if you get hungry. So I'll, um, see you in a few. Oh, and if you and Elise want pictures with the band in front of the backdrop, go over as soon as the reporters leave. That way, you'll beat the crowds coming in with backstage passes."

Brooke nodded and gave him a small smile before turning back to Matt. Her expression turned into a full grin. "So . . ."

Matt looked confused. "What?"

"Thank you for upgrading our flight and hotel! I'm guessing all of *Madness* had a hand in that."

His brow furrowed in confusion, and he shook his head. "As much as I would love to take credit for the upgrades, I don't know anything about them."

Brooke's eyes narrowed, and she glanced back to where Jacob stood with a reporter. *Could it be him?*

"So, Jake. Tell us the real story about your relationship with Mari. You two have both been very tight-lipped, but it's obvious there's something there." The female reporter angled her microphone toward Jacob.

Frozen in her twisted position, Brooke felt like she couldn't breathe. She didn't want to hear him say it out loud. Once those words left his mouth, it would be official. Up until now, she had kept a tiny amount of hope, no matter how unlikely it seemed. Part of her wanted to run from the room, but she had to listen. Better to know the truth now than live with false hope.

"THAT'S the question everyone seems to ask." Jacob smirked as he spoke. "You'll have to stick around for the concert to find out the answer. I plan to make a statement toward the end."

"Are you sure you don't want to give us a clue?" the persistent reporter asked.

"I'm good. Why don't you ask the guys the rest of your questions?"

Brooke exhaled a shaky breath. Matt placed an arm over her shoulder and pulled her close. Leaning into him for support, Brooke contemplated having this tension for the next several hours, until Jacob made his announcement. It seemed as if all the wind had been knocked out of her, but as she began feeling down, she remembered she was not alone. *Thank You, God, for my friends and for being here for me. Walk me through this.* She prayed silently and relaxed a little more against Matt.

"I've got you," he whispered and held her tighter.

Brooke forced a smile. It was going to be a long night. Moments ago, the room was large, bright, and inviting—now, it seemed like a dark tunnel pressing against her with no exit.

Elise moved close on her other side and glared in Jacob's direction. "Fake it till you make it. Oh, look." She pointed to the food table. "They've got some cute little desserts. Let's see if we can find some chocolate."

Brooke was thankful for Elise and Matt. With the two of them and the rest of *Madness*, this trip could still be great. On the table, she found little cups of chocolate mousse and grinned. Even in this dark place, there were good things. "Thank You, God."

CHAPTER

THIRTY-NINE

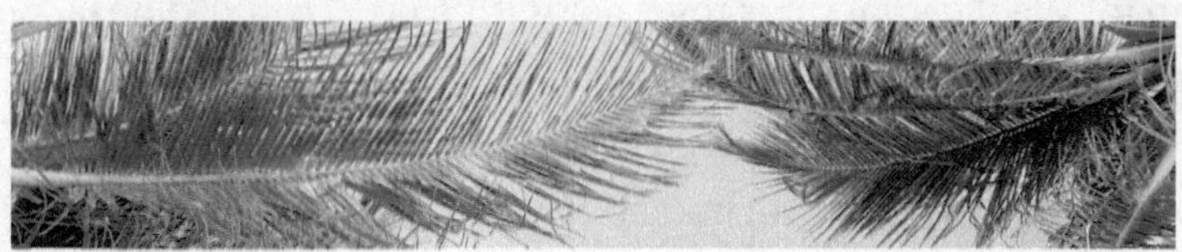

"Okay, you stand here. Ethan, scoot that way. Brandon and Anthony, switch spots." The photographer's assistant placed a hand on her chin and nodded. "Yep, that's it."

Elise and Brooke stood amidst *Nine Days In*, posing for pictures. Brooke felt an arm slide around her shoulder and knew it was Jacob's from the smell of his cologne. She struggled to maintain her smile. The moment the photographer took the last shot, she pulled away and dragged Elise over to *Madness*'s photo spot.

Just as they finished taking pictures with *Madness*, Brooke heard a high-pitched squeal come from the *Nine Days In* line. She looked at Elise and rolled her eyes. "And so it begins."

"Elise!" came a voice from the same direction as the previous squeal.

It was Ally from the plane.

"You have got to be kidding me! Did this girl place a tracker on us?" Elise groaned.

Ally waved them over while earnestly speaking to the photographer.

287

"You know that girl?" Brad asked from behind them.

Elise rolled her eyes. "Plane buddy." She looked behind Brad and saw the line forming. "We'll go see what she wants. Looks like you guys are in demand." She grinned and hugged Brad, then waved to the others. "If we miss you before you go out, 'break a leg'!" Chuckling, she pulled Brooke across the room.

"Elise and . . . Brooke, right?" Brooke nodded at Ally. "You two jump in! We'll get pictures together with *Nine Days In*!" She leaned in closer and winked. "And this way you get to cut past the line!"

Brooke looked at Elise and shrugged, not really wanting to give Ally more reason to attach herself to them.

Elise smiled. "Wow! Thanks." She turned and gave a subtle wink to the band before she and Brooke joined in the photo.

"These are our friends from Orlando! They flew up with us in first class." Ally beamed as she spoke to the band. Laikyn remained quiet.

Nine Days In played along, not giving anything away about their existing relationship with Brooke and Elise. Once again, Brooke felt an arm slide around her, except this time, it was placed at her waist. Tingles shot through her body from his touch. As good as it felt to be near Jacob, it was also torture. After the pictures, Ally tried to get Brooke and Elise to stick with them, but they convinced her that since they had already taken pictures with *Madness*, they needed to move on.

Chuckling, Elise pulled Brooke into a corner. "Oh my gosh. I thought we would never lose them and our cover would be blown."

STANDING in the wings to the side of the stage, Brooke watched in awe as *Nine Days In* worked the crowd. Moments earlier, she had congratulated *Madness* on their performance. It was clear the band had matured during the tour, and she was proud of them.

Matt slung his arm over her shoulder, but as she observed Jacob, her senses numbed to the world around her. Something about Jacob always drew her to him. When he turned his head and winked at her, she felt the familiar flutter. Coming back to reality, she reminded herself they were just friends. Friends was enough. If she said it enough, maybe she would believe it.

"I've been fortunate to sing this next song several times with Mari Stephens." The crowd roared at Jacob's words.

Screams filled the stadium. "Love You Right Now!"

"You guessed it," Jacob replied. "Before we start, though, there's something I feel needs to be said."

Brooke's heart raced, and she wiped sweaty palms on her pants. Matt's arm around her gave her stability.

"I know everyone has wanted confirmation of what my relationship with Mari is, and we've been quiet about it this past year." More roars from the crowd caused Jacob to pause. "Alright, alright, I'm getting there. The thing is, when we first met, we were thrown together, and dating seemed like the natural response. But after trying that, we decided we're better as friends."

Brooke's mouth dropped, and Matt's arm fell from her shoulder. The crowd roared even louder. A few voices broke through, shouting "he's single" and "marry me!"

Jacob's chuckle echoed in the microphone, and he gave the audience a heart-melting smile. "So, with that set straight, let's sing 'Love You Right Now!'" He motioned for the band and they followed his lead.

After the concert, Brooke looked for Jacob, but with the chaos backstage, it seemed impossible. Giving up on finding him, Brooke and Elise joined *Madness* for a ride back to the hotel.

Maddie and Rhys invited Elise, Brooke, and the rest of *Madness* to join them in their suite for a celebration. Brooke agreed, but said she needed to freshen up first.

"What does this mean?" Brooke wondered out loud as soon as the door to their suite closed behind Elise. "I don't know how to feel. Should I get my hopes up? What's going on? He's not dating Mari?

How long did they date and when did they stop? I have so many questions. And does he have the same feelings for me? Is it possible?"

Elise grinned. "It's absolutely possible, but you're going to have to wait for Jacob to give you those answers."

IN BED, Brooke stared at the ceiling for what seemed like hours. It probably *was* hours. How was a person supposed to sleep with so many life-changing questions on their mind? She'd had several heart-to-hearts with God during the night about Jacob, her future, and how she should feel.

Wait.

That was the word that echoed in her mind. Was it an answer from God? Surely not, or she misunderstood in her tired delirium. He is God, after all. He could provide the answers anytime. Why *wait*? She needed to know now.

Quietly sliding out of the bed and into the bathroom, Brooke started her day. Normally, she would give anything for a chance to stay in bed past 6:30 in the morning, but no matter how many times she tried to will herself back to sleep, it wasn't happening. Shocker. Her second shock came when she looked in the mirror. Of all days to have dark circles from a sleepless night . . . At least the matted mess her hair had become from tossing and turning could be tamed. But was her concealer up to the task awaiting it under her eyes?

Examining the soaking tub, she decided a relaxing bath might help turn the day around.

FROM THE MIDDLE of the Bow Bridge in Central Park, Brooke took a picture of the lake, the skyline in the background and several boats on the water. The lake breeze was refreshing in the summer heat.

Elise stood beside her and shoved her phone into her pocket with a frustrated sigh.

"What's going on? You've been texting someone for the last half hour and are clearly irritated," Brooke commented. "You've hardly even paid attention as we've walked through Central Park."

"You're right. I'll leave it."

"Who was it?"

"Huh? Just my mom. It'll be okay. Don't worry."

Brooke wrapped an arm around her friend as they lagged behind *Madness*. "It's too nice outside for us both to be down. So what if Mari showed up and Jacob has to spend the day taking her all over town to prove they're *good friends*? Who cares that I haven't heard from him since his announcement and my heart is in a tumult? So what if your mom is giving you a hard time?" She kicked a stone that was lying on the path. Elise turned to her and Brooke forced a giant smile. "See? I'm happy! Let's be happy!" she said through gritted teeth. The chirping birds, a Buddhist monk offering bracelets of peace for five dollars, and even the man playing the saxophone under the bridge all seemed to mock her.

Elise stared at her with a brow raised. "You're going to be fine. I'm sorry you're having to go through this right now."

Brooke pressed her lips together. She knew she needed to tell Elise what she was thinking. "Listen, I don't want this to affect you, but I'm not up to attending their second concert tonight. It will be bad enough watching them at the play we're all attending this after-noon, but at least then I'll have something else to focus on. That's my limit. If Jacob was interested in me, he would have made an effort to contact me by now." All her doubts resurfaced. "Who knows? Maybe Jacob is really still dating Mari and just trying to get the reporters to leave them alone. Anyway, you can still go to the concert with *Madness* and hang out with them. I'll be fine by myself."

"What's this about *Madness*?" Maddie asked. The rest of the group had slowed down to let them catch up.

After Elise explained, Brad spoke up, "We'd love to have Elise hang with us before the concert." He looked up and winked. "When we're done onstage, we can head back to the hotel and have an early celebration of our own. There's no reason we need to stay while *Nine Days In* plays. Brooke, you can join us at our place." Her spirits lifted at his consideration. "Elise, you don't mind missing the repeat of *Nine Days In* tonight, do you?"

"Nope. That sounds perfect." She nudged Brooke's shoulder.

Brooke smiled genuinely. "Thanks, guys. I don't know what I did to deserve good friends like you."

Matt pulled her into a tight hug and ruffled her hair. "Just keep being you."

FORTY

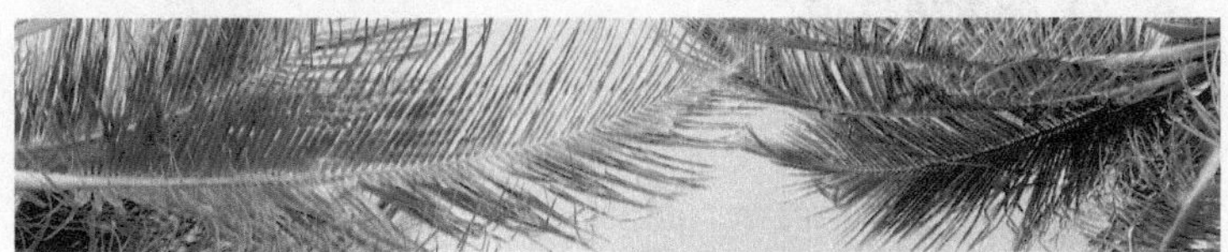

When *Madness* returned to the hotel after opening for *Nine Days In* that night, Brooke hung out with them and Elise as long as she could at their suite, but she was mentally exhausted and needed sleep. She said her goodnights and walked the short distance to her own suite.

Turning into her hallway, she came to an abrupt halt. There, in a crumpled pile on the floor, sat Jacob.

As if sensing her presence, he turned his head toward her and jumped up. Concern filled his eyes, and he pulled her close. "Where have you been? I've been calling and texting you for the last forty minutes. You let Keith off for the night, saying you were staying in your room. I had the manager let me in, only to find it empty. I texted Matt and got no answer. I was about—"

"I was with *Madness* and Elise in Brad and Matt's suite." Brooke pointed behind her.

"What?" He ran his fingers through his hair. "I should have thought of that." Jacob gripped her shoulders and stared at her.

"What's going on?" Brooke tried to keep her mind from jumping to conclusions.

"I . . . um, can I come in? We need to talk," Jacob said flatly.

Brooke tensed. Mechanically, she nodded and opened the door. He didn't look happy to see her and began frantically texting on his phone. After stuffing it in his pocket, Jacob grabbed her hand and walked her to the sofa, patting the spot beside him. He leaned forward on his elbows and rubbed a hand down his face. She closed her eyes and braced herself for his words.

"So . . . where to start?"

Brooke felt him grab her hand, but refused to open her eyes.

"Brooke, I . . . Will you look at me, please," his voice softened, and she opened her eyes. "I want to date you."

"What?" Not what she expected. She furrowed her brows. "I don't—I thought . . ."

"I waited too long, didn't I?" Jacob rubbed a hand over his face again. "Please understand, I believed you wanted me out of your life so you could date Matt. It wasn't until the hospital with Grams that I learned otherwise."

Brooke shook her head. "But I thought you were dating Mari. And . . . she kissed you. And you sang that love song with her. And you never said you weren't dating until last night, even though everyone speculated you were. Are you sure you're not still dating her?" She looked at him accusingly. She needed to know the truth before making herself any more vulnerable than she already was.

With his free hand, Jacob ran his fingers through his hair. "Why would you pay attention to what the tabloids say? We talked about that." His gaze was steely, but lined with hurt. "Our record label asked us to leave the media speculating for a while to help her get more media exposure while she was changing over to singing solo. My friends knew better, so I thought—I figured it was no big deal."

"But she hangs all over you whenever she's around. That's not normal friend behavior." Brooke pulled away in frustration.

"You're right, but it's normal for her," Jacob insisted. Brooke made a face. "I guess I didn't think too much about it, because I wasn't dating you."

Brooke thought about the things he said, but something didn't sit right with her. "We might not have been officially dating, but as much as we were talking and going out, you made it seem like that was the direction we were headed. You sent me so many mixed signals. My head has been a mess."

"I'm so sorry." Jacob leaned in, took her hand again, and caressed it with his thumb. "I never intended to confuse you. I was giving you space. You had just come out of a bad relationship, and I figured you weren't ready for another. I didn't want to be your rebound. I'm really sorry. I've made a mess of this." His hand shot up to his hair again and he pulled at it.

"I was attracted to you from the first moment I saw you, before we even spoke. You sat on Grams' porch, looking like you just woke up. Do you remember? That gorgeous strawberry blonde hair of yours was slightly messy, and those piercing green eyes watched me." He wound a strand of her hair around his fingers. "I knew who you were from our grandmothers, but I didn't expect to be knocked off my feet like that. My soul was drawn to yours. I couldn't stay away after that day, even though I told myself you needed time.

"The other problem was that you weren't a Christian. It wasn't something I'd thought about. But when I mentioned you to my mentor, he told me if I dated a non-Christian and ended up marrying her, it would create problems down the road. I guess that's why I gave mixed messages. It wasn't intentional. I can't think straight around you. I think about you every second of the day, and it's been so hard to stay away from you. Can you forgive me for the way I've hurt you?"

Brooke's emotions had been a tangled mess for so long that the thought of unraveling them seemed impossible. And yet this is what she'd longed for, even when she told herself she'd given him up in her heart. She wanted to place all the blame on him, but she knew she'd played her part in the confusion.

She finally nodded. "I forgive you," she whispered.

"Thank you, Brooke. Will you please give me a chance?"

Brooke couldn't hold back anymore, and the dam of tears broke as she threw herself at him. "I've missed you. I've missed you so much. And Noah, poor Noah's lost all this time with you. I . . ." She could hardly speak through the tears. "I wish I had been honest with you about my feelings. I can't think straight when I'm near you, either."

With both of his arms wrapped around her, he kissed the top of her head over and over again. "So is that a yes? You'll date me?" He cupped her face and smiled softly.

"Yes." It was a strangled cry, then, "Yes," more loudly. "Yes, Jacob." It was barely a whisper the last time as she nuzzled into his chest. A thought hit her. "You paid for our room and upgraded our plane tickets."

His body shook and a sound between a cry and a chuckle escaped from his lips. "I did. I wanted to do something for you, even if we weren't together. Oh, Brooke . . . Brooke, this makes me so happy. I'll make you so happy, and Noah, too." He pulled back again, worry on his face. "But this won't be easy for you. We may not be able to keep it under wraps for long. My job, it will affect you. More than when people believed you were with Matt. Do you still want to give this a chance?"

"Yes," she whispered. Doubts skirted the edges of her mind, but her heart won the battle. "Yes," she said again, feeling more confident in her decision. She had thought it through a thousand times and knew he was worth it. "You're worth it," she said out loud, and Jacob's smile returned, bigger than before.

CHAPTER
FORTY-ONE

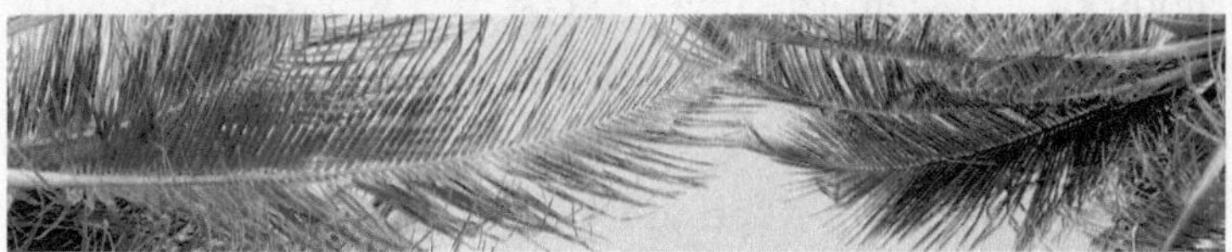

Jacob's fingers interlaced with Brooke's between their front-row seats at *The Phantom of the Opera*. Her feelings tonight were totally different from what they were at the matinee performance of *Hamilton* the day before. Then, she'd been distraught at having to watch Mari hang all over Jacob even though they were *just friends*.

Earlier in the day, during their private boat charter around Manhattan, she and Jacob announced to both *Madness* and *Nine Days In* that they were dating. Everyone except Matt and Elise was enthusiastic about their relationship. She'd told Elise before the boat ride. Elise was mad at Jacob and gave Jacob a stern talk about not hurting her friend.

Brooke learned that when Jacob came to visit her grandmother at the hospital, he had spoken with Elise. He'd explained he was not dating Mari and had plans to pursue Brooke. He'd urged Elise to make sure Brooke didn't cancel the New York trip and to keep his secret until they went to New York. Jacob was who Elise had been texting the day before when they toured Central Park. Elise was angry at how poorly he'd handled the situation with Mari, and the way it affected Brooke.

Matt's negative reaction resulted from different reasons—jealousy and hurt. But by the end of the boat trip, he apologized to Brooke and told them he wished them the best—adding that he, too, would keep an eye on Jacob.

Their grandmothers were thrilled when they called them that afternoon to tell them the news. Jacob and Brooke decided to wait until the following week, when the three of them could be together, to tell Noah—not that he would understand. After that, they planned for Brooke and Noah to fly out to wherever Jacob was each Wednesday and stay until Sunday for the last few weeks of the tour.

Her mind raced throughout the play. Her life had taken numerous twists and turns over the last five months. Such extremes, starting with her mother's death and ending with the birth of a beautiful romance.

After the play, the two bands, Elise, and Brooke, were escorted backstage to meet the actors. It was strange watching the women flirt with Jacob. She tended to forget he was world famous. To her, he wasn't *Jake the pop star. He* was just Jacob—the man she was in love with.

"LOVE IS PATIENT, LOVE IS KIND . . ." Jacob read chapter 13 of First Corinthians to Brooke as they sat in his suite that night after the play. "So now faith, hope, and love abide, these three; but the greatest of these is love." He finished the chapter, then reached up and touched the necklace he had given Brooke.

"Brooke, when I sent you this, I already knew how I felt about you, and even though I believed you were dating Matt, I gave it to you with a hope that there was still a future for us. Since the very beginning of knowing you, I've felt drawn to you in a way that I never have to a woman. To be honest, I didn't think I would ever have a lasting relationship, because I hadn't been raised around healthy ones. But I feel that God brought us together, even though I didn't handle things as I should have. When you became a Christian, it confirmed to me that we were meant to be together. When I saw this necklace, simple as it is, all I could think about was how much I love you, and I had to buy it for you, even if you never loved me the same way."

Brooke's heart raced when she realized what he was saying, and her brows furrowed in question. Did she understand him correctly?

Jacob smiled, as if reading her mind. "Yes, I love you. I love you, my beautiful Brooke, and I'm so happy I can freely say that to you. I love you, I love you, I love you." He grinned, looking as if the weight of the world had been lifted from his shoulders. Without waiting, he reached into a bag that was sitting on the coffee table and brought out a small jewelry box.

Tears rolled down Brooke's face, but when Jacob placed the box on the table and looked at her with concern, her mouth pulled up into a smile and she shook her head. "These are happy tears."

He brought his hand up and placed it on her cheek, wiping her tears with his thumb.

"I feel like I cry all the time around you. Are you sure you want an emotional wreck like me?" she asked.

"I've never been more sure of anything in my life. I am so in love with you and your tender heart, Brooke."

"I . . . I love you, too. I have for a while." She smiled through her tears.

Jacob drew her into a hug and said, "Those are the second most wonderful words I have ever heard you say." When she leaned back and looked at him with confusion, he clarified, "The first were when you told me you became a Christian. Well, I guess I should say you texted me *those* words."

His expression changed, and he held her gaze. "I want to kiss you. May I kiss you?"

She hesitated, stunned by the question, before nodding eagerly.

Within seconds, Jacob placed the sweetest, most tender kiss on her lips. When they separated, she felt flushed.

"That's the first time I've ever asked someone if I could kiss them." He chuckled.

"That's the first time I've ever been asked."

"This is the first relationship I've been in since I've become a Christian. I plan to do things differently than I have before." He grabbed her hands. "Can I pray for us?" She nodded, and he thanked God for her and asked Him to give them wisdom and direction in their new relationship. "I hope this doesn't scare you away, but I want this to be the last relationship I have . . . ever." Her eyes went wide, then Jacob pushed forward the box that had been forgotten. "Open it."

Brooke opened the rectangular box and found a bracelet that matched the necklace, but instead of the three silver circles, it had a circular silver plate, engraved with *"The greatest of these is love."* Jacob flipped over the plate, and engraved on the other side was *JR + BF*.

It felt like a dream. Her heart was full.

CHAPTER 42 EPILOGUE

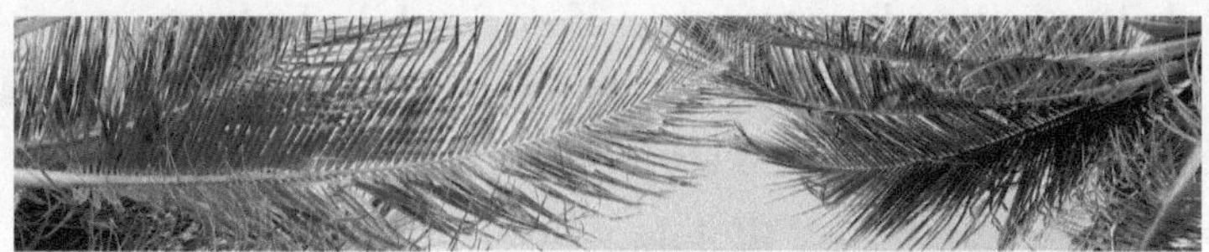

Brooke's gaze drifted out the window, toward the ornamental garden behind the French chateau they'd rented for the week. In only minutes, she would become Mrs. Jacob Reeves. There he stood on the lawn, fully dressed in his tux and more handsome than she'd ever seen him. Noah happily played with a toy at his feet. The minister chatted with Brandon, the best man. Their friends from *Madness* and *Nine Days In* filled the chairs. The scene took her breath away, and she wished she could capture this feeling forever.

The preceding four months passed quickly since they started dating. She never dreamed they would get married so quickly, but Jacob made a convincing argument. They knew each other so well and had already shared so much. And with him going on the road in a few weeks, their marriage would enable Noah and her to travel with him on their own family tour bus. She seized the chance to give up working and spend more time with Noah—and Jacob. Seeing the country was a fun bonus. The thought of being with Jacob every day filled her heart with happiness. Even with the bother of paparazzi and fans following them around, he was worth it. He was worth it all.

Her mind drifted to the day he proposed. They had only officially been dating for a month, so she had no idea he would ask her to marry him. He had set up a weekend at the beach house on Anna Maria Island, where they stayed before. This time, Nan and Grams went with them. He asked Brooke for a walk on the beach at sunset, and their grandmothers took care of Noah while they were gone.

The sun dipped down in the sky, creating a hazy pink glow. Jacob carried a beach blanket and set it out, then turned on music from his phone. It was his voice, singing a beautiful, melodic song she had never heard.

The song told a story—*their story*. A tale of a love that bears all things, believes all things, hopes all things. A love that never ends. One with God at the center.

He took her in his arms, and they danced. He spun her around, and as she faced him again, he was down on one knee. It may have been early in their relationship, but she knew he was the man God intended for her.

"Brooke, Grams and Nan are about to walk out. It's time to head down." Elise's voice drew her from her reverie.

Brooke turned away from the window and smiled at her maid of honor, her thoughts floating back to the present. This was it, the beginning of forever with the man she loved—the man who cherished her and pointed her daily to the God who pursued her and sacrificed all for her.

The End!

THE EPILOGUE IS SHORT, but I hope you will use your imagination to fill in more details!

One of my goals was to highlight how we often make judgments about who we think someone is based on their appearance, what we have heard, or particular run-ins with them. It's human nature. Without knowing them, their backstory, or what is happening in their lives at the moment to make them act a particular way, it is easy to make wrong assumptions about who they are. Certainly, there are times we should heed our intuition or the warnings of others in order to protect ourselves. But it can also cause us to miss opportunities when we might find a good friend, or be the person someone needs in their life to help them through a difficult time. It's important to look beyond ourselves and see—really see—others. I'm talking to myself, too. Sometimes I want to put up walls, be in my own world, and not get involved, but I have to remind myself to see others through God's eyes. Then I remember all He willingly did for me. Surely, I can share some of that love with others.

JOHN 7:24 ESV - "Do not judge by appearances, but judge with right judgment."

THE ABOVE VERSE is spoken by Jesus in the midst of a chapter filled with people questioning who He was and judging Him based on what they saw or heard about Him.

Many people make judgments about who God is, and what Christianity is, without getting to know the truth. It's easy to look at churches, denominations, people who call themselves Christians, pastors, televangelists, and what the media says about Christianity, and think we know the truth. But the truth is found in the Bible.

It's important to compare everything you think you know, or have heard, with what the Bible actually says. People often try to find errors and inaccuracies in Scripture, or say parts of it that really happened are only allegories. But Jesus says in John 17:17, "Sanctify them in the truth; Your Word is truth." Read the Bible and study it to see those truths for yourself. I share many tools to help with that in my newsletter. Sign up on my website: KimGriffin.org

Parts of the Bible are written as poetry and parables, and other sections are written as dreams and visions, but much of it is history. Even when I listen to internationally acclaimed Bible scholars or people who I feel confident have in-depth knowledge of the Scripture, I compare what they say to the Word of God. Don't let the mistakes, hypocrisy, and sins of people professing to be Christian keep you from Christ. Maybe some of those people truly are Christian, but know that until our bodies are renewed after Jesus returns, even we, as Christians, will continue to sin. There is hope in this world, and it is in Christ. If you have any questions, please feel free to email me at Kim@KimGriffin.org.

FOR THE STORY behind the story, go to the special page on my website (find the QR link at the end of the afterword).

Get a free novella: Not Quite Mr. Tilney with newsletter subscription at KimGriffin.org.

AFTERWORD

If you enjoyed this book and its message, I would love for you to write a review on Goodreads, Amazon, and whatever retailer you purchased the book from. As an independent author, I am responsible for all of my own marketing and reviews help my book get seen.

There are two parts to the "story behind the story." Read on for some of that and find more on my website in the special section accessed only by the link at the bottom of this section.

Part 1: This story began with a woman mourning the loss of her mom, and I began writing it several weeks after my mom's death. Like Brooke, I was close to my mom, but unlike Brooke, I started losing my mom 14 1/2 years earlier to Alzheimer's. In many ways, I celebrated her death because she loved the Lord, looked forward to being with Him, and had been "gone" long before she died, yet it was still hard. I had been losing her for so long, but had not fully processed all the years lost while it was happening.

Just as Brooke moved from mourning to joy in the story, writing this helped me to let go and rejoice in the Lord in the midst of my sadness.

We've all been broken hearted at some point in this fallen world, but Jesus gives us hope in all circumstances. Read this beautiful prophecy of Isaiah about the healing Jesus brings.

*The Spirit of the Lord GOD is upon me, because the LORD has anointed me to bring good news to the poor; he has sent me to **bind up the brokenhearted**, to proclaim liberty to the captives, and the opening of the prison to those who are bound; 2 to proclaim the year of the LORD's favor, and the day of vengeance of our God; to **comfort all who mourn**; 3 to grant to those who mourn in Zion-- to **give them a beautiful headdress instead of ashes**, the **oil of gladness instead of mourning**, the garment of praise instead of a faint spirit; that they may be called oaks of righteousness, the planting of the LORD, that he may be glorified. Isaiah 61:1-3*

God offers so much hope and healing! On my blog you can find a study on the fruit of the Spirit. It's in multiple blog posts and the one on joy may be particularly helpful if you are lacking in that area, but be sure to read the preceding ones because they build upon each other. You can find them through KimGriffin.org.

Part 2: In the late 90s I lived in an apartment in Kissimmee, Florida with my husband and toddler son and truly did have a mysterious neighbor (who I eventually found out was famous) coming and going from my building.

To find out more, go to the special Extras page on my website. It can only be opened through this link (or with the QR code at the bottom): https://www.kimgriffin.org/home/books/Extras-DFS

Acknowledgments

First and foremost, I thank God for giving me this story. I have an attachment to all of my stories, but this book is extra special to me because it helped me process my mom's death. She was a woman who loved the Lord and lived it out, and we were close before she succumbed to Alzheimer's. I thought it would take me a long time after her death to start writing again, but only a few weeks later, God gave me this. If you are struggling to process loss or pain, I highly recommend writing (and I always recommend turning to the Lord in prayer and reading His word so it can renew you).

Thank you, Christian mommy Writers and Created to Write for being such an encouragement for me to keep writing and for providing guidance whenever I'm stuck. It's a blessing to have sisters in Christ working alongside me, glorifying God in our writing.

Thank you to my Beta readers who encouraged me with feedback to help this book become what it is: Marla, Caroline, and my hubby who has been so patient with me when I get caught up in writing. And to my wonderful ARC team who has promoted this book and encouraged me with their kind words, thanks so much for joining me in this endeavor!

Thank you Chelsey for pushing and encouraging me as you edited!

To all of you, I greatly appreciate all the prayers for me and this book. May it be to God's glory!

About the Author

Kim Griffin is a former interior designer and homeschool mom who has been leading Bible studies for over 35 years and working in Women's Ministry for over 25. Several years ago, God led her to begin writing words of hope. She writes Christian women's fiction with clean romance and devotionals/Bible studies. Her desire is that her books will draw readers closer to the God who sees all of their imperfections and loves them still.

If you enjoyed this book, please consider leaving a review on Goodreads and Amazon! As an independent author this helps Kim get the word out about her books.

You can learn more about Kim and her books and sign up for her newsletter at her website: kimgriffin.org

ALSO BY KIM GRIFFIN

~

Scan the QR code to see my other books or visit KimGriffin.org

Scan this QR code to **join my newsletter and get a free novella: *Not Quite Mr. Tilney***, a free Gospel of John simple self-paced study guide, and a link to my Fruit of the Spirit Bible Study. You'll also receive updates on my writing, book and author suggestions, discounts on books, freebies, and more!